JF

IRISH PUBLISHER – IRISH STORY

For Mick O'Callaghan
and the village of Schull

MERCIER PRESS
Cork
www.mercierpress.ie

© E. R. Murray, 2016

ISBN: 978 1 78117 452 4

10 9 8 7 6 5 4 3 2 1

Printed and bound in the EU.

Prologue

It was a cool summer night, yet sweat dripped down Zach Stone's back as he waited in the agreed meeting spot. The moon was full and bright, casting a vast yellow halo that reflected on the gentle waves. All was silent.

Perched on the ragged cliff edge of Gallows Island, staring out to sea, Zach felt his heart thump and blood rushed in his ears like a drum beat. As a twig snapped behind him, Zach shivered. A chill ran up his spine and down his arms, turning his fingers icy.

Slowly standing and turning round, Zach met the steely glare of Judge Ambrose. The judge's face looked jaundiced in the moon's light, giving him an eerie glow. Taking a cautious step towards the judge, away from the cliff edge, Zach gave a nervous smile.

'It is almost time,' said Judge Ambrose.

Zach nodded, unsure whether to speak.

'The Reflectory is still guarded, but the Shadow Walkers are ready to march. They're waiting for my command.'

Again, Zach nodded.

'You know what you have to do?'

'Yes, sir,' replied Zach, his voice much squeakier than intended.

'Good. When we unleash the secret weapon, there'll be no stopping us.'

Judge Ambrose turned to leave, but after a few steps, he spun round and fixed Zach with a hard stare. Instantly, a searing pain shot through Zach's body. It felt like a lightning bolt was trapped under his skin.

'You'll make sure there are no mistakes this time, boy?'

The fiery pain surged into Zach's limbs, filtering into every vein and sinew, finally settling around his throat. Zach clawed at his neck, but there was nothing there to grab. He nodded furiously.

When Judge Ambrose was satisfied that his message had been conveyed, he averted his gaze. Zach dropped to the ground, coughing and spluttering.

'I'm glad we understand each other,' called the judge as he walked away.

Zach's eyes narrowed as he watched the figure disappear down the hill. Rubbing his sore throat, he spat onto the ground. But there was no way he was giving up; Zach had waited almost two months for this opportunity – the chance to destroy Ebony Smart and bring his mum back to life. Revenge was within his grasp.

1

Ebony Smart woke to the sound of her own screaming. At first, she could not move her body or stop the noise that surged from her mouth and she wondered whether she was still trapped in her nightmare …

A howling wind.

A dawn sky.

Shadows with angry faces and red eyes hurtling in her direction.

Shadows that can hurt her.

And Ebony, strapped to a slab of cold, hard marble, fighting to break away. Tugging and yanking, desperate to be free, as Zach Stone's laughter grows louder and louder.

After a moment, which felt much longer, the scream died away and with it Ebony regained the ability to move her limbs. As soon as she could, she hauled herself up, the muscles in her arms trembling, and rested on the edge of her huge bed. The imprint of a ghastly face with red eyes hovered everywhere she looked, a ghoulish reminder of her recurring nightmare. Reaching into the cage on her bedside cabinet, Ebony lifted out her pet rat, Winston, for a cuddle. As

Winston snuggled against her, Ebony felt his heart pumping, making his body quiver.

'I'm OK, Winston,' said Ebony, wishing she could believe her own words.

The dream lingered, leaving a sour taste in her mouth. Her body still shaky, Ebony squeezed her eyelids shut as tightly as she could. She clutched at the amulet around her neck – the heirloom that marked her as guardian – and waited until the face melted away. As her breathing calmed, Winston stopped quivering and scurried up her arm to sit in his favourite spot on her shoulder, nestled in her thick black curls.

'It was just a dream,' said Ebony, forcing her shoulders to relax.

Clambering out of bed and into one of the protective outfits her aunt had made for her, its special material moulding itself around her body and instantly warming her bones, she gathered up her best friend. Opening the curtains, Ebony let the bright early morning light flood into the room. A pigeon cooed on her window ledge, its iridescent pink collar glinting in the sun. At the sight of the new day, the memory of the dream began to fade.

'Come on, Winston,' said Ebony, glancing at her bed with a shiver. 'There's no point hanging around here. Let's go see what Aunt Ruby is up to – and if she's finally decided to let me visit home.'

Even though it was only just past dawn, it was breakfast time in 23 Mercury Lane and the kitchen was alive with smoke, sparks and whirring mini-helicopters delivering food to the table. It was the standard fare of eggs, smokey bacon and burnt toast. Uncle Cornelius was seated at the table, greedily licking his lips, his explosive ginger eyebrows trembling with greed. Quietly, Ebony slipped into her favourite spot at the other end of the table – where he couldn't reach to steal her food – and Winston settled into the little place set out for him beside her. It took a moment for Aunt Ruby to realise they were there.

'Good morning. Did you sleep well, dear?' she asked, as Ebony shuffled in her seat. Her aunt was chugging on a finely carved chestnut pipe as she cooked.

'I had the dream again.'

'Was there any change? A lead we can follow?'

'No,' said Ebony, slouching in her chair. 'It was the same as always. I don't think we'll find any leads there.'

Aunt Ruby stopped what she was doing and joined them at the table, the pipe hanging from one corner of her mouth. A piece of toast whizzed past her head and landed in the middle of the tablecloth. It was steaming hot and black all over. Aunt Ruby picked it up and absently started scratching at the burnt layers with a knife, lost in her own thoughts. After a moment, she eyed Ebony carefully.

'Myself and Uncle Cornelius were talking,' she said, scraping the toast in time to her words. 'About your request to go home to visit the Reflectory and those guarding it.'

Brightening, Ebony sat up straight. She had been asking for weeks to go back so she could try to release the souls trapped in stasis and seal the doorway. Last night, they'd eventually agreed to consider her request.

'Great! Are we finally returning to Oddley Cove?'

'I'm afraid not, my dear,' replied her aunt. 'We decided that, even though it's been quiet, we still need to be in Dublin on watch. Which means you need to be here too.'

Stiffening, Ebony picked up her fork and clenched it in her fist. 'But I'm the guardian – if the Reflectory still needs guarding, if the souls are at risk, I should be there. I can stay with Old Joe if you're worried about me being in the cottage alone.'

Uncle Cornelius shifted in his seat and Winston stopped eating.

'The Reflectory is in safe hands with Icarus and Old Joe in charge – but it's a twenty-four-hour job and they don't have time to watch over you too. For now, you should be more concerned about *The Book of Learning* being unresponsive. And when was the last time you heard your grandpa speak? Until the guidance you need returns, you must remain in our protection.'

Ebony gulped. When she had been in danger before, her grandpa's soul had helped her, giving her advice and helping her defeat Judge Ambrose and her cousin Zach. But ever since then, his guiding whisper had been silent. She hoped it was because she was out of danger, but as the days went by, she found that she missed his secret assistance more and more. Part of her almost wished the danger would return so she could hear his gentle whispering once again. But while the absence of Grandpa Tobias bothered her, what her aunt had just said worried her more. Had Aunt Ruby lost faith in her abilities as guardian already?

'You don't think I'm good enough, do you?' asked Ebony, eyebrows knit.

Leaning back in her chair, Aunt Ruby laid her pipe down and shot Uncle Cornelius an odd look. 'You might be *the* guardian – and a capable one – but I'm still *your* guardian, and your safety comes first,' she replied. 'So far, defeating the curse has only made things more dangerous. Now that we've revealed Judge Ambrose's evil intentions to the Order of Nine Lives and they've declared him an enemy, he will be rallying what supporters he has left for all-out war against us.'

'So where is he then?' snapped Ebony.

It was almost two months since Ebony had prevented Judge Ambrose and Zach Stone from snatching her soul and implanting it into another body, and in that time, there hadn't been a single whiff of trouble. Although Aunt Ruby had doubled their spies, implanting cameras into a multitude of summer creatures, including bees and butterflies, they hadn't seen so much as a glimpse of their enemies on the surveillance screens in the basement. The security team guarding the Reflectory had nothing to report either; it seemed like Judge Ambrose and Zach Stone had dropped off the face of the earth.

'Ambrose may have gone into hiding, but I have no doubt that he has something big planned,' replied Aunt Ruby. 'He is still seeking the power of reincarnation and will stop at nothing to kill you and get your soul – and he needs you in the Reflectory to do that, remember? Only he'll want to make sure he has all his pieces ready before he makes his move. I'm afraid for you, Ebony.'

Ebony couldn't argue with that. Before Zach had fled the scene last spring, he had warned her that they'd be coming after her – and Ebony believed this with every fibre of her being. She could sense her enemies watching and waiting. Particularly at night when the nightmare came, Zach's laughter ringing in her ears. Sometimes, drenched in sweat, her heart felt so black after the fear abated that all she could think about was hunting them down and exacting revenge for her grandpa's murder.

'We have to be more cautious than ever,' continued Aunt Ruby. 'Our numbers are few. There's not much left of the Order – sixteen families only – and until we're certain everyone is loyal to us, rather than Ambrose, it's too dangerous to let you go alone. Which means that you must stay here with us.'

'But surely that's even more reason to let me return, so I can start figuring out how to release the souls–'

Aunt Ruby put up her hand to signal that she would hear no more about it. 'You're not going back to Oddley Cove until we can come with you, and that's that. Things are too volatile. You need our protection.'

Ebony felt like reaching out, snatching the toast from her aunt and throwing it across the room; she didn't even know anyone else from the Order besides her family. Resisting the urge, she picked up a piece of bacon and chewed angrily on it.

'However,' continued Aunt Ruby, 'we have got some news that might cheer you up.'

I very much doubt it, thought Ebony.

'It's about Zach's lair.'

Almost choking on her bacon, Ebony sat upright. 'Go on,' she said.

'We're satisfied that it's been completely abandoned. There hasn't been an iota of movement, and we've sent in our best bug spies to check the place out. We've also made a few amendments and I got someone to add a new security system.'

'So, what does this mean?' asked Ebony, excitement bubbling up inside her.

'It means that we've decided you should claim it. You can use it as–'

Before her aunt could finish, Ebony was out of her seat, hugging her. Letting go, she ran upstairs at top speed to gather her rucksack, stuffing it with her most precious belongings: the *Ebonius Tobinius* bronze rose and her grandpa's mahogany medal – which combined to unlock the doorway to the Reflectory – as well as *The Book of Learning*. Checking her amulet was safely secured around her neck, Ebony pulled on a light summer jacket and tucked her pocketknife into her trousers. Minutes later, she was back in the kitchen.

'Let's go, Winston,' she cried, fighting to catch her breath.

Springing up onto her outstretched palm and scurrying up her arm, Winston positioned himself on Ebony's shoulder and clung on as she raced out of the room towards the front door.

'Wait!' cried Aunt Ruby, as Ebony began making her way through the many locks. 'You don't even know how to get in!'

Ebony paused, waiting for instructions.

'Before I tell you,' said Aunt Ruby, eyeballing her niece, 'you must promise me that you'll keep a close lookout. If you see anything out of the ordinary or suspicious, you must come straight home.'

'I promise.'

'And be back within two hours at the most.'

'OK,' said Ebony, tapping the toe of her shoe against the floor.

'We'll have surveillance follow you – you can never be too careful.'

'Fine! Just tell me how to get in.'

After considering her niece for a moment, Aunt Ruby leaned in and whispered the instructions in Ebony's ear. As she listened, Ebony grinned and nodded. Moments later, she was out through the front door, Winston hidden in her curls as they headed straight for the park.

The morning sky was already bright and blue as Ebony Smart scaled the railings of St Stephen's Green and dropped noiselessly onto the dew-soaked grass on the other side. It wasn't even 6.30 a.m. yet, but the shadows were already beginning to stretch. With Winston gripping her shoulder firmly and her rucksack slung over one shoulder, Ebony strode confidently in the direction of the pond, checking behind her whenever she felt a chill run up her spine, or imagined she could feel eyes following her. Despite feeling wary, excitement fizzed through her. She was ready to get one up on her enemies by claiming Zach's lair as her own.

'Let's call it the Hideout,' said Ebony to Winston.

The rat lifted his left paw in the air – his signal for yes – but he trembled on her shoulder as they stopped at the green marble seat near the main entrance of the park. The back of the seat reared up to a point with a bronze bauble on top, while the front curved down into a small basin decorated with an intricate carving of a rose. It marked the secret entrance to Zach's old home.

'It's OK, Winston,' said Ebony, recalling Aunt Ruby's new

security instructions. 'This belongs to us now.'

Reaching out, she grasped hold of the carved rose, but instead of twisting it like Zach had done before, she leaned in close so her eye was in line with the centre of the rose and waited until it opened to reveal a small round lens. Recognising her iris, the familiar hum started up as the mechanism inside the seat sprang to life. The marble began to sink and mossy steps appeared leading down into the ground, small lights automatically blinking on along the edges, showing the way. Breathing in the familiar scents of damp soil and June flowers – elderflower, honeysuckle, wild garlic and plain old dog-roses – Ebony walked down into the earth and paused. Although her aunt's surveillance had been thorough – she wouldn't have allowed Ebony to claim the place unless she was one hundred per cent certain it was safe – being there resurrected some painful memories and put Ebony on edge. Last time she'd been there, she'd still believed that Zach was her friend. Unable to hear any noises from inside, she flicked the switch to seal up the entrance, leaving the park behind.

One deep breath later, blood pounding in her ears and Winston's claws prickling her collarbone as he clung on, Ebony stepped into the main room. She clapped her hands, and the room exploded with light as candelabras flared up with fake flames. Uncertain what to expect, her heart thumped in her chest as her eyes fell on the familiar surroundings. It was almost the same as before; the only difference was that a desk, a computer and an office chair had been added.

Taking quiet, tentative steps, Ebony searched the area to make sure they were alone. She checked under the four-poster bed and inside the cupboards – even though they were too small for anyone to hide inside – and searched the small bathroom. The place was empty. There were signs of Zach everywhere, but it was clear he hadn't been there for some time; the used towel discarded on the floor was stiff and smelled of mould, bubbles had dried on the bar of soap in a moonscape design and the pizza crusts on a plate in the kitchen had turned fuzzy and green.

'It's all clear,' said Ebony, relieved to hear her voice break the silence.

But Winston wasn't convinced. He quivered and shook, using Ebony's thick black curls to hide behind. Gently, Ebony lifted him off her shoulder and held him out in front of her, balancing him across the palms of her hands so he could survey the room.

'Look,' she said. 'I've searched everywhere. We're alone.'

Winston blinked slowly as he checked the place over, wrapping his tail around his body. He licked its stubby tip, the end flat instead of pointy – a battle scar from Zach – then hid it under his tummy. As his eyes fell on a door on the other side of the room, his fur stood on end and he made a strange, low squeal.

'Trust me,' said Ebony, fighting to keep her voice from shaking. 'That door's always been locked. Zach said he had it sealed up when his family left. There's no one behind it.'

Popping Winston back on her shoulder and with her breath held, she headed for the small door. Her throat tight and thick with fear, she reached out and gave the handle a tug. It was firmly locked. Pressing her ear to the door for a moment, trying to ignore the sound of blood rushing in her eardrums, she let out a small sigh.

'See? Just like I said.'

Winston's whiskers twitched. He leaned in and listened at the door also, then scurried down Ebony's arm and rested his front paws on the handle, pressing down with all his body weight. When the door didn't open, his fur flattened and his body relaxed. He did a small somersault then turned to Ebony and lifted both paws in victory. Ebony laughed loudly, her voice filling the room. Finally reassured, Winston leaped off Ebony's palms and headed straight to the sofa to search for spilled crumbs.

As the sun rose higher in the sky, Ebony decided to get to work. If she could figure out a way to get *The Book of Learning* to start working again, or at least find some useful information about the whereabouts of Zach or Judge Ambrose, she might be able to convince her aunt to take her to Oddley Cove. She wiggled the mouse on the computer desk, and the screen lit up; as Ebony had suspected, it was linked to the surveillance cameras in 23 Mercury Lane. There was nothing of interest happening, just Uncle Cornelius washing the breakfast dishes with his tongue as Aunt Ruby scribbled notes about one of her latest inventions.

Opening *The Book of Learning* using the special fingerprint combination – index finger, middle finger, little finger, thumb – Ebony turned to the first blank page. She waited for it to spring into action and show her a clue, just like it had for the last time two months ago when she'd needed help to defeat Zach and Ambrose. When nothing happened, she ran her fingers over the inside cover, tracing the eye symbol and the list of dates of all her past incarnations, as well as the last one representing her own lifespan, not yet complete. When there was no response, Ebony emptied her rucksack of her essential possessions and tried touching each item in turn to *The Book of Learning*'s pages in the hope of triggering something. But nothing worked. Not even the crescent-shaped amulet around her neck could kick the pages into action. The book stayed inert and silent.

Reaching out to Winston for comfort, Ebony discovered he was now snoozing, belly up, his fat tummy rising and falling with his heavy breath.

'Hey!' she said, prodding him gently in the hope that it would wake him. 'I need your help.'

But Winston slept on. Watching her only friend snoozing, Ebony grew irritable. She had expected to feel euphoric once she had claimed the Hideout; after all, it was a small triumph over Zach Stone. Instead, she felt like she was trespassing on his territory.

Turning back to the computer keyboard, Ebony set about making a screensaver. She made the message huge, in fat lime-green block capitals:

THE HIDEOUT
PROPERTY OF EBONY SMART
NO TRESPASSERS

Leaving the message to bounce around on the screen, she folded her arms.

'There,' she said. 'It's ours now.'

And yet, it didn't make her feel any better. Zach was her enemy: he'd killed her grandpa and tried to kill her. With the help of her remaining family and the Order of Nine Lives, she was determined to make sure that he would pay for what he'd done – only then could her spirit be at rest.

Joining Winston on the sofa, Ebony stretched out on her back, trying to calm her fury as she gazed through the glass ceiling of the Hideout, watching the sunlight dapple the pond above it. The pondweed was still, almost luminous in the morning glow, and small schools of tiny glistening fish clung to it to feed. Meanwhile, ducks paddled across the surface of the water with their bright orange feet, dipping their heads for food. Ebony wondered what it must be like for the ducks, looking down at her. Did they even notice her?

As though hearing her thoughts, the ducks suddenly exploded with shrieks and squawks, beating their wings on the water. The water rippled and sloshed, blurring Ebony's view. The Hideout darkened as the shadows of their wings dappled every corner and crevice, lapping like flames. As their shrieks magnified, the room continued to darken. Up above, a huge shadow loomed.

There was a sudden flash of indigo and a blaze of white followed by a barely audible splash; above the water line, Ebony saw two sets of huge, slate-grey claws lifting back into the air. They were open, like they'd just released something. The ducks dispersed, still squawking, a flurry of beating wings. There was a loud clunk and, waking with a start, Winston sat up on his hind legs. Ebony watched as a single drake floated on the pond; from the angle of his neck, Ebony guessed he had been killed during the commotion. Above him, the shadow circled the sky. Whatever the claws belonged to, it wasn't leaving yet.

Once again, the room darkened and, although she knew she was safe, Ebony ducked. Cringing as the claws wrapped themselves around the dead drake and carried it off, she couldn't look away.

An eerie silence followed.

'I've never seen a bird that big,' said Ebony.

Winston was now staring upwards, his attention fixed on something above his head. Ebony followed his gaze to where the water had again settled, clear and sparkling.

Resting on the glass ceiling was a small silver box. On its base, there were words engraved in a curlicue script. Climbing up on a chair and taking her time to decipher the words, Ebony read the message out loud:

Help me find my owner. Do Not Open.

3

Leaping up the gently lit, moss-covered stairs two at a time, Ebony ran out into the daylight, with Winston close behind. Quickly showing her eye to the rose, Ebony waited until the secret doorway closed behind them, then ran to the pond's edge.

'If my estimation is right,' said Ebony, peering into the water, 'it should be just about … there!'

Winston peered in. Turning round, he shrugged. That part of the pond was too deep to see to the bottom.

'I guess there's only one thing for it,' said Ebony.

Stripping off her jacket, shoes and socks, and leaving them along with her rucksack in Winston's care – the park would open soon and she might not be able to get back into the Hideout – Ebony jumped into the pond. Despite the sunshine the water was cold, sending shockwaves through her body that made her gasp. The water went up to Ebony's waist and mud squelched between her toes as she waded away from the edge. Soon, the bottom fell away and she was treading water, the cold water freezing her chest and lungs. Looking down, she saw the water was clearer than at the edges. She guessed that this was the deepest part, above the Hideout.

'H-here goes,' she stammered, taking a deep gulp of air and upending herself like a guillemot. The water was unusually murky from where she'd disturbed the mud in the shallower areas, and it took a moment for her eyes to adjust, but after a minute, Ebony caught sight of something glinting at the bottom. She'd found the right spot; she could just make out the sofa in the Hideout through the glass below.

Heading straight for the small silver box, she swam as hard as she could, but the water seemed to go on and on. The pond was much deeper than Ebony had thought – the glass ceiling had distorted its depth. Determined, she continued down, but still the bottom of the pond didn't seem to be rising to meet her. Then, giving one last almighty kick with her legs, she found the box was finally in reach.

Stretching out her arm, small bubbles escaping her lips and nostrils as she fought to hold in what remained of her breath, Ebony managed to grab the box. Spinning her body round, she tried to use the glass ceiling of the Hideout for leverage to push herself up, but instead of hitting against the smooth surface, her foot caught in something that clamped around it. Ebony tried to pull herself away, but whatever it was she'd got caught in held her fast.

Looking down, Ebony saw fronds of billowing pondweed wrapped around her leg. Stuffing the box in her pocket, she tried to unravel the weeds, her lungs dry and burning, screaming for air.

Frantic now, she kicked and wrestled to get free.

Remembering her pocketknife, Ebony pulled it out and cut away at the binding around her feet. After a couple of seconds, she was able to break free. Swimming up to the surface of the water as fast as she could, Ebony gasped for air as she broke the surface, sucking in huge mouthfuls of oxygen.

'I got it!' she cried, once her breath had returned.

Winston was waiting on the bank, his fur ruffled and his eyes bulging. Ebony made her way over to him and pulled herself out of the water. Crouching so Winston could see, she reached into her pocket and pulled out the silver box, holding it in the flat of her palm. Winston's fur flattened as he examined it.

On closer inspection, Ebony saw that the box was covered in delicate engravings, just like *The Book of Learning*, with a matching key design in one corner. Ebony turned the box around and flipped it over, the inscription face up. The message glinted in the sun.

Help me find my owner. Do Not Open.

'It's definitely the same script as on *The Book of Learning*,' said Ebony. 'I'd recognise it anywhere.' Unzipping her rucksack, she showed both to Winston. 'See? It's made of the same type of silver too – they must have been created at the same time.'

Winston blinked slowly.

'But why does it say not to open it? And how am I meant to know who owns it? Maybe I should just–'

Winston began jumping up and down on the spot on his back legs, waving his front legs about. Ebony understood his meaning right away.

'Do you think it's a trick?' she asked.

Holding up his left front paw, Winston also nodded his head emphatically.

'So, does that mean it's trying to trick me to open it? Or to not open it?'

Letting his paw drop, Winston gazed up at Ebony and shrugged.

'There's only one way to find out ...'

As she tried *The Book of Learning*'s special fingerprint combination to open the box lid, Winston covered his face with his paws. A deafening wail sounded and the box turned so hot that Ebony dropped it. Winston let out a gut-wrenching howl and dived into a pocket on Ebony's rucksack.

Spotting a strange glow inside her bag, Ebony peered in. It was coming from the centre of her bronze *Ebonius Tobinius* rose. As she pulled it out, the rose shuddered in her hand and a bright blue flame, buzzing and hissing, shot out of its centre. The ghostly flare launched into the sky and arced its way towards the horizon where it fizzled out, the light quickly dying.

'What the–?' cried Ebony.

But the awful wailing drowned out her words. Trying to smother the noise, Ebony grabbed her jacket and threw it over the box. The noise stopped instantly and the rose stopped glowing, returning to its usual bronze, its petals shining in the early morning sun. Ebony stared at the rose thoughtfully. It was clearly connected in some way to the box, as it had never done anything like that before. But she wasn't sure why it had reacted that way or what it meant.

Carefully retrieving the box from under her coat – it still felt warm to the touch – she slipped it into her pocket then returned the rose to her rucksack. Checking the ground to make sure she hadn't left anything behind, Ebony spotted a small mound of frost where the box had been sitting.

'Come see this, Winston. The box was hot but it left frost behind!'

Peering out, Winston shook his head. He allowed Ebony to lift him out of the rucksack, but he kept his distance from the frosty mark that now resembled the silhouette of a bird.

'Don't worry,' continued Ebony, putting on her shoes and socks. 'I think we've been given something important and if it's somehow linked to the rose and *The Book of Learning*, I'm sure it won't do us any harm. Let's go and show Aunt Ruby and Uncle Cornelius.'

Winston immediately hopped up onto Ebony's shoulder.

As she headed home – the park gates were now open – Ebony kept her head down and her hands in her pockets, dodging the early morning throng of people walking to work. The rucksack on her back felt heavy, like she was being crushed under its weight, and, shrouded in wet clothes, her body shivered. As her nose started to run, Ebony rummaged in her jacket pockets for a tissue, forgetting to look where she was going and not noticing the man in a suit and tie walking towards her, engrossed in his phone. The pair collided. The impact spun Ebony around and she found herself facing the park again.

A little way back, a hooded figure caught her eye. It was the only still figure in the moving crowd. Everyone else was racing along, eager to get to work or drop their kids at school, but this figure didn't seem interested in going anywhere. In fact, it didn't seem interested in anything other than her. The face was hidden by the shadow of the hood, but whoever it was, they were staring straight back at her. After a moment the figure waved and, without thinking, Ebony waved back. Then, the hood dropped.

It was Zach.

His chestnut hair glinted in the sun, but even from this distance, Ebony could see his face had changed; it looked gaunt and strained. Ebony gasped and felt her heart start to thump. She didn't know whether to run towards or away from him, but before she knew what was happening, a man passed between them. When he moved away, Zach was gone.

As Ebony stood frozen in the street, staring at the spot where Zach had been, Winston tugged on her hair.

'Did you see him, Winston? Did you see Zach?' said Ebony, frantically looking down the street to see if she could spot him anywhere.

Following her gaze, Winston frowned and shook his

head. He made a motion like breaststroke with his front legs, followed by a fake shiver.

'You're right. Maybe holding my breath underwater for so long is making me hallucinate,' said Ebony after a moment. 'I'm just being paranoid.'

Turning in to Mercury Lane, her outfit beginning to dry thanks to Aunt Ruby's specially invented cloth, Ebony was surprised to see her aunt standing on the doorstep of No. 23. Aunt Ruby's flame-red hair glistened as she shielded her eyes, her attention fixed on the sky – she no longer bothered with camouflaging herself now that she didn't have to pretend to serve Judge Ambrose. Instinctively, Ebony ducked behind a wheelie bin to watch. Although she had grown to trust her aunt, she also knew that Aunt Ruby still kept secrets.

After a moment, a shrill cry filled the sky, and a huge headless bird appeared, its wings outstretched. Ebony guessed its wingspan must have been five feet at least; the wings were mainly white in colour, with a rose-yellow tinge and edged with black feathers that splayed at the tips like lots of grasping fingers.

As the creature glided lower, Ebony realised that its head was actually tucked in, swaying from side to side on its long, bent neck as it eyed the ground. Circling for a moment, the creature swooped over Ebony; on closer inspection it looked like a vulture. It had a bald head and neck, purple and scarlet in colour, with a neon-orange wattle on its beak and piercing pale-yellow eyes. When the vulture dipped right above her, Ebony gasped; she recognised those slate-grey claws. It was the creature that had dropped the box in the pond and carried off the dead drake. She'd never seen a vulture so colourful – but what was a bird like that doing in Dublin?

A strange, high-pitched cry sounded from across the street. Looking in the direction of the noise, Ebony spied Aunt Ruby, one hand cupped over her mouth, making the call. In her other hand, she held a dead rabbit. The rabbit had something pinned to its flesh that looked like a note. The vulture dived, dropped an envelope at her aunt's feet and, with its beak, snatched up the rabbit that Aunt Ruby threw towards it, before swooping back up into the sky. Its wings stayed outstretched the whole time. When the bird had shrunk to a dot in the distance, Aunt Ruby picked up the letter. She read its contents, frowned, then screwed it into a ball and jammed it into her pocket before calling, 'You can come out now, Ebony.'

As Ebony stepped out from behind the wheelie bin, her hand hovered over the pocket where the silver box was hidden. If the vulture was going to visit her aunt, why hadn't it brought her aunt the box? Why had it chosen Ebony? Ebony quickly decided that, until she knew exactly what was going on, she would keep the gift a secret.

4

'What was that thing?' asked Ebony, taking a seat on one of the beanbags in the living room.

She was completely dry now, the silver box still hidden in the pocket of her trousers. Aunt Ruby had accepted her niece's story that Winston had slipped off the bank and into the pond, forcing Ebony to go in after him. Winston had played along, somewhat reluctantly, and was now sulking in Ebony's sleeve.

'A King Vulture,' replied her aunt, matter-of-factly, as though she was talking about a common sparrow. 'Usually found in the Central American jungle. A magnificent creature.'

'But this one lives in Ireland?' asked Ebony.

Even though it wasn't long past breakfast, Uncle Cornelius had brought in a tray of tea and cakes for everyone and was tucking in heartily. Winston tried to resist to show how upset he was about lying, until Ebony used a small piece of his favourite raspberry swiss roll to coax him out.

'I haven't seen it for a while but, yes, it lives in Ireland.'

'What is it doing here?' asked Ebony, accepting a hot mug

of tea from Uncle Cornelius. Cupping her hands around it, she let its warmth flood through her body.

'Flying and eating, mostly.'

'I meant, here, Mercury Lane.'

'It was looking for food. Icarus usually leaves it some scraps when it visits the area, but seeing as he's in Oddley Cove, the job fell to me. You don't want to upset a King Vulture – especially when it's hungry.'

Shuddering, Ebony thought of the huge, ribbed claws that she had seen. The claws that dropped a silver box that she wasn't allowed to open.

Sensing her niece's unease, Aunt Ruby continued. 'I think you'll find the King Vulture very interesting ... On occasion the Order uses it as a courier because it can cover huge distances effortlessly, travelling for hours without even having to flap its wings. The Ancient Mayans used to believe that its kind carried messages from other worlds. That it could communicate between the afterlife and this world.'

'Wait – didn't it bring you a message?' asked Ebony.

'Yes, but nothing of importance,' replied her aunt, staring into her teacup.

Suspicious, Ebony looked to Uncle Cornelius, but he avoided her gaze also, pretending to choose his next cake. Why would someone send a message via a dangerous vulture if it wasn't important? And the way her aunt had reacted, handing over a rabbit with a note attached and screwing up the letter she received: she was hiding something.

'So, who were you sending a message to?'

'You have to pay the vulture when it delivers,' said Aunt Ruby. 'That was a thank-you note.'

Ebony didn't believe her aunt's explanation for a second, but she had more questions that needed answering. 'You said the Mayans believed that it could carry messages between the afterlife and this life. Does that mean that members of the Order can use the vulture to send messages to the souls in the Reflectory? And can they send messages back?'

'Our legends do state that this type of bird can carry messages from souls in the Reflectory to those of us on earth and back again. Somehow the King Vulture can penetrate their trance-like state, also enabling the souls to transmit a message in return, but–'

'Really?' Her heart threatening to burst open, Ebony leaned towards her aunt, careful not to spill her tea. Maybe the box had been sent to her by her grandpa – if that was the case, perhaps she could send a reply, seeing as her aunt was keeping her away from the Reflectory. 'That's so cool.'

'It's only a legend, Ebony, not something I've witnessed – though I guess it can't be ruled out. Besides, we don't really need a messenger now that we have our guardian again.'

A sense of relief washed over Ebony. Maybe her aunt hadn't lost faith in her after all. Instinctively, Ebony's hand reached into her pocket. Clasping her fingers around the now cool metal of the silver box, she traced the inscription on the base with her fingertips.

'Have you ever seen parcels delivered by the bird?' asked Ebony.

'Just letters.' Narrowing her eyes, Aunt Ruby chewed her lip. 'Why do you ask?'

'No reason,' said Ebony innocently. If her aunt was going to keep secrets, why shouldn't she?

That night, Ebony decided to investigate the silver box a little more. The room was dark, with only a gentle, flickering light; now and again, Ebony liked to read using a single candle. The heavy brass candlestick holder was from home and using it reminded her of the times in Oddley Cove with her grandpa when storms would cut the electricity.

'What do you think, Winston?' said Ebony, as she turned the box around in her hand. 'Where could it have come from? It looks so similar to *The Book of Learning* – it must be from the ancients.'

His body shoved under the duvet, just his head peeping out, Winston shivered and refused to come out.

'I wish I could open it,' said Ebony, her fingernails hovering over the seam. 'I know it made that awful noise before but we didn't come to any harm. I tried the fingerprint combination already and that didn't work – maybe I should try blood like when I first found *The Book of Learning*?'

Leaping out from under the covers, Winston launched

himself at the box and knocked it out of Ebony's hands, making it bounce across the floor. A sizzle and splutter of light burst from it with every bounce. When the box finally came to rest in the middle of the room, the sparks grew in number, zipping in all directions like fireflies. The box itself was fizzing in the centre like a firework fountain.

'Something's happening at last!' cried Ebony, ducking to avoid a stray spark that smashed against the wall just above her head. 'This is great!'

But Winston wasn't convinced. He leaped onto Ebony's lap and cowered there. Holding him close – she knew animals were always scared of fireworks – Ebony watched as the sparks began to join up, lighting the centre of the room. In the middle of the light, something moved. It was a figure with straight black hair wearing a white robe. Ebony recognised the outfit immediately – her past self from ancient times had worn something similar – but who was this girl she was seeing?

'Hello?' whispered Ebony, wanting to make contact but half afraid it would frighten the image away. Remembering how she'd once connected with a past self by touching the amulet around her neck, Ebony grasped the delicate crescent-shaped locket and stared hard in the direction of the girl. But the girl appeared to be oblivious to Ebony's presence. She was standing on a wind-blown rock, holding a cage in front of her containing what looked like a black falcon. The bird was muscular yet elegant, a blue-grey tinge to its wings and white bars across its breast and legs. It kept opening and closing its hooked beak as though communicating. The girl whispered something to the bird, then checked behind her. Lifting the birdcage up high, she opened the door and set the bird free. The birdcage swung like a pendulum as the weight of the bird lifted, but instead of flying off, the falcon landed on the girl's shoulder, its beak close to her ear.

Smiling, Ebony pointed. 'Look, they're friends, just like you and me.'

Snuggling in, Winston made a small purring sound like a cat. Laughing, Ebony tickled his head while she continued watching.

A tear fell from the bird's eye and the girl caught it, before lifting it to her lips. The bird took off, flapping its wings to gain height, quickly darting up into the sky. The speed and shape of the bird made it instantly recognisable to Ebony: it was a kind of peregrine.

Inside, Ebony's stomach knotted as she was reminded of her animals at home. She missed the dogs, especially Mitzi, the one-eyed shih tzu, as well as her goats, Cassandra and George. The scrapbook she'd brought with her containing all their photos was well thumbed, but it didn't compensate for the smell or feel of warm fur. When she used to take the feed with her grandpa, the animals would run to greet them, tails wagging and eyes bright. Sometimes her grandpa would drop food onto her wellies or her shoulder so the animals would nibble at her. The memory stung.

'I wonder what it means,' she said, her eyes welling up as

she watched to see what would happen next. But the vision blurred and ended, and Winston didn't respond. He was asleep, breathing deep and slow, tiny snores escaping from his mouth.

As the last few sparks fizzled out and the vision disappeared completely, the glow of a single candle no longer felt comforting. Creeping across the room so as not to wake Winston, Ebony collected the box and tucked it under her pillow. Blowing out the candle and snuggling down, she let herself drift off to sleep, silent tears dripping down her cheeks.

'We have more good news for you,' said her aunt in greeting the next morning. 'Something that will help you in your role as guardian.'

Slumped in her chair, Ebony tilted her head to one side. 'News?' Taking a big gulp of lukewarm tea, she waited as her aunt fiddled with a button on her shirtsleeve.

'We thought we might introduce you to more of our kind,' Aunt Ruby answered after a while. 'People your own age.'

Spluttering into her cup, Ebony sat upright. 'Like who?' she asked, when her coughing subsided.

She hadn't thought about there being more people her own age in the Order of Nine Lives, and her aunt had never suggested such a thing before. Of course, there was Zach – but he'd turned out to be a bloodthirsty murderer intent on stealing her soul.

'Recent arrivals from Japan,' said Aunt Ruby. 'A maritime defence expert – a brilliant yet somewhat difficult man – and his lovely wife. They have two children. One boy and one girl. Nice children they are, very smart; I understand that Seamus is quite the genius. We thought they'd make nice friends for you. The children are coming to stay with us while their parents get set up. You can show them around, help them settle into their new city – it's never easy being the new kids in town.'

'So when do I get to meet them?' interrupted Ebony, the issue of the box still niggling away at the back of her mind. She would have to deal with that later.

Uncle Cornelius pulled out his tarnished pocket watch and showed it to her aunt, a big grin on his face.

'Oh, right about now,' she said.

As if rehearsed, there was a loud knock on the front door. The sound resonated right through the house, and Ebony felt the floor shudder, the teacups on the table tinkling like bells. She wondered how big the person knocking on the door could be. From the deep, resounding boom, she guessed that they were giant.

As another knock sounded, Winston appeared from a hole in the wall he'd been excavating and scurried up Ebony's leg, then onto her shoulder, where he hid in her curls. Aunt Ruby hurried out to answer the door. Meanwhile, Uncle Cornelius took the opportunity to scoop every remaining piece of breakfast he could – including those belonging to Aunt Ruby and Winston – onto his plate as a treat for later. It was piled high with bacon and toast – even the crusts Ebony had saved for Winston – like a derelict tower waiting to topple. Ebony chuckled, leaned over and gave it a push. As the food tower slowly tumbled towards the ground, Uncle Cornelius dropped to the floor, opened his jaws wide and caught the whole lot in his mouth in one go. He had so much food in there, he couldn't close his mouth to chew at first. As he tried, his jaws and teeth made loud sucking sounds and his side-burns wobbled, the crumbs wedged in their bristles showering his trousers.

'Eugh! That's disgusting,' said Ebony, shielding her eyes, yet unable to control her giggles.

Uncle Cornelius continued chomping, undeterred. By the time Aunt Ruby's footsteps could be heard returning from the hallway, he was already back on his chair, picking his teeth clean with one sharp claw, his other hand resting comfortably on his podgy tummy. It reminded Ebony of the first day she had met him – only now she knew that he was friendly and he no longer tried to eat Winston.

Cornelius looked up and caught Ebony staring. He winked, stuck out his fat, raspy tongue, then settled his face into a smug grin. Ebony giggled, but her laughter soon subsided as the door burst open, slamming against the wall with such force that Winston leapt an inch off Ebony's shoulder. Uncle Cornelius and Ebony glanced at each other quizzically, then turned their eyes to the doorway.

5

As the door bounced back from the wall, Ebony instinctively tried to tame her wild curls with one hand. In marched Aunt Ruby, gabbling excitedly, followed by a giant of a man with ice-white hair, a matching walrus moustache and tanned skin. He resembled a mountain with snow frosting its peak and his eyes were the greyest Ebony had ever seen – like bitterly cold waves on a winter's day. He looked about as Japanese as tomato ketchup.

But when a boy, who looked about Ebony's age, and a younger girl followed close behind, the connection began to make sense; both had dark, glossy hair and they didn't look a bit like their father. The brother and sister had prominent cheekbones, wide faces, skin the colour of clotted cream and deep, softly lidded eyes. The boy's hair was twisted into long, thin spikes that protruded from his scalp like a sea urchin. The girl was smaller, her hair cut high and sharply across her forehead, bunched up at the side in pigtails. Her silken blue dress with fluted white sleeves resembled a summer sky. Although they had never met before, Ebony recognised the girl immediately from her vision the night before. The thought made her insides tingle.

Last to join the group was their mother, the most exotic-looking individual Ebony had ever seen. Tiny, slight and elegant, a giant white chrysanthemum made of silk in her raven-black hair and wearing a fluffy white coat, she hardly made a noise as she entered the room behind them. It was like she was floating.

'This is Mr O'Hara,' said Aunt Ruby, fighting to keep irritation out of her voice. But as she introduced the others, she softened. 'And then we have Mrs O'Hara, Seamus and Chiyoko.' An impatient grunt from the giant man hurried Aunt Ruby on. She turned to her guests. 'You've all already met Uncle Cornelius, but it was a *very* long time ago. In fact, was it even this lifetime?'

Ebony eyed the brother and sister to see if they would react, but they didn't bat an eyelid. They were obviously comfortable with knowing that they were reincarnated.

'Everyone, my niece, Ebony Smart.' Aunt Ruby held her arms out wide towards Ebony, her voice rising up at the end of the sentence in a flourish.

Mrs O'Hara's face lit up as she stepped forward and took hold of Ebony's hand. The lady's fingers felt like cool, delicate porcelain in Ebony's grip. Mr O'Hara stayed put, offering a barely discernible nod of his head.

'We're very pleased to meet you,' said Mrs O'Hara.

A warm feeling spread over Ebony – finally, she might make some friends – but the feeling soon disappeared as Seamus gave a snort and threw Ebony a begrudging look.

'Seamus, Chiyoko, say hello to the *guardian*!' said Mr O'Hara, his voice as deep and rich as chocolate. He drew the last word out like it was sticky on his tongue and difficult to say.

The girl looked at her mother, then stepped forward and stuck out her hand, but Seamus kept his eyes pinned on his father and, matching his scowl, refused to budge. Despite a cough from his mother, there was no moving him. It was as though his shoes had been glued to the floor.

Ebony rose to greet Chiyoko, but before she could take the girl's hand, Chiyoko squealed and pointed to Winston. 'It's true! She does have a rat! Look, Seamus, it's Wilfred!'

'Winston,' corrected Ebony.

Seamus shuffled and mumbled an indiscernible noise. His mother laid a hand on his shoulder and reluctantly Seamus looked up and caught Ebony's eye.

'Hi,' he said, almost spitting out the word.

Ebony felt her face grow hot.

'Oh, I wish I had a rat like that, he's so sweet!' said Chiyoko, leaning forward and giving Winston a stroke.

Aunt Ruby made a gesture towards the living room and everyone followed her through. They each selected a beanbag, except for Seamus, who seemed to prefer leaning against the wall wearing a sour expression. Mr O'Hara wrinkled his nose as Winston climbed down from Ebony's shoulder to sit in the middle of the coffee table where he could enjoy some extra attention.

'Our gift to you,' said Mrs O'Hara. She placed a small box

on the table. It was a delicate eggshell blue, decorated with golden starfish.

'It's customary to exchange gifts in Japan,' whispered Chiyoko to Ebony. 'It's nothing exciting. Just some sweets.'

'And one for you,' said Aunt Ruby, signalling to Uncle Cornelius.

Jumping up, Uncle Cornelius disappeared briefly, returning with a similar-sized package. Smiling, he tried to bow, but next to Mrs O'Hara he looked clumsy and silly. Ebony giggled, but no one else seemed to find it funny. Aunt Ruby gave her niece a disapproving look. When Ebony caught Mr O'Hara glaring at her, she hid her face to conceal her blushes.

'Now, down to business,' said Mr O'Hara.

'Already?' groaned Chiyoko, but her father ignored her and continued on.

'Status report please, Ruby.'

'We've upped surveillance – the butterflies are proving particularly useful; their flight is so gentle the images they transmit are very clear – but all seems to be quiet.'

'Hmm,' said Mr O'Hara in his chocolatey voice, rubbing his chin. 'That's worrying.'

Ebony wondered why it could possibly be worrying. Boring, perhaps, but worrying? Instead of voicing her opinion, she kept quiet; she doubted her thoughts would be welcomed and being belligerent was no way to make friends. She tried to catch Seamus's eye, but he looked away, clearly pretending not to notice.

'Nothing of any interest to share?' added Mr O'Hara.

When Aunt Ruby shook her head, Ebony smiled inwardly, glad that she hadn't revealed the silver box to anyone.

'And you? Did you discover any activity in Japan?' asked Aunt Ruby. 'Have you made good progress with your research?'

Aunt Ruby was staring at Mr O'Hara with a strange mix of admiration and dislike. Ebony concluded from the way her aunt was acting towards him that he must be a big deal within the Order.

'Huge progress. Huge!' said Mr O'Hara. 'The Pacific Ocean is quiet, of course, thanks to me. Although ...' He raised one eyebrow and straightened up, an accusing eye on Aunt Ruby. 'Things have been allowed to slip here. There are strange happenings on the Atlantic.'

'The Atlantic?' asked Ebony. 'Oddley Cove is on the Atlantic!'

Mr O'Hara looked irritated. 'Why else do you think we've returned?'

Seamus chuckled and scuffed his shoe, but Ebony tried her best to ignore him.

'There are pirates!' added Chiyoko, almost bouncing out of her seat and gazing eagerly in Ebony's direction. 'Father went to find them but–'

'Shut up,' snapped Seamus, and Chiyoko did as she was told.

Determined not to worry about the cold reception from Mr O'Hara and his son, Ebony decided to try to find out more. She had met her own pirate self not that long ago, and if there was the chance to meet her again, then she wanted to know about it.

'Are there pirates near Gallows Island?' asked Ebony, glancing at her aunt. 'If so, they're probably linked to Judge Ambrose.'

'Watch out, world, we have another genius in our midst,' said Seamus mockingly.

His father let out a chuckle.

'Yes, well,' cut in Aunt Ruby, before Ebony had a chance to reply. Feeling the friction between the two adults, Ebony guessed that an old grudge existed there; one she would get to the bottom of and use to her advantage if necessary.

'If the judge is involved, then what am I still doing in Dublin?' asked Ebony, crossing her arms and raising her eyebrows at Aunt Ruby. 'Surely I should go back home.'

'This is your home now,' said Mr O'Hara matter-of-factly. 'And you're better off staying here where you can't cause any more harm.'

'Harm?' asked Ebony. Mr O'Hara was right in one sense – without her grandpa there to welcome her, Oddley Cove was no longer really home – but why was he being so unfair? 'I saved the Order and broke a curse. What harm did I do?'

'It was you that left the Reflectory open and unguarded, wasn't it?'

Guilt and frustration weighing her down – hadn't she asked hundreds of times to be allowed to return so that she could try to seal the gateway back up? – Ebony tried her best to ignore his words. But it was difficult, seeing as she agreed with them.

'Now, off you go, children,' said Mr O'Hara in a patronising voice, 'and let the adults get down to the real work.'

'Aunt Ruby?' tried Ebony.

Her aunt gave a sly wink, violet eyes twinkling. 'Why don't you take your new friends upstairs, show them your room and then theirs?' she suggested. 'Chiyoko can take her pick on the first floor, and Seamus can be next door to you.'

'But—' began Ebony.

Seamus cut her off. 'Our rooms?' he asked, his scowl deepening.

'Ruby and I have agreed that you'll both stay for a week,' replied his father. 'It will give your mother and I time to settle, and then we'll be back for you. How does that sound?'

He gave his son a friendly wink but Seamus acted like he hadn't noticed.

'Do I have a choice?' the boy snapped. He looked at his mum, who gave him a sad smile.

'Now, now, this is no time to be churlish,' replied his father. 'You know I have an important position as maritime defence expert and, as a result, we all have to make sacrifices now and again.'

Speechless, Seamus raised his eyebrows, then shrank back against the wall, glaring at no one in particular.

'You've got a wonderful room, I hear, and you'd only be

bored while myself and your mother get our affairs in order. Plus, I'm sure there's a way you can make yourself *useful*.'

Fiddling with his thumbs, Seamus didn't reply. Winston sat on his hind legs and gave a small squeak.

Mr O'Hara's coolness reminded Ebony of Judge Ambrose and a shudder ran through her bones. Disappointed, but knowing there was no point in arguing, she got to her feet.

'Come on, guys,' she said.

'I'll stay here, thanks,' said Seamus, examining his shoelaces.

'Oh yes. Seamus should stay and listen,' said Mr O'Hara.

Ebony felt the colour in her face deepen. As she opened her mouth to object, Chiyoko intercepted her, grabbing her by the hand and pulling her towards the door. Winston quickly followed.

'I can't believe I'm actually here, touching the hand of the guardian,' said Chiyoko, shooting a look of disgust at her brother before pulling Ebony out into the hallway. Ebony made eye contact with Seamus and gave him her best glare, but the boy looked away without even acknowledging her.

'Just because I'm younger,' continued Chiyoko when they were alone, 'he thinks he knows so much more. Still, who cares about him? I'm your number-one fan. I can't believe I'm actually here. With Wilfred too!'

'Winston,' reiterated Ebony, bending down to scoop him up.

But Chiyoko was too busy chatting to listen. 'Your room's at the top, right?' She darted up the stairs, yanking Ebony behind her. Puzzled – how did this girl know so much about her? – Ebony paused, glancing back towards the living-room door.

'Forget my brother,' said Chiyoko. 'You won't win with him. He's as set in his ways as my father.'

Reluctantly, Ebony allowed Chiyoko to tug her upstairs. Why should she, the guardian, be sent away, while Seamus was allowed to stay with the adults? It wasn't fair. Hoping that her aunt's wink meant that she'd fill her in later, Ebony climbed the stairs.

'Wow, this place is huge!' gasped Chiyoko, taking the stairs two at a time. 'And dark. Is it haunted like they say?' But for all her questions, Chiyoko didn't stop talking long enough for Ebony to reply.

After a moment, Ebony relaxed, forgetting about the frosty reception downstairs. And if Aunt Ruby didn't fill her in, she'd check the surveillance cameras to catch up on any conversations she missed. For now, she was going to enjoy having a number-one fan.

6

Ebony plonked herself on the bed, and Chiyoko copied her, swinging her feet off the end as she looked around excitedly, taking in every detail. Her pigtails bounced in time with her feet. While she was distracted, Winston scurried into his cage to get away from her grasping hands.

'I love your house, it's so spooky,' said Chiyoko. 'In Japan we live in a wooden house on stilts by the sea. Now we're going to be in a line of buildings, people on either side, as well as above and below. I miss the sound of cicadas.'

Although 23 Mercury Lane now felt the same as any old house, Ebony could still remember how big and imposing it had seemed when Judge Ambrose first brought her here. How she had been scared of the noises and shadows, of the locked doors suddenly opening, ghostly footsteps in the dust and prehistoric wildcats in the basement. Now, they were a regular part of everyday life.

'So, is it haunted? Did you really meet the ghosts of your ancestors?' asked Chiyoko, her eyes shining.

Ebony realised the girl actually wanted an answer this time. 'Technically they're not ghosts. And they're not my ancestors. They're past incarnations of me: one was a cowgirl from the 1800s, another a pirate from the 1600s … shouldn't you know all this?'

'The theory, yes, but I've never met a past self. No one else has except you, as far as I know.'

Ebony felt herself puff up with pride.

'A real-life pirate you say?' Chiyoko's eyes were as big and round as saucers as she tried to take it all in. 'Like the ones my father watches for? He hasn't actually met one yet, but he intercepts their communications all the time.'

Ebony noted the failure with a private smile. 'As real as you and me.'

'You're amazing,' said Chiyoko. 'I don't listen to Seamus. I've told him I want to be just like you when I'm older.'

'Why? What does Seamus say?'

'You know … That you aren't a proper guardian. That you should be replaced by the right person.'

'Oh, he does, does he?' said Ebony, balling her fists.

'Yes. Seamus just copies father though; when father set up the AESL, my brother was first to join.'

'The what?' asked Ebony, not sure she wanted to hear the answer.

'The Anti-Ebony Smart League. The group that my father started up to try to have you removed from your position as guardian.'

'But that's impossible! I was chosen as guardian, I didn't ask for the role. There's no way I can be removed.'

'Unless it's proven that you're an imposter, like some people claim.'

Ebony couldn't help wondering whether her aunt knew about the AESL – and if she did, why would she let the O'Haras stay? 'Like your father?' she asked.

Chiyoko looked away, embarrassed, but didn't reply.

Realising she'd never even considered anyone else from the Order of Nine Lives having opinions about her, never mind negative ones, Ebony cleared her throat. 'How many are in this league, exactly?'

'Most of the Order. They're pretty much all against you.'

'They are? But I opened the Reflectory! How can they be against me?'

'My father said that things became too unstable when the judge disappeared. His abandoned supporters were angry and restless and needed something to get their teeth into before all hell broke loose. He believes the AESL has averted a major catastrophe.'

'But why turn on me?'

'They think your aunt had something to do with your opening the Reflectory. That she faked *The Book of Learning* to trick everyone into believing you're the guardian. Some people believe the Reflectory isn't really open at all, that it's all a lie. After all, no one else has seen it.'

'What about the men guarding the doorway in Oddley Cove?'

'They say they're guarding something, but it could be an

illusion.'

'Well it's not,' said Ebony. 'How dare they?'

Uncurling her fists, Ebony realised why her aunt had been keeping her away from Oddley Cove and the men guarding the Reflectory. She thought Ebony could be protected from the knowledge that everyone was against her, but now the secret was out. And there she was, thinking they'd recognise her as their saviour.

'Don't worry,' continued Chiyoko. 'We're on your side.'

'We?' asked Ebony hopefully.

'Me and mum. We believe in you.'

Ebony's heart sank – after all she'd done and all she'd been through, she was still an outsider. Other than her immediate family, she only had two supporters within the Order.

'Hey, don't be sad,' said Chiyoko. Without warning, she snuggled against Ebony. Taken by surprise, Ebony stood up abruptly. Falling on the bed in a heap, Chiyoko didn't seem to care. Rolling onto her back, she waved her arms and legs back and forth on the quilt in sync with each other.

'I can't believe I'm doing bed angels on Ebony Smart's bed,' she said. 'It's amazing!'

Not that amazing, thought Ebony, feeling suddenly drained. But she bit her tongue. This was her only chance to make a friend and to find out what was really going on within the Order.

'Have you always lived in Japan?' asked Ebony, briefly removing the emphasis from herself.

'No. Father's from Ireland. We spent some time here when I was little, but I don't really remember it. Then we moved to Japan for Dad's work. This is the first time we've been in Ireland in years.'

'I thought O'Hara wasn't a very Japanese name.'

Chiyoko smiled. 'No, but Hara is. We switch between the two, depending on what country we're in.'

'And what about your brother's name?'

'He was the first-born and my father insisted on an Irish name. He quickly discovered no one in Japan could say Seamus, so I got a Japanese name. It means "child of a thousand generations". Neat, hey? But enough about Japan. Can I see *The Book of Learning*?'

Chiyoko flipped over onto her stomach, resting her chin on her hands dreamily. Winston flattened himself lower in his cage and shuffled his bum backwards into the straw. Spotting him, Chiyoko laughed and pointed, 'Oh my God, it's am—'

'Yes, it's amazing,' said Ebony, wishing she'd stood her ground and stayed downstairs with Seamus and the adults. If everyone was so against her, she would have to keep a close eye on things.

Deciding it might keep her number-one fan quiet for a moment, Ebony pulled out *The Book of Learning* and threw it onto the bed. Chiyoko gasped and flinched, like she was in danger.

'It won't harm you,' said Ebony. Using her fingerprints to

open the book, she laid it open on the first page, the single eye staring out blankly.

'They said you had to use blood!' said Chiyoko, sounding disappointed.

'I did,' said Ebony, wondering whether 'they' meant the Order, and if it did, how they knew every tiny detail about her life.

Chiyoko looked impressed for a fleeting moment, then her face fell. 'But why isn't it pink and sparkly?'

'Nothing about me is pink and sparkly,' replied Ebony, one eyebrow raised. 'And it never will be. My favourite colours are red and blue.'

'But my sources said–'

'What sources? Who exactly have you–?'

Before Ebony could finish, Chiyoko squealed, making Ebony jump. The amulet that was fastened around Ebony's neck had swung free from her top as she'd leaned in. As Chiyoko reached out for the amulet, Ebony recoiled, covering it with her hand. Without warning, an image of Zach's angry face flooded Ebony's mind. Then his image melted away, morphing into the shadowy red-eyed demon that haunted her dreams, with its clawed, reaching hands and pointed wings. It was so realistic, it was as though the creature was right there in her bedroom, staring into her soul. Unable to move, Ebony watched as its face grew in size, its nose elongating into a snout. Opening its mouth, she saw sharp teeth with saliva webbed across the points.

And then … SNAP!

Chiyoko was clicking her fingers and calling Ebony's name, her voice wobbly. 'Ebony! Are you OK?'

Despite her thumping heart and clammy palms, Ebony nodded. Satisfied, Chiyoko returned to admiring *The Book of Learning*. Lifting a finger in the air, she let it hover near the frozen, crinkled eye in the middle of the page. Ebony found herself willing the eye to move – if things kicked into action, the Order wouldn't be able to deny her position as guardian – but it stayed still and lifeless, like the page of any old book.

'It's OK, you can touch it,' encouraged Ebony.

Chiyoko did as Ebony suggested, trailing her finger over the eye. A tiny spark of glitter twinkled, and Ebony rubbed her eyes, hoping she wasn't imagining things.

'Can I see the Hangman page?' asked Chiyoko.

Ebony was just about to turn to the requested page when she paused. 'Chiyoko, how do you know about all of this?' she asked.

Chiyoko shrugged. 'It's common knowledge.'

'But how?'

'The TV show, of course.'

'TV show?' *This girl is really something*, she thought.

'You're quite the celebrity in Japan. We don't know who leaked the story, but we have a manga cartoon about you. It's already very popular,' continued Chiyoko. Then she lowered her voice to a whisper. 'Thankfully most people don't know about the Order. They think it's just made up. And I think you're much prettier in real life.'

'Where can I see this show?' asked Ebony, her voice turning snappy and irritable despite the compliment.

Ebony didn't even have a TV; her grandpa had always listened to the radio, so she'd grown up without one. It had always seemed like a waste of time, sitting in front of a box watching other people's lives – and made up ones at that! Except for westerns, of course. Westerns were always worth watching. Grandpa Tobias used to take her to Old Joe's cottage so they could munch crisps and drink fizzy lemonade while cheering for the Native Americans. But a manga cartoon about her? She didn't know whether to be flattered or angry – and surely they should have asked permission?

'You can see it on here,' said Chiyoko, pulling out a mini-computer. She switched it on, loaded up the screen, then handed it over. 'Now can I look at the Hangman page?'

'Be my guest,' said Ebony, gesturing without taking her eyes off the screen.

The cartoon started with a catchy theme tune, showing a girl with curly hair billowing in the wind; Ebony guessed that it was supposed to be her. A rat appeared with the name Wilfred flashing across his chest, and the two of them lifted off the ground and flew off into the night. The scene zoomed out, following the silhouette of the girl circling the planet in a Superman pose. When the music stopped, it showed Ebony, dressed in a kimono and drainpipe trousers, charging through Dublin on a motorbike, with several bikes manned by what looked like goblins after her. She pointed her finger and FLASH! A beam shot out, zapping one of the goblins. It juddered and shook, then fell on the ground, dead. If the show wasn't meant to be about her, it might actually have been amusing.

'This is idiotic,' said Ebony. 'I've never seen a goblin. And I can't make beams come out of my fingers.'

'You can't?' asked Chiyoko, sounding both relieved and disappointed at the same time.

Ebony pointed her finger at the mirror. 'See? I've never seen or heard such nonsense.'

Looking a little hurt, Chiyoko retrieved the computer and, switching it off, flung it on the bed.

'So where did whoever leaked my story get their information, exactly?' asked Ebony, knitting her brows.

'Your aunt's reports, of course.'

Ebony crossed her arms. 'My aunt is reporting on me?'

'She has to. Even without a judge in place, events have to be monitored and accounted for.'

'So everyone is reported on?' asked Ebony. 'That's so wrong!'

Chiyoko looked guiltily up at her new friend. 'Not everyone. Just you. Because you have to prove that you're the real guardian.' Biting her lip, she looked like she'd suddenly realised she'd given away too much.

Deciding that having a number-one fan didn't feel that

great after all – it was exhausting – and that it was time to ask her aunt a few questions, Ebony rose to leave.

'Come on, we'd better join the others. I'll get Aunt Ruby to make you some hot choc–'

But Chiyoko didn't move. Her face was contorted, all colour drained from it, staring straight in front of her. For once, she was quiet.

'Chiyoko, what is it?' Following the girl's gaze, Ebony couldn't see anything out of the ordinary, but something pricked at her skin, making the hair on her arms rise. As though sensing the same, Chiyoko broke into a sweat and started trembling. At that moment, the ground and walls also started to shake.

'The m-mirror,' stuttered Chiyoko, staring towards the object in question as though locked in a spell.

Ebony, clinging on to the door frame to keep herself upright, felt her heart pumping. She stumbled over to the dressing table and, hands splayed on the glass top for balance, peered in. Her bottles of *Ebonius Tobinius* perfume jumped and rattled, the lid popping off one of them and pinging across the room. Puffs of its hypnotic scent filled the air.

'I can't see anything!' cried Ebony.

'Can't you hear the whispers?' asked Chiyoko, her voice turning dreamy.

Straining to hear something beyond the tremendous rattling, Ebony checked in the mirror once more. Unable to see anything except herself reflected, she made her way back to Chiyoko and waved her hands up and down in front of the girl's eyes.

'It's so ... blue. And green and rolling.'

'Chiyoko!'

As Ebony shouted, the rattling stopped.

'I can hear a song,' said Chiyoko. 'Something about coffins on the sea bed.'

Ebony strained all her senses, trying to pick up on what Chiyoko was experiencing, but she still couldn't see or hear anything. She held her breath, but there was only silence. Yet Chiyoko remained in a trance.

Seconds later, she heard it – a familiar whispery hush that brought back memories of fishing with her grandpa. Next, the deep, guttural roll of waves, reminding her of when she'd lost their boat, smashing it against the rocks of Gallows Island as she rescued Winston. There was no mistaking the sound of the sea.

Ebony took a deep breath and closed her eyes, squashing down the painful memories. Only when her breathing calmed could she open her eyes. That's when faint voices began to rise and fall, not particularly tuneful but singing all the same:

♪ **Down in the dark depths, pirate souls are restless.**
Their voices carry on the crest of a wave.
Wooden coffins embedded in the sea floor,
Bounty of riches glitter in the sand ... ♩

'I hear it,' whispered Ebony.

Locked in her trance, Chiyoko didn't reply, so Ebony turned to face the mirror again. This time, it looked very different.

Blue-green waves rose, coiled and plunged inside the

glass. The top of the mirror started to darken, turning into a thick, dense cloud. Slowly, Ebony approached. The sky turned completely black and a fat yellow moon began to rise. The waves rose and fell, and the silhouette of a sailing ship pitched and danced on the waves. An old-fashioned ship with masts and sails and something protruding from the front – the face of a dragon, perhaps.

'It's beautiful,' said Chiyoko in a calm, soft voice. She was beside Ebony now, her fingers reaching towards the glass. It was like there was a magnetic field in the air and she was an iron filing being pulled towards it. A speck of light glowed in one corner, drawing her closer.

'It's sinister,' said Ebony. 'There's something not right …'

Could the danger be starting all over again? Feeling a strange mix of relief and fear battling in her gut, Ebony pulled Chiyoko away from the mirror and took hold of her arms. The sound of waves grew louder, crashing about her ears as though she was on a stormy sea with no land in sight.

'Chiyoko? Listen to me, you've got to look away.' She gave Chiyoko a shake, but it had no effect. In the mirror, the song continued, the voices growing louder.

♪ **Skull and bones flying on the main mast,**
Cutlasses and swords ready in hand … ♫

'Winston, help me,' said Ebony. Winston sprang into action. He leapt from his cage, raced across the floor and scurried up Chiyoko's leg, then onto her shoulder. Standing on his hind legs, Winston bit Chiyoko's ear – not hard enough to draw blood but enough for it to pinch. As Chiyoko cried out and grabbed her ear, the bedroom door sprang open and Seamus rushed in. The song and the sounds of the sea stopped abruptly.

'What the hell are you doing to my sister?' Seamus shouted.

Chiyoko, released from her trance and weakened by it, had sunk to the floor. Rushing to her aid, Seamus pulled her to her feet. Her cheeks were dappled with pink and tears streaked down them.

'I'm s-sorry, she was in a trance,' said Ebony. 'We had to get her out of it.'

'You might use blood to open stupid gadgets created by your aunt, but you can't go around using innocent people for your tricks and sorcery!'

'I'm not! What do you mean by tricks and–?'

Seamus pointed to the open *Book of Learning* on the bed. From where she stood, Ebony could see the previously empty page was covered in red splotches.

Carmine red. Blood red.

'But … it wasn't like that before,' she said, rushing over and snatching it up. 'It … it looks like blood. But if it is, it's not hers, it can't be.'

Chiyoko pulled away from her brother's grasp and joined Ebony, peering closely at the page. 'It's true, Seamus. I was the one reading the book and the page was empty,' she said. 'Then there was the sound of waves and–'

As if she had flicked on a switch, the noise started again. It grew and grew until it filled the whole room, forcing everyone to cover their ears.

'What are you playing at?' shouted Seamus.

His sister pointed at the book, looking terrified. The red blood had started to move and swell.

Ebony felt Winston trembling on her shoulder as the blood formed waves like those in the mirror. They rose and fell, dancing and twisting. Ebony, Chiyoko and Winston leaned closer. When the red waves parted, a letter T formed in the middle of the page. Followed by the letter H.

'What's going on, what are you looking at?' asked Seamus, pushing his way in.

The words settled on the page and the sound of waves stopped.

'THEY'RE COMING,' read Seamus aloud, as though it was the least interesting message he'd ever received. 'Who? Some evil baddie that only you can defeat, I suppose?'

'Zach! And the judge!' cried Chiyoko. 'It must be. You will save us, won't you, Ebony?'

Ebony was staring at the book, her ears ringing from the absence of the noise that had threatened to burst her eardrums only moments ago. Feeling a smile spread across her face, she stared straight at Seamus.

'Of course I will,' she said. Grabbing Chiyoko by the

shoulders, Ebony gave the girl a quick squeeze. 'You're my lucky charm. You got *The Book of Learning* working again.'

'I … I am?' asked Chiyoko, her face beaming. 'I did?'

Seamus tutted in disgust. 'You might be fooled by her nonsense, but I'm not,' he said, rolling his eyes. 'It's her aunt's trickery – we all know she's an amazing inventor. The quicker we remove this imposter and find the true guardian, the better.'

'Come on, Chiyoko,' cried Ebony, ignoring him as she slammed the book shut and shoved it in her pocket. 'We've got to tell Aunt Ruby.'

'When the AESL hears about this …' said Seamus.

Ebony stopped dead and turned to face Seamus, her arms crossed and her eyebrows knit. 'I have no idea what your problem is, Seamus,' she said. 'But I'm the guardian whether you like it or not. And I'm here to stay.'

'Sure,' said Seamus, 'whatever you say, *your highness*.'

Turning on her heel, Ebony stomped out of the door and started down the stairs. Winston stalked after her, just as haughtily. Leaping off one of the steps, he caught on to Ebony's shin, scampered up and dropped into the side pocket of her trousers. Like all the special clothes Aunt Ruby had invented for her, they seemed to mould around him.

'Are you coming, Chiyoko?' Ebony called after her.

'Wait, sis,' she heard Seamus hiss. 'I want to talk to you.'

Chiyoko peered into the stairwell and rolled her eyes before returning to see what her brother wanted. 'I'll catch up,' she called to Ebony.

As Ebony headed down the stairs, an idea struck her. There was something about *The Book of Learning*, something not quite right. Pausing two floors below, she opened it up again. 'The page hasn't turned brown like it usually does, Winston,' she whispered, glancing back towards her room. Why hadn't she noticed this detail earlier? 'Whatever's happening, it isn't over yet.'

Just as she finished her sentence, a bright flash from her bedroom lit up the stairwell.

Turning, Ebony raced back up the stairs. As she neared her bedroom, a second flash lit up the room, temporarily blinding her. When her eyes cleared, she took the remaining stairs two at a time and barged her way in. Seamus was on his knees in front of the dressing table, his arms covering his face – he must have got the full force of the bright light – but where was Chiyoko?

Noticing two freshly made, jagged cracks down the front of the mirror, Ebony stared intently at it. Behind the broken glass, there was movement once again. Heart pumping and sweat beading on her upper lip, Ebony approached cautiously. Seamus rose slowly and he too focused on the mirror. Within the glass they could see a dark sky, a rolling sea and a ship journeying across the ocean, all illuminated by the light of a bright yellow moon. This time, Ebony could see it more clearly. It was a three-masted vessel, with two square-rigged forward masts and multitudes of oars sticking out on each side, cutting through the waves at speed. The front was sharp and pointed, like a weapon, with a red-gold dragon figurehead that jutted out from the black hull, glistening as it pointed the way.

'Our reflections,' said Seamus, his voice trembling as he pointed. 'They're missing.'

Before Ebony could reply, there was a roar, followed by a girl's scream. Lifting his hand, Seamus reached out towards the mirror.

'I wouldn't do that if I was you,' said Ebony, putting a hand out to stop him. 'This house has a knack of throwing up unpleasant surprises.'

Spinning round, Seamus fixed Ebony with an angry glare. 'What have you done with my sister?' he asked.

Ebony blinked back at him, not comprehending. Winston popped his head out of her trouser pocket and blinked too. Seamus flicked out his arm and pointed towards the mirror. Suddenly realising what he meant, Ebony set Winston down on the glass top of the table so he could have a clear view of the mirror.

'Is she in there?' asked Seamus.

'I don't know.' Ebony turned to face him, a determined look in her eye and her jaw set. 'What exactly happened?'

'How should I know? It's your room!'

'You were here. I wasn't. Tell me everything,' said Ebony, matter-of-factly.

Seamus's face crumpled into a scowl. 'We were about to follow you. I turned to get her computer and there was a bright flash that blinded me for a moment. When I looked up, she was gone. After a second flash, you appeared.'

'Did you see or hear anything else?'

'No,' he said, glancing at the mirror before lowering his eyes.

'Are you sure she didn't follow me?' Ebony asked, even though she knew it wasn't possible; they would have met on the stairs.

'I'm sure.'

'Could she be hiding?'

'Meeting you is a dream come true for her,' said Seamus snottily. 'In case you hadn't noticed, you're her hero. There's no way she'd hide when you're around—'

'Shh! Listen!' said Ebony, and Seamus reluctantly quietened.

There was a small, barely audible sound that could easily have been missed. Ebony, Seamus and Winston listened, breath held. The sound was just loud enough for the ear to pick up. A gentle sobbing.

'Chiyoko!' cried Ebony and Seamus at the same time.

Turning back to the mirror, they saw that the ship now looked much larger. Although it was dark, a beacon blazed at the prow, illuminating the deck and a small figure tied to the front mast. It was a girl wearing a blue dress with billowing white sleeves, and she was crying. It was definitely Chiyoko, but Ebony couldn't understand how. She had seen visions in the mirror before, but nothing like this had ever happened.

'That's impossible,' said Seamus, his scowl deepening.

'Nothing's impossible in this place,' replied Ebony.

As she tried to relax so she could think more clearly, Ebony noticed a slight tremble in Seamus's lips.

'Will she be OK?' he asked. His voice was gentler, and Ebony felt herself soften towards him. Her mind raced, trying to think of something to say that might make him feel better under the circumstances. Nothing sprang to mind. Instead, she turned towards the mirror and shouted, 'Chiyoko, can you hear me? Are you OK?'

'Don't be so stupid–' started Seamus, but he was silenced by a faint voice.

'Ebony? Is that you?'

'Yes.'

'I can't see you. Where are you? Have you come to rescue me?'

For once, Seamus was speechless.

'Ebony?'

'It's OK, Chiyoko,' called Ebony. 'Don't cry. We'll get you out of there.'

'Can you see me?'

'Yes. I can't reach you yet, but I'm watching over you.'

There was a sudden slamming noise and a movement in the shadows of the ship's cabin. Shuffling footsteps sounded and a dark figure slowly revealed itself on deck. It was almost man-shaped, with thick arms and stumpy legs, but more creature than man. As it lumbered towards Chiyoko, its flesh seemed to swirl and re-form, shimmering like a tar road on a hot summer's day. As Ebony leaned in closer, trying to figure out what this thing was, the creature turned its face towards her, red pinpricks for eyes and yellow stumps where teeth should be. Then it tipped back its head and opened its mouth, letting out a terrifying screech.

'H-h-help!' cried Chiyoko.

The bedroom darkened and a chill filled the air, along with a rotten stench that made Ebony's nostrils sting.

'W-what is that?' whispered Seamus, pinching his nose. 'A pirate?'

'Not like any I've ever seen or heard of,' answered Ebony.

'It's armed like a pirate!'

Peering in, Ebony saw that Seamus was right. The creature held a long, slightly curved blade with a sharp point and knuckle-duster handle in one hand, and in the other, a fat chain with a spiked ball at the end. Fighting the fear that filled her body, Ebony called out, 'Don't be frightened, Chiyoko. We'll get you out of there!'

Hearing her voice, the creature screeched again, smashing its spiked ball against a barrel on the deck, making it splinter into a thousand pieces. Thunder boomed as the creature spun around and thrust the cutlass in Ebony's direction. The blade grew in size and shot through the mirror, making a horrific scratching sound as metal tore through glass. Winston threw himself from the dressing table to the floor, and Ebony jumped back just in time, instinctively covering the amulet with her hand, the blade stopping just inches from her throat.

'You don't scare me,' said Ebony, fighting to keep her voice under control. She could feel Seamus trembling at her side.

The creature cackled, its face stretching and morphing

before settling back into place. Pushing the outstretched blade further into the room, the creature forced its head and neck through the glass in a single fluid movement. Wind whipped around the stunned onlookers as the strange pirate bellowed, knocking Winston off his feet. The rat tumbled and rolled backwards across the floor.

Racing to her bedside cabinet and grabbing her brass candlestick, Ebony lobbed it towards the marauder. It hit the creature in the head, making it pull back inside the mirror. Snatching up a towel that was lying nearby, Ebony threw it over the mirror. For a moment, the shape of the figure's cutlass tip could be seen trying to poke its way back through the mirror – but somehow the towel was preventing it. Eventually, the towel deflated completely and the wind died away. A single slither of shadow spilled from under the towel and onto the floor.

'So, Guardian ... how exactly are you going to save my sister?' asked Seamus, his teeth chattering.

'Me? I'm just a fraud. A cheat. A trickster, remember?' Although she was worried about Chiyoko, she couldn't help goading him. After what his sister had told her about the AESL, it would serve him right.

'So prove me wrong,' he said, a sneer on his face. 'Get her out of there.'

'Fine,' said Ebony, whipping the towel from the mirror. When she did, all signs of the ship and the sea were gone; now there was just the reflection of her and Seamus staring back. But the cracks remained. As realisation dawned, Seamus ran to the mirror and checked it all over with the flat of his hands. He even peered behind it, like he expected Chiyoko to be hiding there in some twisted game of hide and seek.

'Where is she?' he asked, his face stricken.

'That's what we'll have to find out,' said Ebony, pushing past him, 'if you'll let me.'

Running her fingers along the fresh fissures, Ebony closed her eyes; she wasn't sure what she was expecting to happen, but it couldn't hurt. Experience told her that when strange events happened in 23 Mercury Lane, things had a habit of revealing themselves – whether she wanted them to or not. And with *The Book of Learning* back in action, maybe her grandpa's guidance would also return? However, nothing happened when she touched the broken glass, so Ebony turned instead to her book and checked the status of the page – it had turned brown and dry like autumn leaves.

'What I don't understand,' said Seamus, his eyes glued to Ebony's face, 'is why they took Chiyoko at all.'

Ebony swallowed hard. 'It must have been a mistake,' she said. 'They came through my mirror – they'll have been looking for me. *The Book of Learning* warned me, didn't it? "They're coming." That's what it said. Just after that, Chiyoko was taken.'

'So you're to blame.'

'I didn't make this happen,' snapped Ebony. 'But I'll fix it. With Aunt Ruby's help.'

'Your aunt?'

'She'll know what to do,' said Ebony, popping Winston on her shoulder.

'No way,' said Seamus. 'I'm gonna tell my father first.' And with that, he snatched *The Book of Learning* from Ebony's hand and darted out of the room.

9

Ebony had no choice but to follow, charging after him so fast that Winston had to cling on to her curls with all his might using both front paws; it was a long way down over the banister.

'Seamus, wait!' called Ebony, hot on his heels. 'Maybe that's not such a good idea.'

But Seamus wasn't listening. He continued to charge down the stairs like a crazed rhino, with Ebony barely managing to keep up and Winston hanging on for dear life. When they reached the bottom, Seamus skidded to a stop and Ebony had to leap the last few steps to avoid bumping into him.

Aunt Ruby was waiting, her arms folded and a stern expression on her face. Her waist-length red hair gleamed despite the gloom of the long, dark hallway.

'What's all the commotion?' she asked in a loud whisper, glancing nervously at the living room where her guests were relaxing.

Staring up at Aunt Ruby, a blank expression on his face, Seamus clearly couldn't think of what to say or where to start. Taking the opportunity, Ebony jumped in. 'Chiyoko's disappeared.'

Aunt Ruby took a moment to comprehend her niece's words. Then her eyes widened and, glancing once again towards the living-room door, she gave a small mousey squeak. Winston's ears twitched and he looked around him, confused.

'You can't be serious!' said Aunt Ruby in a loud, angry whisper. 'Quick, into the kitchen!'

Herding Seamus and Ebony inside and quietly closing the door behind them, Aunt Ruby rested against the frame. 'Tell me everything,' she said.

'I want to tell my parents, not you,' said Seamus. But Aunt Ruby stood firm, blocking his exit. 'Tell me first,' she said, 'and then I'll help you break the news.'

'Why should I?'

'Fine,' said Aunt Ruby, stepping aside. 'Go ahead and explain to your father how you failed to look after your sister.'

Seamus's shoulders slumped. 'OK. You win. Your house sucked her in.'

'It what?' asked Aunt Ruby incredulously.

'Into the mirror. In *her* room.' Seamus pointed an accusing finger in Ebony's direction. 'Chiyoko's trapped on a ship, but now the ship's disappeared.'

Aunt Ruby looked at her niece quizzically. 'What ship? How?'

'I don't know how it happened. I wasn't in the room at the time,' said Ebony.

Seamus's face reddened and he blurted out, 'I don't know how either. There was a bright light and I was blinded and then she wasn't in the room any more. She was in the mirror, on what looked like a pirate ship.'

'Don't worry,' said Aunt Ruby, looking relieved. 'If it's pirates, we'll sort it out. It'll be a piece of cake.'

At the mention of food, Winston suddenly noticed a large plate of biscuits on a tray on the kitchen table. They were next to a giant teapot and several china cups and saucers. Sneaking down Ebony's back, across the floor and up the table leg, he positioned himself behind the teapot and started munching.

'My sister has been stolen, imprisoned inside a mirror, and you think it'll be a piece of cake?' Seamus burst into a sudden run towards the door, but Aunt Ruby was ready for him. She flipped him round, held him across the chest with one arm and clamped her other hand over his mouth. Taken by surprise, he squealed and squirmed but was no match for Ruby's strength.

'Now, Seamus,' said Aunt Ruby gently. 'There's no need for hysterics. We need to get Chiyoko back. Am I right?'

Seamus nodded.

'And to do that, we have to stay calm, OK?'

Again, Seamus nodded.

'So we're going to sit down and talk this through before we enlist the help of your parents. Are you with me?'

When Seamus nodded again, Aunt Ruby let go. Seamus took a couple of steps towards the kitchen table but then he turned and gave her a swift kick to the shins. Aunt Ruby cried out and Seamus made another dash for the door handle.

Ebony moved fast. Before she even realised what she was doing, she had grabbed Seamus, pulled his arms behind his back and tied his wrists together with a tea towel. Holding her hand over his mouth, she jerked him backwards, dragging him off balance. Aunt Ruby secured a second tea towel round his mouth as a gag.

But it was too late.

The door to the living room clicked open and footsteps headed in their direction. 'Ruby?' came Mr O'Hara's voice from the hallway.

Aunt Ruby grabbed a kitchen chair and jammed it under the door handle. 'Everything's perfectly fine, Jeremiah. I'm just getting us a little snack.'

She clattered a cup against a saucer, making Winston scatter, and signalled to Ebony with her head: the sink. Ebony understood right away and backed up. Seamus kicked out, scuffing his shoes on the floor – but with his arms firmly tied and his body off balance, his efforts proved useless.

The door rattled as Mr O'Hara tried to open it. 'Ruby, I must insist—'

'I'll be right there,' called Aunt Ruby, pushing Seamus's head down so he was below the height of the sink.

Once Aunt Ruby had opened the secret door that led to the basement and Mulligan's lair, Ebony gave Seamus an almighty shove, sending him sprawling inside. Clambering in after him, she sat on his legs so he couldn't kick out. The door swung back in place, leaving them in complete darkness with the sound of dripping water and short, sharp gusts of wind as company.

From somewhere deep in the belly of the basement, there came a low growl. Crossing her fingers, Ebony hoped Mulligan wouldn't find them at the entrance to his quarters. Cramped and cold, Ebony was at least confident that any muffled cries wouldn't be heard – but what was her aunt thinking? It was bad enough they'd lost Chiyoko, but kidnapping Seamus? How would Mr O'Hara react to that?

Ebony heard the door open and Aunt Ruby apologising in her most velveteen voice.

'Sticky door,' her aunt explained. 'Gives us no end of trouble.'

'I thought I heard a yell?'

'Oh, you did. That was me, I'm afraid. That blasted door always puts me in a pickle. I apologise for my outburst.' She lowered her voice to a whisper. 'I'm awfully embarrassed. I didn't think anyone could hear me.'

Ebony chuckled under her breath. Her aunt should be an actor, never mind a transport and travel specialist.

'Now, anyone for biscuits?' asked Aunt Ruby.

The tray clinked and clattered, and Mr O'Hara cleared his throat.

'I'm afraid we'll have to decline your offer,' he said, not sounding particularly regretful. 'We have important business to attend to and must be on our way. So if you could summon Chiyoko and Seamus, we'll say our goodbyes.'

As though a switch had been flicked, Seamus started to squirm. Ebony shifted her weight to keep him in place.

'I checked on them a moment ago and Chiyoko is napping – jet lag, poor thing – and as for Seamus, you just missed him.'

'Missed him?' Suspicion crept into Mr O'Hara's voice.

'They've gone to Ebony's new hideout on my orders. For surveillance. I thought it would be good to enlist his help right away. Ebony wasn't trained in our ways like Seamus and Chiyoko. She will benefit greatly from such distinguished guests.'

'Well, yes, quite right. He can keep an eye on her too,' said Mr O'Hara. 'Make sure there's nothing untoward going on.'

Under the sink, Ebony fizzed with anger.

'I have high hopes for that boy,' continued Mr O'Hara. 'High hopes indeed. He isn't anywhere near up to scratch, but one day, who knows? He could lead the Order. Or even prove to be the rightful guardian … Well, if you can just tell them we said goodbye – we have to get to headquarters. We'll send a car with their things and we'll be in touch.'

Wondering why adults always used ten words when one would do, Ebony wished her aunt would hurry things up. It was growing hot and uncomfortable in the small, cramped space under the sink, and if Seamus started squirming again, either tea towel could fall free. They'd have a sorry time trying to explain why they had Mr O'Hara's son tied up and hidden under a sink while his sister was trapped inside a mirror.

Finally, Ebony heard their footsteps retreating and their voices growing quiet. After a moment, there were several loud clunking sounds as Aunt Ruby secured the many locks on the front door. Behind her, Ebony heard a deep sigh.

'Seamus,' she whispered. 'Don't be scared. We're not going to hurt you. Honest.'

'I know that, you idiot,' said Seamus's voice, loud and clear. 'Now get off me. My legs are going dead.'

Ebony realised that the tea towel must have slipped and he could have shouted out all along. Wondering why he hadn't, she untied his arms and, clambering out from under the sink, eyed Seamus carefully as he got to his feet.

'Don't worry, I'm not going to run,' he said, throwing the tea towels onto the kitchen table. 'What would be the point?'

'The locks are pretty tricky,' said Ebony. 'They'd slow you down.'

'That's not what I meant,' said Seamus, slumping into one of the chairs just as Uncle Cornelius and Aunt Ruby came into the room.

'Sorry about that, Seamus,' said Aunt Ruby. 'I didn't mean to be so rough.'

'Who cares?' said Seamus, shrugging.

'It's just that I don't think your father would take too kindly to what's happened. And when we didn't get a chance to go through the details, I sort of … panicked.'

'My father has that effect on everyone,' said Seamus. 'I'm used to it.' Then he looked Ebony in the eye. 'People panicking because he's a perfectionist, not kidnapping me, that is.'

'Oh, you're not kidnapped,' said Ebony.

'Then what? I'm free to leave?'

Aunt Ruby heaved a big sigh. 'I wouldn't recommend it until we have your sister back. We'll need your help to find her.'

Seamus mulled the request over for a moment. 'Fine. But I'm doing it for her, not you. And if we don't get her back soon, I'm going to report everything to my father.'

Letting Winston scurry up her arm, Ebony tried to ignore the cold look Seamus shot her way.

'That's the spirit,' said Aunt Ruby. 'Now take us to the scene of the crime – and quick!'

10

Racing upstairs, Seamus pushed his way past Ebony so he was up front and leading the group. However much Ebony tried to overtake him, Seamus managed to block her way. He stuck out his elbows and took long strides, positioning himself in the centre so there was no way she could get past. Ebony felt her anger rise but tried to remind herself that this was about finding Chiyoko, not getting one up on Seamus – even if he seemed intent on getting one up on her. When they reached her bedroom, Seamus hesitated. Ebony shoved past and pointed out the mirror that was now calm and uneventful.

'This is where Chiyoko was when we last saw her,' said Ebony quickly. 'These cracks appeared at the same time that she disappeared. Seamus said there was a flash of light and then she was gone.'

Aunt Ruby leaned in and examined the mirror closely. Uncle Cornelius gave the air a sniff, then whimpered. He pointed at the floor. Ebony gasped: on it was a small black skull design that she hadn't noticed before. Bending down, she tried to touch it, but it gave off a searing heat that stopped her getting too close.

'It's burned into the wood,' said Ebony. 'What is it?'

Aunt Ruby stared at the mark, a strange expression on her face. 'Probably something we shouldn't mess with,' she replied.

In the reflection in the mirror, Ebony noticed that Seamus was looking quizzically at her aunt. Aunt Ruby was hiding something, but Ebony knew there was no point dwelling on it now; finding Chiyoko had to be their priority. She could quiz her aunt about the mark later.

'Why don't you demonstrate exactly what happened?' asked Ebony, grabbing Seamus and yanking him towards the dressing table. 'You were the only one of us here.' Feeling him stiffen in her grasp, she let go. As he ran his fingers through his hair, she noticed that his hands were shaking.

'Please,' added Aunt Ruby, gently but firmly.

Reluctantly, Seamus did as he was told. As he talked, the adults nodded and made *umm* and *ah* noises, intermittently checking the area for clues. As Seamus described the pirate that he had seen, Aunt Ruby turned to Cornelius and muttered, 'That sounds like a–' He quickly shook his head and indicated towards Seamus and Ebony, both of whom were watching her expectantly. 'Never mind, go on with the story.'

When Seamus had finished, Uncle Cornelius and Aunt Ruby joined hands in front of the mirror and began to sway.

'We should have this fixed in a jiffy,' whispered Aunt Ruby.

Uncle Cornelius began to sing. It was a beautiful noise, like sunsets and warm bread, and tiny images of dragonflies and birds floated out of his mouth, hovering in the air before they faded or popped. Ebony hadn't heard her uncle sing like that since the time he'd rescued her from her aunt's funny turn in the basement.

'What the …?' began Seamus, too intrigued to finish his sentence. Despite growing up in the Order, he had obviously never seen or heard anything like it.

'They're trying to initiate something,' said Ebony. 'Don't interrupt.' She quickly regretted her words when Seamus gave a snort.

'I'm not stupid,' he whispered. 'And what do you know anyway? I heard your aunt talking to my father in the kitchen. You didn't even get basic Nine Lives training.'

'Ssh!' whispered Ebony. 'Listen.'

'I will not *shush*. Who do you think you are? Just because you have a TV show about you, it doesn't make you any more special than—'

A quiet but definite crack sounded, silencing Seamus. He followed Ebony's gaze to the mirror, where shadows and silver mists were swirling. Stiffening, Seamus stepped back.

As the singing continued and the adults swayed, a moon rose inside the glass. Clouds passed across it like ghosts, and below, waves began to form, the mists turning into sea spray. The prow of a ship came into view at the edge of the mirror, its dragon figurehead rising and dipping in the waves as the oars reached and pulled along the ship's sides. Seamus gasped. The scales of the dragon twinkled red-gold as they caught the moon's glow.

'That's the ship that took Chiyoko! Look!'

Uncle Cornelius and Aunt Ruby continued their singing as though in a trance. Winston peeped his head around the door – he'd finally managed to catch up. Ebony beckoned to him, but he shook his head and stayed put, observing from the safety of the landing. Above their enchanting song, a rowdy tune from many gruff voices rose up inside the mirror.

♪ **Skull and bones flying on the main mast,**
Cutlasses and swords ready in hand. ♫

'That's it! That's the song!' cried Ebony. 'I heard it when the ship first appeared!'

Shoving past Uncle Cornelius and Aunt Ruby, Seamus called out, 'Chiyoko? Chiyoko, can you hear me?'

But the force of his shove caused Aunt Ruby's and Uncle Cornelius's hands to separate. Uncle Cornelius stopped singing, the swaying ended and the scene inside the mirror disappeared. The enchantment was broken.

'What are you doing?' cried Seamus, his lips tight. 'You have to help my sister!'

'We were trying,' replied Aunt Ruby, her eyes narrowing. Uncle Cornelius leaned against her and began to mewl gently. 'Conjuring takes time. Without interruption,' she looked pointedly at Seamus, 'we might have been able to surprise her kidnappers and get her out. But I'm afraid this might not be as simple as I thought. I'm not quite sure what we're dealing with here – these are more than just commonplace pirates.'

'So now what?' asked Seamus, his voice cracking slightly.

'We've done everything we can for the moment,' said Aunt Ruby.

Seamus's face paled then reddened and Ebony saw him ball his fists by his side. 'Can't you try again?' he cried.

'Impossible,' said Aunt Ruby, shaking her head. 'The only way Chiyoko could have been captured through the mirror is via the Shadowlands.'

'The place where people are exiled when they're banished from the Order?' asked Ebony.

'Yes – that's it. But as well as that, in ancient times, when transport was limited and long distances were more difficult to travel, people within the Order used the Shadowlands to get around. Very few know how these days, but I'm certain that's what happened here.'

'So can you get her back?' asked Seamus.

'Our best chance was to take whoever kidnapped her by surprise,' replied Aunt Ruby. 'Unfortunately, we've lost that chance.'

Unfazed by the rebuke, Seamus said, 'Then try something else! You're the transport and travel specialist, aren't you?'

'They'll have closed off this entry point,' replied Aunt Ruby.

'If she was taken through the Shadowlands then can't we get to her that way? How do we access them?' asked Ebony, collecting Winston from the landing and placing him on her shoulder.

Aunt Ruby looked up uncomfortably. 'We don't actually know.'

'Icarus!' cried Ebony. 'He can ride the shadows. We could ask Icarus to teach us.'

Uncle Cornelius shuffled and studied his nails, while Aunt Ruby looked to the floor.

'If you won't ask for his help, I will!' said Ebony. 'I'll go to Oddley Cove and ask him myself.'

'He's not there,' replied her aunt.

'What do you mean he's not there?' Ebony felt her pulse quicken. 'I thought he was guarding the Reflectory. Does that mean there's just Old Joe? And Icarus's supporters from the Order?'

Her aunt kept her gaze averted, a guilty look passing over her features. 'Not exactly. Since Ambrose disappeared, things have been unsettled within the Order. The guards have been recalled to Dublin.'

'But that means the Reflectory is vulnerable. My grandpa's soul is still in there – and your husband's! What if Zach or the judge takes revenge and damages them?'

Ebony's heart quickened as she thought about her grandpa's serene face, positioned in front of his mirror in the Reflectory. All the souls had mirrors, reflecting the good memories and expelling the bad. Ebony had seen herself in his mirror when she'd accessed the Reflectory, a memory of them both taking out the fishing boat. The boat she'd lost in a storm. The pain of it made her anger rise.

'I'm going to the Reflectory,' said Ebony. 'And this time, I'm not going to hear a word against it.'

'There's no point,' said Aunt Ruby. 'It's disappeared. And your Uncle Icarus with it.'

'Disappeared? How can it have disappeared? Has the door closed?'

'We don't know,' replied Aunt Ruby, looking more uncomfortable by the second.

'I told you I should have gone back to the village to protect it. And what about Icarus? Is he OK?'

'All we know is that he was inside when it vanished.'

'What could you have done anyway?' sneered Seamus. 'You're just a girl.'

'I opened it, remember? After it had been hidden for centuries.' She turned to Aunt Ruby. 'You have to let me go back. I have to find it!'

'But why?' asked Seamus. 'If you really can open the Reflectory, which I very much doubt, you can open it anywhere! Shouldn't we concentrate on getting my sister back first?'

Ebony snorted her disdain – what did he know anyway? – but then she noticed her aunt looking sideways at Uncle Cornelius. Putting his head down, Uncle Cornelius rubbed his fat hairy paws, one over the other.

'Is that true?' asked Ebony.

It wasn't something she'd ever considered before, but there was no reason why the doorway had to be static. All she needed was a pure heart under the light of her birth moon and the amulet, rose and medal, which she always carried with her for safekeeping.

'It is, if the door is closed,' said Aunt Ruby. 'But we don't know if that's why it disappeared and you mustn't go in there – not yet.'

'Why?'

'Because when you're in there, we can't help you. The Reflectory protected you last time, but we don't know how powerful Ambrose has become. That's why we've kept you away from the Reflectory for the last few weeks. It will be central to whatever Zach and Judge Ambrose are planning, and we know they can somehow get in, so by keeping you here, we're ensuring that you're safe.'

'Things have changed, Aunt Ruby, the stakes are higher now. Seamus is right – we have to get Chiyoko back. You can't keep me here, wrapped up in cotton wool.'

'It's not just about you,' replied her aunt. 'The future of the whole Order is at stake. Your destiny is linked to the rest of us. Your decisions and behaviour affect us all – and our future. If the judge and Zach achieve their aim and swap your soul, we're all doomed. It'll cause a chain reaction that will destroy the Order of Nine Lives for ever. You have to remember that!'

'How could I forget?' snapped Ebony. 'But we still have to do something.'

'I agree,' replied her aunt, 'but not in haste. You have to know exactly what you're dealing with first and we have to be prepared.'

A weighty silence descended on the room. Aunt Ruby and Uncle Cornelius gave each other awkward looks. After a moment, a loud, shrill cry sounded. It was the cry of a bird. Outside the window, Ebony saw the King Vulture circling, its black wing tip coming close to the window. Following the bird were huge, black clouds, full of menace. The vulture tipped back its indigo head and screamed a second time as it circled the street. At the same time, giant droplets of rain, the size of golf balls, began to fall. The sky blackened and thunder rumbled. After the third cry, lightning flashed and the bird fell silent. In response, Uncle Cornelius tipped back his head and roared three times also. When he fell silent, the rain began to lash so violently that the windows shook as the droplets pummelled against the glass.

'What was that all about?' asked Ebony.

'It's a warning,' said Aunt Ruby. 'Whoever is holding Chiyoko captive sensed our presence. They're telling us to stay away unless we're ready for war.'

'And what did Uncle Cornelius say?'

'The direct translation isn't quite fit for your ears, but it was along the lines of: we're ready.'

'And are we?' asked Seamus.

'Not quite,' replied Aunt Ruby. 'But I know where we can get help. Leave it to me – myself and Cornelius will have to go out for a little while, but stay here together and you'll be safe. Let's go, Cornelius, there's no time to lose.'

11

Before either Ebony or Seamus could protest, Aunt Ruby turned and raced down the stairs with Uncle Cornelius right behind her.

'You!' said Seamus, storming into the middle of the room and pointing at Ebony, his face close to hers. 'This is your fault and I want you to do something about it. Now!'

Ebony had had enough. She felt like punching him in the arm. And hard. Instead, she gave him a shove. Seamus staggered backwards, even though she could see that he tried really hard not to. Shocked, Seamus righted himself and then glowered at her.

'Do that again and I'll—'

'You'll what?' asked Ebony, giving him her best angry stare.

Seamus fell silent, but he didn't back down. Holding her gaze, he reached out and pushed Winston, so he toppled off Ebony's shoulder and landed on the floor in a heap.

'What the hell do you think you're doing?' shouted Ebony, scooping Winston up and checking him over to make sure he was OK. She carefully set him down on the bed, where Winston rubbed his head, looking a little dazed. Unable to contain her anger any longer, Ebony threw herself at Seamus, her weight bearing both of them to the ground. Taken by surprise, Seamus offered no resistance as she flipped him over and ground his face into the floor.

'Never touch my rat again,' she growled, before standing up and collecting Winston from the bed.

'You keep your hands off me,' replied Seamus, getting to his feet and wiping himself down like something very dirty and disagreeable had just touched him. 'When the AESL hears about this, you're going to be sorry you ever got yourself caught up in this guardian stuff. Did you expect me to be impressed? Did you think I'd bow down to the almighty Ebony Smart?'

It took Ebony a second to regain her composure, then she popped Winston back on her shoulder again, crossed her arms and smiled. 'You know what? I've just realised what your problem is. You're jealous!'

'Am not.'

'Yes, you are. You're jealous that I'm the guardian!'

'I am not. So shut up! And anyway, if my father is right and he gets his way …' Seamus bit his lip.

'Your father and the AESL don't scare me. Besides, there's nothing they can do. It's the Reflectory that chose me, not the Order. And just for the record, I don't even want you here. You're only staying here because my aunt feels sorry for you – even though you don't deserve it, because you're a horrible, spoiled brat!'

On her shoulder, she could feel Winston cowering. Glancing in the mirror, she saw he had his paws over his ears. She didn't like to see that. Even worse, she hated that Seamus had managed to get to her. Deciding that it would be better to ignore him completely and not rise to his digs, she turned away. Outside, the summer storm raged, the wind rattling the windows so hard that they threatened to break – Ebony was so caught up in her anger, she barely registered the noise.

'If you weren't such a show off, Chiyoko would never have been in your bedroom. She'd have never seen that stupid mirror or been taken.'

'You keep forgetting, I wasn't there when it happened – you were.'

'That's got nothing to do with it! It's your stupid mirror. It was you they were after.'

'But if you hadn't asked her to come back into the room … it was your stupid fault!'

Seamus rushed towards Ebony and Winston took a flying leap from her shoulder to safety. 'Take that back!'

'I will *not*, until you agree it wasn't my fault.'

'Take it *back*, I said.' Seamus swung at Ebony, thumping her on the arm. Surprised, Ebony squealed, then thumped him back just as hard. Winston darted out of the way as the pair grappled and punched, crashing against the dressing table, neither getting the better of the other and neither willing to back down. They ended up on the ground again, rolling and kicking.

Suddenly Seamus let out a squeal and called out, 'Ouch! It's burning!' Pulling away, Ebony realised they had rolled over the black skull mark on the floor. Quickly checking his back for damage, Ebony found a small hole burned into Seamus's top, but thankfully it had only made it through the first layer. Too tired to continue, and unnerved by the mark, Ebony and Seamus shuffled apart, keeping their distance from each other, panting and catching their breath.

Ebony was the first to stand and straighten. Meanwhile, Seamus climbed to his feet and stayed bent at the waist, his hands resting on his knees, breathing heavily like a runner after a long and fast race.

'I'm sorry. I didn't mean to call you stupid,' said Ebony. 'It just slipped out.'

'It's fine,' said Seamus, making it quite clear with his tone of voice that it wasn't fine at all.

'I mean it. I'm sorry.'

'Sure you are,' said Seamus, giving her a snide look.

'Look, I'm not saying you're right, because you're not. I didn't make your sister disappear. But I do feel responsible because they were looking for me. I'll do my best to help get her back.'

Ebony peered out through the window to check on her aunt's progress. Uncle Cornelius was perched on his motorbike saddle, looking impatiently at his pocket watch and revving the engine – Aunt Ruby was nowhere in sight. Driven by the wind, the raindrops were battering everything in their path, and Uncle Cornelius's fur was already drenched. The desire to chase after them was strong, but Ebony knew that even if she raced downstairs and made it out in time, there was no way they would take her with them. Both the motorbike and the sidecar were only big enough for one.

Glancing up, her anger still ripe and bubbling, she noticed Seamus had red blotches on his cheeks, a wet streak running down one side.

'Seamus?'

He turned his face away and wiped his sleeve across his eyes.

'Are you OK?' started Ebony, placing her hand on his shoulder.

'Leave me alone,' he said in a small voice.

'I'm sorry, I didn't mean … I got angry because I thought you'd hurt Winston.'

Seamus quietened, stubbing his toe off the ground. 'Well, I'm sorry I've given you a hard time. I don't mean to be horrible,' he said, his face averted, hidden half in shadow. 'My father has had this big plan laid out for me my whole life. A big plan that I can't ever live up to.'

I know how that feels, thought Ebony, her aunt's words about her destiny affecting everyone else fresh in her mind. But she stayed quiet and let Seamus have his say.

'I don't mean to be so mean. It just happens. There's no room for failure and I feel so … I guess that's why I've got no friends.'

'That's not true!' said Ebony, swallowing her pride. 'We'll be your friends, if you'll let us.'

Seamus looked up, his eyes watery and glistening and his cheeks blotchy, but Ebony pretended not to notice. His words tugged at her heart. She knew what it was like to be lonely and to make mistakes. Looking down, she noticed Winston nodding too.

'Really? Even after I've been so horrible?' asked Seamus.

'Really. See? Winston agrees too. In truth, I don't have any friends either – apart from your sister, and she's more of a fan club than a friend.'

Seamus laughed. 'I'm sure you'll get on great, if we get her back,' he said.

Ebony corrected him. 'When we get her back.'

Silent for a moment, Seamus cleared his throat. 'Truce?' he offered sheepishly.

'Truce,' agreed Ebony. Seeing a flame of hope in his eyes, she stuck out her hand.

There was a blast of a horn from the street, just loud enough to be heard over the storm, and Seamus dashed to the window with Ebony quickly following. Aunt Ruby appeared, taking her time to clamber into the sidecar.

'They can't really leave us here alone,' cried Seamus, banging his fist against the glass to try to attract Aunt Ruby's attention, but his efforts were useless against the noise of the engine and the thunderous skies. 'What if the pirates come back?'

A smile crossed Ebony's face as an idea struck her. Placing Winston on her palm, Ebony whispered into his ear then set him down on the floor. He raced out of the room as fast as his legs could carry him.

'When they've gone, we should get out of here too. Knowing my aunt and uncle, they'll be gone for a while. Want to see my hideout?'

Although it was the middle of the day, Ebony knew that the unexpected summer storm would have emptied the park. As she grabbed her rucksack, Seamus glanced at the window then at the mirror.

'Sure,' he said, nodding vigorously and carefully stepping around the skull mark as he headed for the door. 'Let's go!'

12

Hurrying along Earlsfort Terrace, past the National Concert Hall with its flat, grey façade and heavy black chains crowning its perimeter walls, Ebony and Seamus raced towards St Stephen's Green as fast as they could, pushing against the gusts of wind. They pulled their coats up over their heads to try to protect their faces from the freezing cold rain. Despite the awful weather, the sting in her fingers and cheeks, and her worries that the contents of her rucksack might get drenched and damaged, Ebony was happy. She couldn't wait to show off her hideout to her new friend.

As she had expected, the park was deserted, so she held her eye to the rose carving on the seat, opening the entrance right away. The usual hum could hardly be heard over the drumming rain, and she raced down the steps, dragging Seamus with her. Seamus was quiet, his eyes darting in all directions as he took in every detail. When they reached the bottom, the mouth of the secret entrance closing quietly behind them, they quickly removed their wet coats. Ebony pointed out the ceiling where the pond water rippled and danced.

'It's a-ma-zing,' said Seamus, and he sounded so much like his sister, Ebony's mood dampened.

'Let's see where my aunt has gone,' she said.

First checking her rucksack to make sure the contents weren't soaked, Ebony sat down at her desk. But when she tried to access the surveillance cameras, they weren't working. The screen showed black, with rows of lime-green lines rolling down.

'The storm must be interfering with the transmitter,' said Ebony, disappointed. 'Let's see if we can find out more about what happened to Chiyoko instead.'

Assigning Seamus the task of double-checking the last few surveillance reports her aunt had given her, she set about testing out her new computer. Her aunt had granted her access to the Order of Nine Lives database, so she typed in 'skull symbol'. The screen went black and a white message flashed across it – CLASSIFIED. A moment later, it flickered back to the standard screen. Trying again, this time searching the term 'pirates with skull symbol', Ebony hit another blank. Once again, CLASSIFIED flashed across her screen.

'This is weird,' said Ebony.

Seamus quickly tired of his task and joined her at the computer. 'Classified? If only we could ask my father. He regularly classifies his own files, so I'm sure he'd know how to get around it. What are you looking for anyway?'

'Let's not involve him just yet. I'm trying to figure out what that skull mark means.'

'Have you tried this?' asked Seamus as he leaned in and started poking at the keyboard.

'Stop it!' said Ebony. 'You're putting me off. Have a look around or something.'

Without another word, Seamus went off to investigate. Behind her, Ebony could hear him opening and closing drawers and doors. Blocking out the noise, she concentrated on searching the Order's files. This time, she tried just 'skull pirates'. Yet again, the term CLASSIFIED appeared on her screen. Only this time, there was a name on the file.

'Seamus, this is one of your father's files. Look!'

Realising Seamus had fallen quiet, she turned round.

Seamus was nowhere in sight and the usually locked door in the corner of the room was wide open.

Grabbing her rucksack and crossing to the doorway, Ebony paused at the entrance to an empty, dusty corridor. On either side of the grey stone walls, tear-shaped bulbs blinked on, secured to the walls by rose-shaped holders with vines wending their way along the stems. She could see four doors, two on each side, and the corridor then curved to the left. But from where she was standing, she couldn't see where it led, or any sign of Seamus.

'Hello?' she called out.

Seamus stuck his head out through one of the doorways, and Ebony jumped so hard she nearly hit the top of the door frame.

'What?' he said. 'These rooms are filled with cobwebs. Don't you clean around here?'

'This door has always been locked,' replied Ebony. 'I've never seen it open. Even when this place belonged to Zach.'

It was Seamus's turn to jump. 'This place used to belong to Zach Stone? You're kidding!' As he glanced the length of the hallway, goose bumps showed on his arms. 'I wonder where it leads?'

'I don't know, but there's only one way to find out,' said Ebony, swallowing nervously.

'After you,' said Seamus, looking terrified. 'It's your hideout.'

'How about we go together?' said Ebony.

Taking a step, hardly daring to breathe, Ebony peered into the rooms that Seamus had already investigated. There was a family-sized bathroom, untouched for what looked like years. The pink facecloth on the sink and a little yellow rubber duck on the corner of the bath were both covered in thick, lacey cobwebs. Moving on, there were two bedrooms and a big country-style kitchen. They were just ordinary rooms, if a little old-fashioned; dark and ugly. It was difficult for Ebony to imagine Zach living here with his mum and dad, as a happy family. Creeping forward together, Ebony and Seamus followed the passageway. As they moved further along, beacons automatically flared, lighting their way as they followed the corridor round to the left. When they turned the corner, a final door greeted them. It was slightly ajar.

'Let me guess, another bedroom!' said Seamus.

As Seamus pushed the door open, they both stopped in their tracks. Inside, a blue light blazed, almost blinding

Ebony as it caught her eye. She looked away, blinking to help her sight adjust.

'Hello?' she called out.

Her voice echoed around the room, but there was no reply so, together, they stepped inside, both shielding their eyes from the eerie glow. The edges of the room were pitch black. As their vision adjusted, they saw the floor was made up of big, old flagstones, like those found in a church, and there was a collection of objects on top of a marble fireplace: a large conch shell, a bird's skull, a photograph and a bucket of ash. The collection was surrounded by candles of varying heights. The blue light was coming from inside the skull, its two eyes lit up like a demon. In the hearth where a fire should be, there was a thigh bone on top of a large drum. And around the drum's base, there were rocks.

Ebony picked up one of the rocks; it had a black skull burned into it. Seamus checked the others – they were all the same.

'What is this place?' asked Seamus.

'It looks like some sort of shrine,' said Ebony, lifting the conch and holding it to her ear.

At first she heard the rushing sound that people said resembled waves, but then she heard something else: voices faint and angry:

♪ **See white horses gallop o'er the ocean,**
Angry pirates with murder in their eyes,

Cutthroats and coffins, rising from the darkness,
Seas awaking, sails point to the sky. ♩

Lowering the shell, her heart pumped. The words were different, but the tune matched the one she'd heard in her bedroom mirror.

'Whatever this is,' she said, 'it's linked to whoever took Chiyoko. Listen.'

Holding the shell to Seamus's ear, she watched as his eyes grew huge. 'I don't like this one bit,' he said.

Stepping forward, he picked up the photograph from the fireplace and looked at it closely before handing it to Ebony, a grim look on his face. Tilting the photograph so she could see it properly in the blue light, Ebony saw an image of herself and Zach huddled near each other in the park bandstand. It was raining and they were sharing food.

'This must have been the first time I met Zach!' said Ebony. 'I thought there was no one else around. This must be the work of Judge Ambrose.'

'But what's it doing here?' asked Seamus. 'I thought Zach wanted you dead. Instead, he built a shrine?'

'Thanks for the reminder,' said Ebony, feeling a chill creep all over her body.

Pointing to the drum and bone, and then the bucket of ashes, Seamus continued. 'And what exactly are these for?'

'I'm not sure – but I bet there's more to discover. Let's check out the edges of the room. They're probably dark for a reason.'

Hands out in front of her while her eyes adjusted, Ebony made her way into the dark edges and corners. Feeling her way around the cold stone wall, she soon found a heavy, plush, burgundy curtain. As she pulled it open, wind suddenly whipped around her. Shielding her face with one hand, and with the other outstretched, she pushed on. As she bumped into something cold and hard, Ebony's hand wrapped around a metal bar. Opening her eyes, she found a door made of bars, like one in a prison. It covered a gaping hole in the wall, and on the other side was another tunnel.

'We've got to open it,' said Ebony, searching the wall with the flat of her hands for a trigger to unlock it.

'What if it's dangerous?' asked Seamus. 'Wouldn't we be better off leaving it?'

'It could lead us to something that'll help us find Chiyoko,' Ebony replied.

As she continued to search the walls, Seamus crouched down and started searching the flagstones.

'I think I've found something,' he said.

Bending to join him, Ebony saw what looked like a lever in the floor to the left of the hole. It was wedged between two flagstones with an inch-wide gap running the length of the stones, enough for the lever to move. Taking hold, she tried to pull it towards her, but she wasn't strong enough. Seamus grabbed hold also, and together they yanked with all their might. The lever groaned and shifted, and the cage bars slid to the left, leaving the entry unobstructed.

'It worked!' cried Ebony, getting to her feet.

'You're not seriously going in there?' asked Seamus as Ebony moved to step into the tunnel.

'You can wait here if you like, but I'm going to see where it leads.'

'Wait!' cried Seamus, running back to the fireplace and picking up the thigh bone. Hoisting it over one shoulder, he gritted his teeth. 'OK. Now I'm ready.'

Letting the curtain drop behind them, and both secretly happy to leave the glaring blue room behind, Ebony and Seamus took a deep breath. The passageway was scooped out of the earth and then strengthened with white plaster, its floor initially lined with flagstones but quickly turning to dirt that was well trodden and dry. It was bitterly cold, but automatic flares like those in the Hideout lit their way, so they could see where they were going. However, the tunnel turned and twisted like a river, so they had no idea what was up ahead.

Each step was as terrifying as the last, and the pair walked close together. Seamus gripped the thigh bone tightly. As a scuffling noise sounded behind them, he turned and held it out in front of him, barely able to lift it yet wielding it like a weapon.

'It's just dirt falling from the tunnel walls,' said Ebony, pointing to a section where earth was visible behind the crumbling plaster. 'It looks like no one has been in here for a while – maybe the door opening after such a long time has loosened it.'

'What if it collapses?' asked Seamus, checking the ceiling. Spotting a section that was plaster-free, roots pushing their way through, he whimpered.

'Let's get a move on so we don't find out,' said Ebony. 'I wonder where it leads.'

Pushing on, the pair hardly dared draw breath. After a while, her confidence building, Ebony quickened their pace. When she looked back to check on Seamus, his face was glistening with sweat, despite the damp, chill air.

'It can't be far now,' she said encouragingly.

Hearing another, more distant noise behind them – this time a rumbling – they paused. Seamus was trembling, even though he was clearly trying to hide it.

'Do you want to go up ahead or behind?' asked Ebony.

'Ahead,' replied Seamus, thigh bone lifted. Walking on cautiously and glancing nervously at the ceiling, checking for bare patches and crumbling earth, he said, 'Do you think we'll have to come back this way?'

When there was no reply, he looked behind him. 'Ebony?'

Ebony could hear Seamus's voice, but she could no longer see him. The world had turned fuzzy and strange, made up of shimmering lines and grey smudges, like a charcoal drawing that had been brought to life. Seamus's voice was slurred and distant so she couldn't make out his words. But she could hear a different voice, a closer voice, as it spoke her name.

'Hello?' she said, not able to see who was speaking, but hoping it was her grandpa. The word sounded normal, but the effort to make it was tremendous. It felt glutinous in her mouth, like mud.

'I have to speak to you,' came the reply, melodic as a bird.

Fighting the disappointment – it wasn't Grandpa Tobias: the voice was female – Ebony tried to look around her, but it felt like her head and neck were trapped in an invisible web. The voice was coming from in front of her, and a figure appeared which looked like a sketch that hadn't quite formed. The image wobbled and wavered, greenish in colour, hurting Ebony's eyes as she tried to focus.

'Where am I?' Ebony asked, blinking her eyes to try to focus properly. The effort was exhausting.

'The Shadowlands,' said the voice.

Ebony knew that the Shadowlands was where the exiles were banished and that her aunt was certain it was the way to get to Chiyoko, but she didn't have a clue how she could have got there.

'We don't have much time, Ebony. Do you have the box I sent you?'

Wondering where she had heard the voice before – was it one of her past selves, perhaps? – Ebony battled to formulate a reply.

'That was you? Who are you? Please, I need to know.'

'I'm a friend. Listen to me carefully. Under no circumstances must you lose that box. Return it to the rightful owner. If you don't, no one will be able to help you.'

'Why? What does it contain?' asked Ebony.

'Something that was stolen a long time ago that needs to be returned.'

'Is it dangerous?'

'Unleashed at the wrong time by the wrong person, yes. Keep it close and keep it safe. You must return it to its owner before Ambrose finds it. If he does, he will gain power so terrible that no one will be able to stop him.'

Nodding, Ebony felt weak. She still had no idea who she was talking to or how she had ended up in the Shadowlands. 'I'll do my best,' she replied.

'Good,' said the voice. 'Because you're going to have to fight for your life like never before. Now go, before we are discovered! Keep going – you're on the right path. But tell no one we met.'

'Who ... are you ...?' managed Ebony, each word a struggle. Her head began to ache and it hurt to speak. 'Who ... do I give the box ... to ... and how do ... I get ... back?' But there was no reply and the next thing she knew, she was sprawled on the floor of the secret passageway, her hands covered in dirt and scratches. As she struggled to her feet, Seamus appeared around a bend up ahead.

'Where were you?' he hissed, his face a mixture of anger and worry. 'I didn't see or hear you leave. I thought ...'

With the warning fresh in her mind – *tell no one we met* – and the truce with Seamus not long made, it was easy for Ebony to lie.

'I doubled back to check on the noise, but I didn't find

anything so I came straight back. Sorry, I should have told you. You weren't scared, were you?'

'Of course I wasn't,' replied Seamus, his face pale. 'But don't disappear like that on me again. Now come on, let's keep going!'

As she chased after Seamus, Ebony's mind raced. Had she really been in the Shadowlands and, if so, how had she got there? And how was she meant to find the owner of the box? As they wound their way around a final corner, her thoughts were interrupted. In front of them was a tarnished metal door; it looked old and heavy, with an ivy design carved around its edges. There was no visible handle, but in the centre a black skull was branded on the metal. Seamus lifted his thigh bone, poised to attack.

'What if there are pirates on the other side?' he whispered. 'That mark is the same as the one they left behind in your bedroom.'

Ebony stepped towards the door and took a deep breath. 'We can't turn back now.'

She tried giving the door a push. When it didn't budge, she began searching for an opening mechanism. There were no flagstones on the floor, just tightly packed dirt, and no hidden lever to be found.

'I don't like this one bit,' said Seamus, making Ebony look up.

Standing on one leg and tipping over to the side, Seamus bent the lifted leg and kicked out at the door. As the sole of his shoe connected with it, the metal groaned. In the centre of the door, the skull design glowed briefly then returned to normal.

'What did you do?' asked Ebony.

'I'm not sure,' replied Seamus, biting his lip.

'Whatever you did, do it again,' said Ebony.

Lifting his leg again and angling it to ninety degrees, Seamus gave another almighty kick in the same spot. This time, the skull glowed and melted away before their eyes, leaving a skull-shaped hole in the door. The teeth formed a jagged handle. Reaching out, Ebony carefully took hold and pressed the handle down, making sure not to cut her fingers on the sharp teeth. But something jabbed her palm, making it sting. 'Ouch,' she cried, pulling back her hand to see the damage. A tiny pinprick of blood showed in the centre of her palm. Feeling silly – the wound was tiny – she gave the handle another try. The door opened with a little jiggling and they stepped cautiously inside.

'Let's leave it open in case we need a speedy exit,' suggested Ebony.

But when they looked back, there was no sign of the door. In its place was a solid-looking red-brick wall that looked like it hadn't been disturbed for hundreds of years. Reaching out towards it, unsure whether it was real or an illusion, Ebony's hand hit against cool, scratchy brick. 'Well, there's no going back,' she said.

Seamus blew out a big puff of air and Ebony gave him a nervous glance. Up ahead, there was a bright light.

As Ebony led the way, a familiar smell, like wet fur, assaulted Ebony's nostrils and she battled her brain to figure out where she'd come across the stink before. A few steps further and everything clicked into place.

'It's OK, Seamus,' she said, as the room opened up. 'I know this place. It's our basement.'

She didn't add that it was strictly out of bounds, that she had no idea why a passageway led from there to the underground lair – or why no one had told her about it.

Looking about him, Seamus fell silent and clasped his thigh bone more tightly. Following his gaze, Ebony realised why. In front of Seamus was a wall filled with television screens. And in front of the television screens was a huge beast. It was hairy, muscular and had very sharp teeth, which right now were bared and snarling at Seamus and Ebony. That was the smell Ebony had recognised – damp prehistoric wildcat. Seamus took a step closer to Ebony.

'It's Mulligan, my aunt's pet and bodyguard,' said Ebony, taking a cautious step sideways, her eyes scanning the room for the whistle her aunt used to control the beast. It was nowhere to be seen, but a coiled leather whip hung on a hook just a few feet away. Pausing, she added, 'Whatever you do, don't move a muscle.'

Seamus did as he was told and stood completely still. Mulligan sniffed the air and gave a low growl.

Taking a few sudden bounds towards the whip, Ebony took Mulligan by surprise. Snatching the whip from its hook, she gave it a quick jerk, a loud crack sounding as it slapped against the floor just in front of one of Mulligan's huge paws. He snarled, showing his huge teeth, but backed away. Seamus's jaw dropped as Ebony slapped the whip off the ground again, and the wildcat retreated. Although the whip was heavy, Ebony quickly got the hang of it, and the third crack tipped Mulligan on the nose, making him roar. Opening his jaws wide, he gave a big, phlegmy snarl, then backed into the darkness. Ebony and Seamus watched the muscles rippling on his shoulders and hindquarters as he skulked away. Ebony recognised the tunnel they'd just come from as the area where Mulligan slept. She had never been down there in case she bumped into him. Now she wondered whether he'd been guarding the brick wall on purpose all this time.

Once Mulligan showed no sign of returning, Ebony led Seamus towards the TV screens, whip in hand.

'Now, let's see what we've been missing,' she said.

14

Jumping into the big squashy chair in front of the screens, Ebony patted next to her for Seamus to sit down. The chair was covered in long silver and black hairs. Picking up a remote, she pointed it at the screens and, thankfully, they kicked into life. Seamus settled himself into the chair, his face alive with excitement.

The TV screens were all joined, like a massive mosaic, each showing a different room. Every area of the house was monitored, including the living room, and every room was empty.

'You can spy from the dungeon?' asked Seamus, a hint of admiration in his voice.

'It's a basement, technically. But seeing as my aunt and Uncle Cornelius won't be back yet, the house is not what I'm interested in.'

Ebony pushed a button and the scene changed. This time, the camera focused on Aunt Ruby's chin; it was bobbing up and down so they were still on the move.

'It's Winston transmitting the picture; he has cameras and a microphone implanted into him,' explained Ebony. 'I sent him along so we could spy. If I could just figure out how to get the volume up and running ...'

She pressed a few of the buttons on the remote and finally there was a hiss, a crackle and then indiscernible noises started to come through. Seamus stared at the screen as though his life depended on it. The picture suddenly zoomed out; Ebony recognised the interior of a giant glasshouse.

'That's the Order's headquarters,' said Ebony. 'Isn't it beautiful?'

'It's huge,' replied Seamus, drawing out the word. Realising he'd just admitted that he didn't know as much as he liked to let on, he quickly corrected himself. 'It doesn't look that big in photos, is all.'

Uncle Cornelius and Aunt Ruby were making their way through the headquarters buildings led by Mrs O'Hara, her hair spilling like oil down the back of her sea-green silk blouse.

'What's Mum doing there?' said Seamus quietly, thinking aloud. 'Shouldn't she be unpacking so we can come home?'

'My aunt must have asked for her help.'

'But it looks like she's taking them to my father. I thought your aunt wanted to keep this whole thing secret?'

'I'm just as puzzled as you are,' answered Ebony. 'Let's watch and see what happens.'

Returning their attention to the screen, Ebony and Seamus watched as the group hastened on, pausing to greet a few people in one of the narrow passageways between the glasshouses. After passing through a couple of rooms filled with giant tropical plants, Mrs O'Hara stopped abruptly, her back to a wall covered in vines. It took Winston a moment to catch up, but he kept his gaze fixed on his target the best he could. Seamus and Ebony watched as Mrs O'Hara checked around them, then beckoned. By the time Winston caught up, the conversation was in full swing. Aunt Ruby's was the first voice they could hear clearly. 'I appreciate this, Mrs O'Hara. I know he'll be reluctant but he's the only person I know that can tell us what we need to know,' she said, her voice filled with urgency.

'You are welcome, my old friend. But remember, tread carefully with my husband. And speak in facts, not riddles.'

Mrs O'Hara swept away the vines. She poked at one of the stones, pushing it all the way in until it fell through to the other side. The other stones around it began to nudge forward until they formed a door shape. Reaching into the hole, she turned her hand so it was palm up. A beam of red light appeared and scanned across it from left to right.

'O'Hara,' announced a computerised voice.

A beep sounded and, grasping the stones, Mrs O'Hara pulled with all her might. Once the door was open, she motioned for Aunt Ruby and Uncle Cornelius to step inside. Before Winston could follow, the door slammed shut and the stones melded back into a wall, with Mrs O'Hara keeping watch in the corridor.

'So much for spying,' said Seamus.

Seconds later, Mrs O'Hara bent down and picked up

Winston. Holding him up in front of her face and staring deep into his eyes, she gave a wide, closed-lip smile. Ebony felt her heart warm as the smile grew huge on the screen.

'Your mum knows about Winston!' she cried.

'My mum's a Buddhist. She's always helping stray animals. There's no way she knows about Winston.'

But Ebony wasn't convinced, particularly since Mrs O'Hara proceeded to set Winston down and open the secret door for him. He scurried quickly into the room beyond.

Filled with an unusual mix of computers and exotic plants, it was a room straight from a science-fiction novel. Between huge leaves and strange blossoms, radars and lists of binary shone out from semi-hidden monitors. Bright yet misty, the room was heated to tropical temperatures, so Winston had to keep blinking his eyes to be able to transmit his recording properly.

Ebony recognised the flora right away from the botany books and encyclopedias she loved to read with her grandpa. And they all had one thing in common – they were carnivorous. There were sundews with their long, sticky tongues, Venus flytraps with their mouths yawning wide and inviting, and pitcher plants that drowned their prey before digesting the decaying flesh of the insects and small creatures that decomposed inside them. As Winston positioned himself near a pitcher big enough to devour a small child, Ebony's heart felt like it was going to leap out of her chest.

'Be careful, Winston,' she whispered.

'Ssh!' replied Seamus. 'Listen!'

Already, Mr O'Hara and Ebony's aunt were deep in conversation. Ebony increased the volume until they could hear the voices clearly, both of which were edged with disdain.

'I'm telling you, Jeremiah. Things are more dangerous than you think. Someone tried to snatch Ebony through the Shadowlands; it has to be Ambrose. Who else would have that power or would even want to try? Thankfully, he failed, but there's more to it than we thought. He has help. A certain mark was left behind – something I recognise from the history books.' Taking a pencil and piece of paper from a nearby desk, Aunt Ruby did a quick sketch and held it up for Mr O'Hara to see. The paper showed a skull.

Mr O'Hara took the paper, crumpled it up in his massive hands and tossed it across the room. Aunt Ruby continued, visibly angry but undeterred, 'I've seen evidence of a pirate ship, but it was quite mysterious. Unlike any pirate ship I've seen before. You said earlier that there were unusual happenings on the seas, but you didn't elaborate. Do you have any idea what's going on?'

'My findings are highly confidential.'

'You said you were here because of pirate activity, but, from what I saw, these are no ordinary pirates – and I'm guessing your work and our potential kidnappers are linked. You have no right to withhold information.'

Next to Ebony, Seamus snorted. 'Because your aunt's so honest!'

Ebony ignored the dig and continued listening to Aunt Ruby.

'I know you're eager to advance your career but refusing to help could look ... disloyal. Tell me what you know!'

'If you're implying I'm somehow mixed up in all this–' spluttered Mr O'Hara.

'I'm imploring, not implying. We need your expertise to protect the guardian. And we need it now. Tell me, these pirates you mentioned ... are we dealing with Shadow Walkers?'

As Mr O'Hara silenced Aunt Ruby with a wave of his hand, Ebony looked to Seamus for an explanation, but his face was locked on the scene, crumpled in concentration with a deep frown lining his forehead. On the screen, Aunt Ruby and Mr O'Hara were interrupted as Uncle Cornelius stepped backwards into a huge lobster-claw *Heliconia*. His fur caught on the colourful spiked leaves and, as he yanked himself away, he pulled the plant and its ceramic base with him. Ebony chuckled, but Seamus was far from amused.

'Shut down the AESL and help us,' continued Aunt Ruby. 'Or at least tell me what my brother and sister-in-law knew about the Shadowlands. If you don't, the judge could succeed in his mission to swap souls – starting with Ebony's – and he'll gain the power of reincarnation for himself. The Order as we know it will die out, including your family, leaving the equilibrium of the world in turmoil!'

'Enough with the melodrama!' cried Mr O'Hara. 'There

is no evidence except your say-so that Ebony is the true guardian. If she is, I will support her wholeheartedly but until this is proven to members of the Order outside your immediate family, I will keep the AESL in place. However, out of respect for Ebony's parents, I shall give you a portion of the information that you seek.'

Even from the weird angle that Winston was transmitting the images, it was clear that Mr O'Hara's face had turned very pinched. With an impatient click of his tongue, he took a pen from his pocket and scribbled something on a pad of paper on his desk. When he had finished, he dropped his hand, and Winston crept a bit closer to take a peek. On the screen, it showed the beginnings of a list.

'Number 1: Find a wide open space,' read Seamus aloud. Then he shook his head. 'The only wide open space my father admires is the sea, and even then, he's never set foot on it.'

Shocked, Ebony asked, 'Never? Then how does he monitor the oceans? Isn't he a maritime defence expert?'

'Gadgets and gizmos, both overland and under the sea. High-powered submarine missiles and seekers roam under the waves gathering data and images, while drones plot positions and on-board activity from above. He's an expert, but he won't leave dry land.'

As Mr O'Hara got to his feet, Winston backed away. Mr O'Hara's white moustache trembled as he handed the note over. Ebony thought he looked nervous. 'This is all I can tell you, though I'm certain it's complete nonsense and I don't want my name attached to it. I haven't made the sacrifices I have, slaved away at my career, for you to get in my way. Now, it's time for you to leave.'

'What's wrong with him?' asked Ebony. 'Why is he so reluctant to help?'

'You don't know my father,' said Seamus, sounding weary. 'He has big plans, and believe me, they don't include you. Or anything regarding figments of the imagination, like Shadow Walkers.'

'If that's what we saw in the mirror, it looked very real to me,' Ebony retorted.

Seamus sighed and shook his head, refusing to say more. Ebony made a mental note to quiz her aunt later as, on screen, Mr O'Hara returned to work, checking the progress of a radar and something that looked like a 3D model made of lights that was too far away for her to make out. Aunt Ruby and Uncle Cornelius turned to leave; the door was clearly visible on this side of the wall. As they passed through, Winston ran for dear life before it could slam in his face. Jamming on his brakes once outside, he made a sharp left and then raced ahead at top speed – he clearly didn't want to be left behind – so he would be first to reach the motorbike. Ebony and Seamus could hear his heart pounding on the speaker as he climbed up and hid in the sidecar.

Moments later, he squealed, making the speaker ring with feedback. A big violet eye filled the screen. As Winston was moved a little further away, Aunt Ruby's face appeared.

'I presume you two got all that?' she asked. 'Meet us at St Stephen's Green – we're on our way!'

'We don't have to go back through that tunnel, do we?' asked Seamus, his voice a bit squeakier than usual.

'No,' replied Ebony. 'We'll stay above ground this time. Somewhere visible.'

15

The late afternoon sun had come out, making everything bright and sharp, a tinge of damp in the air.

'Welcome to the Irish weather,' said Ebony.

Seamus gave no reply; he was too lost in his own thoughts, dragging his feet as he followed. Meanwhile, Ebony took pleasure in the warm breeze on her face. The summer feeling was infectious, and Ebony let it wash over her and seep into her bones. Watching the people they passed, dressed in colourful clothes and with a spring in their stride, Ebony almost felt normal – able to forget her fears and responsibilities for a moment.

But only almost.

'If my aunt said to meet her in the park, there must be a reason,' said Ebony, not sure what else to say as the Leeson Street gates came into view. 'Let's find somewhere we can be easily spotted.'

The sun was shining brightly, so the park was now full of people; it looked like a completely different place from earlier. Some were cutting through to Grafton Street for a spot of shopping, while others were relaxing on the benches with steaming cups of takeaway coffee or a snack. Ebony led the way to a big grassy area and sat in the shade of a huge sycamore. Overhead, small birds and gulls squawked. Ebony picked at the blades of grass and threaded daisies, trying to figure out how to break the uncomfortable silence. Luckily, Seamus began to speak.

'Did you hear my father talking about sacrifices? Chiyoko, Mum and I are the only ones who've made sacrifices. Father's always at the office or schmoozing and he always gets his own way. He couldn't give a stuff about us. All he cares about is his stupid work.'

Ebony was taken aback by the sudden outburst. She set down her daisy chain and gave him a sympathetic smile. 'I'm sure your dad doesn't mean to–'

'Be such a pig?' cut in Seamus.

'Be so busy,' tried Ebony.

'Either way, it's not fair.'

Nodding, Ebony tried to imagine how Seamus was feeling. It was one thing having no one, but another to be ignored by the people around you.

'I'm sure he cares very much deep down,' said Ebony.

Seamus fell silent and Ebony couldn't think of anything to add. Now that she had some time to think, guilt plucked away at her stomach – maybe if she had been more careful, if she'd managed to get Chiyoko out of the trance sooner, the girl wouldn't have been taken. She concentrated harder on her daisy chain, wishing the others would hurry up and get there.

Hearing a squeak, Ebony saw Aunt Ruby approaching with Winston. The pair were making their way across the grass, watching the people nearby. There were jugglers tossing skittles and diabolos, brows knitted in concentration. A group of students with loud, cheery voices sprawled in a circle, not caring about the damp grass as they smoked and laughed. A young boy whizzed past on a scooter.

As soon as Aunt Ruby reached them, Ebony jumped to her feet and reached for her rat, cuddling him close.

'Sending Winston was a good idea,' said Aunt Ruby in greeting. 'I wish I'd thought of it myself. It saves us time. We're one step closer.'

'How?' asked Seamus, a hopeful look on his face.

'That's why we're here,' replied Aunt Ruby. 'We're going to learn how to ride the Shadowlands.'

Looking at each other with confused expressions, Seamus and Ebony turned to Aunt Ruby.

'You said you didn't know how,' said Seamus.

'I don't, or at least, I didn't,' said Aunt Ruby. She flicked out her arm, showing him the list his father had written. 'But your father does. So let's get going! No time like the present.'

'My father doesn't even believe that shadows can be ridden, so how would he know this?' asked Seamus, a quizzical look on his face.

'Because,' answered Aunt Ruby, placing a hand on her niece's shoulder, 'he worked with Ebony's parents for many years, before she was even born, and they had it mastered.

They passed the knowledge on to your father, and even though he dismissed it, he committed it to memory. You know what he's like.'

Seamus nodded. 'A know-it-all. Has to be the best at everything.'

Studying the note, Aunt Ruby read out the first instruction. 'Find a wide open space and seek the most prominent shadows.'

Ebony's heart raced. She had been in the Shadowlands briefly and it wasn't particularly pleasant – but if learning how to access it meant saving Chiyoko, she had to try.

'What about the Shadow Walkers?' asked Ebony. 'What are they? Will they be there? Are they dangerous?'

'I'll tell you all about them later. What you need to know for now is that they live in the Shadowlands, they are extremely dangerous and we need to be wary and avoid coming into contact with them if we get in,' said her aunt. 'But the chances of us succeeding right away are pretty low. Entering the Shadowlands takes great skill. We need to concentrate on trying to master this, so we can then use it to find Chiyoko.'

'We can't do it here in front of all these people!' replied Ebony.

'You leave that to me,' said Aunt Ruby, smiling as she tapped her nose. Putting her finger to her lips, Aunt Ruby listened carefully. 'Uncle Cornelius should have delivered my command just about … Ah, here we go.'

From nowhere, a huddled mass of surveillance bees and wasps appeared. They swarmed in bunches, loud as spitfire engines, targeting people's sandwiches, fizzy drinks and hair. They buzzed and fussed, chasing all the people to the park gates. As Aunt Ruby, Seamus and Ebony headed towards the central area, crowds of people pushed past them, desperate to escape, waving their arms around and screaming, even though the bees and wasps hadn't actually stung anyone. The park warden abandoned his post; Ebony spotted him racing along with the others towards the main gate. Within minutes, they had the park to themselves.

Positioning themselves on a wide expanse of grass surrounded by trees, so they couldn't be seen from outside, Ebony, Aunt Ruby and Seamus sought out the best shadows.

'OK,' said Aunt Ruby to Ebony, reading the instructions. 'Concentrate on the shadow of this sycamore. Stare until your eyes go funny and the thoughts in your brain get so mashed together that your mind can't cope and has to go blank. Then, just as the world feels like it's dropping away, imagine merging with the shadow.'

'Why me?'

'We'll both be trying.'

'I can give it a go,' cut in Seamus.

But Aunt Ruby shook her head. 'We've already mislaid your sister. I'm taking no chances with you.'

'So after I merge with the shadow, then what?' asked Ebony.

'Concentrate on that for now, and if we manage it, we'll figure out the next bit when we come to it.'

'Are you sure about this?'

'Yes,' said Aunt Ruby, a big smile on her face. 'With a manual, how hard can it be?'

Breathing slowly and deeply, Ebony fixed her stare as directed and imagined climbing into the darkness. This was something her parents had mastered, a skill they had tried to pass on, and her aunt believed in her – she was determined to succeed. All she had to do was follow the instructions Mr O'Hara had given them.

Ebony stared until the shadow blurred and danced before her eyes, the sounds of the park and her companions drifting away, until it felt like there was only her and the shadow left.

Her mind felt woozy and strange, her thoughts whirring around her head so noisily and confused that she began to feel nauseous. But still she concentrated and breathed.

Suddenly feeling as though the world around her had disappeared, Ebony gulped and tried to calm her fears. Concentrating on the shadow, watching its darkness grow thick and heavy green lights flaring at the edges of her eyes, she imagined merging with the blackness. Reaching out, her fingers connected with the shadow and she felt something graze her skin. Something cool and light, but hardly there, like she imagined a cloud would feel.

Beads of sweat formed on Ebony's forehead as a mixture of fear and excitement swept through her body. Feeling a pull, like something was tugging at her belly button, she tried to let go, to allow the pull to take her like a current in water. But overcome with dizziness, she started to fall and the lights suddenly hurt her eyes.

When she could focus again, she found that she was still in the park – and so was her aunt.

'Give me a minute and I'll try again,' said Ebony, panting.

Staring at the tree shadow once more, Ebony focused her mind. But it was no use. She couldn't even make the image blur this time.

'You'll never manage it!' said Seamus. Then, as though remembering that they were supposed to be friends, he covered his mouth with his hand and gave an apologetic shrug. Ebony gave it one last try, but Seamus was right, it was useless. She was useless.

Placing a hand on her niece's shoulder, Aunt Ruby smiled, one corner of her mouth barely lifting. 'Don't worry,' she said. 'I doubt that anyone manages it first time.'

'I just need more practice.'

'But not now, you've done enough. You need to get some rest and we'll try again later.'

'Tonight?' asked Ebony.

'Tomorrow. And not without me present, do you hear?'

'But what about Chiyoko?' Ebony and Seamus shouted in unison.

'To succeed, we need our energy levels to be at their highest. We'll be no use to Chiyoko if we reach the Shadowlands exhausted and are easily overcome by the Shadow Walkers. Come. Tomorrow is another day.'

As they started for home, Seamus leaned in and whispered. 'You did better than your aunt. At least you started to turn invisible.'

'I did? In what way?'

'Your aunt might be thin and wiry, but she was solid as a rock. It didn't matter how much she concentrated, nothing happened.'

Ebony chuckled behind her hand but decided that if she'd almost made it then there was no way she was giving up now. As Aunt Ruby and Seamus turned in the direction of home, Ebony hatched a plan.

Lagging behind, but not enough to let them notice, she kept her footsteps quiet. As they headed up the path ahead, reaching a bend to the right, Ebony ran straight across the grass and through a gap in the hedge near the turrets of the wooden play towers. Peeking round the hedge, there was no sign of her aunt or Seamus following. As an extra precaution, she climbed over the fence into the overgrown bog garden and took a deep breath. She had to move quickly.

'There's no way I'll manage it, eh, Seamus?' muttered Ebony under her breath, positioned under a sturdy evergreen oak. Remembering his words only made her more determined.

She closed her eyes and relaxed her shoulders. Then, breathing slowly and deeply, she opened her eyes again, fixing her glare on the biggest tree shadow near her. Fingers grasping the amulet around her neck, she stared until the shadow blurred and moved, the sound of birdsong and distant traffic drifting away. Although she was alone in the park, the claustrophobia she had felt before soon crept over her again, only this time, the shadow began to wrap itself around her.

Concentrating even harder, allowing the darkness to expand, Ebony didn't try to reach out. That had somehow broken the spell the last time. Instead, she let the shadow engulf her. As her whole self immersed, body and mind, beads of sweat formed on Ebony's forehead. A weird mix of fear and excitement rippled through her body, but still she stared, keeping her mind focused. She was almost there.

Suddenly, Ebony was enveloped by a cool, airy sensation, and she imagined herself stepping into the shadow, morphing into the shape of the tree. The world turned dark for an instant before everything lost its colour. Her surroundings resembled a black and white movie – everything was grainy, in different shades and hues of grey. Hardly believing that she'd made it, Ebony kept still and quiet.

She was in the Shadowlands. She'd made it by herself and, unlike accessing the Reflectory, she knew exactly how it was done.

Inside the Shadowlands, things were very different. Ebony could still see the trees and the path through the park, and she could make out the pond nearby, but everything looked flat and without definition, and they were all a strange shade of lichen green, just like her anonymous friend had been. It was as though they had become the shadows and weren't solid any more.

Looking around her, Ebony found even the slightest movement took effort, but to test her theory, she gathered her strength and tried to climb back over the fence. She found that there was nothing to grab hold of; instead, she walked right through, unable to feel the fence at all.

As Ebony stamped her feet lightly, the ground still felt solid, only springier than usual. Looking down, her body seemed the same shape and size, only the colours were different and she didn't look real. Her clothes and hands were made up of grey outlines and shading, like a pencil drawing. It was as though she was a sketch.

Ebony gulped, trying hard not to be afraid. It was obviously the effects of passing into this other world. She would just have to get used to it, but how long could she stay like this? Aunt Ruby had told her not to try to access the Shadowlands without her, and now she realised why – she had no idea how to leave!

Hearing a muffled noise to her right, Ebony looked around. Four shadowy figures were walking towards her. They didn't look a bit like her new form; they were the same unusual shade of green as her surroundings and only vaguely shaped like people, without any features or clothing. But they clearly weren't Shadow Walkers either, as they looked nothing like the pirate she had seen earlier. They were more like the figure she had encountered in the tunnel to Mercury Lane. Perhaps they were the banished exiles? If so, Ebony hoped they could help her leave.

'Hello?' she called, but there was no reply.

The muffled murmuring continued, as they continued to head her way. Maybe they hadn't heard her greeting? Stepping forwards slightly so she would be more visible, Ebony called out again, a bit louder this time. 'Hello there!'

There was still no response. Although it was difficult to walk, her steps slow and heavy, Ebony made her way to the shaky outline of the path and stood in its centre.

The figures would have to see her standing there. They would have to stop and help her.

As she stood her ground, the figures continued coming towards her, at the same speed, without any sign of recognition. Ebony tried waving to attract their attention.

She might as well have been invisible.

Nothing she did worked, even though they were now very close.

Surely they'll bang into me, she thought to herself. *When they feel me, they'll have to stop. Maybe that's what it takes here?*

Planting her feet firmly, she steadied herself and waited. The figures drew so close, she could hear their muffled chatter.

Then, all of a sudden, Ebony felt like she was being ripped in two. Her stomach and head thumped and burned as though they were being pummelled with hot stones. Pain scraped the back of her eyes, and her skin stretched and flexed, like someone was trying to cut it away while she was still alive. Heat rushed over her body, followed by an extreme iciness that made her fingers feel like they were going to drop off. She saw flashes of pixellated stars, and then everything was how it was before: linear, grey, exhausting. Only now Ebony was bent over, panting, and the shadowy shapes were gone.

Gathering her strength, Ebony managed to look behind her. The mumbling figures were walking on as though nothing had happened.

'I wouldn't do that too often,' said a clear voice. 'It's far too unpleasant. And rather dangerous.'

Ebony swung round and gasped with relief. There stood her uncle, Icarus Bean, in sketched form! He was in front of the tree, his features and clothes unkempt and bedraggled, his hair sticking out at all angles from his head and dark circles under his eyes. But what was he doing here?

'Uncle! I was told you'd disappeared!' she cried, trying to run to him but instead toppling to the ground. After what had happened, she was weak.

'Don't be too hasty,' said Icarus, looking about him. 'Or too loud.'

Certain it was all clear, Icarus helped Ebony to her feet. Her head felt light and her stomach somewhat queasy, but other than that, she was OK. 'What happened?' she asked, pointing the direction of the receding figures. 'Are they ghosts?'

'Ghosts?' laughed Icarus. 'Goodness, no. The park has reopened – they're regular people walking through. They just happened to walk right through you, that's all.'

'That's all! But how? I passed through the fence and didn't feel anything.'

'Inanimate objects are easy to pass through, but living, breathing objects of any kind feed off your life source. When you're in the Shadowlands you're part of the shadows. There's no substance to shadows. They're not solid things you can touch or smell – so that's your current consistency.'

'And it makes me invisible?'

'Almost. You take on the form of the shadow you inhabit. You merge with it. Shadows aren't black like many people think; they're grey.'

'So that's why we look like sketches?'

'Precisely. Grey is a very tonal colour. There are lots of shades. When you enter this place, you're no longer a specific colour. You blend and merge.'

'So, those people ...'

'Can't see, or hear you. They don't know you're here. So there's no point shouting like that or putting yourself in danger by letting them pass through you. Drawing attention to yourself in here is not a smart move.'

'I didn't know,' interrupted Ebony. 'But this is cool! Look at us! We look like cartoons,' she said, lifting a hand to see its linear shape move like a black and white animation.

'It's not so cool when you're stuck here,' said Icarus.

As Ebony squirmed and looked at her feet, Icarus continued. 'You do know how to leave, don't you? Surely you weren't foolish enough to enter the Shadowlands without knowing how to get out? I don't know what Ruby was thinking, letting you do this on your own.'

'She didn't exactly let me ... but now you're here, you can show me!' cried Ebony, looking up hopefully at her uncle. His expression didn't make her feel any better. Icarus let out a huge sigh, setting alarm bells ringing in Ebony's brain.

'What's wrong?' she asked.

'Ambrose's power is strengthening,' said Icarus, hatred apparent in his voice. 'Things have changed. I used to be able to move about freely. It took a lot of effort, but I managed. Now ...'

'Now?' questioned Ebony.

'Now, it's not so easy. I can get in fine, but getting out is the hard part.' The look on his face was tense and stark, chilling Ebony to the bone.

'So why are you here?' she asked.

'There was a lot of unrest among the men while we were guarding the Reflectory. Lots of strange talk.'

'About the Reflectory not being real and me not being the true guardian?'

'You've heard?' answered Icarus, his brow furrowed. 'The men that used to be loyal to me have grown secretive and question my judgement – as well as yours. One of our men, Jeremiah O'Hara, has recently returned from Japan; he's the ringleader and has some bizarre ideas. Unfortunately, the men are listening to him. They even wanted me to join them.'

'Against me?'

'Exactly. So I decided to sneak away. So few people can access the Shadowlands, it's the best place to hide.'

'Leaving the Reflectory unguarded?' asked Ebony, feeling her anger grow.

'Hidden, actually. It was a fluke, but it's safer that way. Who knows where this strange talk might lead. But there's no time to explain any more. The Shadow Walkers – the creatures that live in the Shadowlands – have given their allegiance to Ambrose. He can access this place freely, being the one with the power to banish people from the Order here as punishment. But I've seen him training the Shadow Walkers to fight and inciting them to hatred. He taunts them with talk of a secret weapon and they bow to his orders. They're on the move at his command, sucking the energy from all around them in the Shadowlands. As each day goes by, I find my movements more difficult.'

'But you've been riding the shadows for years.'

Icarus looked away and mumbled something under his breath. Although Ebony couldn't make out the words, she could tell by the tone that it wasn't complimentary.

'You shouldn't be here, Ebony,' growled Icarus after a moment, shaking his head. 'I don't know if I have enough power to get us both out.'

'I had to do something,' Ebony replied. She explained to Icarus what had happened to Chiyoko. 'Aunt Ruby seems to think travelling the Shadowlands is the key and I'm not going to sit around and wait for Chiyoko to be hurt.'

Icarus shook his head. His clenched jaw trembled slightly, and Ebony felt her anger rise. He was treating her like she was a stupid child, not the guardian of the Reflectory. She felt her face heat and wondered what it looked like in monochrome and whether Icarus could see it. If he could, he showed no sign.

'Why do you always think you know best?' he asked.

'You all tried to prevent me from opening the Reflectory …' began Ebony, her voice trailing off as she started to feel weak again.

'This is no Reflectory, Ebony,' said Icarus Bean, his lips curled and twisted. 'You were safer there. The Reflectory is a place of healing and recuperation, full of good energy. It protects you, just like the souls in its care. This place–' He stopped mid-sentence and held up his hand. 'Ssh! Listen.'

Ebony strained her ears. There was a faint *putt–putt*, like a distant punt engine starting up. The sound grew a little louder and clearer, revealing a definite rhythm. It wasn't an engine after all: it was a crowd of marching feet. On the horizon, their slippery forms resembled a herd of giant cockroaches.

'Shadow Walkers,' said Icarus. 'They're on the march.'

'What will they do if they catch us?'

Before Ebony knew what was happening, Icarus was up close to her face, his jaw wide open – wider than a person could usually open their jaw, dislocated almost – and he was drawing deep breaths in front of her mouth, breaths so deep and rasping they sounded like they were going to be his last. She only realised her own mouth was also open when a sudden and very terrible feeling overcame her, like her insides were being pulled up towards her throat so hard they might spill out of her mouth. Her stomach, her brain, her heart – they were all being yanked by a powerful invisible force. She couldn't move or scream or stop the feeling. Just as she thought the pain was never going to end, it stopped. Her body jolted as everything fell back into place, but it felt like her insides were on a rollercoaster, shooting downwards far too fast.

She looked at Icarus aghast, rubbing her chin and neck to alleviate the last bit of pain; a slight but sharp tingle.

'Sorry,' he said, 'but you asked.'

'You could just have told me,' she grumbled.

Icarus shrugged, a dark glint in his eye. 'Telling you

things rarely seems to get the point across. But at least now you know what to expect when the Shadow Walkers come looking for you.'

Ebony shook her head. 'When I go looking for them, you mean,' and she turned to follow the shapes in the distance. A jolt ran through her body as she came to a sudden stop.

'Don't be hasty, Ebony,' said Icarus, holding onto her rucksack to pull her back. 'What exactly are you planning to do?'

'I'm going to make them tell me where Chiyoko is, so I'll be able to save her!' Even as she said it, she knew her plan sounded sketchy.

'All by yourself,' replied Icarus incredulously. 'You have no idea what you're dealing with here. If you try to face the Shadow Walkers on your own, the results will not be pretty.'

The marching sound grew louder and clearer. Ebony listened for a moment, and Icarus stood stock still, one ear cocked. Without warning, he yanked Ebony back towards the green blob of tree. She let out a small squeak of surprise and Icarus quickly covered her mouth with his hand. As the noise grew louder still, Ebony realised that she didn't need to go looking for the Shadow Walkers – they were coming their way.

'Squeeze your eyes tight and imagine you are back in the park,' said Icarus in her ear. 'Concentrate your energies on the shapes and shadows, and focus on the park's sights and smells. We have to get out of here. I'll follow you, but I have to make sure you get out first.'

Ebony tried following her uncle's vague instructions, but nothing happened. She tried again, only this time she imagined herself beyond the tree, back in the golden sunlight, amidst the sweet melody of birdsong. She tried using all five senses to conjure the image; its colours, sounds and smells, the taste of sweet nectar on her tongue after chewing pink clover, the feel of grass and gravel underfoot. But no matter how vivid she made the image, she failed. Realising time was ebbing away, she shook her head vigorously and made a muffled sound. Icarus uncovered her mouth.

'What?' he snapped. 'We don't have time for this!'

'It's not working!' said Ebony, alarmed.

'Then you'll have to merge with your surroundings. Imagine becoming part of them and quick!' said Icarus sternly. 'Watch me!'

Ebony observed, looking for clues on what to do. Icarus closed his eyes and frowned, deep in concentration. His face seemed to turn a darker shade of grey than before. It was like a 5B pencil had shaded him in. Narrowing her eyes, Ebony couldn't help staring as his skin continued to darken. He was changing before her very eyes – and then he was gone, completely camouflaged by his surroundings. Ebony tried to copy him. Screwing up her eyes and concentrating really hard, she checked her hands, but nothing had changed. She looked exactly the same as she had since she'd arrived in the Shadowlands. By now, Icarus was completely invisible, melded with the background.

'Uncle?' she said quietly, her heart racing.

But there was no reply. Desperate, Ebony squeezed her eyes shut. Breathing slowly and deeply, trying to gain control over the situation, she opened her eyes and fixed her stare on the blurred outline of the tree Icarus had merged with. The drumming of footsteps grew louder. The army was heading in their direction.

'Quick!' hissed Icarus's voice, seemingly from thin air. 'If they find you, you'll be captured.'

'OK,' said Ebony. 'Here goes.'

As she concentrated hard, she felt herself darkening, fading into the shadows. Then, just as she was certain she was about to succeed, something went wrong. Instead, of melding with the tree, she started to lighten again, right in front of the oncoming army.

'Help me, Uncle,' cried Ebony.

Icarus lowered his voice as more soldiers came into sight in the distance. 'Try *The Book of Learning* if you have to, but hurry!' he said, reappearing. 'The Order can't afford for you to be in the clutches of the enemy.'

Ebony did as she was told and tried using the fingerprint combination to open the book. The book was exactly the same, it hadn't turned into a sketch-like outline like she and Icarus had, but it no longer recognised her. *It must be because of my Shadowlands form*, thought Ebony, hastily shoving the book back into her pocket.

'Do something!' said Icarus. There was a mild panic in his voice that made Ebony's heart pump faster.

'Trust me, I'm trying,' she said, her uncle's demonstration of what the Shadow Walkers would do to her if they caught her playing on her mind.

'For hope's sake, girl,' said Icarus through gritted teeth.

The footsteps were a loud thrum now. She squinted her eyes into the distance until she could see a company approaching. There were forty figures, if not more. They were huge, shadowy forms, with angry red eyes and stumpy yellow teeth. They had a determined march and were armed with spiked balls on chains, clubs and long, curved blades, just like the pirate that had taken Chiyoko.

'It's too late,' said Icarus. 'Get behind me, I'll try to camouflage you. Quick!'

The soldiers were almost upon them now. Ebony slipped

behind her uncle, hoping his long trench coat would hide her. As her uncle melded into the shadows in front of her, shielding her from view, she stayed stock still, breathing as quietly as she could. The footsteps turned into a loud clamour. *Stomp. Stomp. Stomp.* Then, the worst thing imaginable happened.

The stomping stopped. Right in front of her uncle.

Ebony held her breath, made herself as small as she could and closed her eyes. She felt her uncle tense. Felt her own body tense too. If her uncle moved even an inch, she was lost.

After a long, silent pause, the marching started again. Ebony hardly dared hope that they were moving on, but moments later the footsteps began to grow quieter. When they had faded to a dull hum, Ebony felt Icarus's shoulders slump and saw him start to reappear. She knew they were in the clear.

'They'll be back again soon,' said Icarus. 'So if you can't get yourself out, we'll have to bring the outside world to you.'

'How can you bring the world to me?' asked Ebony.

'You just … ride the shadows,' said Icarus. 'That's what you do to travel any distance or to exit the Shadowlands in a different place to where you entered – it's a good method, and the Shadow Walkers can't leave this way. The constraints of their exile prevent it, so they can't follow you. But I warn you, it's time-consuming and energy sapping.'

'What are we waiting for?' asked Ebony, panic building.

'We'd better get a message to your aunt first, to let her

know where you are.' Cupping both hands around his mouth, Icarus made a high-pitched screeching sound that made Ebony jump.

'Ssh,' she whispered, checking in the direction the Shadow Walkers had marched. 'They'll hear you.'

'They'll think we're a vulture,' replied Icarus, repeating the call again.

Seconds later, the King Vulture appeared in the distance, its wings outstretched and end feathers splayed, heading in their direction. Like *The Book of Learning*, it hadn't changed form; the bird's colours were as bright as ever, forcing Ebony to shield her eyes. Icarus held out both arms and the vulture landed, wrapping a set of claws around each forearm. The bird stooped its bald purple head towards Icarus, and Ebony watched as her uncle whispered in its ear. The vulture blinked its piercing eye, then nodded. Using all his might, Icarus flung the bird into the sky; the vulture lifted off, flapping its wings twice, before stretching them out and soaring into the distance. As the bird disappeared, Icarus silently dropped to the ground in a crouching position. 'Can you remember the direction of Mercury Lane? You always need to know the direction you want to travel in to aim correctly.'

Ebony pointed behind her, away from the tree. She had definitely come from that way. Or had she? Although she hadn't moved far since crossing over into the Shadowlands, her brain felt confused, like a big city river filled with sludge and sediment, her thoughts jumbled up in the murk. She just wanted out of there; the sketch-like surroundings were starting to make her head hurt.

'Good,' said Icarus, confirming that she was right. Checking around him in all directions to make sure it was safe, he took out a penknife and drew a line across the earth. Just like he was scoring through coloured card, a white line showed where he had dragged his knife. Sitting back on his heels and surveying the mark, he then stood and moved close to Ebony.

'We score a line at right angles to where we want to go, then tear the ground up. It will start to ripple, then as momentum builds, these will turn into waves; when you see the third wave form, leap on top of the moving ground, keeping your destination in mind. That's how you ride the shadows.'

'Hurry,' snapped Ebony. She had no idea why, but she suddenly felt extremely grumpy. It was like a scene from a cartoon where a big black rain cloud settles over a character's head, threatening to strike them with lightning and a downpour. Instinctively, Ebony looked up. Sure enough, there was a huge cloud above her, just like the one that had followed the King Vulture earlier that day. Icarus paused, followed her gaze, then shook his head and sighed.

'We'd better get you out of here,' he said. 'It's getting to you.'

He extended the line in the ground at both ends to make it even longer. When the line was the length he wanted it, he scored a small arrow at each end, both pointing in the direction of Mercury Lane. Ebony looked on, trying to ignore the angry feelings stirring within her and threatening to spill over. She bit her lip and watched – she had to stay focused.

'OK,' said Icarus, finally happy with his markings. 'It can be slow to start with, but once it gains momentum, things happen pretty quickly.'

Icarus caught one of the corners he'd created with his penknife and teased it until it lifted from the ground. There was a gaping white hole underneath. 'Are you ready?'

'Yes,' said Ebony.

Icarus continued teasing the section of the path facing home until it all lifted from the ground.

'Stand close beside me,' he said, 'and face the way we're going.'

Ebony did as she was told.

'And then, after three, I'll pull. One, two, three ... HEAVE!'

As he called out the last word, he yanked hard on the earth he had lifted, his voice straining with the effort. There was a loud tearing sound as the ground in the Shadowlands lifted, ripped up from its roots, making a massive rippling strip of earth that looked like someone was shaking out a big carpet. The effects were small at first, but then the ripples turned into huge waves of ground that began to lift and fold under, silent as a wisp of smoke. Ebony counted them under her breath.

'Jump!' cried Icarus, grabbing Ebony's hand.

Together, they threw themselves onto the rolling shadow ground. Slipping and sliding on her belly, racing along at top speed, Ebony checked on her uncle; he had managed to swing his legs round and push himself upright into a seated position. Ebony tried to copy but found it too difficult, so she stayed on her stomach instead, concentrating on 23 Mercury Lane. Up ahead, she saw the waves spreading. Time and again, she rose up on a huge mound of earth before slamming back down again, only to rise up once more. It was like riding a bumpy slide, only more dangerous and unsteady. Ebony tried to catch hold of something for balance.

'Relax!' shouted Icarus as he began to inch ahead. 'Ride it like a water slide.'

Understanding, Ebony let go of her fears and tried to relax her body and mind. She allowed the folding and rolling earth to control her movements, guiding her this way and that. Although she wobbled and bounced, she realised she was quite safe; Icarus had scored the earth wide enough for them both to fit, the edges several feet away on each side so there was no danger of falling off. Beside her, Icarus looked calm, his legs out in front and his hands resting on his knees, like he was guiding a giant, invisible toboggan. Finally feeling more confident, Ebony managed to scramble to a sitting position. The ride became much smoother. Soon, the ripping sound stopped and Ebony saw a wide, flat ribbon of earth cascading towards them. Realising they were nearly at the end, she looked to her uncle, her eyes wide.

'What happens when it ends?' she cried out.

But it was too late. Icarus grabbed Ebony's hand and they hurtled up, up, up, as high as Ebony had ever been before. All of the sketch-like scenery dropped away and the world turned completely blank. Ebony could barely see Icarus beside her, his outline and features were so faint. She looked down at her body for a brief second, too scared to keep her eyes off her surroundings for long, and she too was growing fainter.

'Icarus?' she cried. Her words fell on emptiness; Icarus was gone.

In the next instant, Ebony landed on cold, hard ground. The impact jarred her tailbone, but when she opened her eyes, the colours burned and she quickly closed them again. Feeling with her hands, she realised she was sitting on cold concrete. A jackdaw cried overhead, nearly splitting Ebony's eardrums in two. She was back in the real world, with noise and colour and 3D shapes. It was almost too much to bear. Opening her eyes and looking around, she spied Icarus sitting on the steps up to 23 Mercury Lane.

'You did it!' she cried.

All Icarus could do was nod, his head resting in his hands. His shoulders drooped and he looked like he was completely wiped of energy. Ebony stumbled to her feet, but her legs felt as unstable as a newborn calf's and she slumped down beside him, equally drained. Noticing how dark it seemed, Ebony looked up. The black cloud hovered over her head menacingly; it had followed her.

'Don't worry about that,' said Icarus, sensing her concern even though his head was still resting in his hands. 'It'll disappear as your mood improves.'

'But you don't have one – how come?'

'It's the effects of the Shadowlands on an outsider. You don't get them as an exile, as you're not meant to leave. Since the judge hasn't lifted my banishment, as such, I'm still officially in exile.' Looking up, he gave Ebony a serious stare. 'We'd better not make a habit of this.'

'No,' lied Ebony. The Shadowlands had sapped Ebony's energy; it had been difficult to move, to speak, and her mood had darkened, but already she was trying to figure out how much power it would take to make that initial tug to start the ground rippling. 'Are we safe?'

'Safer,' was Icarus's reply. 'But you should learn to either keep out or leave at will. Riding the shadows takes time and effort. That move I demonstrated earlier, when it felt like I was sucking the life out of you? That's how the Shadow Walkers will take from you what they've lost. They don't necessarily understand what it is they seek, but they hunt it down anyway.'

'Hunt what exactly?'

'Belief, dreams, hope. Feelings of excitement, of love. All this is lost in the Shadowlands over time. The Shadow Walkers avenge their incarceration by sucking out what is good and pure in people. The fact that they took Chiyoko by mistake means they're already hunting you at Ambrose's command – if they find you in the Shadowlands, you'll make it much easier for them to take you.'

A heavy silence fell between them.

'Where is everyone?' growled Icarus moments later, frowning as he checked his watch. Worry was etched into his face and there was sadness and regret in every line. Ebony's heart lurched as she realised how much pain he must be in. She'd lost her grandpa and it had broken her heart in two, leaving a constant, dull ache, but at least she had gained a family. Icarus had lost almost everything – his wife, his father and his son.

'They're probably on their way,' said Ebony, hoping she was right and they hadn't been ambushed. 'Unless they're inside or they're still in the park, looking for me.'

'I told them to meet us on the steps. They should have been here at least half an hour ago.'

'But it's only minutes since you sent the message!'

'Time doesn't work the same way in the shadows,' said Icarus. 'Shadows are fluid, they don't have the same solidity as earthly things. Time can be speeded up or slowed down, shifted around as needed.'

'Could we have done something wrong?'

'No,' said Icarus, but his face showed some uncertainty. Then he leaned in and grabbed Ebony by the shoulders. 'Promise me you won't be foolish enough to go back there alone; it takes time and skill to master travelling the Shadowlands. You don't want to be trapped there, do you hear me?'

'I promise,' said Ebony, straightening her clothes as Icarus let go, a thought hitting her – if she needed to use the Shadowlands to rescue Chiyoko, she'd need to know how to get out with her. 'But tell me everything I need to know. Anything that might be of use, just in case something happens. Like, how do you pull others out of the shadows?'

'The more you visit the Shadowlands, the more honed your senses become. For instance, those people you couldn't see properly? I could hear them, see their colours. If I wanted to, and I was strong enough, I could yank them into or out of the Shadowlands, simply by taking hold of them and imagining them passing through with me. It takes real skill though, and double the effort. You can also pull people out when riding the shadows, just like I did with you.'

'I guess it takes practice. But you said something about colours; the people I saw were green, like the pond and the path.'

'You saw green when you were looking at the outside world, but as your eyes get used to the Shadowlands over time, more colours become apparent. Soon enough, you begin to distinguish people by their colours.'

'And what about objects?' said Ebony, thinking about how *The Book of Learning* had failed to respond to her fingerprints. 'Am I right in thinking that if you have the objects with you when you enter the Shadowlands, they'll travel in too?'

'Yes, but they don't always work the same in there. The most useful thing to learn is how to leave – and as a back-up, how to ride the shadows. It's not a well-known technique these days, but it was used more frequently in ancient times. It was dangerous, but useful – and those banished to the Shadowlands couldn't escape that way, so our kind used to chance it. The only place the Order couldn't access via the shadows was the Reflectory, and that's why people used to send messages to their family souls via the King Vulture.'

'So how come you know how to ride the shadows?'

'I spent a lot of time in exile, but because I wasn't trapped in there, it didn't affect me the way it did the other poor souls – I didn't become a Shadow Walker. Your grandpa taught me the theory behind riding the shadows when I was a small boy, and once inside, I had plenty of time to practise. Master this, and you can go wherever you want from inside the Shadowlands – simply concentrate on where you want to go and pull your destination towards you. Then ride the earth to get there. I often travel long distances in short periods of time using the shadows. You see, shadows stretch and move, and they're always there. It's a great system. Better than the New York or Paris undergrounds when you master it.' Looking up, Icarus smiled. It was the first time Ebony had seen him smile. The corners of his lips turned down and trembled slightly, like they wanted to go up but didn't know how.

Ebony's mind raced with possibilities; being able to travel the shadows opened up a world of opportunities, but how could she use it to help Chiyoko?

Icarus jumped to his feet, jolting Ebony out of her deep thoughts. She saw Aunt Ruby and Seamus crossing the road. Aunt Ruby's faced was red and blustery. 'I told you not to try that without me!' she chided.

'But I did it!'

Aunt Ruby shook her head and pointed a finger at her niece. 'What if Icarus hadn't been there? You're as stubborn as your grandpa. Your behaviour was both stupid and dangerous. If you can't be trusted, I'll have to keep you under lock and key. Do you hear me?'

'Sorry,' replied Ebony, the seriousness of her actions sinking in. But the thrill of entering the Shadowlands lingered, making her stomach flutter. Catching Seamus's eye, she gave him a small smile. Seamus responded with a secret thumbs up, visibly impressed. Above her head, Ebony could see that the cloud that had followed her had almost disappeared.

'I'll give you one last chance,' said Aunt Ruby. Turning her attentions to her brother, Aunt Ruby rushed to him and held a hand to his face. 'Are you OK? I got your message, but where have you been? I received word from the Nine Lives men in Oddley Cove that you and the Reflectory had disappeared and I've been worried sick ever since. We didn't know what had happened.'

'I'm sorry, Ruby, but that's what I wanted the Order to think,' said Icarus. 'The Reflectory is still there, I've just … hidden it.'

'How?' asked Aunt Ruby and Ebony in unison.

'It was a complete accident,' said Icarus. 'We were ambushed a few nights ago by three Shadow Walkers and I went inside to protect the entrance. As I was waiting for one of them to try to break through, I noticed a lever near the doorway and curiosity got the better of me. I thought it couldn't hurt to give it a try. It didn't seem to do anything, but as I peered outside to assess the situation, the men from the Order were going crazy. The Shadow Walkers were nowhere to be seen – they must have returned to the Shadowlands but I didn't get a chance to ask; the men were too busy shouting about how the doorway had disappeared, and me with it. Yet when I looked behind me the sky world was there as normal. After a while the men left – there was no point in guarding a door that was no longer there – and when I stepped through the doorway into the night air, I saw that they were right. The entrance to the Reflectory could no longer be seen.'

'And you kept it that way?' asked Aunt Ruby.

'Yes. I placed a marker on the ground so I'd know exactly where the entrance is. I was explaining to Ebony earlier, there's been a lot of funny talk from the AESL, and it's gained a lot of supporters. They were trying to persuade me to take up a position in headquarters that would have me under AESL control.

'Think about it,' continued Icarus. 'What better form of defence can we have than it seeming like the Reflectory has disappeared once more?'

Jumping to his feet, he sighed. 'I'd better go,' he said, his bloodshot eyes searching around warily. 'I'm hiding for a reason – and although it's getting difficult for me to move around in there, the Shadowlands is still the best place for me.' And before anyone else could say a word, he took off. In seconds, he was gone; it was like he'd disappeared before their very eyes.

19

'Aunt Ruby, tell me more about the Shadow Walkers,' said Ebony later that evening, her mouth full of chips. 'Icarus and I saw a group of them marching like an army and I need to know what I'm up against.'

'An army of Shadow Walkers?' said Seamus, wide-eyed. 'You're not serious.'

'About forty of them. It doesn't sound much, but the size of them … they'd be difficult to overpower.'

Beside her, Winston tucked into his own small meal of rat food while Uncle Cornelius piled his plate as high as he could with fish fingers. Seamus poked at his beans, shifting them around his plate. Every couple of seconds, Uncle Cornelius checked Seamus's progress, eyeing up the perfectly browned fish fingers and golden chips with a grin.

'Maybe Seamus would like to explain?' said Aunt Ruby. 'I believe he excelled in his history training.'

'The Shadow Walkers,' Seamus sighed, trying to disguise his shaky voice, 'are supposedly creatures that exist and move in the shadows.'

'But who are they? Where did they come from?'

'Surely you know of the Order's punishment for wrong-doing?'

'Banishment to the shadows. So the Shadow Walkers used to be members of the Order? They're the exiles?' offered Ebony.

'More like what's left of them,' said Seamus. 'If you believe that kind of thing. They're ghouls made up to scare kids into behaving, that's all.'

'But you saw one yourself – it came through the mirror.'

'That was a pirate,' scoffed Seamus.

'A pirate that can reach through glass?'

Seamus glanced at Aunt Ruby. 'In the Shadowlands, anything is possible. And if you can enter the Shadowlands, why can't a pirate? My father says that people only believe in superstitious nonsense because they're not strong enough to take responsibility for their own lives.'

'Well I saw them, so whether you believe me or not, I know they're real.' Ebony turned back to her aunt.

'Living in the shadows affects Nine Lives souls rather negatively,' said Aunt Ruby, taking up the story. 'Icarus describes it as a darkening of the soul – he wasn't always so sullen and melancholy. And he's the lucky one; he wasn't permanently trapped in the shadows during his banishment like the others. Until recently, before Ambrose decided he could put the Shadow Walkers to good use, they couldn't leave the Shadowlands. Even now, with their exile still in place, they can probably only exit with his permission.'

'But how do they change so much? Aren't they just people who have been banished from the Order?'

'They are. Or more correctly, they were. The Shadowlands has the opposite effect to the Reflectory. Unlike the Reflectory, which takes away bad memories, in the Shadowlands memories are heightened, rather than removed. This is a place of punishment, don't forget, and the things you are forced to remember are not exactly the things you want to remember. Some of the things Icarus has told me ...' Aunt Ruby shuddered. 'The Shadowlands absorb all your happy emotions, leaving only the bad ones behind.'

Hand to her chest, automatically reaching for the amulet for comfort, Ebony considered the demonstration of Shadow Walker behaviour that Icarus had shared. The feeling of her brains and heart being sucked out still felt very real.

'So if an army of Shadow Walkers actually exists, who has assembled it?' asked Seamus. 'They're meant to be quite stupid, all their energy focused on anger.'

'Judge Ambrose,' replied Ebony. 'Icarus has seen him giving them orders.'

'He must have been planning this for a long time,' said Aunt Ruby. 'His recruits are the people he banished over the years. Banishment used to be the punishment for those who attempted to access the sky world, our sacred place where souls prepare for their next life, but for some time now, more and more people have been sent to the Shadowlands under Ambrose's orders, their crimes undisclosed. I'm beginning to wonder if they did anything wrong at all, or if was he just building his army.'

'And they'd join him willingly? Even though he is responsible for their imprisonment?' asked Ebony.

'I'm guessing he's promised them their freedom. It's a bit like a master tormenting a starving dog,' said Aunt Ruby. 'It's a terrible life in there. Those poor souls will do anything to get out.'

'But they're not out. They're still in the Shadowlands. I saw them!'

'And I don't believe for one minute that they'll ever get to leave permanently,' said her aunt. 'They'll be allowed out of the shadows to do the judge's bidding – but that will be all. Once he is done with them, I've no doubt he'll return them and leave them to suffer.'

Ebony scowled, thinking back to how the judge had managed to convince Zach that it was his duty to kill her, that it was for the good of his mother and the future of the Order. As though reading her mind, Aunt Ruby continued. 'Just like the judge tricked Zach and convinced him he's special, he has tricked these souls too. He dangles rewards like carrots, and the poor fools fall for it. Meanwhile, keeping them trapped in the Shadowlands turns them into hateful, murderous creatures, driven by desperation and anger.'

Ebony bit her lip. 'The longer they're there, the meaner they get,' she said.

'Yes,' answered Aunt Ruby. 'The revenge they'll seek on the Order if they manage to get free won't be pretty.'

'But then why would such a place exist at all?' asked Ebony.

Irritated by the way the conversation was going, yet unable to keep his knowledge to himself any longer, Seamus slammed his fork down with a clatter, making Winston jump. 'Legends from ancient times say that the sky world needed to give our people some form of control, so that order could be kept. Banishment to the Shadowlands was such a terrible threat that it was meant to minimise the chance of uprisings against the sky world – to help prevent the revolts of earlier times from reoccurring.'

Aunt Ruby smiled. 'Thank you, Seamus. Moreover, it was meant to be a temporary punishment. It wasn't designed for people to be in exile for so long.'

'But because the judge has been hatching his plan to take control of Nine Lives souls,' continued Ebony, getting the gist, 'he is keeping people there for good?'

'Exactly,' replied her aunt. 'Some for a lifetime, some for several lifetimes. Many probably don't even remember what it's like back in the real world. Living as part of the Order, having the chance to aim for Ultimation – it'll all seem like a dream to them now, if they remember at all.'

'So the Shadow Walkers are monsters after all?' asked Ebony.

'Somewhere deep inside, they're still people, just like us. But barely. They've had so much of their personality sucked out of them, they're more like empty shells.'

Ebony lowered her fork, letting it rest on the edge of the plate. She was too deep in thought to notice Winston lean over and lap up some of her bean juice and steal a nibble of a fish finger. 'Can we defeat them?'

'We will try.'

The room fell silent, each person lost in their own thoughts. Uncle Cornelius stuffed a chip in his mouth and chewed noisily. Looking slightly disgruntled, Seamus pushed back his chair and got to his feet.

'I can't listen to any more of this talk. Shadow Walkers indeed. If we don't get a sensible lead soon, I'm calling my father. Now, where am I sleeping please?'

'It's only 7.30,' said Ebony, frowning slightly.

Aunt Ruby threw Ebony a look. 'Your room is next to Ebony's,' she said.

'The one with the ghosts and goblins,' added Ebony with a chuckle, letting Winston clamber onto her sleeve. When Seamus's face turned pale, she regretted her words instantly. Holding on to Winston, she jumped to her feet. 'I'm joking! Come on, I'll show you.'

Reaching the bedroom, Seamus seemed reluctant for Ebony to leave; he checked under the bed, then in the wardrobe.

'I'm not tired,' said Ebony. 'Let's see if *The Book of Learning* can tell us anything more.'

Pulling out the book, she noticed relief warring with concern on Seamus's face. Joining him on the bed, she opened the book up, pausing on the warning that had appeared earlier. The words 'THEY'RE COMING' sat there bold and red and angry.

Continuing on to the next blank page, Ebony opened the book wide so they could all see. Winston positioned himself with one paw on the book, and Seamus joined them, his back stooped and his shoulders slumped.

'So, what are we waiting for?'

'If I knew that—' started Ebony, but the page gave off a shimmer, as though it had heard her words.

Winston did a somersault and Ebony grinned. 'Just like old times, eh? Right, let's see what you have for us.'

A rock formed on the page. The sun blazed at full height behind it, golden beams reaching out in all directions. The page began to sizzle, turning a pale yellow colour.

'It can't be drying up already!' said Ebony. 'It hasn't shown us anything.'

But instead of the page drying, the sun lowered and a gentle breeze blew across the page.

'I can feel that,' said Seamus, holding out his hands to the book like it was a campfire. 'That's so amazing!'

Once again, he sounded so much like his sister that it made Ebony even more determined to find her. Putting her finger to her lips, she pointed to the page as little figures crept into view, dressed in white robes with ivy headdresses and carrying offerings of fruit, flowers and small figurines. Next to them the rock's true size could be discerned; it was, in fact, a mountain.

'Those are the ancients,' she explained, 'the original Nine Lives tribe – I can tell by their outfits. It looks like they're worshipping something.'

'I can't believe what I'm seeing,' said Seamus. 'It's real! Just like on the TV show. Can you point your finger and–'

'No,' interrupted Ebony, feeling an acute sense of déjà vu. 'I can't shoot killer beams out of my fingers.'

'Pity,' said Seamus, watching the figures on the page. 'We could do with a guardian with killer beams.'

Ignoring the slight, but hoping with every fibre of her being he was beginning to believe in her as guardian, Ebony watched as the figures began to dance and sway, just like Aunt Ruby and Uncle Cornelius earlier. Holding hands, the revellers began circling the mountain. The mountain seemed to tremble and small chippings sprayed off the sides.

'It looks like it's coming to life!' gasped Ebony.

As she spoke, the mountain split in the centre of its base, the crack riding all the way up to the top. The figures danced and jumped, their movements more frenzied and excitable. Seamus was leaning back now, holding his hands in front of him like a protective shield.

Fast, rhythmic drumming started, like an angry crocodile's tail beating on the skin of a swamp. It was so strong it made *The Book of Learning* vibrate. As the drumming grew louder and more rapid, the mountain on the page began to shake violently. A giant boulder dislodged itself from the top right corner and tumbled down, bouncing off the sides as it went. The people drummed and danced harder. Singing filled the air.

A new figure appeared on the scene, sporting a shock of black curls. The scene zoomed in to show the face; it was

Ebony's past self, dressed in a ceremonial robe and headdress. She was being pulled against her will, closer and closer to the rock. The dancers seemed to be weeping now, their movements turning frenzied. The mountain answered with an almighty rumble, followed by an explosion. The summit split open and a thick black vapour spewed out of the mountaintop like volcanic lava – only it had two red slits for eyes and, as it plunged down, a set of wings spiked out from its back and a hideous mouth formed.

'That's it! That's the demon I've been seeing in my dreams,' cried Ebony, shivering. 'What is it?'

'I've no idea,' replied Seamus in a crackly voice.

The creature plummeted at top speed towards the ground, pointed wings pinned back as its sharp, clawed fingers grasped and reached. In seconds, Ebony's past self had been snatched up and, in a flash, dragged back towards the mountain – the ghoul and its captive were sucked back inside in the blink of an eye.

The music and dancing stopped. The other figures fled, slipping off the sides of the book and under the page edges. The mountain scene was still once more.

'I don't understand,' said Ebony, lifting the page to see whether there was anything she'd missed. 'I think I've just seen how my original incarnation was murdered, but how does that help us find Chiyoko?'

Seamus winced at the sound of his sister's name. Then he pointed at the book as a figure crept out from behind the dislodged boulder and picked up his bow. Attaching something to the arrow, he turned and fired. The arrow shot out of the page and whizzed past Seamus's head, making a high-pitched whirring sound as it skimmed his ear.

'What the …?!' cried Seamus, diving to one side.

The arrow struck the wall directly behind them and stuck there quivering. A spiral of wide, flat ribbon dangled from its shaft. Where the arrow had shot out of the page, there was a small bunched mark like a belly button.

'I think you'd better get that,' said Ebony, judging how high it was lodged in the wall. 'You're taller than me.'

20

Trembling, Seamus got to his feet. Clutching a pillow in front of him as if it would protect him if the arrow somehow came free and decided to shoot itself in his direction, Seamus stretched up onto his toes. With gentle encouragement from Ebony, he eventually plucked the arrow from the wall and held it at arm's length. Ebony saw there was writing on the ribbon, but she couldn't make it out from where she was sitting.

'Read it!' she called excitedly. She watched him trace the words with his eyes, his lips moving soundlessly. Then he scrunched up the ribbon and threw the arrow to the ground.

'It can't be!' he shouted, making Winston jump. 'The Deus-Umbra. Is this your aunt's doing? Some trick to back up her story?'

'The day-uss-what?' asked Ebony.

'An old legend. The stuff of nightmares!'

Rushing over and grabbing the arrow, Ebony took a moment to study the message. Behind her, Winston hopped up and down, impatient to know what information *The Book of Learning* had provided this time.

'Beware the Deus-Umbra,' read Ebony in a puzzled voice, taking time over the name to make sure she pronounced it correctly. 'The Deus-Umbra? But what is it and why should we–?'

Winston moved fast, clambering up Ebony's body onto her shoulder. There, he put his paws over her mouth as if to stop her from saying the name again. Nudging him away with her chin, she turned to Seamus, who was looking rather shaken.

'Are you going to tell me what's going on?'

'There's no point,' said Seamus. 'It's a pile of nonsense–'

'Tell me! Can't you see this is real?'

'My mother would agree with you, but my father says it's all fairytales and superstitions.'

'Forget what your father says for a moment.'

'But he's never wrong.'

'Just tell me what you know!' growled Ebony, ready to shake him.

Shaking his head, Seamus replied in an impatient voice. 'If any of the legends are to be believed, what we just saw was an ancient sacrifice to the most terrible mythical beast that ever lived. Mythical being the important word in that sentence.'

Just as he finished speaking, Aunt Ruby and Uncle Cornelius burst into the room.

'What's going on?' said Aunt Ruby, looking around. 'It sounded like a herd of wildebeest stampeding.'

'*The Book of Learning* just sent us this,' said Ebony, holding out the arrow.

Taking hold of the arrow, Uncle Cornelius gave the ribbon a good sniff. Ebony watched his hair stand on end. After reading the message, he carefully handed the ribbon to Aunt Ruby. His movements were careful and calculated, like the ribbon might come alive and bite him. As soon as Aunt Ruby finished reading, her face darkened.

'It's just a myth!' scoffed Seamus.

'If only that were true,' replied Aunt Ruby, a grave expression on her face. 'The Deus-Umbra is indeed legendary, but it's as real as you and me. Once mistakenly worshipped as a god, the ancients believed that it was in charge of mountains, storms and shadows. They gave it offerings of fruit and flowers to keep it happy. It was terrified of birds – especially birds of prey, as they often formed groups and attacked the creature – so our ancestors kept these birds caged.'

Ebony thought back to the vision the silver box had shown her. It had involved a caged peregrine falcon, but the girl – a past incarnation of Chiyoko – was releasing the bird, not caging it.

'Why did they do that?'

'So the creature would keep away natural disasters,' replied her aunt. 'The Deus-Umbra is a demon from somewhere beyond the worlds that we know. It sees, hears and knows everything and has a special affinity with the universe.'

'Like when we go through Ultimation and mingle with the universe, helping to replenish its good energy?' asked Ebony in an uncertain voice, wishing she didn't look so ignorant in front of Seamus. She chanced a peek at him; his eyes were narrowed in concentration, a frightened look on his face. She could tell that he was starting to believe.

'Similar, I guess. That's why our people mistook it as a god and gave it that name: Deus meaning god, Umbra meaning the shadows of an eclipse. There was peace when it first arrived – the Deus-Umbra wasn't always vengeful.'

'So what changed? Something must have happened.'

'Things were harmonious for many decades. But then an adventurous child from one of the original Nine Lives families accidentally stumbled on the Deus-Umbra's home. Terrified, the child ran and, in its haste, fell from the mountain and was killed. Devastated by the death, and blaming the Deus-Umbra for it, our ancestors refused to give any more offerings to the demon-god. When they were plagued with storms, avalanches and floods, they realised their mistake. They had turned the Deus-Umbra against them.'

'Really?' asked Seamus, leaning in.

'Tell us more,' urged Ebony.

In an excited whisper, Aunt Ruby continued. 'The story goes that, deprived of its offerings and worship, the Deus-Umbra reacted with great fury, causing many deaths. Storms raged and vicious floods destroyed everything: crops, livestock and people. Even when the ancients started sending offerings again, there was no end to the devastation. In a desperate attempt to appease the Deus-Umbra, the village chief decided to offer their most precious commodity and sacrifice a child. The death and devastation quickly ended, but the plan went terribly wrong – the Deus-Umbra tasted blood and liked it. Not long after the initial sacrifice, the demon-god appeared in the village and demanded a yearly child sacrifice.'

Holding a paw to his head, Winston looked like he was going to faint.

'Not knowing what else to do, the Order of Nine Lives obeyed. The practice continued for many years until, one day, our people decided that it couldn't be a god after all – a god would protect, not harm – and there was a revolt. The Deus-Umbra was imprisoned in a volcanic mountain deep under the sea, and until recently it was assumed that the demon had died. But now it seems the demon lives on.'

'And it's haunting my dreams – but why?' added Ebony. Remembering what the strange person in the shadows had told her – he will gain power so terrible, no one will be able to stop him – she gasped. 'Judge Ambrose! This must be the secret weapon that Icarus heard him mention. This is how he's strengthening his power. Could the Deus-Umbra help the judge to enter the Reflectory or swap souls?' asked Ebony.

'I believe so,' answered Aunt Ruby. 'Before it was imprisoned, the Deus-Umbra could enter places and do things we've never dreamed of. It was the only creature that could move between the eternal realms of Ultimation and Obliteration. It could communicate with exiles, with souls, with those who had received their final judgement.'

'What if it could still communicate in those realms even when imprisoned?' cried Ebony. 'If so, the creature could have met with a soul, like that of Zach's mum, and used it to lure the judge to its prison, knowing Ambrose would be power-greedy enough to help set it free.'

'What's Zach's mum got to do with it?' asked Aunt Ruby impatiently.

'Wait, I know this,' cried Seamus. 'Her story was in the manga cartoon. Zach's mum was killed in the line of duty during her last life, and she hadn't achieved her destiny, so she was heading for Obliteration. The judge had signed her final decree, but Zach didn't want to lose her, so he offered her up for the soul-swapping experiment.'

'Yes, yes, but how does that link to the Deus-Umbra?' asked Aunt Ruby.

'The judge retracted his signature and built some kind of life-support machine,' continued Ebony. 'Then he came after me. Maybe the demon communicated with her in some way and, when the judge made his retraction, used her to get to Ambrose.'

'Do you really believe that Judge Ambrose has joined forces with the Deus-Umbra?' asked Seamus, running his fingers through his hair.

'Yes,' replied Aunt Ruby softly, laying a hand on the boy's arm. 'I believe Ambrose is trying to gain the demon's cooperation to increase his power so it will be easier to defeat Ebony.'

Paling, Seamus put a hand to his chest. 'Now that he has Chiyoko, do you think he'll sacrifice her to the Deus-Umbra, like the girl we saw in *The Book of Learning*?'

'I can't say for sure. All I know is that Judge Ambrose clearly hasn't succeeded in freeing the Deus-Umbra yet. If he had, we'd know about it.'

Resting his face in his hands, Seamus was quiet for a moment. Everyone in the room was still. Not a breath could be heard.

'Well, I don't scare easily,' replied Ebony. 'And if the Order got rid of this menace once, we can do it again.'

'There's a problem,' said her aunt. 'We don't have the full story. We don't know how close Ambrose is to setting the Deus-Umbra free and we don't know how or where the original Nine Lives families managed to imprison it. Without this knowledge, how can we succeed?'

It wasn't yet light when Ebony opened her eyes, pinned to the bed in terror and her palm aching. Sweat soaked every inch of her skin, yet she shivered. In her dreams, the murderous red eyes and the gaping mouth of the Deus-Umbra had been right on top of her, sacrificial drumming in the background. Rather than a dream, it felt like a warning. Knowing she wouldn't be able to sleep any more, Ebony instinctively rubbed at the mark on her palm where the skull door handle had pricked her, as she ran through everything she'd learned so far to see if she could come up with a plan.

- She had been given the task of returning a mysterious box to its rightful owner but didn't know who that owner was.

- Chiyoko was still missing, about to become a snack for an ancient demon.

- Worst of all, how was she expected to defeat Zach and Judge Ambrose and their Shadow Walkers, as well as the ancient demon, when her own people didn't even believe in her?

If only her past selves or her grandpa could help her! They had helped to save her life before, why were they quiet now?

A rogue tree branch scratched at Ebony's window, making her heart thud. Reaching for Winston, she tucked him under the covers with her and closed her eyes, as though pretending to sleep would make her feel safer. Trying to block out her jumbled thoughts, she waited for daylight to arrive.

When it reached 5 a.m. and Ebony heard the first bird sing, she decided she'd had enough. Rain lashed at the windows and the sky was slate grey. Her thoughts were still fighting for attention as she climbed out of bed, exhausted. Then she had an idea. Both Icarus and her aunt had mentioned the King Vulture's ability to deliver messages to the Nine Lives souls – she could try to send an S.O.S. to her grandpa!

Grabbing a pen and paper, Ebony wrote a quick note:

Dear Grandpa,
Please speak to me again – I need your help.
I love and miss you,
Ebony xxx

Although she had watched both Icarus and her aunt contact the vulture, she had no idea whether she would manage it herself – but it was worth a try. Folding the note carefully, Ebony added Grandpa Tobias's name to the outside and dressed quickly. She collected her rucksack with all her necessities, including the silver box, and carefully stepped around the skull mark on her bedroom floor. She crept past the other rooms, leaving everyone else to sleep – all except Winston, who was tucked up snug and warm in her sleeve. Reaching the front door, she opened the locks as quietly as she could and stole out into the pouring rain.

It didn't take long for Ebony to reach the Hideout and her heart felt lighter as she bounded down the steps – it was as though the rain had washed away some of her worries. But on reaching the bottom of the steps, Ebony jerked to a stop. Winston popped his head out of her coat pocket, quickly pulling it back inside when Ebony pointed to the scene in front of her.

On the floor, there was a set of muddy footprints that led across the floor and beyond the previously locked door, towards the secret tunnel. Looking behind her, she realised that, whomever they belonged to, that person had entered from the park. She'd been in such a hurry, she hadn't waited for all the candles to light so she hadn't seen the muddy trail on the stairs.

As a cough sounded from somewhere deep in the passage-way, Ebony's body tensed. There was no time to run or hide.

21

Seconds later, a black figure stood in the doorway: thin and spiky, with hair sticking out like twigs.

'S-Stay back,' stammered Ebony, wishing she had a weapon to hand.

The figure lifted its hands in a gesture of surrender, then stepped forward. In the glare of the blue light, with his bloodshot eyes and paper-thin skin, Icarus Bean resembled a ghost.

'Uncle! What are you doing here? How did you get in?' asked Ebony.

'Your aunt added me to the security system,' said Icarus. 'I was hiding out and looking for clues on when Ambrose might strike. Come with me.'

He led her down the passageway and they stopped in the last room, taking a moment for their eyes to adjust to the blue glow.

'What is this place?' asked Ebony, gesturing around her once she could see. 'And why does it lead to 23 Mercury Lane?'

'It used to be our games room – we played pool and darts

and table football.' A wistful look passed over his features, then his face clouded. 'But the tunnel wasn't in use back then – we thought it was unsafe. How did you open it?'

'Seamus triggered something – he kicked it and a handle appeared.'

His forehead creasing, Icarus continued. 'Did you see the mark on the door? The skull?'

'Yes.'

'Whatever you do, don't touch it.'

'Why?'

'Because it might be a trap. This is the work of Ambrose.'

Feeling a shiver run up and down her spine, Ebony replied, 'I already did. When Seamus triggered the security mechanism, the skull transformed into a handle, and I was the one that opened it.' Secretly rubbing her palm, she didn't mention the pinprick; it was only tiny, after all. 'Did you know that Ambrose is trying to make a pact with the Deus-Umbra?'

Icarus nodded grimly and pointed at the bucket of ash. Ebony dipped her hand into it; rubbing the ash between her fingers, she found small, brittle chunks. On closer inspection, she realised they were bits of charred bones; the ashes had once been a living creature. Jumping back, she looked to her uncle for an explanation.

'It looks like some kind of sacrifice,' said Icarus. 'Ambrose must have been trying to communicate with the Deus-Umbra.' His gaze fell on the conch shell. 'The conch is also a powerful method of communication.'

Ebony's blood ran cold. 'What if we destroy the shrine? Would that help?'

'It won't make any difference. What's done is done. There's no going back now. Let's close the place up – it gives me the shivers.'

Hesitating, Ebony picked up the conch shell and raised it above her head, ready to dash it to the ground.

'I wouldn't do that,' said Icarus, holding up his hands and edging nearer. 'That's a powerful piece of magic and if you destroy it, who knows what would happen.'

Lifting the shell to her ear instead, Ebony once again heard the swish of waves, the rumblings of sea breeze. 'Last time I heard a song,' she said, holding it out.

'Did you talk back?' asked Icarus, carefully taking the conch.

'No. Should I have?'

'It depends on where it's connected to. This conch is enchanted with ancient magic. In times past, tribal chieftains could create a kind of sound link to home through the conch shell. Everyone knows you hear the sea if you hold a conch to your ear – and with old magic, the ancients harnessed this power so travellers could always communicate with home.'

'Like an ancient telephone?'

'Exactly. The formula has been lost to us, but once the conch had been connected, the bearer could listen to the sounds of home whenever they chose. And when they spoke into it, their voice would ring across the skies in their village, for all to hear.'

'So how did Zach get hold of one?'

'It must belong to Ambrose – a family heirloom perhaps. Or stolen. I'm surprised they were foolish enough to leave it behind. Look after it. That shell might come in useful.'

Herding Ebony out into the corridor, Icarus closed the door to the shrine behind him and they headed back to the main room of the Hideout, closing the second door also. Shuffling uncomfortably and running his fingers through his hair, so giant clumps stuck up on end, Icarus looked like he wanted to say something but the words wouldn't come.

'What are the AESL saying, Uncle? Is that who you're hiding from?'

Carefully placing the conch on Ebony's desk, Icarus rubbed his chin with his hand and scowled, backing away to the exit. 'Believe me, you don't want to know. But you won't see me again unless it's absolutely necessary. And don't tell anyone I was here.'

It was only after he'd left that Ebony remembered about her note to her grandpa. However, there was no point chasing after him – she knew from experience he'd be long gone. She'd just have to try for herself. Tipping her head back and cupping her mouth, she tried a practice run, copying the noise she'd heard her uncle make, but the pitch was wrong and the tone off-key. She sounded more like a strangled duck. She tried a second time, but there was no improvement and the effort made her throat hurt.

Deciding to consult *The Book of Learning*, Ebony slung her rucksack down and laid Winston on the pillow of the four-poster bed, where he dozed off, his tummy gently rising and falling with his deep breaths.

'If you have anything else that can help me,' she said aloud, seating herself at the desk. 'Then let me see it. I know it's not going to be pretty.'

Flicking to the next empty page, Ebony sat and waited. The page turned an unusual wash of grey and red, and a long and continuous line, like that on an Etch A Sketch, started to appear around the perimeter. It continued its path until it formed a perfect rectangular frame. Into the frame flew a flock of gulls, their grey wings outstretched as they circled and squawked. Another flock joined them, and another, flapping and gliding and circling. A familiar rushing sound began and the red and grey swirls formed the crests of waves; Ebony recognised the sound of strong swells. She knew them as well as she knew her own breath. The noise woke Winston and he ambled over, climbing the desk legs and positioning himself close to the book so he could see what was going on. The background turned blood red, frosting the tips of the waves; on the page, dawn was breaking.

'I'm hoping it will show us Chiyoko's location,' said Ebony, trying to ignore the guilty feeling that threatened to engulf her. 'Or how to beat the Shadow Walkers.'

Winston nodded, keeping his eyes on the swirling image. Two gulls swooped across the page, squawking and hollering as an arrow followed their path, piercing one of the gulls through the heart. The gull dropped from the sky, the other diving after it as if trying to avoid the same fate, only to be pierced with a second arrow. Winston squealed and Ebony averted her eyes. When she looked back, there was a huge ship making its way through the waves, heading towards them.

Ebony squinted at the image – was this the same ship that had carried Chiyoko away in the mirror? She didn't think so. The other one had felt more sinister. As the ship neared, it became clear that it was definitely different. The three masts were much higher and more upright, and the deck had a shallower draft. There were cannons, rather than oars, showing at the sides, and on the front, a beautiful black falcon gleamed. Its proud chest was curved and muscular and its regal head lifted as though searching for the safest passage through the waves. The bird's outstretched wings were delicately patterned with gold leaf to show feathery details, and its eyes sparkled red, a ruby for each. Two strong legs, each tipped with a giant set of claws, jutted from the prow, as though ready to pluck something from the waves. The craftsmanship was so exquisite, the figurehead looked like it would flap its wings and fly up into the sky at any minute. Underneath the carving, in elegant capital letters, were the words THE BLACK PEREGRINE.

'It's beautiful!' said Ebony.

She'd seen many vessels on the ocean but never such

refined craftsmanship or attention to detail. The ship must have been built a long time ago – the 1600s maybe – but the prow was strong and powerful, cutting through the waves at a speed she wouldn't have thought possible without an engine. Every time the ship got close, the book adjusted its distance and made it look far away again. It was like one of those training devices that swimmers used, strengthening their strokes without actually going anywhere.

Then, as Ebony and Winston watched, a huge freak wave splashed against the hull of the ship, lifting it high into the air. Crashing down, the angle changed so that the deck was visible. At the prow was a familiar face that Ebony had seen before: her pirate self.

'Hello. Can you hear me?' called Ebony.

There was no reply.

Winston leaped onto the page and pawed at the pirate's face. The pirate girl sneezed, but nothing else changed.

On the page, the pirate girl fiddled with the cutlass that hung from her hip, staring out to sea as she searched for something. Her mouth moved as she muttered under her breath, but there was no sound so her words remained secret. As she turned to leave, a band of rowdy pirates suddenly appeared on deck. Raising her cutlass aloft in a show of power, the pirate girl shouted. In response, the pirates cheered, and the girl turned and stomped triumphantly towards the cabin. When she disappeared her crew started to jeer at one another, raising their fists and their weapons. One held up a pair of dead gulls. The pirate girl reappeared, hands on her hips and her mouth wide, yelling orders. Quickly, the men returned to their duties.

'I must have been the ship's captain in my past life,' said Ebony. 'It looks like the rabble answered to my commands.' Winston did a little flip, making Ebony laugh. 'I like the idea too – but how does this help us or Chiyoko?'

As the words came out, the ship started to roil out of control, rocking and heaving as though being attacked by a freak storm, although no such storm was visible. The sky was cloudless, the sails were down and gulls glided by the masts easily, so Ebony knew the air must be calm.

The pirate girl leaped up onto the deck, lifted her telescope and began to survey the surrounding area. Checking the horizon, she swung this way and that, searching for what was causing the commotion. Winston leaned in, but when the telescope turned in his direction, the pirate girl suddenly dropped it in alarm and stumbled backwards. She rubbed her eyes and hesitated before picking up the telescope again.

'Did I – I mean, she – see you? It's happened before, a connection like that,' said Ebony, her voice high-pitched with excitement. 'The conch! Remember what Icarus said. Maybe we can use it to communicate with her, like Icarus explained.'

As the pirate girl peered through her telescope once more, Ebony positioned herself right in its path and, lifting the conch shell to her mouth, shouted, 'Can you hear us?'

The pirate girl reeled, dropped the telescope and clasped

her hands to each side of her head, as though blocking out a terrible, ear-splitting noise.

'It worked! She heard my voice, Winston! I'm certain of it.'

Winston nodded emphatically, leaping over the book with excitement. The bright light in the Hideout meant he cast a huge shadow over the page, and all the pirates stopped what they were doing. Freeing their weapons, they made ready to fight.

'Careful, Winston,' giggled Ebony, but her laughter soon died away.

The pirates weren't reacting to Winston after all. It was another ship. A huge black ship, with a red-gold figurehead, that looked big enough to swallow up *The Black Peregrine*. A ship that appeared empty and lifeless as it powered through the water. Ebony's palm started to burn and a strange sensation followed, like cold fingers walking on her skin. She felt the icy tips work their way up her arm to her throat, a sudden searing, yet familiar, pain encircling her neck, fire filling her throat and blocking her airways. Feeling like she was going to choke, Ebony tugged at her neck as her palm began to sear. Winston watched her, alarmed but unable to help. Then, just as quickly as it had started, the pain stopped.

'It's Ambrose,' croaked Ebony, rubbing at her throat and checking her palm – the black dot had grown in size. 'I don't know how, but I think he's on board that ship.'

Leaning in, she squinted, looking for any sign of her enemies, but all she could see were dark shapes that seemed to slip and slide around the ship, moving too fluidly to form a person. At the front, Chiyoko was tied to a mast pole, her head rising to peer over the ship's edge every time it dipped with the waves.

'She looks weak, but at least we know she's still alive,' said Ebony. 'But what I don't understand is how the ship with Chiyoko and *The Black Peregrine* can be in the same image. *The Black Peregrine* would have been around centuries ago.'

At the nearest point on the deck of the enemy ship, Ebony spotted movement. A figure made of wisps of slate-grey smoke. Its eyes were tiny pinpricks and it hardly had a face, yet it emanated anger and hatred.

'It's a Shadow Walker,' whispered Ebony.

She watched as the Shadow Walker slipped over the edge of its ship and down on to the deck of *The Black Peregrine*, where it formed a dark puddle. The puddle slithered across the deck until it was positioned behind the pirates, where it bubbled and expanded, thick tar-like tendrils poking their way out of the murk. The figure re-formed and made its way towards the unsuspecting pirates, who were all fixated on the strange ship looming over them. A single spot of black remained where the figure had appeared – in seconds it morphed into a skull, just like the one on Ebony's bedroom floor and on the door in the Hideout's secret tunnel. As a pain shot through her palm, she checked it again: the mark in its centre was still just a dot, but definitely bigger than before.

'Look how many oars there are,' said Ebony in a small

voice. 'There must be lots of them on board, Winston! And if they're on the open sea, it means they've left the Shadowlands.'

Quickly, Winston leaped back over the scene towards Ebony, squealing with fright. But as he did so, he accidentally caught the edge of *The Book of Learning* with one of his back feet and flipped it over.

'Be careful! We haven't got the whole story yet!'

As the book slammed shut, the image of the miniature black ship popped up out of its cover and Ebony shuffled back in fright – this had never happened before. Ebony noticed that the oars on the ship had stopped moving. On the deck, several Shadow Walkers lumbered, each carrying weapons and displaying angry red eyes. Winston cowered, keeping his distance. Without warning, one of the Shadow Walkers stopped in its tracks and slowly turned its head towards Ebony and Winston. Lifting a telescope, it opened its mouth wide enough to show stumpy yellow teeth and began to cackle. As the mark on Ebony's hand began to burn, the other Shadow Walkers stopped and stared also.

'Can they see us?' whispered Ebony, rubbing her palm to try to soothe the pain.

The cackle grew louder, and the Shadow Walker lifted a small barrel, then began to pour something that looked like oil onto the deck in swirls. Following the movements with her eyes, Ebony realised the Shadow Walker was using the oil to form letters.

'That looks like a Y,' she said aloud, 'and an L.'

Moments later, the Shadow Walker put the barrel down, took out a match and struck it against the side, then threw it onto the oil it had just poured. The oil flared, sending out a strange, blue and fizzing light. A fiery message lit up the deck.

YOUR LIFE FOR HERS

The flames grew bigger, and even from a few feet away Ebony could feel the heat they gave off. Pulling Winston close, she scooted back further. Then, just as she was starting to panic, the flames disappeared and the image of the ship with it. Panting with fear, Winston ran up Ebony's arm onto her shoulder and sat, trembling.

Only when there was no sign of the image returning and she was certain it was safe did Ebony quickly open the book again to check the page. The pirates on *The Black Peregrine* were now frozen in fear as the black ship loomed over them, and it looked like one man was wounded – but the page had dried, turning sepia, so Ebony wouldn't find out what happened next.

'It looks like we'll have to make a trade, Winston. But where exactly are they and can we trust them to hand Chiyoko over?'

Shaking his head emphatically, Winston stamped his foot. His fur and tail shook and shivered, his ears trembling as he climbed down onto Ebony's lap and curled into a ball.

Running her fingers through her hair, Ebony thought

hard. The solution to getting Chiyoko back was obvious, but if she gave herself up to Ambrose, the soul-swapping curse would come true for certain and she couldn't let that happen. But if she didn't, what would happen to Chiyoko?

Booting up her computer, she typed the words *The Black Peregrine* into the search box, hoping to find out some information about the ship – when it existed and what seas it travelled. That might help her to find Chiyoko's location. Again, the same CLASSIFIED message filled her screen. Looking up, Winston frowned.

'If I can't get access to the information I need, it means someone in the Order is hiding something. Let's go to the National Library and see what we can find out there.'

Winston nodded and climbed down her arm, onto her hand.

'Actually, I have an idea. Aunt Ruby and Icarus both said that riding the shadows takes plenty of practice, and if that's the key to reaching Chiyoko, why don't I give it another try?'

Winston gave his head a good strong shake.

Ignoring him, Ebony continued. 'It might take a while to figure all this out, so I should use this time to hone my skills. Let's see if we can get from here to the National Library using the Shadowlands.'

22

Positioning herself in the centre of the Hideout, directly under the pond where the water dappled the floor with moving shadows, Ebony gripped her pocketknife tightly and stared at the shadow of the desk on the floor. She wasn't worried about trying to ride the shadows from indoors – she'd already passed through a fence without feeling anything, so she was certain it would be safe.

'You'd better stay here,' she said. 'I'm not sure what effect it would have on rats. I don't want you hurt.' Winston stamped his foot, shaking his head again, and Ebony relented. 'Icarus said it takes double the effort, but you're only little. OK, let's give it a go.'

Concentrating on the shadows, breathing slowly and deeply, Ebony let her heart and mind relax. The shadows began to shimmer and merge, but she almost dropped the knife, breaking her concentration. As she tightened her grip on the knife and relaxed her mind once more, the shadows also tightened. Breathing even more slowly, Ebony tried again, this time letting herself be wrapped into the gentle grey hues. Slowly, the Shadowlands emerged and the walls of the Hideout dropped away. Finding her hands and body had turned fully sketch-like, she checked on Winston. He was grey and linear, reminding Ebony of the old *Tom and Jerry* cartoons she had sometimes caught her grandpa chuckling at in Old Joe's cottage as they gutted fish for dinner. Taking one last big breath, Ebony set to work.

'Here goes! Which way is the National Library from here, Winston?' Winston pointed and Ebony nodded agreement, before sliding him into her pocket. 'I don't want us to get separated.'

Then, crouching to score a line in the floor like she'd seen her uncle do, she made a perpendicular line at each end and added an arrow with the tip of her knife, pointing towards the library. Not quite able to remember what the arrows looked like, she did her best; one side was a little wonky, but she didn't have time to worry about that. She could feel herself tiring already.

'Fingers crossed,' she said, taking hold of where she'd scored and lifting the ground to reveal a slash of white below. 'One, two, three.'

On three, she gave a hard tug, but instead of ripping up the ground like last time there was a small, pathetic sound, and then – nothing. Feeling her mood dampening, Ebony tried to think of what might be wrong. Tugging again, she found the ground wouldn't budge.

'My uncle is much taller and stronger than me. Maybe that's what's wrong? I haven't loosened it enough?'

She retrieved her pocketknife and, dropping to the ground, used it to cut away underneath where she had scored. It wasn't easy, but by the time she had finished, she had a decent length of the ground pulled away. Taking it in her hands, she widened her stance for balance, then counted again and yanked with all her might.

This time, she found herself sprawled flat on her back in the Hideout. Winston had tumbled out of her pocket and was near the leg of the four-poster bed, looking dazed.

'What did we do wrong?' asked Ebony, sitting up.

Getting to his feet, Winston zigzagged his way towards Ebony. Instead of stopping and climbing up onto her leg, he bumped right into her.

'We'll have to try again.'

Collapsed in a heap and flattening himself to the floor, Winston gave a small shake of his head. Seeing he was in no state to go through another trial, Ebony sighed.

'Fine,' she said, popping Winston into her sleeve where they could communicate more easily. 'We'll just have to walk.'

Ebony passed though the library's metal detectors and placed her rucksack into a locker. Before stuffing everything else inside, she slipped *The Book of Learning* into her pocket.

'Let's hope no one notices,' she said into her sleeve, where Winston was hiding.

Just as she'd slammed her locker shut and added a security code – 1304, her birthday – a hand clamped on her shoulder. Spinning round, Ebony was greeted by a tall, blue-haired woman. Ebony recognised her immediately as Miss Malone, the toady-faced librarian she had met before and one of the judge's sympathisers. Ebony recoiled as the librarian looked about her uneasily.

'Yes, yes, miss,' she said in a shrill voice, loud enough for everyone to hear. 'That's no problem at all. Come this way.'

Grabbing Ebony's wrist and dragging her along so Ebony had no choice but to go with her, Miss Malone stopped just before the entrance to the reading room.

'I need you to pass some information to your aunt, and I also have an important message for you,' she whispered. 'In thirty-three minutes exactly, go through the door marked STAFF ONLY. It's cordoned off with blue rope, to the right of the computers. You can't miss it.'

With that, she turned and rushed away before Ebony could say a word.

'What do you think, Winston?' asked Ebony.

A small squeak sounded from her sleeve.

'OK. But only if you're sure.'

The reading room was vast and round, with rich carved wood panels and white angel frescoes peering down. Fat grey reading pillows and warm green lights graced every desk, and curved bookcases marked with Roman numerals ran the length of the walls. The domed ceiling was capped with racetrack-shaped glass windows, and everywhere the walls were minty green. Heading straight for the computers at the side of the room, Ebony typed *The Black Peregrine* into the search box. The first result was not terribly relevant, but the second caught her eye:

Peregrine, Black – *Encyclopedia*, bird species

See also:

Peregrine, Silent – *Bird Myths and Legends of West Cork*

Clicking on the description, Ebony read under her breath: 'The legend of a mythical giant bird that guarded the seas of Ireland's south-west shores.' Ebony scribbled down the details on a slip of paper and rushed to the counter where a short, pudgy-faced man with a long brown beard waited. Taking the note, he shook his head.

'You've missed the next collection,' he said, pointing at a timetable taped to the counter. 'It takes time to find and gather the books, so we locate them in shifts for collection at set times. Your request won't be available for another two hours.'

'Two hours? But I need it now!'

She must have spoken more loudly than she'd meant to because several heads turned to look at her, and someone tutted their disapproval.

'I think we can take care of it; phone the request through, Roger.' Miss Malone appeared from the back. Despite her colleague's protests, she shooed him over to the telephone and then leaned in to Ebony. 'Twenty-four minutes and counting. Don't be late!'

Positioning herself in the quietest part of the room, right at the back, Ebony pulled out *The Book of Learning*. She could feel Winston growing fidgety and agitated in her sleeve, but there were too many people close by to let him out: an old lady with pinkish curls, a bald man with huge eyebrows reading a newspaper and a few students in ripped jeans and colourful jackets.

'Sorry, little guy,' she whispered, 'you'd better stay in there for now.'

Bird Myths and Legends of West Cork arrived ten minutes later, a beautiful old manuscript with elaborate blue and silver lettering in the title and an oversized decorative letter starting each page. The writing was tricky to read, but Ebony persevered. The beginning was academic and wordy, using archaic language that Ebony found confusing to cite other academic sources and explain the intentions of the text. Uncertain where to begin, she began flicking through the pages in search of something interesting. As she moved to close the cover, about to give up, there was a loud crack and, snake-like, a leather whip shot out in front of her and slapped against the page.

Looking around to see where the whip had come from, Ebony spotted the heel of a spurred boot and a shock of black curls beneath the rim of a wide-brimmed hat passing through a nearby doorway. The cowboy incarnation of her past self was disappearing through a door marked STAFF ONLY with blue cords in front of it: the door Miss Malone had told Ebony to go through. It wasn't quite time for their meeting, but her past self obviously thought the page was important enough for Ebony to read properly, so she leaned in and read it carefully, whispering the words softly to Winston.

THE SILENT PEREGRINE

A legend that was once well known on the shores of West Cork, but has since been rendered almost extinct through the loss of oral tradition, the story of the Silent Peregrine dates from before the ninth century. The Silent Peregrine was one of a giant and magical species of the falcon family that was believed to guard the shores of West Cork from devils and demons. Local people revered the species and the birds held a special place in the coastal society. They were treated as demigods, with extra attention and care given to their keep as well as festivals and statues in their honour. The special role of bird handler fell to one person, usually a girl; this is thought to be because these birds were particularly combative and easily provoked, yet very true and affectionate, and so a gentle nature was required for successful handling. Specific details are lost, but something altered within the village and suddenly the village chiefs demanded that the birds be caged. The people obeyed, but without their freedom and unable to hunt or exercise, the species began to die out, until only one remained. The bird *would cry and cry for its fellow birds, a melancholy sound that reverberated around the village, driving its inhabitants almost insane. Then, one day, the village came under attack and the handler released the bird so it could use its call to garner help from far and wide. Again, the details are sketchy, but the bird's intervention worked and the village was saved. Only, when the peregrine falcon returned, one of the village chiefs removed its vocal chords. He knew the bird would probably die from grief sometime soon and that the village would be left unprotected. He believed that taking the vocal chords while the bird was alive meant they would retain their magical properties, and this magic would keep the village safe. This is when the last of its species became known as the Silent Peregrine.*

As soon as Ebony finished reading, the words lifted off the page of the original manuscript. Each letter formed a tiny black bird; they encircled her head, then popped like a bubble. The page was now blank.

'That's it?' whispered Ebony under her breath. 'After what we saw in the vision, I'm sure this is referring to one of Chiyoko's past lives. But what does that have to do with anything?'

Closing the book quickly before anyone noticed the page was now blank, Ebony jumped as Winston popped his head out of her sleeve and gave her finger a gentle nip.

It was time.

She returned the book, her nerves jittery as she checked

around her, then sneaked through the heavy double doors for her meeting. Miss Malone was waiting, leaning on a giant orange umbrella, but there was no sign of Ebony's cowboy self. Away from prying eyes, Ebony put Winston on her shoulder.

'Come!' urged Miss Malone, her voice breathy and anxious.

'Why should I?' asked Ebony, thinking back to the time at the Botanic Gardens when the judge and his people, including Miss Malone, had been shooting at her. Instinctively, her hand reached for her pocketknife, but it was stashed in the locker. If Miss Malone attacked her now, she was defenceless.

'Because things are desperate. The judge may be in hiding, but I believe he has something nasty up his sleeve. He'll want to regain control of the Order and will return when he thinks he can't be beaten.'

'You should know, you're one of his supporters!' said Ebony.

'I was until I saw the error of my ways. I'm on your side and, although the AESL has some of the Order confused, you still have support and it's growing,' said Miss Malone.

'And this message – why can't you give it to me here?'

'I'm just following orders. I don't actually know what the message is. I have to bring you to the rooftop, and the message will be delivered there.'

Miss Malone sounded so earnest, Ebony couldn't help softening. If she had more supporters, she had better find out who they were, and fast. Curious, Ebony followed, her throat dry and her heart leaping like a spring lamb.

Beckoning, Miss Malone led Ebony and Winston through a couple of dark and dusty rooms, down a level, through a door and then up several flights of a winding staircase until they reached what looked like a fire exit. As Miss Malone pushed the door open, they all paused; rain was now lashing down outside.

'How do I know this isn't a trick?' Ebony asked, hesitating.

'I admit I supported Ambrose,' said Miss Malone. 'But I didn't know what was happening. I was just doing my job as a member of the High Court.'

'You expect me to believe that?'

'Yes, because it's the truth.' Miss Malone's face creased with desperation. 'I honestly thought I was carrying out official Order business.'

'Like shooting at me?'

'That wasn't me or the colleagues I'm friendly with,' said Miss Malone. 'And it was quite a shock for us to see that he would shoot at some of our own, let me tell you. That was when we first started to realise that things were not what they seemed.'

'How do I know I can trust what you're saying and this isn't some trick of Ambrose's to draw me out?' asked Ebony.

'I know I can't prove it, but you have to believe me,' replied the librarian. 'At the time we had no idea you were the guardian. And we didn't know the judge was planning to swap souls or that he was holding some of our kind in stasis. Now we hear he's controlling the Shadow Walkers. You can't think that anyone in their right mind could support that!' She shook her head vigorously, her blue hair catching the light like mackerel scales under ocean waves. 'Now, please! Let's go and recover this message.'

Miss Malone opened her umbrella and stepped outside, and, after a moment, Ebony followed, tucking under the umbrella's warm amber glow as the rain thudded against it. They were on a platform that overlooked the entrance to the library. It had a white spiral staircase that led to other areas of the building, probably for maintenance men and emergency services, and behind them, there was a smooth, green dome, but no sign of any message or messenger.

'While we're waiting, what do you want me to tell my aunt?' asked Ebony, looking around her.

'Tell her that I'm acting as Icarus's messenger until he comes out of hiding. We are seeking ways to reduce Ambrose's power. Icarus found a clause in our laws that states if a judge is absent for longer than sixty-five days – and that's just days away – we can call an emergency meeting and vote him out.'

'I don't think that will scare him much.'

'No, I don't suppose it will. But the sky world will recognise the vote and remove his ability to sign decrees and banish people into exile. He'll no longer have any sway over our eternal destinies.'

'What can I do to help?' asked Ebony.

'Let us worry about the vote; you must release the souls that are in stasis in the Reflectory. Only you have this power and we need our missing Nine Lives families to be reborn again. There should be a hundred families at all times – and there must be a reason, known only to the sky world, for this number.'

'But the souls will be reborn as babies, and only when their family situation naturally allows – we could be waiting decades for our numbers to return,' replied Ebony.

'I realise that. But if we can restore our numbers for the future, the Order stands a better chance of continuing. Holding the souls in stasis must be adding to Ambrose's power in some way – otherwise, why would he bother? It could also help to sway those among us who doubt your abilities.'

Her stomach knotting and excitement bubbling inside her – this could be the excuse she needed to persuade her aunt to let her return to Oddley Cove – Ebony gritted her jaw.

'I will try,' she said, not mentioning that she'd have to convince her aunt first. 'I'll tell my aunt. Now where's this message?'

'I'm not sure. I was told that it was vital and we had to be here at this time.'

'And who gave you this message exactly?'

'It was delivered anonymously,' answered Miss Malone, looking suddenly worried. 'On official paper. By King Vulture.'

A clunky tune from an ice-cream van rang out below, but neither of them took much notice at first. The roads always filled with traffic when the rain came, and they had a message to locate. Then, from below, a voice called out.

'Ebony.'

Winston's fur stood on end, and his ears pricked up. Ebony's skin felt like it was crawling with lice and Miss Malone paled.

Looking down, Ebony saw a face sticking out of the van window, surrounded by images of ice-cream and lollies. She would recognise those penetrating green eyes anywhere.

Zachariah Stone.

Before she knew what was happening, Zach pulled out a gun and fired in their direction. At first, Ebony thought she had been hit, but as her face struck the cold metal platform, she realised that Miss Malone had pushed her down to safety. Poor Winston bounced out of her sleeve and bumped along the wet floor on his bum, slipping off the side of the roof. Ebony could see his tiny front paws clinging on for dear life, but she couldn't move; Miss Malone was heavy.

Zach opened fire once more, the bullets hitting high up on the dome. Ebony knew that Zach was a crack shot – she realised that he couldn't be trying to hit her. The shots were some kind of warning.

Stretching out her arm, Miss Malone managed to reach Winston and hook him back onto the platform. With a low howl he scampered, slipping and sliding, back towards Ebony to hide. Once Winston was safe, Miss Malone concentrated her efforts on shielding Ebony, pinning her to the ground.

'What do you want, Zach?' shouted Ebony, barely able to squeeze enough air into her lungs to be heard.

'You know what we want. Your life in exchange for your little friend's.'

'Chiyoko? You'd better release her Zach, or–'

'Or what? You're in no position to bargain, Ebony. You might as well give up now; your soul belongs to us. My mother is prepped and waiting and we have dark and ancient powers on our side this time.'

'Over my dead body, Zach Stone.'

'That's exactly the intention,' cried Zach and aimed one last flurry of bullets above them.

Waiting for the shooting to stop, Ebony made a mental note to make sure her most precious belongings were always with her and that she was armed from now on – if she explained the situation to her aunt, she might even be allowed to carry one of the Order's guns for protection.

Down below, the ice-cream-van engine cranked up, tyres screeching and a clunky tune ringing out as Zach pulled away. When she was certain it was safe, Miss Malone clambered off

Ebony. Right away, Ebony inspected the damage that Zach had inflicted on the National Library's domed roof. The bullet holes formed a familiar message in capital letters:

YOUR LIFE FOR HERS

After a moment's pause, Ebony turned to Miss Malone and frowned. 'Are you sure you didn't know that Zach was going to appear?'

Miss Malone's cheeks lit up like a lamp. 'I had no idea, I swear it. I thought I was helping.'

Winston tugged at Ebony's trouser leg and jumped to the floor, squashing himself as flat as he could, while looking up earnestly.

'Winston's right. Your instinct was to save my life,' said Ebony. 'They're probably trying to make it look like I can't trust you – that's how Zach tricked me before, but it won't work this time. I'll give you another chance, but if you double cross me, trust me, you'll pay.'

Miss Malone gave a small smile. 'I won't let you down. I swear it.'

As Ebony bent to gather up Winston, she found him with his front paws crossed, tapping one foot, his nose scrunched up. Scooping him up, Ebony added, 'And thank you, Miss Malone, for wanting to save my life.'

A proud smile crept onto the woman's face and her cheeks

blushed. 'Let's get you home. I think it's best that you don't go alone.'

After seeing Zach for certain for the first time in months, Ebony's legs wobbled and her mind felt fuzzy. She was in no mood to argue and happy to have the company.

24

Miss Malone dropped Ebony to 23 Mercury Lane in a small pea-green car and waited outside. Uncle Cornelius's motorbike and sidecar were parked outside the house, so Ebony knew they were home. Clutching her rucksack close, she climbed out of the car, raced across the road and began tackling the locks, her hands shaking. As she reached the final lock, Ebony heard a screech of tyres. Spinning round she saw a sleek midnight-blue car with the number plate N1NE L1VE5 hurtling around the corner, two of its wheels lifting off the ground.

Ebony gasped: it was Judge Ambrose's car – she recognised the number plate immediately. Scrabbling at the last lock, she twisted the key.

Across the road, Miss Malone sprang into action. Leaping out of the driver's seat, she broke into a run towards the oncoming car. Ambrose's car screeched to a stop in the middle of the road, diagonally across both lanes, missing her by just inches. Miss Malone yanked the driver's door open and grabbed whoever was behind the wheel by the scruff of the neck. Pulling and tugging, she managed to drag the driver out into the road. Ebony heard his complaints before she spotted his shock of white hair: it was Mr O'Hara.

'What are you doing?' he shouted, swatting a now very apologetic Miss Malone away. 'Headquarters is under attack. We need all hands on deck. Ebony, go and get everyone.'

Finally the key turned and, jittery as a bag of frogs, Ebony dashed inside, her mind twisting and turning with worry as she yelled for her aunt. 'Aunt Ruby! Mr O'Hara is outside. HQ is under attack! They need our help!'

Within seconds, her aunt was on the staircase, her violet eyes flashing. Uncle Cornelius came running out of his study snarling, a variety of weapons protruding from every pocket, a helmet tucked under his other arm.

'I was at the National Library and I saw Zach. He fired at us!' said Ebony, blurting it out.

Racing down the stairs, Aunt Ruby took hold of her niece and held her at arm's length. 'Are you OK? Are you hurt?'

'I'm fine,' replied Ebony. 'It was just a warning. He wants me in exchange for Chiyoko.'

'That doesn't surprise me. Try not to worry, we'll come up with a plan.' Aunt Ruby peered through the door. 'But right now, we'd better go and help headquarters, and quick. I'll travel with you, Seamus and O'Hara in the HQ car, and if Uncle Cornelius fetches our car, he can bring Mulligan. Collect Seamus and I'll sort out some weapons.'

Quick as a flash, Uncle Cornelius dashed outside. Racing up the stairs, Ebony called out for Seamus. He was already on his way down.

'I'm ready!' he cried, nudging his way past.

By the time Ebony caught up with him – Winston firmly planted on her shoulder, twitching his whiskers as he clung on to her curls – Seamus was in the hallway, hopping with impatience. Aunt Ruby soon reappeared with a gun for Ebony and a bow for Seamus. Seamus snatched it up, a nervous look on his face, and slung it over his shoulder. Meanwhile, Ebony secured the gun in her pocket and her rucksack on her back. Outside, Mr O'Hara began tooting the car horn. As though a starter pistol had sounded, everyone raced into the street.

'Where's Chiyoko?' shouted O'Hara. 'I said all hands–'

'I told her to stay inside,' intervened Aunt Ruby. 'She's too young. And we don't have time to argue.'

Ebony and Seamus jumped into the back of the midnight-blue car and Aunt Ruby into the front. As O'Hara pulled away, tyres screeching, Ebony looked back; Miss Malone was close behind in her pea-green Mini.

'Do you know how to use that thing?' Ebony asked, pointing at the bow and wondering where the arrows were.

'Of course he does,' snorted Mr O'Hara from the driver's seat. 'If you'd had proper training from your family, you'd know how to as well.'

In the front seat, Aunt Ruby took a single deep breath. Seamus glanced at his father, shook his head and scowled. Seated in the back of the car with Seamus pulling his best stony silence, the journey to the Botanic Gardens seemed to go on forever. As they left the city behind, its busy streets and one-way system turning into a row of houses that snaked opposite the canal, Ebony familiarised herself with the gun. It had been a while since she had used one and it felt alien in her grip. Trusting in its abilities and hardly able to practise in the back of the car, she concentrated on calming her mind, trying to prepare for what they might encounter at headquarters.

Reaching a barrier that prevented cars from turning in to the road that led to the gardens, O'Hara blasted the horn angrily. The sound made Ebony jump and she tightened her grip on her weapon. There was a sign next to the barrier that read:

BOMB SCARE
EVACUATED AREA

Ebony knew it was a cover-up; the Order couldn't allow civilians to witness the attack. A man in a luminous yellow jacket was leaning into a car just ahead, and Ebony guessed he was explaining alternative directions to the driver. But as O'Hara blasted the horn again, the man waved the other car on, spun on his heels and marched towards where they were waiting.

'Imbecile!' spat Mr O'Hara.

Suddenly recognising him, the man gave an apologetic wave and quickly lifted the barrier. Taking a deep breath as the gardens came into view, Ebony readied herself. But nothing could have prepared her for the sight as they drove through the wrought-iron gates and headed straight for the giant glasshouse.

The second they passed through into the gardens, they were shrouded in complete darkness, even though it was still daytime. A single bright spotlight was switched on, lengthening the shadows and highlighting the carnage. Everywhere, there was chaos. Several windows at the top of the domed glasshouse were smashed, with acrid smoke curling in tendrils from where the panes had shattered. Without waiting for the car to stop, Aunt Ruby threw open the door and leapt out, heading straight into the fray. Members of the Order were running in all directions. Some were throwing grenades or fighting what seemed like imaginary attackers; Ebony couldn't see what they were battling against, but they lashed out, ducking and firing their guns. Others were lifted by an invisible force into the air and thrown, screaming as they arced through the sky, while more lay still on the ground. One woman covered her ears and frothed at the mouth, writhing like a worm.

Jamming on the car brakes, Mr O'Hara opened his door.

'What's going on, Father?' asked Seamus. 'Where's Mum?'

But Mr O'Hara was already gone; Ebony guessed he must have joined in the furore, although she couldn't spot him in the crowd. She could see her aunt wrestling with an invisible something near the headquarters' entrance; she held her arms open wide, as though fighting something far bulkier than herself. Focusing her eyes, Ebony could just make out a shifting, vaporous outline. Suddenly Mulligan burst onto the scene and knocked the assailant flying, tumbling after it before quickly getting to his feet and holding it captive in a corner, roaring and snarling. Nearby, Miss Malone was throwing things at a slippery, shady target.

'Shadow Walkers,' spat Ebony. 'Come on, Seamus, let's help!'

They jumped out of the car and, spotting Uncle Cornelius wrestle something to the ground, Ebony ran towards him, Winston clinging to her shoulder for dear life. Realising she was running alone and hearing something loud crashing towards her, Ebony stopped and crouched down, looking around and trying to focus on the shadows to see what was coming her way. A noise above her, accompanied by an icy breeze, made the hairs on the back of her neck and Winston's fur stand on end. The ground shuddered around them and then they both saw the grass being flattened by what looked like a giant footprint. This Shadow Walker was huge!

Following the gigantic footsteps, Ebony checked where the creature was headed. She spotted Seamus frozen to the spot directly in its path, his eyes wide as he looked towards the creature approaching him. He could see it but was clearly too stunned to react.

Ebony raced back towards Seamus, taking care to dodge round where she thought the next giant footsteps would land. Just in the nick of time, she grabbed Seamus around the waist and yanked him out of the way. Seconds later, they saw the grass where he had been standing was completely squashed flat.

'I could have handled it on my own,' said Seamus, bow in hand.

'You can thank me later,' said Ebony, getting to her feet.

Spying Miss Malone in the distance, pinned against the wall but still fighting, Ebony took off towards the smoking building, but she didn't get far. After just a couple of steps, she felt herself being lifted into the air, her legs still running but no ground underneath.

Instinctively reaching for Winston, she found he was missing. He must have fallen off when she had tackled Seamus. A beam from a spotlight flashed over the ground, improving Ebony's view. She spotted Mr O'Hara crouching behind his car and, at the headquarters' entrance, Mrs O'Hara was helping Aunt Ruby to her feet. Looking down, Ebony realised she was more than ten feet off the ground, with Winston staring up at her.

'Run!' screamed Ebony as she felt the creature lift its leg. 'You'll get squashed!'

Doing as he was told, Winston ran straight towards the thickest section of fighting, where Aunt Ruby's hair could easily be seen, blowing wildly behind her as she grappled with a Shadow Walker.

Twisting around, Ebony fired her gun at where she thought her captor's head might be. But as they entered the beam of the spotlight, she figured she must have missed –

the creature was unharmed. As its outline grew visible in the spotlight, she realised its body was huge, but its head was tiny in comparison. It had a face like melted rubber, its eyes set in loose folds of skin and its nose drooping, a slobbering crack of a downturned mouth open, revealing small, stumpy yellow teeth. Instead of looking angry, it looked sad. Lowering her gun, Ebony remembered what her aunt had said about the Shadow Walkers: that they were once human and part of the Order.

'Let me go and I won't hurt you,' said Ebony, trying to reason with the creature.

In reply, the Shadow Walker lifted Ebony high over its head with both hands, ready to fling her into the battling crowd.

There was a gentle whooshing sound and a cry. When Ebony looked up, an arrow made out of green lights was sticking out of the Shadow Walker's eye. As the creature howled with pain, it flung Ebony around like a cocktail shaker. Feeling the strap on her shoulder slipping off, Ebony tried to cling on to her rucksack, but a few more shakes and the bag broke free, falling from her grip. Another whooshing sound filled the air and the creature roared as a second arrow hit its eye. It dropped Ebony, using both hands to try to yank the arrows from its eye socket. Feeling herself falling through the air, Ebony let out a scream. But instead of landing on the hard ground with a thump and a shattering of bones, she hit soft fur and a muscular rump, before rebounding onto the grass. Her shoulder hurt from the impact, but as she rolled away, she gave Mulligan a thumbs-up.

Lifting her gun, her eyes now accustomed to the Shadow Walker's fluid, shadowy form, Ebony fired two shots. A pair of tiny, see-through bullets hurtled towards the creature, one hitting its heart and the other its brain. The creature's internal organs should have imploded, but instead, it simply looked down and rubbed at the spot where the bullets had entered its body.

She had missed earlier but this was a direct hit and she realised that her bullets couldn't harm the Shadow Walkers – Seamus's arrows had more impact.

As the creature reacted angrily, stomping on the ground, Seamus pulled back the string on his bow again, and a green arrow automatically appeared. As the arrow hit the Shadow Walker, driving it back, Ebony crawled out of the way just in time.

'Now we're even,' said Seamus. 'We've saved each other.'

As his words died way, there was a piercing screech from above. Looking up, Ebony saw the outstretched wings of the King Vulture overhead, its shrill cry echoing for miles around.

'My rucksack. Have you seen it?' asked Ebony – she couldn't afford to lose *The Book of Learning* or her bronze rose and seeing the vulture reminded her of her note to her grand-pa. Maybe, if the message worked, he would be able to reveal something about setting the souls in stasis free.

As the cry rang out, Ebony watched daylight creep back

overhead, blue sky pushing away the darkness like a wave. As the sky brightened, the Shadow Walkers seemed to melt away. Men on the ground began to unfurl themselves one by one, like flowers after the rain. The writhing woman pushed herself to a sitting position to survey the damage. Those that were fighting suddenly stumbled and staggered, as their opponents unexpectedly disappeared.

'The Shadow Walkers, they're leaving!' cried Ebony as Aunt Ruby limped to her side. 'Did anyone see Ambrose or Zach?'

Aunt Ruby and Uncle Cornelius shook their heads.

'I don't understand. They've got the upper hand,' continued Ebony. 'Our weapons are useless against them. Why are they leaving?'

Sensing something tall looming behind her, Ebony spun round, her gun lifted.

'Watch what you're doing with that thing,' snapped Mr O'Hara. He was completely unscathed; there wasn't even a scrap of dirt on him. Ebony guessed he'd been hiding the whole time.

Miss Malone joined the group, a gash on her cheek pumping blood. She had Winston carefully cupped in her big, stubby hands. As she handed him over, Ebony noticed blood on his ear. There was a small nick where a piece of flesh was missing.

'Judge Ambrose must have called the Shadow Walkers away,' said Miss Malone, her eyebrows knit.

'But why?' pressed Ebony. 'That makes no sense.'

The sky was once again blue and filled with fluffy clouds; the darkness had completely lifted. Only the puffs of smoke still chugging from the glass dome, the broken weapons and limping people indicated there had been anything wrong just minutes before.

'Who cares? At least we won the battle,' said Mr O'Hara triumphantly, opening his arms wide and gesturing at his surroundings. 'I myself saw several of the Shadow Walkers off,' he continued, puffing up his chest.

Ebony scowled. She had seen Mr O'Hara hiding – he hadn't helped at all and now he was acting like he had led them to victory. But she kept quiet, knowing that an outburst would give him more ammunition against her for his precious AESL. She noticed that Seamus was looking at the ground, shaking his head, and wondered if he had seen his father hiding too.

'That wasn't a battle,' replied Aunt Ruby. 'It was a warning. Judge Ambrose was giving us a taste of his power.'

'And we barely managed to hold them off,' said Ebony. 'I definitely saw more troops in the Sh–'

Aunt Ruby shook her head covertly and at exactly the same time Seamus nudged her and pointed to a nearby bed of roses. 'Your rucksack! Look!'

Realising her error – her aunt clearly didn't want Mr O'Hara to know about the Shadowlands – Ebony retrieved her rucksack. The zip had stayed tightly shut, so she knew that her most precious belongings were safe. As for her grandpa's note, the vulture was long gone and the chance to send it had been missed.

As Aunt Ruby turned away from the smoking building, Mr O'Hara cried out. 'Wait! There's a little business we have to attend to.'

Gritting her teeth, Aunt Ruby shook her head. 'You can't be serious, O'Hara. We need to help the wounded and tidy this mess up before outsiders start to notice something is wrong.'

'I'm completely serious,' said Mr O'Hara, taking a step towards headquarters. When no one followed, he added, 'Trust me, this will interest all of you.'

As Mr O'Hara strode ahead, leading Ebony with Winston in her pocket, Aunt Ruby and Uncle Cornelius up the spiral stone stairs to the meeting room at the top of the glasshouse, Seamus dragged his feet and held back. Beside him, Miss Malone whispered conspiratorially; looking back, Ebony did her best to hear what they were saying, but their echoing footsteps drowned out any chance that she had.

When they reached the top of the stairs, the door was locked, puffs of smoke escaping from under it. Taking out a huge rusted key, Mr O'Hara forced the lock to turn, then ushered everyone inside. As they stepped through, Mr O'Hara at the back of the group, it took a moment for the smoke to clear. When it did, Uncle Cornelius mewled and dashed across the room.

Icarus Bean was waiting. He had the same dark expression and bedraggled hair, but he was dressed much more smartly than earlier. He wore a suit, complete with waistcoat and overcoat. Had Mr O'Hara locked him in while they were under attack and, if so, why? Ebony glanced at her aunt for an answer, but Aunt Ruby seemed just as surprised to see him; she was chewing on a thumbnail, a big frown creasing her forehead.

Despite Icarus's tidied appearance, Ebony noticed his movements were laboured and awkward as he stepped forward to rub Uncle Cornelius behind the ears. She guessed it was the effects of his stuffy clothes. Noticing one of his jacket sleeves was singed and smoking, she hoped he wasn't hurt. As soon as Icarus saw O'Hara, his jaw clenched.

'If you ever pull a trick like that again, O'Hara, I swear I'll–'

'What?' asked Mr O'Hara in an innocent voice. 'I was simply protecting you from the kerfuffle outside in the name of the Order. We were under attack and we can't afford to lose another judge.'

'Perhaps it slipped your notice that this room was also under attack?' shouted Icarus, spit flying. 'There were grenades and exploding bullets showering the place.'

'Another judge?' enquired Aunt Ruby, her words slow and sticky, like she was trying to figure out what they meant as she spoke them.

'Yes!' cried Mr O'Hara. 'We've placed Icarus at the head of the Order, as Acting Judge.'

Seeing Miss Malone's eyes widen, Ebony remembered the message she hadn't yet had a chance to give to her aunt. There was no need for the plan now – it seemed that the Order had already moved on Ebony's behalf, putting Icarus in place to help her.

Turning to her uncle, Ebony grinned. 'That's great news!' she cried. 'You're in charge? That should strengthen our stand against Ambrose!'

Shaking his head, Icarus replied, 'Acting Judge. Nothing more than a puppet.' Averting his eyes, he looked to the floor.

'What do you mean, brother?' asked Aunt Ruby, walking over and laying a hand on Icarus's shoulder.

'Despite his absence, Ambrose is technically still the official judge, so he retains the power to sign decrees and exile people,' replied Icarus, his voice bitter.

So, Miss Malone's plan could still be important, thought Ebony. She caught the woman's eye and gave her a sly wink. Miss Malone's shoulders relaxed and she smiled back, giving a less secret wink in return.

Keeping quiet for now and deciding it would be best to relay the message to her aunt when Mr O'Hara wasn't around – she didn't trust him and suspected he would try to scupper the plan – Ebony tried to figure out why Icarus seemed so angry. She tried to catch his eye to offer support, but her uncle refused to look at her. He was purposely avoiding her gaze.

'So what's the point of the position?' asked Aunt Ruby.

'Exactly,' replied Icarus. 'I was asked to take up the role just before the Reflectory disappeared.' He flashed his sister and Ebony a look that reminded them to play along – he still wanted the Order to believe the place was missing. 'Of course, I couldn't oblige – I had to go in search of the Reflectory. However, when I didn't succeed, the Order caught up with me. It seems they've voted me in without requiring my say on the matter.'

'No prizes for guessing who did the electing,' said Aunt Ruby, turning an accusing gaze on Mr O'Hara. 'These things have to be put to a democratic vote. I certainly wasn't asked.'

'Apparently, the AESL,' Icarus spat the words like they were too disgusting to have in his mouth, 'is so big now that no one else needs to be included in a vote to make a majority.'

Aunt Ruby threw a look of pure disgust in Mr O'Hara's direction. 'That's unheard of! I won't stand for it.'

Ebony felt like running from the room – were the people against her really that powerful? She caught Seamus's eye – an original member of the AESL – and he shuffled uncomfortably, looking apologetic.

'Now, now,' said Mr O'Hara. 'There's no need to be hostile. I think you're all underestimating the importance of Icarus's newly elected position.'

Icarus stepped forward towards O'Hara, his fists balled. Just as it looked like he was about to strike, footsteps sounded and people began to file into the room. Spinning around, Ebony estimated that around thirty in total entered, many of them wounded from the battle. What was going on?

Mr O'Hara was grinning now, his hand clasped around a tightly rolled scroll. As he handed the item to Icarus, he said, 'I'll let you do the honours.'

'I'm so sorry, Ebony,' said Icarus.

'For what?' asked Ebony. Popping out his head, Winston

gave a squeak. Lifting him out and cuddling him, Ebony frowned. 'Can someone please tell me what's going on?'

'Read it,' said Icarus, his eyes flashing angrily as he held the scroll out to his sister. 'It's a case of divide and conquer; the AESL still don't believe in Ebony's rightful position as guardian. They think that by appointing me, they can keep an eye on me and figure out how we faked it all along. At the very least, they hope that causing a rift between myself and Ebony will weaken our family ties and influence.'

Ebony looked at Mr O'Hara, expecting him to protest, but he remained tight-lipped, one eyebrow raised. Taking the scroll from her brother, Aunt Ruby unravelled the tight coil and read aloud:

The Order of Nine Lives High Court hereby summons
Miss Ebony Smart
To a hearing on the charges of
Endangering the Order & Impersonating a Guardian
Date: 12 June
Time: 3 p.m.

Signed:
J. O'Hara (on behalf of the AESL)

Countersigned:
Icarus Bean (Acting Judge)

'What?' cried Ebony, looking at her uncle incredulously. 'You signed this? I thought I was helping the Order by beating the curse!'

Head hung low, Icarus gave no reply.

'He has no choice,' intervened Aunt Ruby. 'As Acting Judge he must do the bidding of the majority. And unfortunately, it looks like all your good intentions have been undermined.'

'Because of your reports!' cried Ebony, turning to her, hands on hips. 'Telling them every little detail has only made our actions seem more implausible. I wouldn't believe half of it if I hadn't been there!'

'How do you know about those?' Aunt Ruby's gaze fell on Seamus. 'Ah, yes. OK, I've been reporting on you, as I ought. But I didn't expect this to happen! When they sent me a warning by vulture about the summons, I didn't think they'd go through with it – and I certainly didn't know about my brother's new position …'

Her words tailed off as she shook her head. So that was the message the vulture had brought, making her aunt angry! Ebony calmed her own temper – at least it meant her aunt was still on her side.

Turning to the group behind Ebony, Mr O'Hara waved his hand. 'The decree is now issued. You are all witnesses. Until the summons is met, Miss Ebony Smart will no longer be considered or referred to as guardian and will not be permitted to undertake any duties or responsibilities associated with said position.'

Ebony refused to turn around or waver as the room filled with shuffling and scraping sounds. She kept her back straight and her head held high.

'Stay strong,' said the small melodic voice of Mrs O'Hara, lightly squeezing Ebony's shoulder as she passed by.

'Keep your chin up, Ebony,' whispered Miss Malone, also turning to leave.

Ebony followed her advice. Even when the last of the people had left the room, leaving just herself, her family and the two male O'Haras, Ebony kept her shoulders back and fought the tears that threatened to fall.

'What am I going to do?' whispered Ebony to Winston. He snuggled into her neck, but it didn't make her feel any better.

'I'd like you to leave, O'Hara,' said Icarus, stepping forward and shoving his face upwards, level with Mr O'Hara's chin. 'I want to speak to my niece. Alone.'

Despite his height advantage, O'Hara backed away, his face resembling a bulldog chewing a wasp. Heading towards the stairwell, Uncle Cornelius escorting him like a sentry, Mr O'Hara threw Icarus a wicked smile.

'Remember my warning, Icarus. You'd be a fool to test me.'

'What does he mean?' asked Aunt Ruby.

Icarus glared back at the man, clearly seething. Shifting from foot to foot, Ebony could only think of getting away.

'Ignore him. You need to leave also, Ruby, Seamus. This is between me and Ebony,' said Icarus. Spotting Winston on Ebony's shoulder, he added, 'You too, little man.'

Icarus lifted Winston onto his sister's shoulder. Aunt Ruby and the others left the room, with Winston clinging on to Aunt Ruby's hair, staring back in an affronted manner. Only when the footsteps had retreated, when Icarus was certain everyone was out of earshot, did he take a laboured breath and start talking.

'If you thought things were bad before, Ebony, this is even worse. But whatever happens, you have to know that I'm on your side.' Grabbing her arms, he gripped tightly, his fingers pressing into her muscles, making them throb. 'Whatever it looks like, I'm supporting you.'

'OK,' said Ebony, trying to dislodge herself from his grip.

Icarus let go of her and rubbed his chin, a pained look on his face. 'It's not a good idea for us to be seen in public together from now on, but I'll help whenever I can.'

'Why? What's the problem?'

'Like Ruby said, as Acting Judge I'm beholden to the needs of our people. I have to do as they request. If they decide against you, or if they think I'm acting on your behalf, well let's just say the results could be catastrophic. For the meantime I have to be seen to comply.'

'But don't you have any power? The judge – I mean, Ambrose, had lots of power and–'

'Abused it. So, I will be watched very closely. If we want things to go our way, if we want to beat the curse once and for all, keep you alive and save the Reflectory, we need to garner the support of the Order and win over the AESL. The only way I can think to do that is from the inside – that is why I came out of hiding and accepted this role when I realised O'Hara meant to go on with this ridiculous charade of a trial. This has to be our priority. Otherwise, Judge Ambrose will take advantage of our weakness and crush us when we splinter.'

'But most of the Order hates me! We're already splintered. What can I do?'

'Miss Malone has had a word with you already?'

Ebony nodded.

'She's gathering your supporters and she will also act as my messenger. Because she was one of Ambrose's strongest supporters, no one in the AESL will suspect her.'

'So when Zach and Ambrose come, do you think we'll be ready?'

'We'll have to be, Ebony. We have no choice. Our lives and the future of the Order are counting on it.'

'Uncle, can you do something for me?' asked Ebony, seeing her chance. Reaching into her bag, she handed him the note she'd written for Grandpa Tobias. 'Can you send this to my grandpa via vulture?'

Without even reading it, Icarus tucked the note into his sleeve. 'I'll try.'

'How will we get home?' asked Ebony, joining the others at the bottom of the stairs, nodding her head towards Mr O'Hara. 'I refuse to travel with him.'

'I think you'll find you have no choice,' replied Mr O'Hara. 'I want to make sure my son gets home OK, and as it appears the Shadow Walkers are indeed real and on the loose, it's a case of safety in numbers. I'll be waiting in the car.'

Tipping a fake hat, he walked away. Staring after him, Seamus shook his head.

'Let's go,' said Aunt Ruby, catching Ebony's expression. 'Our priority right now is to get everyone home in one piece.'

Handing Winston back to Ebony, Aunt Ruby pushed open the main door and peered outside, her gun held up, ready to use. When she was sure all was clear, she stepped outside and motioned for everyone to follow. Striding quickly away, Aunt Ruby was followed by Uncle Cornelius, then Miss Malone. Ebony took a deep breath and made to follow.

'Wait!' said Seamus, putting out a hand to stop her. 'Come with me first! Help me to find Mum. She beckoned to me as she was leaving and I didn't see her outside. She must be here somewhere.'

Intrigued, Ebony crept silently after him, checking back now and again to make sure no one was following. Her instincts told her she had nothing to fear, but Seamus was still part of the AESL – could she trust him now she'd witnessed their power? She'd trusted Zach and look how that had turned out. What if Seamus was a traitor just like him?

Pushing the thought away, Ebony followed Seamus along a couple of corridors and small atriums into a room filled with giant lilies, cacti and leafy plants with flowers bigger than a human head. Seamus gestured in front of him, before continuing deeper into the depths of the vast glass structure. Pausing below a passionflower, Ebony put away her gun and grabbed his arm. She could hear Aunt Ruby calling her name.

'I'm not going any further,' she said, 'unless you tell me what's going on.'

'I think Mum wants to tell me something. It must be important if she was trying to keep it secret from Dad.'

In the corridor up ahead, Ebony spotted something on the floor. It was a large white chrysanthemum, its silk petals catching the light and gleaming. 'Look! Isn't that your mum's?'

Racing forward, Seamus snatched up the flower. Clipped inside was a note. 'Seek what your father is hiding. X marks the spot,' he read aloud. Looking around him, he added, 'Do you remember the secret room we saw on the surveillance cameras?'

As soon as he said it, Ebony recognised the stone-walled corridor instantly. It was where Mrs O'Hara had brought her aunt, and it concealed a hidden office. Lifting the heavy, trailing vine, Seamus ran his fingers along the wall, looking for the stone that triggered the secret door. Winston, who was perched on Ebony's shoulder, tugged on her ear and, understanding, she placed him on the floor. He scampered to the area where he'd been hiding as a spy and pointed upwards. Following his directions, Ebony soon located a stone marked with a white chalk X, but when she pushed on it, nothing happened. Joining her, Seamus added his weight and the stone began to sink into the wall.

'But what about the scanner?' asked Ebony. 'We could set off an alarm or something.'

'When we watched Mum on the cameras, the security system announced her surname. I'm an O'Hara too – and I'm sure Mum wouldn't suggest it if it meant we'd get in trouble.'

Taking a deep breath, Seamus placed his palm face up in the hole. Seconds later, red lights scanned from left to right. Ebony and Winston stared from the sidelines, breath held.

'O'Hara,' announced the security voice, and everyone let out a huge sigh of relief.

Moments later, a beep sounded and Seamus yanked the door open using all his strength, and the three hurried inside.

'What are we looking for, exactly?' asked Ebony as they approached the computers hidden amongst the exotic shrubbery.

There were moving targets on radars, cascading lists of binary numbers, video footage of seabeds, but none of it made much sense to her.

'Something to do with the Shadow Walkers, I'm guessing,' replied Seamus.

'But I thought your dad didn't believe in them, until tonight at least, so why would he have any information about them?'

'I thought that too, but I suspect he was lying to us,' said Seamus. 'My father is an expert marksman, and yet I saw him cowering behind a car during the fight. He's no coward. The only reason he would do that was if he knew our weapons were useless against them. How could he know that if he hadn't encountered them before?'

Stunned, Ebony considered the possibility. Seamus was also lost in thought, and he jumped when she laid her hand on his shoulder.

'We need to be quick. My aunt was calling me earlier – they'll be frantic by now.'

'OK,' replied Seamus. 'But let's try to find out what we can while we still have the chance. My father's a workaholic. I doubt we'll get the opportunity to snoop in here again.'

Examining the various records strewn around the desktops, and checking some of the hidden computer monitors, Ebony shook her head and growled with annoyance. 'I can't figure any of this out or what it has to do with the Shadow Walkers,' she said. 'It's too complicated.'

'I can't make sense of it either,' said Seamus. 'But let's keep going.'

Spotting Winston jumping up and down on the spot, Ebony rushed to see what he'd found. On the screen in front of him was a computerised diagram of a ship – a ship with a ghastly dragon figurehead that Ebony recognised only too well. Staring at the ship, Ebony realised Mr O'Hara knew about the ship and so, not only did he know about the Shadow Walkers, he might also know about Chiyoko. As the diagram turned on the screen, making the ship visible from all angles, Ebony spotted an outline of a girl tied to the front mast.

'Seamus!' she cried. 'Quick! Look!'

Rushing over and also recognising the ship where Chiyoko was being held, Seamus banged his fist on the desk. 'He knows! He's known about my sister all along! That's why he's been extra awkward. When my father faces a problem he doesn't know how to solve, there's no living with him.'

'We have to tell my aunt,' said Ebony.

But Seamus shook his head. 'I think we'd better keep this to ourselves,' he said. 'My father asked for Chiyoko when he came for us. That means either he hasn't noticed her on this image yet, or, more likely, he's trying to pretend that he hasn't. My father may be hiding something, but, if that's the case, there has to be a good reason.'

'Like there's a good reason for trying to remove me as guardian?' sniped Ebony. 'You have more faith in him than I do. What if you're wrong?'

'His daughter has been captured! We're talking big stakes.'

'You said yourself that he doesn't care about you or your sister; that he only cares about work.'

'Forget that. I was just being childish. Now I understand why he's so fixated on his work. The appearance of that ship on the seas must have warned him that the Shadow Walkers are starting to move into our world. And since he knows our weapons are futile, he must have been trying to figure out a way to defeat them. Now that they have Chiyoko, it will only make him more determined to succeed.'

'So what do we do?'

'Let my father continue his work and hope for the best.'

On the desk, Winston lifted up his left paw, seemingly in agreement with Seamus's plan. Holding her hands up in surrender, Ebony stepped back. 'Your father seems more concerned with bringing me down than defeating the Shadow Walkers and rescuing Chiyoko. Despite the fact that as every hour passes it becomes more and more likely that your sister will become lunch for the Deus-Umbra. But I'm not going to let that happen. I won't interfere with your father's work, even though it would be better if he'd work with us instead of against us, but I refuse to give up on trying to find a way to rescue Chiyoko.'

As Seamus smiled, his face lit up. 'Thank you,' he said. 'But for now, we must play along. Even though we're friends, I must pretend to take my father's side. That's the only way

I might persuade him to share what he has learned with me. Agreed?'

He held out his hand and Ebony shook it. 'Agreed.'

As they stepped into the corridor, the door concealed itself amongst the stonework once more. Seamus gave Ebony a serious look. 'When all this blows over, I'll make sure my father knows what a great guardian you are,' he said.

At precisely the same time, Mr O'Hara appeared. 'What's going on? Why didn't you follow us to the car?' he boomed, stepping into the corridor, his head almost hitting off the top of the door frame. He loomed over Ebony, his huge bulk casting a shadow over her as she stared up into his cold face. 'What is the meaning of this guardian talk, son? Didn't you hear me in the upstairs chambers?'

'We were looking for a toilet,' replied Seamus, standing to attention. 'If you hadn't interrupted just now … I was buttering her up, trying to get some inside information.'

Knowing he was trying to throw his father off the scent, Ebony turned on her heel. 'I'm off to join the others,' she said.

'The sooner you admit,' Mr O'Hara called after her, 'that it's time for you to stop this charade, the better. The true guardian is still out there – and while you and your aunt are determined to continue your trickery, you are endangering all of our lives.'

Stopping in her tracks, Ebony turned to face Mr O'Hara. 'What more proof do you need? I'm the one that faced up to Judge Ambrose and Zach last time, I'm the one that defeated the curse and opened the Reflectory–'

'That's what you and your family say,' said Mr O'Hara, cutting her off. 'But what other witnesses do you have? I believe that Seamus, here, could be the rightful guardian.'

His face beamed with pride but, beside him, Seamus burned bright red.

'That's what all this is really about, Mr O'Hara? You want your son to be guardian? Well, that's impossible. Your bullying tactics might usually work, but this is something even you can't control.'

Seamus gave her a secret shake of his head, reminding her of their plan to let his father continue his work while trying their own approach in secret – but Ebony was too angry to back down.

'It's my destiny!' she yelled. 'You can't just take someone's destiny and claim it as your own! The Reflectory won't allow it. I've been the guardian since the time of the ancients.'

'Well, if that's true, perhaps you could provide some concrete proof,' said Mr O'Hara. 'If you opened the Reflectory, you must know where it disappeared to, for instance. Or has it disappeared because that doorway you say you opened wasn't to the Reflectory at all – it was nothing more than a faked concoction dreamed up by your aunt?'

Knowing that she couldn't disobey her uncle by telling the

truth, Ebony shook her head slowly. 'No. I don't know where it is,' she replied.

Before Mr O'Hara could gloat any further, she turned and walked away, biting her lip harder with every step.

'Where were you?' cried Aunt Ruby as Ebony stepped out into the fresh air. Dusk was settling across the sky like a veil. 'I have the others scouring the grounds for you. We thought the enemy had returned and snatched you! Have you seen Seamus?'

'Did you know that Mr O'Hara wanted Seamus to be guardian?' asked Ebony.

'I had an idea – especially when he set up the AESL. That's why I asked them to come to Dublin.'

'You did what?' cried Ebony.

'Although, seeing O'Hara's ambition, I now have no doubt he would have come anyway.'

'You asked them to come, knowing full well that they'd try to push me out? That they'd already set up the AESL? Why on earth would you do that?'

'Yes, well … Mrs O'Hara is an old friend and I thought it would be best to keep her husband close. He is an intelligent man and necessary to our cause – and troublemakers are much easier to watch when they're on your doorstep. Anyway, I believe Mr O'Hara is on the verge of a great discovery.'

'A great discovery? About what? The only thing he's discovered is how to make a fool out of me and remove any back-up we had against our enemies. Thanks to you, it seems! If only you hadn't brought the O'Hara's here …'

'Now, now, dear,' said Aunt Ruby, lowering her voice to a whisper. 'All will become clear. He worked closely with your parents and they were good judges of character. We have to trust in that.'

'You've lost it,' replied Ebony. 'And there was Miss Malone cooking up a plan to help us, when all along, you're making things more difficult than they need to be by bringing people here that are against me!'

'What plan? No one told me of any plan.'

As Ebony relayed the idea of releasing the souls while waiting out the next few days to vote out Judge Ambrose, Aunt Ruby's eyes grew wide.

'That's not a bad idea,' she said. 'And it might work. But that means you'll have to return to Oddley Cove and visit the Reflectory. I don't know if I can let you do that. The danger is mounting.'

'And it'll only get worse. We need to act before the AESL intervenes any further. I could probably still sneak away – they won't be expecting me to act right now. Though you should have let me go back weeks ago!'

Part of her was hopeful that her aunt would let her return home, but the other part was wary – what if she didn't succeed? Any confidence she'd felt was draining away, just like her supporters.

'We can't act rashly, but I promise to think on it,' said her aunt.

As she finished speaking, the search party returned. When they saw that she was all right, Uncle Cornelius gave Ebony a hug, and Miss Malone flashed a secret smile. Even Mulligan brushed against her leg. Her temper calming, Ebony began to feel better, until she spotted Mr O'Hara, with Seamus in tow.

'So, you're still staying at my house, even though you're a traitor?' said Ebony, giving Seamus a sly wink before turning abruptly and stomping back to the car. As Seamus climbed in next to her, she kept her head turned and her gaze fixed on the window, only half pretending that she wasn't interested in anything anyone had to say.

All the way home, Ebony seethed. How dare the AESL call a summons against her? What right did they have? But as they pulled up outside 23 Mercury Lane, there was an even bigger shock waiting. The door to the house hung open, dangling from one of its hinges.

'Let your uncle go first,' said O'Hara over his shoulder, watching as Uncle Cornelius and Mulligan pulled up behind them.

Uncle Cornelius released Mulligan and was out of the car in a flash. Together, the two wildcats leapt up the steps and pushed their way in on all fours, growling loudly. Aunt Ruby clambered out and pushed her face to Ebony's open window. 'Wait here,' she said.

'No way,' said Ebony, already climbing out. 'I'm coming with you.'

As Seamus went to follow, his dad stopped him. 'You stay here, son.'

'But they might need my help,' said Seamus.

'I said, wait here.'

Ebony heard Mr O'Hara mutter something else under his

breath but couldn't make out the words. She also heard the automatic locks on the door click into action.

Seamus splayed his hand against the glass and Ebony recognised the look of frustration on his face – he really did want to help. Ebony gave him a sympathetic nod. Then, with her gun held close to her chest, Ebony followed Aunt Ruby inside, her back pressed to the wall.

The place had been ransacked. Sketches from Aunt Ruby's room had been torn from the walls and thrown over the banister. Books from Uncle Cornelius's study littered the stairs, and some of the helicopters that delivered breakfast had been ripped from their wires and stamped to pieces on the hallway floor. Ebony and Ruby skirted the length of the hallway, breath held; they could hear Uncle Cornelius and Mulligan racing around upstairs, growling and howling.

Kicking the kitchen door open, Aunt Ruby signalled for Ebony to follow her into the basement. Heading straight for the sink, they pushed through the little door on all fours. With Aunt Ruby in the lead, her slim silver lighter held aloft so they could see, they reached the dumbwaiter and heaved on the ropes together to lower themselves as quietly as the squeaky pulley would allow.

Downstairs, all was still. The surveillance screens were switched off and Mulligan's chair in the centre of the room sat empty.

'It's all clear,' said Ebony.

'Let's check the cameras,' said Aunt Ruby. 'We'll view the

live feed of the rooms first, then the recordings.'

Ebony jumped into the chair while Aunt Ruby leaned against the back. Picking up the remote, Aunt Ruby pointed it at the screens and they crackled into life. They checked each room in the house in turn, including the attic and the roof, where Uncle Cornelius was now standing, sniffing the air for a trail. Meanwhile, Mulligan had his nose squashed to Aunt Ruby's bedroom carpet, trying to identify a scent. Finding each room otherwise empty, Aunt Ruby skipped back in fast rewind.

They'd only gone back an hour when they spotted movement. It was Zach Stone – while they'd been fighting for their lives against Shadow Walkers at headquarters, he'd been searching through their home.

'The attack was just a decoy!' cried Ebony.

'Yes, but what did he want?' asked Aunt Ruby, skipping the recording back further and further until the moment Zach broke in.

He'd come in from the roof, using a small bomb-like device with a timer to blast the attic window away.

'That must be the scent Cornelius has picked up,' said Aunt Ruby.

The first place Zach had checked was the room Seamus was staying in, but it had very little to search so he quickly moved to Ebony's. Certain she saw his hand quiver as he reached for her door handle – was he afraid of her? – she watched as Zach pulled out drawers and yanked everything from the wardrobe. Ebony clutched her rucksack to her chest, thankful she'd had the foresight to keep her most precious belongings with her.

'I bet he wanted *The Book of Learning*,' said Aunt Ruby. 'Or the bronze *Ebonius Tobinius* rose.'

'But why?' asked Ebony trying to detach herself from the scene as she watched Zach tear a page from the scrapbook of her animals and rip it to shreds, his face crumpled with rage. Inside, her own rage bubbled and blistered. 'The judge can get into the Reflectory without my rose – he farmed his own, remember? And the only time Zach ever looked into *The Book of Learning*, he saw such horrors I don't think he'd ever want to go through that again.'

'But what if things changed when you opened the Reflectory? What if your rose turning to bronze has altered things? Or maybe something happened when Icarus hid the door?'

Ebony considered her aunt's words for a moment. 'You mean they can no longer get in?'

'The ambush Icarus spoke of – the Shadow Walkers didn't go inside the Reflectory. Maybe they're stumped?'

Shaking her head, Ebony kept her gaze on the screens and Zach's ransacking. 'I don't know. It seems too good to be true. You said yourself that with the support of the Deus-Umbra Judge Ambrose is stronger than ever before.'

'Yes, but only when that support is secured,' said Aunt Ruby, scrutinising the scene before her as Zach destroyed her room before moving on to Uncle Cornelius's study. 'So I think we still have time. If only we knew what he was looking for.'

Gripping her rucksack tight, Ebony remembered that her anonymous 'friend' in the Shadowlands had said that Ambrose wanted the box – that must be what Zach was seeking. Almost blurting it out, she stopped herself in the nick of time. As Icarus had said about the Reflectory, keeping quiet was the best form of defence.

She had to figure out what the box was for, and fast. It was somehow central to everything that was happening, and even though Ebony was banned from guardian activity, she had no intention of not completing the task she'd undertaken. She would continue with her quest to find the box's owner and rescue Chiyoko – hopefully damaging Zach and the judge's plans along the way – with or without the support of the Order.

As Ebony hugged her rucksack closer, her aunt pressed a button and returned the surveillance cameras to real time. The attic room was now boarded up with rough slabs of wood and protruding nails.

'Uncle Cornelius is clever, but DIY never was his forte,' said Aunt Ruby, grimacing.

Another screen focused on the kitchen, where Mulligan was pushing his way under the sink. Uncle Cornelius now had his face shoved inside the fridge, tucking into something with gusto. Shaking her head and chuckling, Aunt Ruby moved on. All the other rooms were completely dishevelled, but they were empty – except for the living room, where Mr O'Hara and Seamus were now tucked up close together, seemingly bickering. Every now and again, Mr O'Hara checked around him, in case someone was coming.

'Interesting,' said Aunt Ruby. 'Let's turn that volume up a little.'

Mr O'Hara was first to speak. 'I've been trying to track some unusual ships that are showing up on radar, but one minute they're there and the next minute, poof, they're gone! It's like they just disappear – I've never seen anything like it. A lot is at stake here, son – more than you realise. I'm the maritime defence expert and I can't be made a fool of in this way. If only you could expose Ebony and claim your rightful position, it would deflect from my own situation and buy me time.'

'You're the one that believes I'm the guardian, not me.'

'So what if you're not really meant to be guardian? It seems the position is there for the taking, so why shouldn't it be you? If that slip of a girl can fool people … Well, she can't fool me. That aunt of hers is a very capable inventor and I know she's mixed up in this. Do you know, I bet those disappearing ships are somehow linked to the pair of them. A decoy to distract me from my AESL duties.'

Ebony bristled. The ships weren't her doing, but Chiyoko's disappearance was, even if it was by accident. The message she'd received – YOUR LIFE FOR HERS – still weighed heavily on her mind.

'What if she isn't lying, Father?' asked Seamus, his eyebrows knit. 'What if the things her aunt has reported are true? I saw *The Book of Learning* in action. I saw pictures appear and move–'

His father clenched a fist and banged on the mantelpiece.

'You're beginning to sound like your mother, Seamus. Of course she's lying. The book works for all members of the Order when it wants to. And didn't I tell you that her parents were just the same? See where that got them!'

Taking a sharp breath, Ebony leaned in closer. Wasn't Seamus meant to be playing along with his father? And what did her parents have to do with this?

The conversation was interrupted by the sound of footsteps as Uncle Cornelius appeared in the living room, his facial hair dotted with bits of ham. Ebony chuckled and glanced at Aunt Ruby. Her aunt looked far from amused. Her face was clouded over, her fingers twisting around each other as she glared at the screen.

'Why did you call him here, making trouble for all of us, if you dislike him so much?' asked Ebony, now that Mr O'Hara and Seamus had fallen silent.

It took a moment for Aunt Ruby to reply. When she did, her words began with a deep sigh.

'Mr O'Hara was working with your parents when they disappeared, Ebony. We suspect he knows what happened to them, but he refuses to say anything about it. It's been easy for him to hide away in Japan, but I thought that by bringing him here, by keeping an eye on him, we might learn more.'

'But the way he's behaving – the Anti-Ebony Smart League and rallying the Order against me. Could he be working with Ambrose?'

Aunt Ruby shook her head wearily. 'No. He's ambitious and arrogant, but he's always been against Ambrose. Even when Ambrose was in power.'

Every inch of Ebony was screaming out to tell her aunt about what she'd seen in the secret room in HQ, but she had promised Seamus that she'd keep quiet for now, so she resisted temptation. 'What about removing me from my duties as guardian?'

'He has no real power to do that – just as Icarus's position as Acting Judge is essentially powerless, so is Mr O'Hara's place at the head of that stupid league. He'll forget all about that,' said Aunt Ruby, frowning, 'when the real trouble starts.'

'It's coming,' said Ebony. 'First the Shadow Walkers' attack, then Zach ransacking the house. It's close. I can feel it in my bones.'

'Me too,' said her aunt. 'You'd better keep your gun with you from now on, just in case. I think things are going to get hairy.' Her gaze lingered on Ebony for a bit longer than Ebony felt comfortable with. 'You know, your grandpa and your parents would be really proud of you.'

Blinking back the sting in her eyes, Ebony pointed at the screen. 'Uncle Cornelius is leaving. Let's see what else they have to say.'

As soon as Uncle Cornelius disappeared out of the door, the conversation struck up again in hushed voices.

'You should give Ebony a chance to show you her abilities,' said Seamus.

'But you're the best we have. When you take over as guardian, it will bring great honour to our family and we will achieve great things for the Order.'

'It won't happen,' said Seamus, his voice cracking as he stared his father in the eyes. 'Like Ebony said, the role of guardian is not something you can control, no matter how hard you try. You're wrong about her.'

'I'm never wrong. I have spent my life preparing you for this role.'

'And what about what I want? It's my life. I can't face down Ambrose, Zach Stone and an army of Shadow Walkers!'

'We – the Order – will protect you.'

'Like you protected the Reflectory that disappeared? And headquarters? I saw you hiding behind the car! You didn't fight at all, didn't even take a shot.'

His tanned skin turning pale, Mr O'Hara bent down so his face was level with his son's. He spoke through gritted teeth, his fat moustache quivering like a small bird caught in the wind. 'Did anyone else see?'

'I don't think so,' lied Seamus.

'Good. Let's keep it that way. I have enough issues with disappearing ships and a disobedient son. I must maintain my reputation within the AESL.'

'Why? What's wrong? Why is the AESL so important to you?'

'I can't tell you, son, but I made an important promise. You have to trust me.'

In the basement, Aunt Ruby turned to Ebony. 'I'm sure that promise is linked to your parents. We need to find out – I want to know what happened to them.'

For the first time ever, Ebony felt something stirring inside her gut. She'd always just accepted her parents' disappearance without question because she'd never known any different, and she'd had her grandpa's love and support instead. But now, with her grandpa gone and all the strange and life-threatening events going on, and especially after meeting Mr O'Hara – the only person who might know what had happened to her parents – something inside her had changed.

So do I, she thought.

By the time Ebony and Aunt Ruby reached the living room, Mr O'Hara had already gone and Seamus was slumped on a beanbag.

'I thought you were going to play along with your father?' said Ebony.

'So did I,' said Seamus, looking miserable. 'But I couldn't quite manage it. At least I didn't mention Chiyoko's disappearance.'

Seeing how worried he looked, Ebony decided she should give him a break. It was his father's ambition getting in her way, not his, and she knew what it was like to be forced into things against your will. He would also be missing his sister and, like Chiyoko, the cicadas of home.

Heading to her room, leaving her aunt and uncle to tidy up downstairs, Ebony set to removing all traces of Zach's presence. Her ruined scrapbook she shoved to the back of a drawer. Once finished, she plonked herself on the bed and heaved a big sigh. 'OK, Winston, let's review. We have the silver box I'm not allowed to open that Zach was probably looking for – we have to find out who it belongs to and return it. We have a vision and a legend about Chiyoko setting a bird free. We have Chiyoko stolen by Shadow Walker pirates under Zach and Ambrose's command, needing to be rescued. And then there's the Reflectory – I have to figure out how to get back in and release the souls. The question is, how do I do it all, and what do I do first?'

Squashing himself down so his head rested on his paws, Winston flattened his ears.

'I'm going to take a hot shower,' said Ebony, hearing Seamus close the door to his room beside hers. 'Hopefully it'll help wash the cobwebs away.'

Even though Ebony had the temperature piping hot and blasted the water on super strength, holding her face under the streaming cascade, the shower didn't help. Quickly drying herself and climbing into a fresh outfit, she grabbed her rucksack.

'One last think before dinner,' she said, joining Winston on the bed and yanking the bag open.

As she started pulling out the contents, throwing them onto the bed without taking much notice, Winston gave a loud squeal.

Looking down, Ebony saw why right away.

Peering up at her with shiny, glassy eyes, was a small figurine. It was a type of doll, with black, sharply fringed hair, two glossy pigtails and a clotted-cream complexion. Its body – a blue and white dress with fluted sleeves – was made of tinted paper, and the limbs were hinged. It was a replica of Chiyoko, and in its hand it held an eggshell-blue origami swan, decorated with seahorses. At first, Ebony didn't dare to pick it up. Winston's cowering didn't help; it set her nerves on edge.

'What harm can a doll do, Winston?' she asked, trying to make herself feel braver.

Hand trembling, she lifted it. The figure was light but strong. Turning it over and examining the craftsmanship, Ebony began to feel less nervous. It was intricately made and exquisite. Although its hands and feet had metal loops on each end, any intended attachments were missing.

'It's a puppet,' said Ebony, her heartbeat back to normal. 'It's beautiful.'

Winston peered out from under the pillow where he was hiding and nodded. Clapping his paws together, he hopped up and down, trying to get a better look. Ebony lowered her hands.

'Look at the swan! I'm sure it's made of the same paper the O'Haras used as giftwrapping. Seamus is here and Mr O'Hara is hardly likely to give me a gift. Do you think Mrs O'Hara somehow put it in my bag?'

Snatching the swan from Ebony's hand with his mouth, Winston attacked it with his teeth and claws. The swan began to unravel: first a wing and then its head and neck.

'Winston!' cried Ebony. 'What on earth are you doing? I hope you'll help me put that back together!'

Dropping the unfolded paper on her lap and panting, Winston sat back on his haunches. Inside the swan was a message. It was written in beautiful, calligraphic script:

Why don't you look out of the window?

'Strange message,' said Ebony. She sidled up to the window from one side and peered out cautiously, just in case Zach was waiting. But the street was empty. Noticing Winston jumping up and down on the spot beside her, Ebony bent over and picked him up.

'What is it?' she asked. Following his paw, which was pointing skyward, and sheltering her eyes with one hand, Ebony spotted a small and raggedy-looking red aeroplane flying by.

'It's just a toy aeroplane!' she said. 'It's big, but you've seen smaller versions of those before.'

Winston shook his head insistently and continued to point.

The aeroplane was making a loud putt-putting noise as it did a loop the loop above the houses opposite, before circling back. Ebony pushed her face closer to the glass for a better look. Winston lowered his paw and climbed up onto Ebony's shoulder, seemingly entranced by the air show.

'What's that got to do with ...' started Ebony, but then she noticed that the aeroplane had begun to release canary yellow gas behind it.

As the aeroplane ducked and twisted, looping and spinning, a message began to form in the coloured gas. T. H. G. Next, the letters I and N appeared.

'THGIN?' said Ebony, as the letters began to fade away. 'What does that even mean?'

As more letters formed, Ebony hatched a plan. 'We'd better write these down! You memorise the next few letters while I look for some paper and a pen.'

A few moments later, Ebony returned with a shop receipt and a stubby pencil. 'You keep those letters in your head, and I'll get the rest,' she said.

Several more letters spewed out, as well as a few numbers, and Ebony wrote them down. When the aeroplane had finished, it gave three small bursts of smoke and disappeared off into the distance.

'Right,' said Ebony. 'What letters did you collect?'

Holding the pencil to the paper, Winston used his body to nudge it around the page. The letters he added were big and shaky, but they could be easily read. Once finished, Ebony read out their message:

THGIN OTMP03 7ORTSI BENIRGEREP TNELIS

'It makes no sense,' said Ebony. 'Unless … SIL … ENT. That's it! We have to reverse them!'

Sitting on the paper now, Winston began to spin round excitedly. Working together, they reversed the letters. When the words were eventually assembled, Ebony frowned.

'Silent Peregrine Bistro, 7.30 p.m. tonight,' she said. 'The Silent Peregrine is the name of that legend we found in the National Library. And it's similar to the name of the ship *The Book of Learning* showed us – the one my past self was in charge of. Do you think they're related?'

When Winston shrugged, she sat back and rubbed her eyes. 'Let's tell the others,' she said. 'Aunt Ruby will help us.'

Repacking her rucksack, including the puppet, she headed out of her room, bag and message in hand. Pausing for a moment at the top of the stairs, she resisted the urge to knock on Seamus's door to ask him about the puppet. Deciding it was best to give him some space, she quietly headed downstairs. Winston quivered on her shoulder and checked behind them every step of the way. Only when they reached the kitchen, a strong smell of something burning wafting its way under the door, did he finally relax.

Just as Ebony pushed her way into the kitchen, Aunt Ruby rushed out, a flurry of camouflage pants and goggles, sending Winston scurrying into her curls. Ebony winced as his claws pricked the back of her neck.

'Quick! We have been summoned!' cried Aunt Ruby, turning and running back into the kitchen. Ebony hurried after her aunt, quietly closing the door so that the commotion wouldn't disturb Seamus. At the table Uncle Cornelius was tucking into a plate of fried eggs, their edges blackened and the yolks sloppy, like soup.

'Aunt Ruby, stop running around like a headless chicken and tell me. Summoned where? By whom?'

Finally calming down enough to speak coherently, Aunt Ruby rested both hands on the kitchen table and leaned forward. 'A letter was just hand delivered. The man with a crooked face has requested a meeting to discuss you and the future of the Order. But we don't yet know when or where.'

Ebony shouldered her bag. 'How about the Silent Peregrine Bistro at 7.30 p.m. tonight?' she said, throwing the message on the table. 'We just got this lead.'

'Wonderful!' cried Aunt Ruby. 'Problem solved!'

Leaping down, Winston landed on the table and started lapping up some spilt yolk. Meanwhile, Uncle Cornelius pulled out his pocket watch and let it swing, pendulum like, from his paw. Up on his hind legs and his head moving from side to side, Winston did his best to read the clock face. But after several attempts, he began to wobble, eventually toppling over into a heap. Trying to right himself, he stumbled and fell back down, covering his head with his paws as he tried to dispel the dizziness.

Reaching out and grabbing the watch, Ebony confirmed the time. 'That's just thirty minutes from now!' she cried. 'Where is this bistro? I haven't heard you mention it before.'

Uncle Cornelius stuffed as many eggs into his mouth as possible and pushed back his chair so he could rub his fat stomach with a hairy hand.

'Fitzwilliam Square. It's an old Nine Lives' haunt,' continued her aunt. 'Used to be a smugglers' den and has been used as a meeting place for many years by our members. The owner's family inherited it decades ago and have kept it going. They get paid well to help us meet in secret there, so they ask no questions. There'll be no prying eyes or ears.'

'Why haven't we been there before?' asked Ebony, her

interest lit like a fuse.

'With so many of us missing, the place has been a bit of damp squib of late, to be honest.'

Winston twitched his nose excitedly. Ebony nodded. Then an idea hit her square in the jaw. 'But who is the man with the crooked face? Can we trust him?'

'We won't know until we go there,' said Aunt Ruby.

'And if he's followed by the AESL? Or it's a set-up?'

'It's a place that O'Hara avoids; he thinks it's beneath him. And with the threat of Shadow Walkers, the AESL will be on their guard, rather than on the prowl. As for a set-up? I think Judge Ambrose has bigger things on his mind. Seeing as Zach was ransacking this place, there must be some important piece that he's missing to carry out his final plan. I don't know whether we're safe, so we'll go armed just in case.'

'How will we recognise this man?' asked Ebony.

'It shouldn't be difficult to spot a crooked face. Now let's go! We don't want to miss this opportunity.'

Ebony grimaced. 'What about Seamus?'

'Mulligan is downstairs – he's safe. I'll tell Seamus we're going out on an errand and we'll bring him back a pizza. I think it's better if he sits this one out.'

As Aunt Ruby headed off upstairs, Ebony had an idea. 'Winston, you stay here and keep an eye on Seamus too,' she whispered, setting him on the ground.

Sulkily, Winston scampered up the stairs, his ears flat and his tail hanging low.

29

The Silent Peregrine Bistro was hidden away in a dark dead-end alleyway on the edge of Fitzwilliam Square. On either side of the alleyway, tall buildings towered high, blocking out the evening sunlight and the last of the early summer warmth, making it feel more like a cool winter's day. Litter lined the cobbled ground and mice scampered from crevices in the walls, along the cobble cracks, into the heaving bins. After the sighting of Zach Stone in her house earlier and his appearance at the library, Ebony didn't want to be hanging around outdoors, especially in grimy alleyways where she didn't feel safe. The shiver in her bones and the sensation of being watched warned her that Zach could be near.

'It's been a while since you came, Aunt Ruby. Maybe you've gone the wrong way?' she asked, keeping her voice as polite as she could manage.

But after a few more metres, Aunt Ruby clapped her hands together and smiled. 'Here we are!'

Ebony looked about her, confused. Then, in a tiny window, she spotted a sign with the bistro's name that flickered on and off in red neon. The Silent Peregrine looked closed;

the shutters were down and the red metal door was locked. Ebony looked at Uncle Cornelius and her aunt suspiciously. But when Aunt Ruby rapped her knuckles four times on the door, it slid open and a slender, serious-looking waiter greeted them. Aunt Ruby showed a card embossed with a falcon carrying a sprig of golden ivy in its beak, and they were led through the door. Inside, Ebony had to blink to adjust to the darkness. When she could finally make out some shapes in the low candlelight, she saw that the restaurant was made up of small, isolated cubicles.

'Mr and Mrs Von Blanc, your usual table awaits,' said the waiter. 'Please come this way.'

'Usual table? I thought you didn't come often?' asked Ebony.

'I said we hadn't been here recently, but it was a popular haunt once upon a time. Your mother and father loved it here. In fact, this is where they met in their most recent incarnation.'

Ebony tried to picture the scene; it struck her that it was weird not knowing what her parents were really like. She had seen glimpses of their faces in visions and a photo or two, but not knowing how they laughed or smiled, or how they would catch each other's eyes and give little signals – it left a dull ache in her stomach. To try to take her mind off it, Ebony surveyed her surroundings.

Each cubicle had a stained-glass surround. Every inch of the place was designed to keep the conversations of the diners private – if there had been any diners. Ebony imagined pirates or highwaymen bargaining and plotting there; it felt more like a smugglers' den than an eatery.

Aunt Ruby, Uncle Cornelius and Ebony followed the waiter to their cubicle. The stained-glass surround was adorned with what Ebony guessed must be hunting peregrines, their wings outstretched as they searched for prey and pulled back as they dived, silhouetted against a red, dusk-filled sky. She looked around anxiously. There was no sign of a mysterious man with a crooked face.

'Would you like your usual order, Mr Von Blanc?' asked the waiter when they were all seated.

Uncle Cornelius clapped his hands together and grinned, even though he must have just munched his way through his own body weight in fried eggs.

'Yes, please,' said Aunt Ruby. 'And berry lemonades all around.'

'I'll see to that immediately. And I'll get menus for the rest of the party.'

'What do you think?' asked Aunt Ruby as the waiter walked away.

'It's ... discreet,' said Ebony, her stomach rumbling. 'How does anyone know about it?'

'It's by special invitation only,' said her aunt. 'It's the last remaining Nine Lives social quarters in Dublin.'

The waiter returned with three bottles of berry lemonade and two menus. Ebony stared at the words without really reading them. Her nerves were racing around her body at top speed and she wished Winston was with her to help calm her down. Aunt Ruby eyed her niece carefully for a moment and then returned her attention to the menu. The waiter waited patiently.

'I'll have the fish special,' said Aunt Ruby. 'And a pepperoni pizza at the end to take away.'

'Spaghetti Bolognese,' requested Ebony.

Soundlessly, as though he was floating, the waiter took the menus and disappeared. Ebony checked around the room, noticing a shifting shadow in the corner. Her skin broke into goose bumps. Half expecting it to grow red eyes and yellow teeth, she couldn't look away.

'Could the Shadow Walkers get in here?' asked Ebony.

'They can get in anywhere,' said Aunt Ruby, looking around nervously and shuffling in her chair. 'But security is tight.'

'Where is this guy?' growled Ebony.

Aunt Ruby mumbled nervously – something about her latest inventions, a twirling spork that doubled as a tranquilliser gun – but Ebony zoned out, trying to think of what to do if the informant didn't show. Suddenly realising that her aunt had stopped talking and Cornelius had stiffened, Ebony followed their gaze to the door behind her. The silence seemed magnified in the tiny, dark cubicle, but as Ebony turned, there was a collective sigh from the others.

'False alarm,' said Aunt Ruby casually. 'Ah, here's the food.'

A moment later the waiter appeared, slipping a steaming

plate of Bolognese onto the table. It looked delicious. With Aunt Ruby's permission to start, Ebony tucked in.

It was the most delicious Bolognese Ebony had ever tasted. The meaty sauce was thick with tomatoes and the spaghetti was cooked just the way she liked it, with small clumps of strands stuck together. Ebony wolfed her food down, hardly chewing at all. Aunt Ruby's special arrived next. It was a huge flat fish, baked on a dish shaped exactly the same. The skin sizzled, wafting the scent of the ocean in its steam, reminding Ebony of all those evenings after fishing when her grandpa cooked up the day's catch. Barbecues had been her favourite. She stopped eating momentarily and inhaled deeply.

It wasn't until Ebony and her aunt had almost finished that Uncle Cornelius's special dish − a plate full of spit-roasted rats − arrived. The poor creatures were speared to the skewers whole, their bodies blackened and charred. Uncle Cornelius tucked straight in, chomping and crunching on bones and swallowing down fur.

'That's disgusting!' cried Ebony, her face flushed with fury and pleased that Winston wasn't there after all. 'What sort of restaurant serves rat?'

'They eat guinea pig in Peru,' said her aunt, chewing a mouthful of fish. 'And water beetles in Cambodia. Live octopus in Japan.'

'Enough!' cried Ebony.

In the corner of the bistro, two heads bobbed above the cubicle; there were other Nine Lives people in here after all!

As much as she tried, Ebony couldn't make out their faces. A loud crunch across the table made her shiver.

'Aunt Ruby, make him stop.'

'I'm sorry, dear,' said Aunt Ruby in a low whisper, 'but he is a wildcat!'

Feeling her own food churning inside her stomach, Ebony couldn't eat another bite. She sat in silence as her uncle munched his way through his plate of rat carcasses. After a short while, Ebony couldn't stand the noise any more. The cubicle, with its thick curtains and tall surround, closed in until it felt like a coffin. All Ebony could think about was Winston, about how he and Cornelius were meant to be friends.

'Can I be excused?' she asked, already pushing her chair back. 'I need the bathroom.'

'This way,' whispered the waiter, appearing from nowhere.

'Thank you.'

Following the waiter with her nose in the air, Ebony vowed that she would never, ever go to a restaurant with Uncle Cornelius again.

'He's not even my proper uncle,' she muttered under her breath.

Indicating a door, the waiter backed away. Ebony headed towards the toilets, relieved to see that the shadow she'd spotted earlier belonged to a huge leafy cheese-plant, used to conceal the toilet entrance. The plant's massive leaves shone a dark, glossy green.

As she pushed her way through the door, Ebony jumped, clutching at her chest. Waiting for her, was a small, graceful figure in a mask. The mask was made of papier mâché; its left eye and the left side of its mouth turned down at the edges, as though melting away.

It was the man with the crooked face.

'You!' cried Ebony, recognising the figure instantly. 'You're the man with the crooked face?'

Mrs O'Hara gave a small bow. Her long, loose hair gleamed like spilled oil, decorated with a yellow silk lily.

'Why all the secrecy?'

Stepping forward, Mrs O'Hara put a finger to her lips and Ebony quietened. Then she clasped Ebony's hand in her own and walked over to the sinks.

'I do not want my husband to know I'm here,' she said. Her voice was even gentler than usual through the mask, and Ebony had to strain her ears to hear her words. 'He is a good man, but stubborn. I fear that if he finds out that I'm helping you, his actions may prevent us from ever getting Chiyoko back. My husband is a man of facts, not faith. Do you understand?'

'You know about Chiyoko? How come everyone knows, yet pretends otherwise and does nothing?'

'Ah, so you found your way into my husband's office? Good – at least you know you're not working alone. Trust me, I am doing all I can to find her. In his way, her father is too.'

Unable to control her disdain, Ebony snorted. 'Not working alone? We're hardly working together – your husband is turning everyone against me!'

'I know you are angry with him,' continued Mrs O'Hara. 'The AESL is wrong – and I think my husband knows it too, deep down. But despite being reincarnated, despite being part of the Order, he does not believe in things until he has concrete proof. Something tangible that he can understand.'

'What about the things that cannot be proved?' asked Ebony. 'Things that require belief?'

'That is my role,' answered Mrs O'Hara. 'And one day soon, I know, my husband will come to our aid. But these things cannot be forced. When the battle begins with Ambrose and all who follow him – a battle that is very close – the truth will become clear to my husband, and I have faith that he'll support you.'

'And in the meantime?'

'In the meantime, you must rely on your own strength, as well as that of your family and your few supporters, including me.'

Straightening her back, Ebony tried to remain positive. 'Was it you that put the puppet in my bag? I thought I recognised the origami paper.'

'Yes. Show it to Seamus. He will teach you what you'll need to do with it when the time comes.'

'Why didn't you just give it to him?'

'My husband wouldn't approve.'

'Why will I need a puppet anyway? What use is that?'

'Come. I've something to show you,' said Mrs O'Hara, heading silently for the door, not answering Ebony's question.

'I'll be right there.'

After quickly running to the loo, Ebony splashed water on her face, then dried it with a paper towel. She leaned in to the mirror and stared at herself closely. In the corner, a tiny speck of light glowed then whizzed around the mirror like a comet. The glass seemed to wobble slightly, a ripple of shadow crossing over her reflection.

As she moved away from the mirror, her reflection stayed then turned sideways. Ebony realised the face in the mirror was wearing a strange hood, with white wings flicking out at the side. Although the curls were hidden, it was one of her past selves.

The face in the mirror covered her mouth with a hand covered in a bloodied bandage then, letting go, opened her lips – the sound they released was more like birdsong than a human voice. As the song ended, the image in the mirror melted away. Trying to figure out what her past self had been trying to tell her, Ebony hurried back to join the others.

Mrs O'Hara was seated at the table, straight-backed, her beautiful hair spilling down her shoulders like a blue-black waterfall. She was still wearing the mask.

'We've found our man,' said Aunt Ruby brightly, trying to disguise the confusion in her voice.

'Why do you still need the mask?' asked Ebony. 'We know who you are.'

'It's not for your benefit,' replied Mrs O'Hara. 'It's how I see into and manipulate the shadows. Come. There is something I need you to see.'

She stood up and moved towards a pair of saloon-style swing doors that Ebony hadn't noticed before. The edges were made of cast iron with heavy gold corduroy stretched across. Leaving their food behind, Aunt Ruby and Ebony followed. Uncle Cornelius stayed behind to polish off the leftovers on everyone's plates.

On the other side of the swing doors there were chairs facing a large white paper screen, framed with bamboo. It was about seven feet high and ten feet wide. Ebony and her aunt took their seats and looked at each other with equally puzzled expressions. After a moment, some gentle music started up, a melancholy cello, and Mrs O'Hara disappeared behind the screen. On the white paper, the outline of a seascape formed: a cut-out held up by Mrs O'Hara, controlled by thin rods, with its colours shining faintly through.

'I wasn't expecting entertainment,' whispered Aunt Ruby. 'I would have preferred some information. Does she know about Chiyoko, I wonder?'

'She knows. Just watch,' replied Ebony.

'Well, I hope this doesn't go on for too long.'

'Stay alert,' said Ebony, shuffling closer to her aunt as Uncle Cornelius arrived and took his seat. Catching a whiff of chargrilled rat on his breath, Ebony tried to block it out by focusing all her concentration on the show.

The seascape moved to the left of the screen. Mrs O'Hara pulled on a rod to make it look like the waves were moving, and then a bright moon appeared in the sky. Although Ebony knew it was just a torch, the effect was beautiful. A flock of geese flew across the sky in a V formation and Mrs O'Hara made the waves dance with such skill, using her own hair to add depth, that Ebony could almost believe she was watching a real ocean during a storm. As another shape was pulled into the scene, the audience was suddenly looking out over a cliff edge towards land in the distance.

'It's Gallows Island,' said Ebony. She recognised the shape of the cliffs and the way the shoreline curved. 'And in the distance, that's Oddley Cove. I'd know its outline anywhere.'

The seascape then dropped away, the scene switching to an image of a crater filled with fire. Ebony felt drawn to the edge of the crater. Hooked, she leaned closer, certain she could feel the heat from the flames on her skin. Down in the crater, it resembled a moonscape with a mountain rising up in the centre that shook, spitting chippings and boulders. Flames rose from the mountain's belly and thick, black plumes of smoke swirled around the top.

'That mountain looks like the ancient home of the Deus-Umbra,' said Ebony. 'This story must be set long ago, and his home must have been where Gallows Island now stands!'

Mrs O'Hara made the rock split open with a crack, and

the black plume of smoke rose, growing in size until it formed a monstrous creature, with fangs and claws, massive wings with sharpened tips and red eyes. The creature swooped angrily in the air, and a strange drum sounded, high pitched and haunting. The atmosphere was so oppressive that Ebony, Uncle Cornelius and Aunt Ruby pushed back into their chairs; Ebony felt Uncle Cornelius's hairs stand on end as they brushed against her skin.

Suddenly, two figures appeared. Even though they were featureless, puppets made of shadows, they were instantly recognisable.

'Judge Ambrose,' said Aunt Ruby.

'And Zach Stone,' added Ebony.

Uncle Cornelius let out a small, low growl as, marching in time to the drum, an army arrived on the scene. The puppet Mrs O'Hara used was a long stick with lots of figures attached – they had wobbly heads that moved and arms holding weapons: scythes, spiked balls on chains, clubs and electrified whips that sizzled and sparked. It was like a real, live army of Shadow Walkers was coming right at them. Ebony chewed at her thumbnail as a chill ran down her spine. The army was dragging something behind them. As they deposited the figures, they moved on quickly, checking around them as they scurried away. It was like they were scared. Ebony saw that they had left two girls: one with wild, unruly curls, the other with hair bunched up at the sides.

'It's me and Chiyoko,' cried Ebony, shivers creeping up

her spine. 'Or it could be our past selves. What are we doing there?'

The melancholic cello music scratched and whined as the scene changed again, and Ebony felt herself mesmerised. Instinctively, she rubbed her amulet between thumb and forefinger, so engrossed that she could imagine herself falling into the shadows.

But she must have concentrated too hard on the dark figures before her.

In one breath, Ebony was watching the show from the audience, and in the next, the world had turned grey and shaky, smudged and blurred, with heat blasting at her from every direction. She was in the puppet show – and it looked just like the Shadowlands!

By her side, a human-sized Chiyoko puppet with lifeless eyes was shivering, despite the heat. Knowing she was somehow inside the puppet show with the Deus-Umbra nearby, Ebony tried to turn and run but it was impossible. Unlike her experience in the Shadowlands, she had no control over her legs at all. Suddenly she felt herself begin to step forward towards a small rocky ledge – somewhere in her woozy brain Ebony realised that Mrs O'Hara was controlling her movements. She had to trust she would be OK.

Arriving at the edge of the platform and peering over, her head throbbed as she stared down at a familiar scene: a moonscape with a mountain spewing fire. The Deus-Umbra was waiting, its face full of hatred and anger. As it spotted

Ebony, it screeched loudly and rivers of saliva dripped from its fangs.

Ebony tried to think her way out of the puppet show but, just as she had failed in the Shadowlands, she found herself trapped – and this time there was no Icarus to help. Clutching the life-sized Chiyoko puppet's hand tight, she hoped Mrs O'Hara would somehow make everything OK. But the Deus-Umbra shook out its blade-like wings and took flight, racing towards the girls like a thunderbolt. Reaching the platform, it snatched up the Chiyoko puppet and chomped down, biting off her head. Then it bore down on Ebony, just like in her dream. Ebony tried to cry out for help but found she couldn't make a sound.

'No!' cried a voice. Ebony recognised it as Aunt Ruby's, only she sounded very distant. 'Stop this!'

Suddenly, Ebony was back in the Silent Peregrine. Shocked out of her dream-like state, she watched the puppets behind the screen fall away, the scene dissolving. Letting go of the amulet around her neck, she rubbed her eyes, trying to make sense of the situation. What would have happened if her aunt hadn't cried out?

'What's the meaning of this?' demanded Aunt Ruby as the music stopped.

The puppets disappeared from view, and Mrs O'Hara stepped from behind the screen to take a bow, finally removing her mask.

'This is what will come to pass if the guardian fails,' said

Mrs O'Hara gently, her cheeks pink and her face glistening with sweat. 'I have seen it.'

'Seen it?' asked Ebony.

'Mrs O'Hara has visions,' replied Aunt Ruby. 'Like an oracle or witch doctor.'

She looks more like an angel, thought Ebony.

'So how does it help us?' asked Aunt Ruby, her voice rising in pitch and volume.

'Ebony holds the key,' answered Mrs O'Hara. 'She just has to figure out how to use it. Help me get my daughter back. We don't have much time. The Deus-Umbra is coming.'

Aunt Ruby's violet eyes flashed dangerously as she stood up to leave.

Keeping quiet as all eyes turned to her, Ebony's heart sank. Was the silver box the key or freeing the souls? Averting her eyes, she waited until her aunt led the way out of the bistro, Mrs O'Hara following them as far as the door.

As a parting gesture, Mrs O'Hara pressed the mask into Ebony's hands and said, 'Don't lose faith. Give this to my son, it belongs to him – he will know what it means.'

31

'If Mrs O'Hara knew that Chiyoko was missing,' said Ebony, hugging the warm pizza to her body, 'and the puppet she gave me can help, why didn't she use it herself?'

'That's a good question,' answered Aunt Ruby, as they pulled up outside 23 Mercury Lane. 'I'm guessing she needs you and Seamus to work together. Deliver the pizza and explain everything.'

'I'll try,' said Ebony, biting her lip. 'We called a truce and things seem OK, but his father still has great influence over him.'

'And so does his mother. Don't forget the power of a mother's love.'

Uncle Cornelius whimpered, remembering his own mother, while Ebony quietened. She had never known such a thing, so what was there to forget?

As they entered the house, the place was in complete darkness; either Seamus wasn't there or he hadn't left his room. Quickly switching on as many lights as she could, worry creeping along her spine, Ebony raced upstairs. Relieved to see a crack of light under Seamus's door, she gave it a small knock.

'Come in,' called Seamus in a shaky voice.

Had he been crying? With his sister missing, a terrible fate awaiting her and the problems with his father, it came as no surprise. Pushing her way in, Ebony found Winston on his back on the bed, legs splayed, while Seamus tickled his tummy. The place was still strewn with clothes – Seamus hadn't even bothered tidying up after Zach's intrusion. Ebony guessed that he must have been feeling pretty low. Handing over the pizza, she waited for an invitation to sit down. When none came, she turned to leave.

'Wait!' cried Seamus. 'Don't go! I mean … do you want some pizza?'

'I'm stuffed,' said Ebony, reaching for Winston and hugging him tight, her mind filled with images of chargrilled rat.

Seeing the look of disappointment on Seamus's face, she placed Winston back on the bed and demonstrated a few of her favourite tricks with him. She asked him to somersault a few times and, when he got too dizzy doing that, she let him use her curls likes vines, swinging on them like a little ratty Tarzan. To her surprise, Seamus was giggling in seconds. Now that his spirits were lifted, Ebony decided to tackle the puppet issue.

'Seamus, I need to speak to you,' she began, unzipping her bag a little, ready to show him the puppet and mask. 'We've just seen your mother and–'

'My mother was here? I had no idea. Why didn't she come and see me?' Hurt filled his face, even though he was trying to hide his emotions.

'She didn't come here,' Ebony reassured him. 'She summoned us to a bistro.'

'But why you and not me?'

'We didn't actually know it was her before we got there, that's why we didn't ask you to come along. But listen – it's important. She showed us a puppet show and she somehow took me into it. I couldn't do anything – it was like I was under her power.'

'I wanted to tell you but I didn't know if you'd believe me,' said Seamus. 'Mum manipulates the Shadowlands all the time without my father knowing. People know she has visions, but no one realises she's a Shadow Custodian: it's a special kind of protector and seer. She uses shadows like a crystal ball to watch the past, present and future to prevent harm – she can even see into the Shadowlands. She can't go inside, but she can bring things into and out of the places she protects and use her puppets to affect what happens there.'

'So why were you so reluctant to believe in the Shadow Walkers?'

Colouring, Seamus shrugged, hanging his head. 'Mum talked about these creatures, but I'd never seen them with my own eyes, even during her lessons. I guess I'm a bit too much like Dad.'

'Lessons? So you can affect the Shadowlands too? You knew I was trying to get in – why didn't you show me what you knew?'

'I'm only a beginner. Mum started teaching me, but against my father's will. He doesn't believe in what he calls mumbo-jumbo traditions – when he found out what we were doing, he banned us from continuing. So we only practise when we can, always in secret.' Pausing, Seamus gave a heavy sigh. 'I'm not very good. I'd have only embarrassed myself.'

'If your mum's job is to protect via the shadows, why doesn't she stop the Shadow Walkers?'

'She says they have grown too powerful.'

Suddenly, a thought hit Ebony. If Mrs O'Hara could manipulate the shadows but couldn't access the Shadowlands, was it possible that she was the 'friend' that had sent her the silver box? After all, the voice was female and the figure had been green, like objects and people in the outside world. Pulling the box out of her bag, Ebony held it out on her palm.

'Did she give you that too?' asked Seamus.

'I don't know for certain. It was delivered by King Vulture and your mum didn't say anything when we met. But I think she might have. Do you recognise it?'

'Maybe not that one, but we had one like it that mum used to let Chiyoko play with when she was a baby. The birdsong always calmed her down, even when she was teething. Mum used to sing along to the tune.' Absentmindedly, he began to sing a sweet yet melancholic melody. 'But one day, Mum had a vision linked to the box. She said it would bring harm to Chiyoko. After that, it disappeared.'

'Birdsong?' asked Ebony, making a mental note that once again Chiyoko was linked to birds.

'Sure!' said Seamus. 'The box we had played music. Why? What does yours do?'

'I don't know.' Ebony handed him the box, turning it over so he could read the inscription.

'I don't remember that being there, so they can't be the same.' He inspected the box more closely, then began to laugh. 'No, wait! It is. See these marks?' He leaned in, showing Ebony three sharp chips along one edge. 'I'd recognise these anywhere. I made them trying to get the box open to find out where the birdsong came from. But how did that writing get there?'

'Your mother must have put it there as a message for me. I know she gave me the box before Chiyoko was taken, but I think it's linked to your sister. I'll take the box to Chiyoko when we rescue her. Will you help?'

'It's obvious Mum doesn't trust me,' said Seamus sulkily. 'Why don't you ask *her*?'

'Because I'm trusting you and I've got more to lose,' said Ebony. 'You have the AESL behind you. Meanwhile, I have Zach and the judge after me, and practically no support. If I'm to rescue your sister, I need your help. And anyway,' Ebony held out the mask, 'your mum told me to give you this. She said you would be able to show me what to do when the time comes.'

'My mask! I haven't seen this in a while!' cried Seamus.

His face lit up, and his whole body seemed to relax. 'It's the mask that a Shadow Custodian wears and a powerful piece of protection. It gives you access to the shadows, but also helps to hide you from those that dwell in the places you're spying on – which can be very useful when you're poking your nose into the future. Mum has one too; only hers has gold around the eyes to show her status. Is that really what Mum said?'

'Yes,' said Ebony, eyeing the mask carefully. 'And she said it like you were an essential part of the plan. She also gave me this.' Ebony pulled the puppet of Chiyoko out of her bag.

'Then she must be entrusting me with helping you to use it – even though the puppets are powerful.' Jumping up and running to grab something from a drawer, he asked, 'Do you want me to show you what I know?'

Returning with two wooden sticks, each with metal clasps at the end, he took the puppet from Ebony and threaded the rods onto the limbs. Next, he put on the mask. Holding the puppet up in front of a small bedside lamp, he cast a Chiyoko-shaped shadow on the bare wall.

'The top one is to move it from side to side and up and down, and gives the puppet its presence,' he explained. Then he lifted the other stick. 'This one, you hook onto other parts of the puppet to make it move and look 3D. This is for depth and character.'

His movements were graceful, almost as skilled as his mother. Ebony could tell from his eyes that he was smiling.

'If you want to make the puppet small and intense,'

explained Seamus, taking hold of a small bedside lamp and moving it closer. 'You make the light near. To make the figure seem big, you move it away.'

He demonstrated with the lamp and puppet, and Ebony began to understand the effects that were possible, but she couldn't see how it could help save Chiyoko. Or what it had to do with the Shadowlands. After watching for a few minutes, Ebony decided to have a try. It wasn't as easy as it looked, but she could make the puppet move and alter its size. Only under her command, the movements were clumsy, not fluid, and she couldn't attach the second stick while manipulating the first.

'I guess it takes some practice,' she said, handing the controls back to Seamus. 'But why do we need it? It's hardly a weapon.'

'It may not look like much, but the effects can be powerful. As you already experienced, you can be brought via the shadows into the puppet show and, likewise, the puppets can be brought out into the real world. You're working with pure shadow; it's incredibly strong yet flexible.'

'Back at the Silent Peregrine, one minute I was watching your mum's show, the next minute I was inside it, staring into the eyes of the Deus-Umbra.'

'You see? It's powerful. I think mum is trying to tell us that this could help you defeat the Deus-Umbra,' said Seamus.

Holding up the puppet so it hung limply, Ebony raised her eyebrows. 'Sure. Like this is going to terrify that huge creature,' she said.

'Elephants are scared of mice,' replied Seamus.

Winston puffed himself up and marched around like a sentry, making the pair laugh.

'I thought you were a rat,' said Seamus.

Winston puffed up even more as he lifted his left paw, proudly.

'My father wouldn't even consider this as an option, but I've come to the conclusion that he's not always right. He's all about modern gadgets and gizmos, but sometimes the old ways are the best,' said Seamus.

'Back home, we use the sky and the way our animals behave to predict the weather,' replied Ebony. 'If Gallows Island looks closer than usual, and we can count the posts on its pier, we know that rain is coming. It's more accurate than the forecasts.'

'Exactly! And the most powerful magic can lie in the simplest of objects,' continued Seamus.

'Like *The Book of Learning*,' said Ebony brightly.

A knock on the door interrupted them. It was Aunt Ruby in a purple satin dressing gown, her pipe in hand.

'Is everything OK?' she asked, taking a quick chug of her pipe and blowing the smoke out in little rings.

As though embarrassed, Seamus hid the puppet in his quilt. Aunt Ruby peered over but said nothing. Feeling suddenly exhausted, Ebony yawned, setting off a chain reaction. Even Winston opened his mouth wide and scrunched up his nose, a noisy puff of air escaping from his small throat. Unsteadily, he plopped off the bed and headed out the door. Ebony could hear him haul himself up onto the bedside cabinet and into his cage next door.

'That's a good idea, Winston,' called Aunt Ruby. 'I think everyone should get some sleep. Who knows what dangers tomorrow might bring?'

Carefully, Ebony returned the puppet to her backpack. As she stood, Aunt Ruby headed to the window to close Seamus's curtains. When she reached the window, she let out a small squeal. Leaning closer to the glass, she threw her pipe down on the window ledge and reached instinctively for her pocket, but she was in her dressing gown so her gun wasn't there.

'Dammit!' she cried.

'What?' asked Ebony, her heart thumping. Then she felt a familiar tug on her mind – it was Zach, trying to read her thoughts. And judging by the strength of the icy tendrils probing her brain, he was right outside. Pain crippling her head, Ebony tried to clear her thoughts, but it was no use. All she could picture was the secret silver box – he was trying to locate its whereabouts. The risk he was taking made it clear to Ebony that his earlier break-in was an attempt to find it. It left no doubt in her mind that the box was the key to defeating the Deus-Umbra.

Aunt Ruby raced from the room and thundered down the stairs. Ebony could hear her clattering around, searching for her gun, and then the sound of multiple locks opening.

Paralysed with pain, Ebony fought with all her might. Feeling Zach's presence lessen, she gasped with relief and fell back onto the bed, knocking her rucksack to the floor. A strange scratching noise sounded – it seemed to be coming from the floorboards. Seamus tucked his feet up onto the bed, his eyes almost popping out of his head.

'Stay there, Seamus,' said Ebony. The pain in her head receding, she grabbed the lamp as a weapon. 'I'll deal with this.'

32

The scratching sound grew louder, and Ebony located it next to the bed. Peering over the side, she saw that it was coming from her rucksack. *The Book of Learning* was shimmering with silvery light, shaking and rattling against the bronze rose. As her palm began to ache, Ebony put down her weapon and reached over, picking up the rucksack. Setting it on the bed near Seamus's feet, she took out the book and tried the fingerprint combination but, rather than opening, it sparked and leapt out of her hands back into the bag, like it was trying to get away.

Next, there was an almighty explosion: blue light and sparks lit up the room, and acrid smoke filled their lungs. The light died away, leaving Ebony and Seamus coughing and spluttering, trying to breathe properly. When the smoke had cleared, Ebony discovered there was a black skull on the floor that hadn't been there before.

'The Shadow Walkers have left another mark,' she whispered.

Cautiously Seamus moved to the edge of the bed and looked at the floor. As they watched, the skull began spewing a black tar-like substance that bubbled and boiled, growing in size. Wide-eyed, Ebony stared, unable to move. Seamus took a sharp intake of breath and shuffled backwards as a head appeared, then a shoulder – a Shadow Walker. It was much smaller than the ones that had attacked headquarters, only about a foot tall, but its eyes were just as red and hateful, and it was climbing into the room!

Seamus's shuffling jolted Ebony into action. Remembering the gun, she rifled manically through her rucksack until she found it. Grabbing the gun, she fired, hoping that the weapon might be effective against a Shadow Walker so small. The tiny, almost invisible bullet hit the creature in the heart and made him explode. Black goo splattered all over the walls, and Ebony let out a huge breath. But the relief she felt quickly waned as Seamus cried out, 'They're moving!'

The bits of goo were slowly making their way back to where the skull had been. In just moments, the figure had re-formed, its eyes red-hot and piercing. Ebony fired again, and the same thing happened. The creature exploded but began to re-form right away – even against a Shadow Walker of this size, it seemed the gun was largely useless.

Out of the corner of her eye, Ebony saw another movement. Turning and pointing her weapon, she realised it was Seamus; wearing his mask, he'd snatched up the puppet and was quickly attaching the rod that had come loose.

'Seamus, this is not the time for games!' cried Ebony, turning her attention back to the Shadow Walker that was now nearly completely re-formed.

'The gun isn't working, we have to try something else,' he replied.

A Chiyoko-shaped shadow appeared on the wall. Then an amazing thing happened: it pushed itself away from the plaster and headed straight for the Shadow Walker. Unable to tear her eyes away, Ebony watched the two shadowy figures face off. Seamus raised his puppet's arm to strike. On impact, the Shadow Walker stumbled and staggered back. As the creature regained its strength and pushed forward to attack, Seamus moved the lamp closer, making the puppet shadow grow smaller but more intense. This time, when he made a strike, the Shadow Walker was floored.

'Quick!' cried Seamus. 'Do something now while it's weakened.'

Without thinking, Ebony fired at the skull shape on the floor and it exploded, splattering the walls. The bits of goo turned from liquid to gas, rising in vapours. Each blob twisted and spiralled upwards, turning paler as it ascended until it had disappeared completely, leaving nothing but smokey smudge marks on the ceiling.

The creature gave an ear-splitting scream – it was unharmed but frantic. Rather than attacking, it began searching for an exit point. It tried moving towards the closest shadow, but the puppet stepped in its way. Unable to escape, the tiny Shadow Walker beat its chest and roared. Ebony kept her gaze steady, gun in hand, as Seamus made the puppet advance, getting larger and more intimidating. The puppet hit out several times, and although the Shadow Walker stumbled and staggered with the impact, no amount of force seemed to hurt it. In a desperate move, Seamus made the puppet pin the creature to the wall.

'Good work, Seamus,' said Ebony. 'Keep it there, I have an idea.'

Grabbing her rucksack, she quickly emptied it out onto Seamus's bed. Leaping from the bed, and taking the creature by surprise, she jammed the open rucksack over the Shadow Walker's head. As the puppet withdrew its hold, she yanked the bag right down over its body, then snatched up the bag and secured its zip. She held fast as the Shadow Walker struggled inside.

'I wonder if destroying the skull mark has somehow weakened its power. But how did the puppet become real?'

At first, Seamus didn't reply; he was too busy removing his mask and wiping the sweat from his face. But once he'd recovered, he took a long, deep breath.

'I have no idea – I just followed my mum's instructions. That's the first time I've managed it alone,' he said, eyeing the rucksack carefully. 'It certainly seems like the creature is weakened. And we worked well as a team. I want you to know … I believe you're the rightful guardian. I've never wanted the responsibility and I don't have the skills. And after what I've seen?' Seamus shook his head.

'Thank you,' said Ebony. 'I appreciate that, but people have helped me every step of the way. I can't do it alone. If only we had the AESL behind us, imagine how much more we could achieve.'

'My father thinks he can bribe his way through life, bullying anyone who stands up to him. But I'm sorry I ever joined the AESL – I just did it to please him. I'll do everything I can to see it disbanded.'

'Your mother thinks he'll come round when the battle begins.'

'I hope so. He's not a bad man but his ambition …'

'I understand,' replied Ebony. 'But you're not your father. You can help me and make a real difference – just not the way he expects.'

'He'll probably disown me,' said Seamus glumly.

'I think he'll be proud,' said Ebony.

Seconds later, Aunt Ruby returned with Uncle Cornelius in tow. They were out of breath, their faces etched with a mixture of anger and frustration. Ebony was still in the same position, gun poised. When Aunt Ruby spoke, her voice was brimming with emotion.

'Zach was outside,' she said, confirming Ebony's suspicions. 'Only this time, there were Shadow Walkers with him.'

'There was one here too,' said Ebony, lifting the rucksack high. There was no longer any sign of struggle.

'You caught one?' gasped Aunt Ruby.

'We couldn't kill it, and capturing it was all we could think of,' replied Ebony.

Uncle Cornelius mewled, avoiding the bag. Dropping to the floor on all fours, he sniffed out where the black skull had been and snarled. Mulligan softly padded his way upstairs and joined in with a vicious growl. As his huge head peered over the top stair, Seamus stood his ground, one eye on the wildcat and the other on Aunt Ruby.

'I'm going to study this specimen,' said Aunt Ruby, taking the rucksack and cautiously opening the zip a little to peer in. 'It might give us some clues about how to deal with them. For now, you two need to rest.'

'You won't hurt it, will you?' asked Seamus. When all eyes turned to him, he added. 'Well, it is still part human, you know. It's not the creature's fault that Ambrose has kept it in the Shadowlands for too long.'

Aunt Ruby gave a small grunt. 'There's no fear of that,' she said, ripping the zip wide open and tipping the bag upside down. 'It's gone.'

Rushing over, Ebony and Seamus checked inside.

'It must have melted back into the shadows,' said Seamus glumly.

'Forget it,' said Aunt Ruby, her voice tinged with disappointment. 'Into bed, both of you.'

'I'm not sleeping with Zach on the loose,' said Ebony, her jaw set.

'Don't worry, we'll stand guard,' replied Aunt Ruby.

'Well, if you hear anything, call me,' said Ebony, gathering up her things and heading for her room.

'Me too,' added Seamus. Noticing the puppet on his bed, partly concealed by a ruffle in his quilt and forgotten by Ebony, he sat down on the bed right in front of it, to hide it from view. 'Call us both.'

Later, as Ebony drifted off, only one thought remained: she was going to put things right, even if it meant risking her life.

It was almost 1 a.m. when Icarus Bean crashed into Ebony's bedroom, landing on the floor in a heap and waking her with a start. As she jumped up, there was a loud roar and Mulligan leapt through the door. He soared through the air, landing on Ebony's bed, his tail swishing and his teeth showing. Aunt Ruby appeared in the doorway, holding her gun, and close behind her was Uncle Cornelius, gripping a fat, curved dagger.

'It's just Icarus,' cried Ebony. 'Uncle, what's happened?'

Looking up, panting, Icarus took a moment to gather his breath and formulate his reply. He had the conch shell from the Hideout under one arm.

'I have word from Mrs O'Hara that the judge has managed to free the Deus-Umbra,' he said. 'It will be hungry.'

'And Chiyoko?' asked Seamus, overhearing and rushing in.

'That's why I'm here. Chiyoko has been located in Oddley

Cove and there isn't much time,' said Icarus. 'They're taking her for sacrifice and the Shadow Walkers are hunting for the Reflectory – we think they are trying to take it over. You must come with me right now.'

His legs giving way, Seamus grabbed hold of the door frame to steady himself. Clinging on and taking deep breaths, Ebony could see he was trying to hold his nerve. Icarus approached the boy and held out the huge conch with both hands.

'This might come in useful,' he said.

'Let's go!' cried Aunt Ruby. 'Everyone downstairs, quick!'

Not needing to be told twice, Ebony threw on some clothes and grabbed her rucksack, shoving everything she might need back into it: *The Book of Learning*, her bronze rose, her grandpa's mahogany medal, the silver box and her pocketknife. Checking that the amulet was safely fastened around her neck, Ebony shoved her gun into a trouser pocket and grabbed Winston. Seamus, who had gone to get dressed, joined her on the landing. He looked pale but determined, grasping the conch with both hands.

Racing downstairs together, they ran outside to where a wide silver hatchback with blacked-out windows was parked, engine running. Uncle Cornelius was positioned at the wheel and Ebony could see through the window that part of the back seat was piled with weapons – crossbows, handguns and something that resembled a mini rocket launcher. Seamus clambered into the remaining space and shuffled across as best he could. Ebony handed Winston over to him, smiling.

'Get ready for the long ride. I'll see you on the other side,' she said. Instead of climbing in, she remained on the street.

Aunt Ruby turned round, flustered. 'What are you doing, Ebony?' she cried. 'You have to come too.'

Ebony looked at Icarus and, understanding her plan, he nodded. 'I'm going via the Shadowlands so I can get to the Reflectory as soon as possible,' said Ebony. 'I have to make sure it's secure. If it's not, then all the fighting in the world won't save us.'

'But you can't!' replied Aunt Ruby. 'Your grandpa wouldn't have allowed you to go there without back-up, knowing that Ambrose and Zach are still after you and likely to be waiting.'

Ebony straightened her back and tried to compose her face. 'I think my grandpa would understand. I'll make sure the place is OK and then I'll close the doorway and find you in Oddley Cove.'

'She's right,' said Icarus, his voice barely a croak. 'There's no other way.'

'But the Shadowlands will be extra dangerous right now,' said Aunt Ruby, on the verge of tears.

'We're at war,' replied Icarus. 'And this way, we'll move faster.' Turning to Ebony, he gave her a slight nod of the head. 'I'll come with you.'

'Let's go,' said Ebony, hoisting her rucksack across both shoulders.

On the back seat, Winston fought to get out of Seamus's

grasp, but the boy held on tight. Ebony reached in and stroked Winston's head. 'You should stay here, it's too dangerous.'

But Winston bared his teeth then stood to attention, his right paw in the air – his signal for no. Ebony thought about all they had been through together and as Seamus held the rat out on his palm, it felt suddenly wrong to leave him behind. Hoping she was doing the right thing, she let Winston run up her arm and onto her shoulder where he perched proudly.

Seamus leaned across. 'Please hurry,' he said. 'Save my sister.'

Nodding, Ebony slammed the car door shut and watched it pull away, heading west.

'Come,' said Icarus putting his hand on Ebony's shoulder.

'Where will we go?' asked Ebony.

'Somewhere safe, somewhere we won't be disturbed and can have whatever time it takes to get into the Shadowlands.' He pointed to Aunt Ruby's motorbike and sidecar. Two helmets were dangling on the handlebars. 'We'll get there quicker than on foot and we can't chance losing the moon – you'll need it to access the Reflectory.'

Looking up, Ebony saw a sliver of moon in the sky. Taking a deep breath, she hunkered down in the sidecar. As her uncle revved up the engine and took off, tyres squealing, she opened the helmet visor so the cold breeze could pummel her face and help calm her mind.

33

As they cruised along, leaving the busy central streets of the city behind and following a snaking canal, the journey started to look familiar. Certain they were following the same route as yesterday, Ebony tried to figure out where they were headed – surely Icarus wasn't taking her to Headquarters?

She couldn't wait to see the Reflectory again, but her heart was filled with fear. What if she failed to reveal the hidden doorway? To open the Reflectory, she had to demonstrate that she had a pure heart. She'd done it once before, but with so much at stake and under pressure, would she succeed again? On her lap, she felt Winston's warmth as he snuggled in, and she relaxed. She might not have the rest of the Order behind her, but like Mrs O'Hara had said, she could rely on her family and Winston. With their help, there was a chance she would succeed.

When they reached a high wall that led to some wrought-iron gates and skidded to stop, Ebony recognised where she was immediately: Glasnevin Cemetery. She stared over at the tall, grey tower that was lit up, fronting vast rows of gravestones.

'Why here?' she asked, climbing off her bike, removing her helmet and putting Winston on her shoulder.

'The Shadow Walkers have accessed the house twice already and left their mark, making it easy for them to return. This tower offers a bit of protection because if the Shadow Walkers come looking for us, it'll take a while for them to find us. If things don't go according to plan right away, we have time to try again without being disturbed.'

Icarus cut the locks on the gate and pushed it open. The weighty metal creaked and groaned, its noise carrying in the black night. Icarus checked around him. A bat fluttered overhead, but otherwise the night was still. Beckoning, Icarus led the way.

All around, giant crosses and carved angels peered down, glowing eerily under the fake lighting of the park. As their shadows passed over the gravestones, it looked like the angels' heads were moving. Averting her eyes, Ebony concentrated on following her uncle's back. When he stopped suddenly, Ebony bumped into him. Winston poked his head out of her curls and squeaked.

'Sorry!' said Ebony.

'Shh!' hissed a voice from somewhere nearby.

They were at the top of the steps that led to the entrance of the tower and it sounded like the voice had come from there. Ebony could just make out the word 'O'Connell' written above the tower door. The door was open slightly and creaking. On it there was an official-looking sign: 'Danger.

Broken Stairwell. Strictly Official Personnel Only. Closed for repairs.'

'Is it safe?' asked Ebony, as Icarus headed down towards the door, gesturing for her to follow.

'That's Miss Malone's doing. I asked her to secure the area. We might decide to travel back this way, and who knows when that will be? Just in case, the sign will stop us from frightening the life out of any unsuspecting tourists!'

Checking around him first, he ushered Ebony and Winston inside. When they were all in the small, cool space, dimly lit with a yellow bulb, the door slammed shut.

'Miss Malone!' cried Ebony, surprising even herself as she stepped forward and gave the woman a hug.

Miss Malone blushed and held a finger to her lips. 'Let's go up there,' she said, pointing above her head to the higher reaches of the tower.

Ebony looked up to see a narrow winding staircase; the bare bulb revealed a floor-to-ceiling stream of dancing dust motes.

'The moon will only be visible for a few more hours,' said Icarus, looking up at the ceiling, which contained a circular window.

'OK,' said Ebony, following his gaze, 'let's go.'

On her shoulder, Winston began to quiver. 'What's wrong with you? Are you scared of heights? There's a handrail, it'll be safe.'

Miss Malone led the way. Tucking Winston in her sleeve, Ebony took her time climbing the double helix staircase, clinging to the handrails as they got higher and higher. They were at least a hundred feet off the ground when they reached the top. There were four windows, looking out in each direction across Dublin and beyond, and above her head a small circular window showing the pale crescent moon. Ebony joined Icarus and Miss Malone on a sturdy wooden platform, and Winston peeked out. Looking over the edge, he made a strange gagging sound. Ebony hoped he wasn't too scared; they were, after all, pretty high up for a rat. But to Ebony, it was beautiful.

Soon she would be back amongst the glittering mists of the Reflectory. Ebony was certain that, with her uncle's help, she'd be able to release the souls and then locate Chiyoko, but she was less sure that when it came to confronting Judge Ambrose and Zach, with their heightened powers and demon ally, she would be able to beat them again. But first things first, she still had to get to Oddley Cove by riding the shadows.

'Right,' she said, swallowing hard. 'Here goes.'

As Miss Malone turned out the light, Icarus Bean called out, 'Get ready.'

Hastily taking out her pocketknife, Ebony secured Winston in her trouser pocket. Positioning herself next to Icarus, rucksack on her back, she concentrated on the shadows. Keenly aware of her earlier failure, she felt sweat bead on her upper lip. Like last time, she found it difficult to clear her brain of worries, but with so much at stake, she forced her mind to empty, and soon the world around her seemed to drop away. Whether it was down to her uncle's presence or her own sheer determination, Ebony couldn't be sure, but moments later, she passed through without any further complications and could see the outline of the room they'd left behind. This time, Miss Malone didn't look green – she had a faint purple hue around her head.

'I can see colours!' cried Ebony.

'You're improving,' replied Icarus from beside her, checking above him. 'But don't waste the energy you have. The moon was part of the formula for opening the Reflectory doorway, wasn't it?'

'Yes. But the door's still open.'

'It's still best that we move quickly while the moon is still visible, in case it's also part of the formula for locating the hidden Reflectory doorway. We don't have any records of this being done before!'

Icarus began to score into the ground and made a line wide enough for the two of them to ride the shadows without slipping off the sides. When he was finished he added lines that pointed in the direction of Oddley Cove. Taking hold of one side of the scored earth, Ebony lifted it slightly. Icarus lifted the other side. Then he counted them in. On three, they yanked.

The ground began to move. Watching the waves carefully, Ebony took a leap as soon as she saw the third appear, her uncle by her side. Hurtling along, sliding forwards on her belly at top speed, Ebony steadied herself and pushed into a seated position. It was still difficult to control her slide, but the invisible toboggan feeling soon returned. Although she found it a little bumpy, riding the shadows was easier than last time. Side by side with her uncle, she gave him a thumbs-up sign when he checked on her progress. As a ribbon of colour cascaded its way towards them, Ebony held her hand over Winston's pocket and crossed her fingers.

Landing with a thump, Ebony's face hurt and her stomach felt like a professional boxer had pummelled it. Unable to breathe properly, she realised she was face down on hard, cold ground. Managing to move her fingers, she sought out the pocket Winston was in; he nudged her with his nose to let her know he was safe. Although it was hardly a graceful landing, at least they were alive, but had they landed where they wanted to?

A shadow fell across her and she gritted her teeth. As she rolled onto her back, Icarus peered down. 'Are you OK?'

Scrambling to her feet, her head light and dizzy, Ebony looked around to get her bearings. It took a few moments to figure out where she was. They were in the small lane leading to her grandpa's cottage in Oddley Cove. Smelling the burning turf and spotting a thin line of smoke chugging out of the cottage chimney up ahead, she realised how much she had missed home.

'Never better,' she replied, a huge grin spreading across her face.

Almost expecting her grandpa to come outside and greet her, Ebony pressed her hand to her chest. Even though she knew it was impossible, her heart yearned for him to appear.

'Not quite on target, but we're close,' said Icarus. Catching Ebony staring at the cottage, he added, 'There'll be plenty of time to visit later. Let's go release those souls.'

The ascent to the woods was harder than Ebony remembered; it was only a couple of months since she'd moved to Dublin but she was no longer used to the steep incline or the unstable ground. Feeling alien in her surroundings, she stumbled after Icarus, trying not to lose her temper every time she tripped over a tree root or snagged her clothes on a briar. On her shoulder, she could feel Winston shifting his weight to keep his balance. Soon they reached the off-road shortcut into the woods where she had left the gateway to the Reflectory open.

Feeling a sudden surge of energy, Ebony pushed ahead; she couldn't wait to see the Reflectory again. As she stormed into the small copse of oak trees, there was a series of clicks as several rifles pointed in her direction, their safety catches released.

'It's OK,' said Icarus, as he stepped into the clearing. 'It's me, Acting Judge Bean. I bring the guardian. But what are you doing here? I thought you'd all gone home?'

There was a series of mumbles and mutters as the Order of Nine Lives men slowly lowered their weapons one by one.

'We decided to return,' said a man wearing glasses; with

the moon reflected on his lenses, he resembled a giant bug. 'After the attack on HQ, we realised O'Hara wasn't necessarily a reliable source of information; if he was wrong about the existence of Shadow Walkers, then maybe he could be wrong about the Reflectory not being real. So we decided to come back and see if we could find some answers.'

'Against O'Hara's wishes?' asked Icarus.

The man looked around nervously and shrugged in reply.

'And has there been any activity?'

'Not here. We thought we saw something out on the ocean but then it … disappeared.'

'Seems like too many things are disappearing around here,' said another man before spitting on the ground. 'We need some answers.'

In the dim light, Ebony saw that purple bruises flowered on each of the men's faces and their eyes were shifty and untrusting. The Shadow Walkers had clearly done damage during their attack. From their body language and nervous glances, Ebony could tell they'd injured more than just the men's bodies – the Shadow Walkers had also damaged their nerve.

The men stared past Ebony, straining their eyes as though looking for someone else. Behind them, Ebony knew the doorway to the Reflectory was hiding; all she had to do was reveal it and she'd be able to win the men's trust. But where was it?

Combing the ground, Icarus searched for his marker, but it was nowhere to be found. He looked up at Ebony and shrugged. 'It's around here somewhere. I know it is!'

But Ebony knew there was no time to waste. She'd have to try to make the doorway visible once more another way. Although she wasn't sure it would work, Ebony decided to use the same method as when she'd originally opened the Reflectory. It was worth a try.

Ignoring the pressure crushing her chest, Ebony took out her bronze rose, removed the amulet from around her neck and wrapped its chain around the stem, then closed her eyes. Concentrating on an image of Chiyoko, the smile of her grandpa and the support of her family, her heart warmed. Opening her eyes, Ebony lifted the rose and held it under the light of the moon. A sliver of its light beamed down, but nothing happened.

'It's not working,' she whispered to her uncle.

The men from the Order shuffled and murmured.

'Try again,' replied Icarus, his voice commanding and firm, like an officer.

Gritting her teeth, she tried again. Still nothing happened. Frustration rising, she tried to hide her emotions from the men who were watching her closely. She had all the paraphernalia she needed and a pure heart under the moon – what was she doing wrong? Last time she had thought Winston was dead and had cried. This time there was nothing to cry about, but surely determination was just as pure of heart? Looking up, she saw that the moon was still high. They had another few hours before dawn.

Holding out the rose once more, picturing Chiyoko, then

her grandpa's face, Ebony wished with all her might for the doorway to reappear. Unexpectedly, an image of the Deus-Umbra came to mind, flooding her heart with hatred. As she pushed the dark feelings away, the rose began to burn blue. Sparks shot out, towards where the doorway was hidden. At first, they flickered and died away, but after a moment, they began to splutter, like something being welded. The sparks began to stick in the air, forming an outline – bit by bit, the gateway emerged.

'The girl ... she's made it reappear,' cried one of the men.

Watching the huge ivy-covered stone with a giant mahogany door in its centre appear, Ebony's heart warmed. The door had thick black bolts and a small peephole, and it was wide open, just like she'd left it, a silver-grey mist swirling behind.

Drawn to the glittering mist, Ebony walked slowly towards the doorway, her hands clutching the straps on her rucksack. On her shoulder, Winston wiggled and squirmed excitedly. Ebony stepped closer and closer, until something cold and hard jammed into the side of her head and she stopped dead. She heard Winston give a small gulp.

'Where do you think you're going?' asked a voice in her ear.

'You,' said Icarus bitterly. 'How did you get here?'

Not daring to move her head, Ebony shifted her eyes right. Mr O'Hara was holding a gun to her head; it was like he'd come from nowhere.

'I put a tracker on Icarus to monitor his movements. I followed you to Glasnevin and forced Miss Malone to tell me where you were going,' answered Mr O'Hara. 'Then I used the Shadowlands to follow you.'

'You can ride the shadows?' asked Ebony.

'Of course. Your parents gave me the instructions, remember? And if you can ride the shadows, anyone can.'

Despite the bravado in his voice, Ebony felt the gun shake slightly against her skin. She wondered what was bothering him – had he overheard the men's disobedience?

'I'm going inside,' said Ebony.

'Not while I'm breathing, you're not. No one's to go inside except for the guardian and seeing as you've been banned until further investigation, I don't think you qualify.'

'I am the guardian,' replied Ebony, sounding much braver than she felt. 'You just saw me reveal the doorway. You can't deny that.'

'I saw a fine example of your aunt's trickery. When are you going to realise how deluded you are? You're nothing but a piddling little girl!' replied Mr O'Hara. He laughed nervously, trying to keep his gun steady as he looked around at the others. When no one else joined in, sweat broke out on his forehead.

'O'Hara!' called Icarus, stepping forward. 'She's telling you the truth. You know what you just saw.'

'But she's just a girl. And a scrawny one at that.' His voice was higher-pitched than normal.

Ebony drew herself up tall and flexed her fingers. She didn't feel scrawny. In fact, every time Mr O'Hara opened his mouth, she felt stronger. On her shoulder, Winston puffed himself up also. He stuck his head out towards Mr O'Hara and bared his teeth.

'If she's so scrawny then why do you need to hold a gun to her head?' continued Icarus.

O'Hara considered his words and then shoved Ebony towards her uncle, but continued to point the gun towards them. 'How are we meant to defeat Ambrose with a little girl leading us?' he asked, addressing the men. 'A girl with a mangy rat?'

'Let me explain …' said Icarus, stepping towards him with his hands raised in a non-threatening gesture. Then, in a blur of movement, he spun round and kicked the gun from O'Hara's hands before grabbing him in a headlock. Gasping with the effort of holding O'Hara, who was struggling in his grasp, Icarus shouted, 'Now, Ebony, do what you need to.'

Ebony had counted seven men in total guarding the surrounding area, each with rifles, but none of them made any move to help O'Hara; they all stood watching Icarus manhandle him. She pulled the medal out of her rucksack, zipped it up and hoisted it back on her shoulders. With the rose and medal in her pocket she said, 'I'll go check things out. And when I've done what I need to, I'll be back to seal the entrance up.'

'But you can't–' came a muffled cry.

Clapping his hand over O'Hara's mouth, Icarus motioned with his head. 'Go on,' he said. 'You won't get any hassle from these guys.'

Squaring her shoulders and taking a deep breath, Ebony stepped towards the swirling mists. Although she had no idea how to close the gateway, or how to release the souls trapped in stasis, she had to try. She had managed to ride the Shadowlands with her uncle and she had revealed the Reflectory – it had to be possible. Pausing in the doorway, she looked back at Icarus. Her uncle mouthed, 'Be careful,' and Ebony nodded. Lifting her gun, she stepped inside.

As soon as Ebony was through, only the mist remained. There was no sign of her uncle, of the guards from the Order or the door she had just passed through. Instead, there were lush trees and blooming flowers everywhere, with a single black rose glinting like crystal. The surroundings felt instantly familiar. Reaching out to touch the *Ebonius Tobinius* rose, Ebony was shocked to find that it was solid. Taking hold and twisting it, the door suddenly appeared again.

'It's the way out!' said Ebony. 'We have to find our way back to this rose.'

Nodding, Winston took a deep sniff of the air.

Spying the lever that Icarus had spoken of, Ebony marched over and gave it a shove to hide the doorway again. 'Just in case,' she said. 'We don't want anyone else coming inside after us. Now, keep your eyes peeled for anything unusual.'

Winston began to slide down Ebony's arm and she crouched to let him jump off. He hopped merrily alongside her on the soft, springy earth, head held high as he sniffed the warm Reflectory breeze that smelled of freshly cut grass. Now and again he stopped and stared off into the distance, continuing on only when he was satisfied it was all clear.

'It's just as wonderful as I remember,' said Ebony, looking around her. 'I didn't realise how much I missed this place.'

Ebony strode on. Soon, the pair reached the sound of waves and the foliage disappeared, leaving just the mist. Each step felt like she was walking on wispy clouds, her body turning sluggish and cumbersome. She had forgotten how the Reflectory had made her feel last time; soon it would start affecting her memory. Just as she was imagining what it would be like to step out of her body, there was a loud crash and Ebony ducked just in time as a transparent knife went spinning past. It whirled and twisted before popping like a bubble.

'That must be one of the bad things a soul is trying to forget,' said Ebony, feeling her voice slow. 'We're nearly there.'

In the distance, a tiny but growing light glowed. Ebony pointed.

'Look! Can you remember where grandpa's soul is, Winston? I want to check he's OK before we visit the Emergency Room where Zach's mum is.'

Nodding and pointing, Winston led the way, with Ebony following close behind. When they reached the rows of bulb-trimmed mirrors, each with its own luminous soul gazing into its reflective glass, something in Ebony stirred.

A cold feeling crept along her flesh and she paused. The Reflectory was a place of regeneration that kept the good memories and erased the bad. Creeping flesh shouldn't be possible. Ebony checked cautiously about her.

'Do you feel that, Winston?' Glancing down, she saw her pet rat's fur was standing on end.

Breath held, they waited. A moment later, the feeling passed.

'It must be our imagination,' said Ebony. 'Let's go, while we can still remember what we're doing here!'

With every step, her mind turned hazier, and she had to fight to keep her thoughts focused.

'You're on a mission, Ebony Smart,' she repeated to herself, over and over. 'You're on a mission.'

Glancing over the souls she passed, everything looked fine. Nothing looked like it had been tampered with. The souls simply gazed into their mirrors with dazed expressions, shuddering now and again as a bad memory was expelled.

Up ahead, Winston began jumping up and down on the spot, and Ebony quickly realised why. Her heart flooding with an intense mix of joy and sadness, she rushed to join him as quickly as her body would allow, straight to the soul of Grandpa Tobias. Reaching out for her grandpa's hand,

Ebony felt a gentle warmth as her fingers passed through his. Wetness dripped down her face and it took a moment for Ebony to realise that she was crying. Her grandpa's expression was frozen and calm, just like the first time she had encountered his soul, only it no longer looked peaceful and there was a grey tinge to it that made her shudder.

Checking around him, Ebony's heart ached; she knew that Judge Ambrose had placed her grandpa's soul in stasis along with the rest of them, but what effect was it having? And how could she release him? Her grandpa's soul had been in the Reflectory for just over two months and, unless there was something else at work, staying in stasis was taking its toll. It looked like Miss Malone was right; Ambrose was using the souls in some way to benefit himself. Ebony guessed that he was somehow harnessing their energy, but she couldn't figure out what he was using it for.

'Why don't you speak to me any more, Grandpa?' asked Ebony. 'I miss you. I promise I'll listen this time.'

When there was no reply to her question, she stared into her grandpa's mirror as though she might find the answer there. But inside the glass were just a few distant memories; her grandpa's fat, calloused hands frying sprats in a pan, Ebony dropping lines off the side of the fishing boat that now lay smashed to pieces on the ocean floor, two smiling faces she hardly recognised, teary, as though saying goodbye.

'My parents!' cried Ebony, but as fast as it had appeared, the image melted away, replaced by one of a storm brewing on the horizon. 'Please, speak to me again, Grandpa!'

Sinking to her knees, Ebony wept freely. Her tears crystallised as they flowed, glistening bright blue and making a tinkling sound as they hit the ground, sparkling like gems.

Feeling something tug on her trousers, Ebony looked down to see Winston pulling something towards her. It was a piece of paper with familiar writing. Her note to her grandpa had been delivered but clearly he hadn't been able to read it or respond. Ebony wiped her eyes dry on the back of her sleeve. Picking up the note and tucking it into the corner of her grandpa's mirror, she turned to Winston.

'OK, let's move on,' she said. 'I'm sorry, Grandpa,' she said. 'I have to go now. But I'll come back and release you. I won't leave you in Ambrose's power.'

Feeling as though her heart was going to break in two, Ebony reached out to hug him. Although she knew she wouldn't be able to touch him, at least it would feel like some kind of connection before she left him behind. As her right hand brushed the back of her grandpa's neck, her fingers touched something cold and hard. Walking around her grandpa's soul, Ebony spotted something she hadn't noticed before: there was something hidden at the nape of his neck, peeping out from under his hair. It was button-sized, shiny and red, with a black skull on it – the mark of the Shadow Walkers. Ebony could see two prongs sticking into her grandpa's translucent flesh, like it was some kind of plug.

'What's that?' she asked, lifting Winston up on her outstretched palm for a better look.

The rat peered in, then flattened his ears. Then he gave a small growl and made a pulling motion. Guessing what he was miming, Ebony moved to pull the object out, but stopped, her hand hovering over the plug.

'Do you think it's safe for me to remove it?'

Lifting his left paw, then his right, then his left again, Winston finally gave up and shrugged.

Deciding she had to at least try, Ebony decided to risk it. After all, it wasn't like she could kill him again. Taking hold with one hand, the red plug firmly in her fingers, she gave it a yank. The second she did, the soul of Grandpa Tobias fell forward, limp and lifeless looking.

'What have I done?' cried Ebony. 'I should have left it alone!'

But then her grandpa's soul began to tremble and something shot out of his mirror. It was the face of Judge Ambrose, sneering. And then another image: Zach Stone lifting his gun to fire. Next: Zach and Ambrose conspiring. This was followed by another and another; her grandpa's bad memories were being expelled and they were all images of Zach and the judge.

'We did it!' cried Ebony. 'I don't know how, but it's working – I think we've released his soul from stasis – quick! Let's check the others!'

35

Racing around the rows and rows of souls, Ebony pulled out the shiny red plugs one by one, Winston in tow. After every release, the soul fell forward, with more bad memories than ever before spewing out. Soon, the Reflectory was filled with hateful images of Zach and Judge Ambrose; it was as though the souls had been living with their bad deeds for so long, they couldn't wait to expel them.

Tired, her vision blurring, Ebony realised she needed to conserve some energy to rescue Chiyoko and give her the silver box.

'Look, there's the Emergency Room, Winston,' she said, pointing at the light flashing in the distance. 'Once we've checked in there, we'd better get out of here and seal the place up.'

Ebony pushed on towards it, with Winston following closely behind. As she approached the door, her stomach flipped and her mouth turned dry. Last time she was here, Zach had almost killed her. Pausing and listening to make sure it was all clear, Ebony pushed open the door.

Inside, two souls sat in their chairs, both badly damaged

and sickly looking, as they had been the first time she had seen them. Checking behind her first, half expecting Zach to step out of the shadows, Ebony approached the soul of Aunt Ruby's husband – the man her aunt had named her youngest wildcat after – so she could take a closer look. Her aunt would want to know how he was doing.

The soul of the real Uncle Cornelius was yellow and gnarled, his face contorted and lifeless, and it had deteriorated since last time. Something else looked different too, but she couldn't quite put her finger on it. Then she realised that his mirror was crackling with black and white dots; there were no images showing. It was like a broken TV set.

Tentatively, Ebony moved across to the soul of Zach's mum. She was still attached to a pressure pump that was keeping her soul out of Obliteration. As Ebony got closer, dark thoughts entered her mind. *If this soul didn't exist,* she thought, *if I yanked away the wires to the pressure pump, Zach and Ambrose wouldn't be able to swap my soul.* As tempting as it was, she fought the cruel thoughts away. Zach's mum was innocent and Ebony wasn't going to stoop to his level.

'It all seems OK,' said Ebony. 'Let's get out of here and close the place up.'

But Winston stayed where he was, gazing up at the soul of Zach's mum, his shiny black eyes almost popping out of his head.

'What is it?' asked Ebony, hardly daring to breathe.

Moving closer to inspect the woman's soul, she'd only

taken a couple of steps before she realised: the machine wasn't moving. Last time she had been here, it had risen and fallen in slow, rhythmic movements, hissing like an angry snake as it expelled air. This time, the pump was silent and motionless.

Taking a sudden leap, Winston landed on the woman's soul.

'Get down, Winston! That's disrespectful.'

But Winston ignored her words. Instead, he jumped up and down, putting all his weight behind the movements. There was a crack, then a tearing sound, like a fissure travelling through ice, and a moment later, Winston was gone.

He'd fallen into the soul. Except it wasn't a soul at all, Ebony realised. Reaching out to touch the damaged shell, Ebony's fingers were coated with white powder – this wasn't Zach's mum: it was a plaster model. At some point, Zach and Ambrose must have made a swap – but when, why and where had they moved the soul to? And what was the point of leaving a replacement? The only reason Ebony could think of was that they knew she'd come back to check on the souls and they didn't want her to know Zach's mum had been moved. The hairs on Ebony's arm stood on end, and she shivered. She had no idea what their actions meant, but she knew it wasn't a good sign.

A small black blob shot across the room in front of Ebony's face, quickly followed by a second that she swatted away. Another one appeared, this time bigger and shaped like a hand. She ducked as it flew by. Hearing a strange squeak, Ebony looked for Winston; he had climbed out of the plaster cast and was against the wall, his back flat against it and his teeth bared.

'Don't worry – it's just the souls getting rid of bad memories–'

But then she froze.

Her uncle's mirror wasn't working, and there were no other mirrors in this room. Her palm began to hurt and Ebony realised this always happened just before an attack.

'Shadow Walker!' Ebony cried.

The whole room turned black and a terrifying chill filled the air. Winston ran for the open door, with Ebony in hot pursuit.

As they reached the main room, they heard an almighty scream, like metal scraping against metal, and scooping Winston up, Ebony ran for her life. With the effects of the Reflectory in full swing, she wasn't as fast as usual, but she was determined to escape. Racing through the lines of souls and mirrors, the endless images of Zach and Judge Ambrose's face, Ebony felt a chill at her neck. Feeling icy tendrils take hold of her, Ebony ran harder. As she broke free of the Shadow Walker's clutches, the creature gave out a terrible screech that pierced deep into Ebony's core.

With Winston clinging on for dear life, Ebony ran and ran, as fast as her legs could carry her, without any idea of where she was going. She had been expelled from the Reflectory last time; this time she just had to hope that she could find the exit. Thankfully, Winston's powerful sense of smell kicked into gear. Squealing, he pointed left, and Ebony followed. Soon, she spotted a silver mist shimmering up ahead. Seconds later, Ebony passed through to where the trees and shrubs were blossoming. The black rose glistened and gleamed; heading straight for it, Ebony twisted the rose to make the doorway appear, then yanked it open.

This time, the bloodcurdling scream sounded further away. Ebony chanced a look back; the Shadow Walker was having difficulty passing through the mist, but she wasn't sure how long it would hold. If the creature broke through and followed her out of the doorway, would it be powerful enough to kill the men who were waiting there, including her uncle? And yet, what damage might it do to the Reflectory if she left it trapped inside?

Ebony decided she would have to risk it. She couldn't endanger the men and she would just have to trust in the power of the Reflectory. There was no time to lose – she had to seal the doorway, and fast. But how?

As with the Shadowlands, Ebony decided her best bet was to reverse the actions that had originally opened the door to the Reflectory. Pulling her grandpa's medal out of her pocket, her fingers trembling, she placed the medal in the peephole on the outer side of the door. As a glowing crescent-moon-shaped hole formed in its centre, Ebony looked back into the mist. The Shadow Walker had broken through and was hurtling towards her, blackening everything in its wake like a giant storm cloud.

All fingers and thumbs, Ebony couldn't undo the clasp on the chain around her neck, so she yanked the amulet free, snapping the chain. She thrust the locket part into the medal on the outer side also, taking care not to lose the chain by holding both ends. Although unable to see the real world in front of her – it was like the doorway wasn't a doorway at all – she tugged on the chain and slammed the door shut behind her as she jumped through the opening.

Landing on wet grass, Ebony stumbled away from the door, freeing the medallion and amulet from where they were lodged. Without thinking, she pulled the bronze rose from her pocket and lifted it high in the air, at the same time calling out, 'There's a Shadow Walker chasing me. Take cover!'

But the men stayed put and raised their guns, ready to strike – all except Mr O'Hara, who hid behind the nearest tree.

Ebony hoped with all her might that something would happen and suddenly a loud clunking and clattering sounded as the rose clicked into action. Its centre lit up and the petals began to chime. One at a time the petals unfurled, secret grids and codes appearing in lights, before slipping onto the ground, forming a web of coloured beams. Stretching out like fingers, the beams attached themselves to the rock. The doorway groaned like a hungry belly and the lights began to blink out one by one. As the final light disappeared, so did the entrance to the Reflectory.

'It's gone!' cried Icarus. 'You did it.'

'She saved us!' shouted another voice.

Ebony checked around her. Winston was on the ground a few metres away, flat on his back and his tongue sticking out. The men from the Order were wide-eyed, their rifles hanging limply by their sides. Stepping out from behind his tree, Mr O'Hara raised a pointed finger. Ebony noticed his cheek was red raw and he had a bruise around one eye.

'She trapped a Shadow Walker inside!' he bellowed.

'At least she did something,' replied a man with black hair and sea-blue eyes. He rounded on Mr O'Hara with the others, and they closed in. 'What exactly have you ever done that's of any use to the Order?' He raised his gun, pointing it straight at O'Hara.

'Wait!' cried Ebony, thinking of Seamus and Chiyoko and the secrets Mr O'Hara knew about her parents. She had to stop the men from hurting him, even if it meant lying. 'He told us the secrets of riding the shadows. I wouldn't be here if it wasn't for him.'

Mr O'Hara, looking as stunned as the men, took advantage of their momentary surprise to back away. The men began to mumble amongst themselves, but then a loud and vicious yell silenced them.

'Ebony Smart,' shouted Zach, his voice filling the air. 'Over here!'

Accepting a pair of binoculars from one of the men, Ebony turned to where it seemed the voice had come from and spied the outline of a ship bobbing on the waves. Using the binoculars she zoomed in on its deck. There, at the front of the ship, above the figurehead's sinister face, was Zach Stone, his hair blowing in the sea breeze and a megaphone pressed to his lips. Next to him was Chiyoko, her hands tied and a knife held to her neck by a fearsome-looking Shadow Walker.

As Zach laughed, Ebony lowered the binoculars.

Across the bay, fireworks exploded. Gold and green fizz lit up the night sky. After several rounds, a screeching rocket took to the air. It boomed then combusted, a challenge glittering like multicoloured stars:

COME AND GET HER

'How do we get to that ship?' asked the man with black hair and blue eyes.

'Surely we're not going to risk our lives for a girl we don't know?' said another.

'We have no choice,' replied Ebony. 'They have one of us held captive on board and we have to save her.'

'She's only a young girl,' added Icarus.

The black-haired man looked at Ebony questioningly and pointed out to sea. 'Well?'

'We row,' said Ebony, picking up Winston and taking off at top speed on the fastest route towards the harbour.

Icarus ran straight after her and, one by one, the men, including O'Hara, followed. Sliding and skidding her way through the dark woods, hoping she wasn't squeezing Winston too hard, Ebony leapt over the tangled roots and raced towards Oddley Cove harbour, the sound of the men behind her spurring her on.

'Old Joe has a punt moored at our quay,' yelled Icarus as they ran. 'Head for the cottage!'

As they hit the laneways, Ebony pounded the tarmac.

Powering her way over the field towards the quay, Ebony hoped her aunt and the others would arrive soon – they needed all the help they could get. Icarus was ahead of her now, his matted hair blowing out behind him as his long legs stretched, carrying him over the field. By the time Ebony and the others caught up, he already had the ropes untied, his muscles straining as he pulled against the draw to keep the boat at the quayside.

Joe's punt was old and without an engine so, leaping in, Ebony grabbed a set of oars, handing another to Icarus so he could push away from the shore. Three of the Order of Nine Lives men managed to jump into the boat before it was pulled away by the tide.

'Go to the main pier and ask one of the fisherman for another boat,' shouted Ebony. 'Tell them I sent you.'

The four remaining men, as well as O'Hara, turned and ran towards the lights of the harbour in search of a second craft. Deftly swooshing their oars through the water, Icarus and Ebony steered straight towards the enemy ship. Being back on the sea, Ebony felt like she was finally home. Beside her, Winston sat on the wooden seat, sniffing the salty air.

'You realise this is a trap,' cried one of the men.

'Of course it is,' said Ebony. 'It's a ship full of Shadow Walkers.'

The men looked at one another, their faces determined as they turned back towards the sea. Above the ship, a stray firework boomed and exploded, showering golden sparkles onto the ocean. Although Icarus and Ebony were rowing as fast as they could, their progress was slow. The water was calm but the undercurrents were strong, and for every heave, the current dragged them back a few inches. Soon, their arms tired.

'Swap oarsmen,' ordered Icarus Bean, holding his oars out for someone to take. 'We need maximum speed at all times.'

The two new oarsmen rowed with all their might, but no matter how much power they put into their strokes, the ship holding Chiyoko seemed as far away as ever. Then, without warning, there was a terrible wrenching sound as the bottom of the punt struck something.

'There are no rocks here,' yelled Ebony. 'I know these seas. There are no rocks!'

The men continued rowing, but instead of moving towards the ship, their small vessel began to lift upwards, out of the water.

'What the …?' said Ebony, looking over the sides.

She was unable to see anything below except for gently flowing waves, their tops christened with white crystal tips. After a moment, she spotted something like a mast surfacing from the water up ahead. Looking back, there was another one behind.

'We're caught on a ship!' cried Ebony.

Down below, striped sails jutted out on either side of their rowing boat, billowing wildly as they broke from the water and the wind caught them, causing the ship to race forward.

It quickly became clear that they had been speared by the main mast of a ship that was rising from the waves.

'Is it friend or foe?' asked Icarus, shielding his eyes and squinting down as a deck covered in kelp and starfish emerged.

On deck, heavy, purposeful footsteps sounded, and everyone, including Winston, watched quietly as a squat figure slowly revealed itself on deck. The pirate wore a blue scarf tied into a knot at the back of his head and big knee-length boots that clapped off the wooden deck with every step. As he made his way to the front of the ship, he didn't look like he was made of shadows, but Ebony couldn't be certain. Suddenly, the ship lurched as it burst completely free of the water and Winston lost his grip. He flew up into the air, then plummeted, his small body spinning and tumbling towards the deep, rolling ocean.

'Man overboard!' cried a voice.

Looking down, Ebony saw her own face staring back, cutlass held high and a bandana holding her black curls in place, preventing them from blowing across her face. Next to her was the cowgirl. Watching Winston's fall, she lashed out her whip at just the right time, catching hold of Winston's tail and dragging him back to the ship's deck.

'They're friends!' cried Ebony, happy to see her past selves had come to help her. 'Let's go!'

Clambering out of the boat, she swung her legs back and forth until they caught the main mast. Wrapping her legs around it, she shimmied her way down. When she was within a few feet of the deck, she dropped onto it. Icarus and the Order's men followed close behind. By now, the deck was filled with armed and wary pirates.

'Thank you for coming,' cried Ebony, rushing over to her past selves and scooping Winston up in a hug. 'Your timing is perfect!'

'We've been patrolling these waters for weeks,' replied her pirate self. 'We received warning that an important member of the Order was in huge danger, but we hadn't come across anything until now.'

Realising that *The Black Peregrine* was what Mr O'Hara must have been trying to monitor, Ebony hugged each of her past selves in turn. No wonder O'Hara was confused – when *The Black Peregrine* sank beneath the waves it must have seemed like it was disappearing. But what she didn't understand was how the ship had been travelling backwards and forwards through time. She would have to ask later – right now there wasn't a moment to lose.

'We have to save Chiyoko! They're holding her captive on the other ship,' cried Ebony, turning and pointing to where it had been. Only now, the ship was nowhere to be seen.

'Where has it gone?' asked her pirate self.

They all hushed, hardly daring to breathe as they looked around, trying to locate the enemy ship by sight or sound as dawn broke over the horizon. Feeling a stabbing pain in her hand Ebony glanced at it and gasped – the mark had grown again. Now the size of a garden pea, the edges had shifted shape. It resembled a small skull.

Hearing her gasp, Icarus grabbed Ebony's hand. 'What's this?' he demanded, his face full of dismay.

'The door in the secret tunnel. I think you were right – it *was* a trap. Somehow, it marked me, and every time the Shadow Walkers are near, it hurts.'

'Then we must use it to our advantage,' said Icarus.

'But does it mean they can sense me also?'

Icarus didn't need to give a reply; his dark expression said it all. Rubbing at her hand, Ebony tried once more to remove the mark – but it wouldn't budge and a searing pain shot through her every time she touched it.

'We'll ask Ruby for help later. Does it hurt now?' asked Icarus.

Ebony nodded.

'Keep your eyes open and your hands steady, men,' called the pirate captain.

A slight breeze arose, carrying with it the sound of several crackly voices joined in song.

♪ **Down in the dark depths, pirate souls are restless.**
Their voices carry on the crest of a wave.
Wooden coffins embedded in the sea floor,
Bounty of riches glitter in the sand ... ♫

'They're coming,' said Ebony.

The singing ceased abruptly and everything darkened.

Some of the men cried out, and Ebony looked up. The enemy ship was rising out of the ocean, seawater pouring from its deck and seaweed swinging from the crossbeams. Rail to rail, it engulfed *The Black Peregrine* and Shadow Walkers lined its side ready to board the smaller ship.

The pirate captain and her crew quickly prepared to defend their ship, joined by the men from the Order. Searching around, Ebony found Icarus in the thick of them, his suit waistcoat looking as fine as a gentleman's amongst the rowdy bunch.

The sea swelled as Shadow Walkers began spilling onto the deck. They fell in black, tarry puddles, re-forming like putty as they lumbered towards the men, their red eyes gleaming with hatred as they brandished their weapons.

As the Shadow Walkers advanced, the crew of *The Black Peregrine* roared, waving their swords. Faces contorted as they psyched themselves up for battle, they ran screaming towards the enemy.

The first to make contact was a huge, burly pirate with a giant scar that ran from the corner of his mouth to his ear; he was on a Shadow Walker in seconds and slashed at it with all his might. Seemingly unconcerned by its wound, the Shadow Walker reached out, lifted the pirate like he weighed no more than a bag of sugar and threw him overboard.

Ebony listened until the shrill cry of the pirate plummeting towards the waves was abruptly cut off and cursed under her breath. Although the Shadow Walker had a massive slash down its chest, its pace didn't slow as it made its way across the deck past Ebony, grabbing anyone in its way and flinging them out of its path. *Whatever happens*, thought Ebony as an idea struck her, *I'm going to win this battle.*

Tucking herself into a corner near the cabin, she checked inside her rucksack for the puppet Mrs O'Hara had given her. It was the only thing she had seen that could successfully defeat the Shadow Walkers, and while she might not have Seamus's skill, she was still prepared to try. But as she scoured the contents, she discovered the puppet was missing.

'It's not here!' she cried to Winston. 'I must have forgotten to take it back from Seamus.'

Peering in, Winston blinked up at Ebony, his head tilted to one side.

Meanwhile, the battle raged on, the Shadow Walkers growing in number, seemingly multiplying before Ebony's eyes. But the ship's men were putting up a good fight.

A movement in the far corner of the stern caught her eye, as a small figure dressed in a black cap and short trousers made her way, crouching, to hide behind a barrel; Ebony recognised the figure as one of her past selves. From behind the barrel, her past self rolled something in Ebony's direction: an olive-green hand grenade with the pin still in it. Snatching it up, Ebony yanked out the pin and threw it into the enemy ship. There was a loud crash, a flash of white, and splintered wood showered *The Black Peregrine*'s deck. But no more grenades appeared.

'What do we do now, Winston?' asked Ebony.

Inside the bag, *The Book of Learning* began to shimmer

and, whipping it out, she had it open in seconds. Turning to the first blank page, she saw a grid with numbers 1 to 10 across the top and letters A to J down the side. Underneath, the words 'Choose a square' formed.

'This isn't the time for games,' shouted Ebony, frustrated. But, out of ideas, and with her friends being steadily beaten backwards, she had no other option.

'B5,' she shouted over the noise of the battle.

A small explosion rang out at the far end of the ship, with a blast of white heat. Planks of wood lifted into the air, leaving a wide, blackened, sizzling hole.

'We're hit!' cried Ebony, looking about her. 'They must be using cannons!'

Looking back at the page, the word HIT had appeared in square B5.

Something stirred in Ebony's memory and she had a sudden idea of what might be going on. Studying the grid she called out, 'E4.'

This time, as a massive spray of seawater spouted to the left of the ship, the word MISS appeared in that square.

'I know what this is! We used to play this game with Grandpa, Winston,' cried Ebony. 'It's Battleships. I must have hit our ship on the first go! I'll give it a go, but we have to be careful not to hit Chiyoko.'

Studying the grid carefully, Ebony made her next call.

'B6,' she called out.

This time, an explosion sounded on the deck of the neighbouring ship, and a red blast lit up the sky. Looking at the grid, the word HIT had appeared. Trying A6 and C6, she saw two more explosions. HIT. HIT. The second was huge: several planks of wood flew into the sky, their flaming mass forming a giant fireball that left a fat billow of acrid smoke. The explosion must have caught some gunpowder; thankfully she had positioned the hit just right and it was far away from where Chiyoko was tied.

Over the battle cries and screams, Ebony heard the enemy ship groan and creak, like a cry for help, but it remained afloat. 'Just one more and I should create a big enough distraction for us to sneak on board and rescue Chiyoko,' said Ebony.

However, just as she was about to give another command, a massive wave washed over the ship, drenching her and the book, and the grid began to bleed down the page.

'D6,' tried Ebony, but this time nothing happened.

The lines of the grid had turned into a runny mess, the pattern like marble-effect icing on a cake. Then the page turned dry, the marbling frozen in place.

'No!' cried Ebony, desperately turning the page to see if anything else would happen, but it stayed stubbornly blank. She thrust the book into a pocket in her trousers and looked around for inspiration.

'Take the wheel!' called her pirate self and, unable to help in any other way, her spirits sinking, Ebony did as she was told, Winston by her side.

The lightning was sudden and unexpected, a bright sheet of violet that lit up the sky. Seconds later, thick black clouds covered the brightening sky and the route ahead was completely blacked out as sheets of rain poured down. The wind rose quickly and waves started to smash against the side of *The Black Peregrine*, sending violent sea spray over the deck and the crew and washing Winston away from the ship's wheel. Salt water lashed at Ebony's face, making her eyes and skin sting, and no matter how much she blinked, she couldn't clear it from her eyes.

'I can't see beyond the end of the ship!' yelled Ebony, clinging on to the wheel, trying to keep it straight. It was much bigger and stronger than the one she was used to on their old fishing boat, and as she steered, it fought against her guiding hand.

'No one can,' cried one of the pirates. 'More Shadow Walkers!'

Spotting her past self in the middle of the fray, she watched as the captain thrust her sword deep into the heart of one of the Shadow Walkers, twisting it and yanking it sideways and down. The creature should have been disembowelled, but instead, it simply looked down at the wound, gave an evil laugh and swiped the pirate girl across the chest with a flick of its arm. She flew backwards, skidding along the deck like a fawn on ice, unable to stop herself. Her head smashed against the fat central mast and she slumped to one side, unconscious. Nearby, Ebony spied Winston weaving his way between stomping and kicking legs, trying to get back to her.

Fighting the urge to run and rescue him – losing control of the ship would not help anyone – Ebony gripped the wheel with all her might and tried to keep it steady, while searching for a replacement. Icarus was too busy helping a pirate hold back a Shadow Walker, and the men from the Order were lost in the fray. Spotting a cabin boy hiding up one of the masts, she called to him. Terrified, he looked away and pretended he hadn't heard her. Meanwhile, the fighting continued. Metal flashed as the combat raged, but one by one, the pirate crew was overcome – either tipped over the ship's edge, screaming as they fell, or slammed against various parts of the ship, blood spurting out where skin was gashed or heads were split open. She spotted the man from the Order with black hair laid flat on his back, out cold. Unable to just watch any more, Ebony called out to the boy again. 'Take this wheel so I can fight!'

The boy looked from Ebony to his unconscious captain, a puzzled look on his face. But not daring to disobey her any longer, he climbed down from the mast, legs trembling. He took the wheel and Ebony kept hold until she was certain he had it under control. Although it looked like the other ship was now empty, someone had locked the two ships together with grappling hooks so it was being pulled along with *The Black Peregrine.*

Winston arrived, panting, his breath steaming in the cool air, and Ebony lifted him onto her shoulder. As she took a step towards the fight, a familiar feeling crawled over her skin and prickled the hairs on her neck: Zach Stone was nearby, trying to enter her mind. She could sense that he was still seeking the box. Resolute, Ebony fought against him, trying to picture the box hidden somewhere and not in her rucksack, to stop him from attacking her. It took much more effort than she expected; he was stronger than before.

Still battling Zach, Ebony moved Winston to her pocket for safety and began firing at the Shadow Walkers, sending streams of tiny, see-through bullets into the fray. They wouldn't kill the creatures, but they might slow them down and buy the others some time. She fired until the ammunition ran out. At the same time, Zach released his grip.

'What will we do, Winston?' cried Ebony, ducking behind a mast, taking a moment to think.

Winston popped his head out of her trouser pocket and pointed deep inside.

As Ebony yanked *The Book of Learning* out of her pocket, the ship lurched to one side and she staggered, dropping it. It slid across the rain-soaked deck. When the ship lurched the other way, Ebony tried to grab it as it slid past again but missed. Bashing against the other side of the ship, it started to slide back in her direction as the ship righted itself. Then something landed on the ship's deck, blocking its way. *The Book of Learning* settled against a heavy boot.

Zach Stone. He must have seen her drop the book and leapt across from the enemy ship. Picking up *The Book of Learning*, Zach held it out for her to see. 'Thank you very much,' he said. 'What a thoughtful gift.'

'Give that to me,' cried Ebony.

She was surprised when he threw it in her direction and she reached out for it. But just as she was about to catch it, a rogue hand appeared from nowhere and snatched it away.

As she spun to shout at the culprit, she found herself, instead, on her knees, writhing with pain. She could just hear Ambrose's dark, sinister laugh over her own gasps. But she didn't cry out; she wasn't going to give them the satisfaction.

When Ambrose released her and the pain died away, Ebony staggered back to her feet, her hand reaching for her gun before remembering it was out of bullets.

'You're weaponless, Ebony. You're going to die.'

'I know you need me alive to swap souls, Ambrose,' cried Ebony. 'That's if you can, now the other soul you need has gone from the Reflectory.'

His lip curling, Ambrose narrowed his eyes until the grey hair on his forehead formed a visible V shape. 'I see you discovered our little ruse. That means you've been back in the

Reflectory. Tell me, how is your precious grandpa doing? He wasn't looking so hot the last time I saw him, and neither were the rest of them.'

Ebony gave a triumphant smile. 'He was looking much better after I removed the implant in the back of his neck. In fact, I removed them from every soul. They're all free of your influence Ambrose, so whatever power you were getting from them, it's gone.'

Ambrose laughed, as if genuinely amused. 'You mean to tell me that you and your supporters still haven't managed to figure it out? I do wonder how you managed to foil my plans in April.'

Zach sniggered as Ambrose continued, 'It was the regenerative power that I have been extracting from the Reflectory's souls that allowed me to free the Deus-Umbra. I no longer need them now that my greatest ally is free to walk the earth. And by the time they are reborn, we will have a guardian we can use to control them. So, don't worry, my trusty assistant here and I still have the same plans for you. Now, hand me the box.'

'What box?' asked Ebony, trying to keep her voice from quivering.

'Don't play games with me, girl,' snarled Ambrose. His eyes flashed and he seemed to grow taller as his anger flared. 'I know you have it.'

As Ebony tried to look innocent to buy some time, Ambrose laughed cruelly.

'Zach saw you retrieve it from the pond in St Stephen's Green – only he couldn't act because by the time he caught up with you there were too many people around. And since he couldn't find it in your house, I realised you must be keeping it with you.'

Knowing she'd been caught out, and surrounded by enemies with no hope of immediate escape, Ebony grimaced. 'If you want it, you'll have to come and take it.'

'It'll be our pleasure,' said Zach, taking a step closer.

In the blood-red sky of early dawn, a terrible rumbling sounded, followed by a scream. Louder than a foghorn and shriller than a vulture, the scream stopped everyone, including the Shadow Walkers, in their tracks.

'The Deus-Umbra!' cried Ambrose, a crazed look on his face as he lifted his arms in the air and cried out in reply, his eyes scanning the horizon.

Grinning like a wild beast, Zach copied him. As Ebony glanced up to see what they were looking at, she spotted the cowgirl high up on the front mast. Ebony watched as the cowgirl used her whip to catch hold of the rigging on the Shadow Walkers' ship and swung across, disappearing from sight. Ebony had to hope that she was safe and one step closer to rescuing Chiyoko. Thankfully, Zach and Judge Ambrose were too busy staring up into the dark sky to notice.

A second scream sounded, but no matter how much Ebony squinted her eyes into the darkness, she couldn't see any sign of what was making the noise.

The Deus-Umbra was coming, there was no doubt about that, but she wasn't going to wait around for an introduction.

While the judge and Zach were distracted by the noise, Ebony crept across the deck. Even though the cowgirl was on her way to rescue Chiyoko, there was no guarantee she'd succeed. Ebony would have to try to get onto the enemy ship also. Checking around her, she saw that most of the crew was down; the remaining pirates were putting up a good fight, but Ebony was soon going to be the only one alive or conscious. The other ship was too high up for her to jump across – she would have to copy the cowgirl. As she paused to take a deep breath, a quiet voice appeared in her mind.

Climb and jump, it said.

Ebony's heart started to pound. 'Grandpa?' she whispered, afraid to say his name too loudly in case it scared him away or alerted her enemies to her escape.

Climb and jump, it said again, even more faintly.

Glancing up, Ebony figured that if she jumped across to the other ship from higher up she'd have more chance of landing safely – from this height, the ship would only have to lurch an inch or two and the other deck would be too high, making her plummet to the waves where there was a risk of getting crushed.

Shimmying up the ropes and the mast, eventually reaching the crossbeam, Ebony put her arms out for balance. Quickly, she ran along the slippery beam, barely managing to stay on her feet, and leapt from the end of it towards the other ship.

'Hold on tight, Winston,' she cried, flying through the air metres above the ocean. Although she'd been aiming for a rope hanging from a crossbeam on the other ship, she landed instead on the sail of the black ship and, unable to catch hold, began to slide down it at breakneck speed. Pulling out her pocketknife, she jabbed it into the sail and as it tore down through the material it slowed her descent. Reaching the bottom of the sail, she let go of her pocketknife and hit the deck with a thud, missing by inches the massive hole she had blown in the deck. Her heart felt like it was trying to burst out of her chest. She was certain it was her grandpa who had spoken to her.

Around her, the ship was still and silent; all the Shadow Walkers were on *The Black Peregrine*. Towards the prow of the ship, Ebony could make out one of Chiyoko's dress sleeves billowing in the breeze. The cowgirl was there also, crouched low, untying the bindings that held Chiyoko to the mast.

Running to join them, Ebony tripped and landed face down, sprawling on the deck. Looking back, preparing for a fight, she saw a stray length of rope snaking across the deck. The deck was empty and still, so she checked Winston was unharmed and then raced towards the front of the ship, where Chiyoko was now free and rubbing her wrists. Back on *The Black Peregrine*, Ebony could hear Judge Ambrose still crying out the Deus-Umbra's name.

'Are you hurt?' asked Ebony.

Looking up, a confused expression crossed Chiyoko's face. She looked from one Ebony to the other and back again.

'There's two of you!' she cried. 'I knew you'd come, Ebony, but I didn't expect … It's amazing!'

Laughing, Ebony gave the girl a hug then took hold of her hand and pressed the silver box into it. When Chiyoko looked at her, puzzled, Ebony pressed her finger to her lips.

'Come on, let's get you out of here,' she said.

Pulling Chiyoko to the gunwale, she looked out to see if there was any sign of the second contingent of men from the Order of Nine Lives – they were certainly taking their time. Spotting them nearby, cutting through the water at speed, she guessed they would be at the ship's prow in minutes.

'We had trouble finding a boat!' cried one of the men, fighting to bring the boat close enough to collect the girl. Ebony was surprised to find that Mr O'Hara wasn't on board. 'But we're here now. Your aunt and Uncle Cornelius are on their way too.'

Squinting into the distance, Ebony saw a small fishing boat approaching. She guessed that Mr O'Hara would be on that vessel.

A third scream sounded; this time it was so loud, it threatened to burst their eardrums. Ebony, the cowgirl and Chiyoko covered their ears.

'What is that?' asked Chiyoko, trembling, when the noise had died.

'The Deus-Umbra,' replied Ebony. 'A terrible ancient demon that Ambrose has made a pact with. But I can't see it! Where is it?'

'I think the noise is coming from over there,' said Chiyoko, pointing out to sea.

In the distance, smoke was billowing into the sky. It looked like Gallows Island was harbouring a massive fire. As

Ebony turned back, she jumped in front of Chiyoko and put her hands out protectively. Judge Ambrose had followed her. He stood with one hand outstretched and the other holding *The Book of Learning*.

'The box, Ebony.'

'I don't have it – I threw it into the sea,' she said, looking around for Zach. She had to hope that Chiyoko would keep quiet.

'I don't believe you,' said Ambrose, his voice flat and cold. 'Maybe this will help you to cooperate.'

Without warning, he smashed *The Book of Learning* against the ship's side, cracking the silver casing in two. Ebony gasped; she'd assumed the book was invincible. Tears mingled with the rain on her cheeks as, reaching in with his long, thin fingers, Ambrose wrenched the casing open and ripped the book down the spine. Once the pages were free, they began to tear away, one by one.

'No!' cried Ebony, dashing across the deck towards him.

Ambrose glared at her and a bolt of lightning shot through her body once again, the pain intense. It felt like a plaster cast of fire had been moulded around her, searing the bones and muscles in her body. Unable to take the pain any longer, Ebony fell to her knees, hugging herself, trying to stem the agony. Ambrose stepped forward and tried to search her, but the pain kept her crumpled and rigid. Stopping his assault, Ambrose yanked the rucksack from her back and rifled through it. Meanwhile, Ebony groaned as pins and needles attacked her limbs. Whistling to make her look up, Ambrose gave a thin, mean smile as each page loosened itself from the book's binding. One by one, he threw them over the side.

'Stop it!' cried Ebony.

'Not until you give me the box.'

Without the help of *The Book of Learning* Ebony knew that her chances of ever defeating Ambrose were almost zero, but she couldn't give up their only weapon against the Deus-Umbra. Staggering to the side of the ship, Ebony watched as the pages began to slap against the ship's figurehead, sticking to the beastly dragon. A smattering of silvery glitter shimmered from each page as it made contact. Ebony's stomach twisted in knots. She cursed herself for being so clumsy and dropping the book.

A ghastly creaking sound, like the groan of falling masts, interrupted her thoughts. Looking up, Ebony shielded her eyes, expecting to see the masts toppling, but they were secure and undamaged. When half of the pages were gone, Ambrose lifted one side of the silver casing to his lips and gave it a kiss. Then, without another thought, he hurled both sides of the cover overboard. Ebony took a step forward, her heart sinking as she watched the book and all its clues, all its power, spiralling towards the waves.

'Did you really think that you could beat me?' snarled Ambrose.

At the same time, the discarded section of *The Book of Learning* that still had pages attached began hurtling back towards Ebony at full speed, a leathery tendril wrapped around it. She grabbed hold of it, snatching it out of the air as the whip released, and quickly shoved it in her pocket.

'I still will,' she replied, sounding much braver than she felt.

A loud splintering sound, like a thick plank splitting, filled the air, followed by a distant chuckle. Pulling Chiyoko close, Ebony gave her shoulder a squeeze to try to reassure her. She could feel the girl's body trembling. The splintering noise resounded again, followed by a ripping sound. Ebony wondered if, after the damage she had done to the ship earlier, it was finally coming apart.

Peering past Ambrose into the hole, Ebony could see that the majority of the damage had been to the cabins and deck – the hull, while a little battered looking, was still in one piece and she could see no leaks. But still the creaking and groaning continued, as though the ship was in pain.

Zach dropped noisily onto the deck, his face pale and wan, his skin thin on his skeleton. 'You'll never escape,' he said. 'Just give up.'

Ebony took a step back as Zach moved forward, a wild grin on his face. He seemed too fluid, too fast, almost like his body was moving in a different time to Ebony's. Was he turning into a Shadow Walker? What had the judge done to him?

'OK. You have me now. It's a fair swap. Let Chiyoko go.'

'No,' said Chiyoko, shaking her head. 'I'm staying with you.'

'Such loyalty, how very sweet – only, why would we let her go when we have such big plans for you both?' replied Ambrose.

Throwing back his head, Zach gave an almighty roar of laughter. Ambrose joined in and turned his gaze to the ship's prow. Pointing, he shouted, 'Rise!'

As his words ended, there was a massive wrenching sound at the front of the ship. Whoever or whatever Ambrose was commanding, it was down there. Unable to resist, Ebony peered over, half afraid of what she might find but also needing to know what she was up against.

'Don't!' whispered Chiyoko. 'You don't know what's down there!'

Leaning out a little further, Ebony screamed. Covering her mouth with her hand to try to stem the noise, she realised it was too late. The dragon on the figurehead turned its head towards her, its eyes glowing white hot. Opening its mouth wide, the dragon exposed a long, thin tongue made of cold-looking blue flames.

Judge Ambrose hadn't been randomly tossing the pages of *The Book of Learning* away as Ebony had thought; he'd been harnessing their ancient power to give life to the dragon. Where the pages had stuck to the figurehead, they fizzed and crackled and glowed red hot, breathing life into the ancient beast. Before her eyes, the creature's face began to cool, changing to white, then grey, then red-gold.

Spotting the men from the Order pulling up alongside

the ship, Ebony pushed Chiyoko towards her cowgirl self. 'Take the girl, now!'

But Ambrose was too fast. He reached out and grabbed Chiyoko by the hair and held her fast. Without hesitation, the cowgirl leapt up onto the gunwale and then, to Ebony's surprise, dived down between the two ships. Hearing a splash, Ebony had to hope the cowgirl was making her way to the other boat to get help.

An icy cold wind whooshed past Ebony's face and, checking back on the figurehead, she realised the whole thing was gone. A squall of wind whipped around the ship, making Ebony shiver. The next thing she knew, a hand clamped over her mouth. Zach yanked her backwards, throwing her off balance, then wrapped his other arm tightly around her shoulders and chest so she couldn't move her arms. Ebony gagged on the faint whiff of rotting flesh that emanated from him and struggled against his grip, but he was too strong. He pulled her back until they stood side by side with Ambrose and Chiyoko. As Chiyoko whimpered, an unearthly cry rang out above their heads and, high up in the sky, a bright flash streaked through the early morning light. Seconds later, the dragon could be seen swirling and swooping in the air, its red-gold scales shimmering. Opening its jaws wide, the creature roared, sending another blast of wind towards the ship; this time it whipped around the deck in icy circles. In reply, the Shadow Walkers raised their heads and their arms to the sky and roared.

At the far end of *The Black Peregrine*, just in her line of vision, Ebony noticed that her pirate self was back on her feet, wounded, with blood trickling down one side of her face near her ear. Like the rest of her crew who were conscious, she stood stock still, staring up towards the screeching creature. The ships bobbed on the ocean, and Ebony now heard the familiar rumbling of a fishing boat approaching; her aunt and Uncle Cornelius were getting nearer. As she looked around, something bright red and glinting caught her attention: a ruby eye in *The Black Peregrine*'s figurehead. In the momentary stillness, Ebony had an idea. If Ambrose could raise a figurehead with *The Book of Learning*, why couldn't she? After all, the bird in the vision with Chiyoko had looked very similar. It was worth a try.

She bit down on Zach's hand as hard as she could. As he yelped and let go of her mouth, she ripped herself free of his other arm and stumbled away from him, then turned and punched him as hard as she could, knocking him to the deck, stunned. Yanking the damaged part of *The Book of Learning* from her pocket, she ran to the railing of the ship. Ambrose let out a cruel snigger as he watched.

'You'll never be able to manage it!' he snarled. 'You're not strong enough.'

Although it broke her heart to do it, Ebony ripped out the pages, throwing them towards the figure of the bird. Caught in the strange, swirling wind, the pages slapped against it and stuck, but nothing happened. Not giving up, Ebony continued until all the pages were gone. Then she threw the broken casing over the side too, just in case it held extra power.

As the casing smacked against the figurehead with a loud clunk, suddenly the bird blinked its eye. Its body began to glow blue and it opened its beak as though to cry out, only it didn't make a noise. And unlike the dragon, the peregrine didn't pull away. The muscles on the shoulders of its wings trembled and quivered as the bird tried to break free, but it wasn't strong enough. All but the very tips of its wings were still stuck to the ship.

'*The Book of Learning* has no more pages,' said Ebony, her stomach churning. 'There wasn't enough magic left.'

'It's OK, little bird,' called Chiyoko in a soothing voice, tears in her eyes.

The bird looked their way and Ebony saw its eye glint – did it recognise Chiyoko's voice?

'We have to help it!' yelled Chiyoko, suddenly kicking out at her captor. Taking him by surprise, she broke free, clambered up onto the ship's side and leapt across before Ebony or anyone else could stop her.

'No! Wait! We have to stick together–' cried Ebony.

'Foolish girls,' said Ambrose, folding his arms as he watched Chiyoko on the other ship, leaning over the prow and stroking the struggling bird gently as her tears spilled onto its neck. Then, tilting his face skywards, he called out, 'Take them to your master!'

As Ambrose finished speaking, Zach grabbed hold

of Ebony again and there was a loud tearing noise as the peregrine finally seemed to gather enough strength to wrench itself away from the ship. As she watched it fly up, Ebony saw a dark shadow to its right hurtling towards her and Zach. The dragon was moving so fast that it left trails of vapour in its wake, like a fighter jet. Its evil white eyes were upon her, its flaring nostrils only a breath away. Reaching its front legs forward, the dragon snatched Ebony and Zach up in one set of claws. Swooping across *The Black Peregrine* at top speed, it caught Chiyoko in the other set and carried them all high into the sky at such speed that Ebony felt her nose start to bleed. Squirming to break free – she'd rather die at the hands of the ocean than Judge Ambrose's monster – she started to feel dizzy and sick. Twisting her head, she saw that Chiyoko was already unconscious. The speed was too much to handle and Ebony heard Zach vomit just before she slipped into unconsciousness.

Ebony struggled to open her eyes as she regained conscious-ness; when she finally managed, her eyelids heavy and sore, she found that she was lying flat on her back, on cold, hard stone, a long, droning noise mixed with an inhuman hiss fill-ing her ears. The air around her was hot and humid, like a smokehouse.

'Hello?' she called out, but her voice was little more than a dry, cracked croak. At first, she thought she was back on *The Black Peregrine*, listening to the hull creak as the wind and waves blasted its giant hulk, but then the memory of the dragon stealing her away came flooding back. 'Chiyoko,' she called, but the only reply was a distant screeching that echoed around her, making Ebony shiver despite the heat.

It was a screech that she recognised: the Deus-Umbra. And she knew deep down that it wouldn't be long before the demon came for her.

Her eyes finally focusing, she recognised the sparkling granite cavern yawning above her like a starving mouth, a stretch of scaffolding spreading along the wall leading to the exit. She was in the same cave on Gallows Island that she had rescued Winston from earlier that year – and she was about to die. But where was Chiyoko? And Winston? He'd been in her pocket but she couldn't feel any movement there – she hoped he hadn't fallen into Zach's clutches.

Trying to sit up, Ebony found she couldn't move; thick leather straps bound her to a marble slab. She could only lift her head, and when she did, she could see needles that had been inserted into her skin all over her body – her chest, her legs, her temples: they were everywhere. These were connected to tubes of liquid that were hanging beside each of her arms. More tubes pulled off in another direction, and a strange droning sound, like a trapped and angry wasp, could be heard nearby.

As her senses returned fully, Ebony realised that the droning sound was coming from the machine she was attached to. The machine had a large red button that glowed threateningly.

Twisting her head to the right, Ebony realised that there was another figure attached to the machine – she recognised it instantly as Zach's mum's soul. Her soul was weak, relying on the pressure pump on the machine to keep her life force charged. So this was where they'd moved her – but what had changed? She thought they needed the Reflectory's power to complete the soul swap.

Ebony squeezed her eyes shut again. The heat was suffocating. She had failed and it was all over. She was going to have her soul removed and implanted in another body, giving the power of reincarnation to her enemies. Her family would be obliterated and the Order of Nine Lives would be destroyed.

Footsteps reverberated in one of the cave's tunnels, and Ebony faked unconsciousness as the rhythmic thuds grew louder and closer. When a blast of cold water hit her face, Ebony gasped and opened her eyes. Zach Stone was leaning over her, grinning wildly, an empty glass in his hand.

'You want to know what will happen?' he asked. He must have been reading her mind, only she was so dazed she hadn't realised.

He stared at her intensely, and although she tried to pull her gaze away, she was too weak to resist him this time. But instead of reading her mind, he somehow began to transmit images – a sign of his growing power. Her brain throbbed as she soaked up the images: Zach, dressed resplendently and leading a group of uniformed men and women, straight-backed and focused. They marched, speedily and in time, to a podium where Zach's mum was waiting, her golden hair gleaming in the sun, a huge smile on her face as she addressed an auditorium of people waving flags, each bearing Judge Ambrose's crest.

But then something happened, and Zach's images splut-tered and died away. Instead, scenes of horror filled Ebony's mind. Screams and flames, zombie-like drones in army ranks, souls ripped apart and flung aside, unable to fulfil their des-tinies. The world shuddering and fighting back; volcanoes erupting, destroying and reshaping whole continents, and tidal waves wiping out entire islands. Ebony had no idea where the images were coming from, but it was like they were being channelled through her.

'Stop it,' growled Zach. 'That is not how it will be. Ambrose has shown me the glory we will achieve together.'

'It's all lies,' spat Ebony, wrestling to break free, her arms wrenching against the straps that secured her. 'You know Ambrose is just using you. Give me Chiyoko and set us free – the Order of Nine Lives won't harm you if you help us.'

'Harm me? With the Deus-Umbra on my side?' Zach laughed. 'I'm not interested in what you have to say. You just want to keep the powers of the Reflectory to yourself.'

But the images continued and Zach seemed unable to ignore them: people running and screaming in terror as a vast army of giant Shadow Walkers stampeded the land, ripping up the ground and tearing people apart. Finally there were only ash-filled wastelands with blackened tree stumps in a green haze left. The world was alive with anger and decay, with no sign of happiness or joy, only dark, sullen faces creeping in the shadows, neither man nor Shadow Walker.

'I won't let this happen,' said Ebony.

In response, Zach laughed, his teeth bared. The sound bounced around the cave, magnifying its intensity, fuelling Ebony's determination even further. Then there was a loud click as Zach flicked the machine to ON, and instantly

Ebony felt an ice-cold sensation flood her veins as whatever fluid was inside the tubes began to infiltrate her body.

'Zach, no!'

Zach simply folded his arms and watched, a thin smile that hardly resembled a smile at all on his face.

'Please!' cried Ebony, even though she knew it was pointless.

'Ebony Smart, pleading for her life,' said Zach, turning a dial on the machine to increase its power. 'I'm going to enjoy this.'

'At least set Chiyoko free. Her life for mine – that's what you said.'

'Only to trap you. We knew you wouldn't be able to resist playing the hero. We need you both. You for the soul swap, and Chiyoko to feed the Deus-Umbra; the demon has asked for her specifically. She, or one of her past selves at least, is responsible for its imprisonment. When we deliver her, the Deus-Umbra will help us take over the Order and defeat our enemies.'

'You think it'll give you the power, rather than take it for itself? You're a fool, Zach Stone.' But inside, she felt the glow of hope. Zach's words told her that Chiyoko was alive. There was still time to rescue her.

Angrily, Zach reached out to the machine and turned the dial. The icy feeling washed over Ebony in a sudden flood. It filled every part of her body, from her toes to her fingers. She could feel the freezing tendrils send shockwaves through her brain, reaching into every nerve and fissure.

'Just a minute more and then we can start the soul-swapping process.' Zach turned another switch. 'That should do nicely. It's much easier now we can feed off the power of the Deus-Umbra – this place is much more accessible than the Reflectory and here we don't have to worry about the place fighting against us. After what happened last time, I'm not convinced that the Reflectory itself would have let us carry out our plan.'

Her anger rising, Ebony squirmed to break free, but a fireball of pain raged through her body and she screamed. Unable to concentrate on anything other than hurting, Ebony writhed and yanked and pulled, but she was firmly secured. There was no escape. After a moment, a signal sounded and Zach hit the pause button.

'We need to swap your souls bit by bit – my mother is too weak for the original procedure we devised.' He held up a small black device that Ebony had seen before; it was no bigger than a matchbox, with data running across its screen. Zach read the screen and grinned. 'We will capture your soul gradually in here, and slowly drain my mother so we can implant the bit of your soul that reincarnates with what's left of hers.'

As the fire gradually left her body, Ebony heard Zach reach for the dial that controlled the life force of his mother's soul.

'Zach, no!' cried Ebony. 'She looks too weak.'

But Zach didn't listen. He turned the dial to its strongest

and Ebony watched, her breathing slowly recovering, as his mum's soul convulsed and jerked, lifting from the bed in violent bursts.

'Did it hurt you as badly as it looked?' Zach asked Ebony, his voice sounding small and vulnerable.

'It hurt like hell,' replied Ebony between shallow breaths. 'Don't do this to her.'

But Zach let the machine continue, wiping his mother's brow tenderly. 'It'll be all over soon and then you can be guardian and start your nine lives over. I won't let anyone hurt you ever again,' he whispered.

Lying still to conserve energy, Ebony searched her brain for one last crumb of hope. But she could feel her strength and coherence seeping away by the second, tangling her thoughts. *How long will Chiyoko be kept alive? Is there anyone left to help me or are they all dead?* The effort it took to think made her feel dizzy and the room began to spin. In her mind, her thoughts tumbled like kelp in a storm.

How do I get out of here?

Where is Aunt Ruby?

What happened to Winston and the others?

Will anyone rescue me?

Just as she began to feel like there was no hope left at all, something brushed against her wrist.

Only just able to move, Ebony looked to where her hands were strapped down. There was Winston, nibbling at the leather, his small teeth gnawing their way slowly through the straps. Not wanting to draw Zach's attention to him, Ebony lifted her gaze. As she did, she saw the profile of a shadowy black figure on the wall above the scaffolding. The figure lifted a finger to its lips, then pushed away from the granite, slowly and stealthily making its way down the scaffolding towards the cave floor.

Quickly checking to see whether Zach had noticed, Ebony found that he was too busy attending to his mum, frantically trying to offer her some comfort. Returning her attention to the mystery figure, Ebony felt the strap on her wrist loosen. Winston quickly scurried around the opposite side, tucking himself between her arm and body to stay undetected, and started work on the other strap.

As Zach looked up, the figure on the scaffolding stopped, camouflaging itself in the shadows between the pipes. A pinging noise sounded, and the light on the machine turned green.

'Are you ready?' asked Zach, reaching out towards the glowing red button. 'After this, enough of you will be gone that you'll lose consciousness, so I guess this is goodbye, cousin.'

The second wrist strap fell free and Ebony summoned the last bit of energy from every inch of her body. Bolting upright, she head-butted Zach in the face. He staggered back, holding his nose as blood spurted through his fingers. At the same time, Ebony started to yank the needles and wires from her body.

By the scaffolding, the black figure dropped silently to the ground and a voice Ebony thought she recognised shouted her name. Turning just in time, Ebony saw a bow twirling through the air towards her. Even though she had never used one before, she had seen Seamus use his and knew that the arrows would automatically appear. Catching the bow and pulling the string taut, an arrow appearing instantly, she fired at the soul-swapping machine twice in quick succession. Even though her movements were clumsy, she was too close to the target to miss.

'No!' shrieked Zach, pulling his mother's soul close to his chest fearfully as the second arrow hit.

His cry lingered in the air as the machine rumbled, shuddered and then exploded, sending shards of metal and debris blasting outwards. Ebony covered her eyes and shielded Winston with her body. Feeling the last bits of debris settle around her, she looked up to see Chiyoko with her back to her, untying the straps encircling her ankles.

'Are you OK?' asked Ebony as the young girl turned, her hair covering her face as she lifted Ebony into the air. 'Woah! How on earth can you lift me?'

When Chiyoko looked up, her face was cold and blank. There were no features. It wasn't Chiyoko at all; it was a life-sized shadow of her puppet. Gritting her teeth, Ebony checked around her for clues; the real Chiyoko still had to be found – and rescued.

40

Realising it must be Seamus controlling the puppet – which meant that she had outside help – Ebony relaxed into the puppet's arms and let it carry her. Winston ran ahead, stopping briefly to beckon for them to follow him. He stopped at a gaping hole in the wall, signalling that they should go deeper into the belly of the cave. It was an area she'd never been to before, but she had to trust her friend.

Zach shrieked again. He had set his mother down and was tearing at his hair and skin with his fingers, no longer watching Ebony. This time, as his cry echoed throughout the cave, an almighty screech replied.

The Deus-Umbra was nearby. If they didn't get out of there fast, Ambrose could still sacrifice Chiyoko to appease the demon's hunger. As the puppet carefully put her down and turned back towards Zach, placing itself like a guard in front of the hole, Ebony found enough energy to stand on her own two feet. But when she tried to walk, her legs gave way beneath her. Landing on the floor in a heap, she motioned for Winston to leave her.

'Go!' she mouthed. 'I'll follow.'

But Winston stopped in his tracks and shook his head vigorously. Fighting to stand, Ebony winced. Scrunching up her face, she tried again. Winston hopped up and down on his back legs impatiently. Glancing over her shoulder to check she was still safe, Ebony saw Zach leaning over his mum's soul, tears mixing with the blood from his nose. Thin rivulets of diluted red were dripping onto her skin. Her body, already sallow and turning more greyish-yellow by the second, was completely limp. Carefully laying her down, Zach began to snatch up pieces of machinery and try to fit them together. Realising his actions were useless, he fixed Ebony with the most hateful glare she had ever seen. His bloodied cheeks and red-rimmed, bloodshot eyes gave him the look of a devil.

'If she dies,' he spat, 'I'll hold you responsible.'

As he spoke, Ebony could see the soul yellowing further. Zach took hold of his mother's hand gently, but a long, thin hiss sounded and the soul flattened to a body-shaped piece of skin. The features on her face melted away to nothing so she was completely unrecognisable. Ebony shuddered. She knew she didn't have much time if she wanted to survive.

Gathering all her strength, she managed to climb to her feet and stepped through the hole. The heat was even worse here, making Ebony's chest contract. There was a fierce red glow from somewhere below, lighting the way, and steep, roughly hewn steps carved out of the granite that spiralled down. Sections sparkled like crimson gems in the strange light. Wheezing, Ebony squeezed her eyes shut and concentrated on mustering any energy she could. Seconds later, Winston tugged on her trousers and beckoned, his eyes dull and his ears flat. Pushing herself to her limit, Ebony started to stumble down the steps. The heat burning her lungs, she coughed and spluttered as she descended as fast as she could. Screeching sounds echoed all around, but Ebony forced herself on, despite the agony in her bones and the raging fire in her joints.

Feeling like she was going to collapse with every inch of progress, she stopped to catch her breath. As she sucked in air, Zach shouted at the top of his voice, his words filling the cave, 'She's dead! My mother's dead!'

Looking back to the top of the steps, Ebony could just make out some shapes scuffling as Zach tried to come after her and the puppet blocked his way. Blood pumping and head throbbing, she pushed on, but her progress was slow; Winston had to stop periodically so that she could keep up. The spiralling descent made her head spin, and the heat sapped what energy she had left, but still she continued. Finally reaching the bottom of the steps, Ebony leaned over and took a few deep breaths. Straightening up, she found herself in another cave. It was searingly hot, the walls seemingly wobbling with the heat, and a blast of smoke welled up from the ground, clouding her vision. It took a moment for the smoke to clear and her eyes to adjust.

A few metres in front of her was a giant crater, twenty metres across. Just beyond it was an exit – through it she could see the tips of frothy waves in the distance. As another blast of smoke rose up out of the crater, the exit sucked the fumes out. Ebony guessed that was why the island had looked like it was on fire. She had no idea where this exit had come from; she had fished around Gallows Island many times and had never seen it before. Judging by its jagged shape and the rocks that lay scattered around it, it was recently made, the cave wall blasted away by man or demon, she didn't know which.

A tongue of red flame flew up out of the crater and, flattening herself against the wall, Ebony gulped. Suddenly, the earth rumbled and clumps of rock spewed from the hole. Covering her head with her arms, Ebony crouched down and waited for the shaking to stop. Winston pointed into the crater. An awful screech sounded from its red-hot depths; tentatively, Ebony stepped closer and leaned over the edge.

Just as in Mrs O'Hara's puppet show, a mountain was rising up in the middle of the crater, with wisps of smoke circling its summit and flames lapping in all directions. About five metres down from where Ebony was standing, she spotted Chiyoko, shivering on a small ledge formed from jutting rock. She had her back pressed against the crater wall, too scared to open her eyes. At Ebony's feet, Winston gave a nervous squeal. It was a long, long way down to the bottom.

'Chiyoko, it's me,' spoke Ebony as loudly as she dared.

Opening one eye and looking up, Chiyoko's body trembled. She was trying to speak but the words wouldn't come.

Instead, she shook her head and closed her eyes again, pressing back into the wall with all her might.

'Listen to me, Chiyoko, I'm going to get you out of there.'

As a scream rang out, Winston shivered, and flattened his ears. Without warning, he turned tail and fled towards the exit as fast as his legs could carry him.

'Winston! Wait! I need your help!' called Ebony.

But Winston kept going. Seconds later, he was gone.

Ebony's eyes stung; he had never abandoned her before. Unable to follow – she had to save Chiyoko – Ebony peered down at the girl.

Studying the crater wall that Chiyoko was pressed against, Ebony could see small wedges of stone jutting out. They weren't very big, but Chiyoko was light and small. If she took her time, she should be able to climb out. It was risky, but also their only hope.

'Chiyoko, I need you to be brave and climb out. See those rocks?' Chiyoko chanced a peek and nodded. 'You can do it. I know you can.'

'You haven't seen that thing, Ebony. I'm scared,' managed Chiyoko.

'Me too,' admitted Ebony, hoping it would spur the girl on. 'But if we stick together, we'll be OK.'

Too frightened to even try to turn round, Chiyoko called out, 'I can't, Ebony. I'm sorry. Just leave me here and save yourself.'

Whether it was the effects of the machine wearing off or

adrenaline kicking in, Ebony felt a surge of energy fill her body. There was only one thing for it. 'No! I'm coming to get you, Chiyoko,' she called. 'You hold tight.'

'Be careful, Ebony!'

Lying on her stomach, Ebony shuffled backwards towards the crater until her feet hung off the edge, then swung her legs down, looking for footholds. Feeling a small bit of stone jutting out under one foot, she slipped over the edge into the blasting heat. Looking down, she saw a black plume of smoke leave the mountain and circle its summit. Taking a deep breath, Ebony began to climb down.

The descent was slow and it was difficult to breathe. As flames lapped up the centre of the crater, Ebony clung on for dear life, waiting for them to pass. She could smell the hairs on the back of her neck singe. From another area in the cave, Zach's voice rang out loud and clear. 'We're coming for you, Ebony, you murderer.'

'I didn't murder her, Zach. But now you know how it feels to lose someone you love,' she shouted back, tears stinging her eyes as she searched for another foothold. 'You killed my grandpa, remember?'

The only reply was a barrage of footsteps. She had to move fast.

Climbing down slowly, one wedge of stone at a time, Ebony eventually reached the ledge. There was just enough room for two as she dropped to Chiyoko's side. Ebony pulled the girl into her arms and Chiyoko clung on. Realising that this was where they had been in the puppet show Mrs O'Hara had shown her, Ebony knew that if they didn't move quickly, Chiyoko would soon be a goner.

She looked deep into Chiyoko's eyes. 'You can do this,' she said. 'You go first and I'll be right behind. When you reach the top, don't look back. You'll see a cave mouth when you climb out of here and that's where you're to go. No matter what happens, run for your life.'

Barely able to nod, Chiyoko let Ebony turn her to face the wall and she started to climb. Her legs were shaking and her grip was weak, but with a shove from Ebony she managed to pull herself up and start the ascent. Unable to resist, Ebony peered over the edge of the ledge. Below, a fiery heat surged and a black swirling mass of smoke twisted and wended its way around the mountaintop.

Checking on Chiyoko's progress, Ebony heard a terrible screeching and peered over the edge again. The wisps of smoke began to thicken, forming two terrible red eyes and a gaping, fanged jaw.

It wasn't smoke at all – it was a creature. A demon. The Deus-Umbra had been watching them all along – and just like in the puppet show, it was coming for them.

41

'Keep going!' yelled Ebony. Above her, Chiyoko was making slow and steady progress. 'And remember, don't look back, just run!'

A terrible cry rang out from below and Ebony's skin puckered into goose bumps; time was running out. Losing her footing, Chiyoko screamed and Ebony shielded her face from the spattering of chippings that showered down upon her. When the chippings stopped falling, Ebony looked up; Chiyoko was higher, not far from the top. Exhausted, every sinew screaming with pain, Ebony continued to grasp and pull at the protruding parts of the cave wall, hoisting herself up. Arm over arm, she scaled the wall, the screams from below spurring her on. Yet, no matter how much she tried, she couldn't climb quickly enough, and her strength was beginning to fail. Pausing to take a breath, her heart beating at an incredible speed, Ebony watched Chiyoko climb out. But instead of running like she was told, the girl stuck her head over the edge and held out a hand.

'I'm not leaving you,' she growled through gritted teeth.

'I said run!'

'No! Come on, Ebony!'

Determined to escape, Ebony scaled the final part of the wall. But as she reached out to grab the waiting hand, Chiyoko was suddenly wrenched back out of view.

'E-Ebony–' began Chiyoko, but she was unable to finish her sentence.

A chuckle rang out and Zach peered over into the crater where Ebony was barely managing to cling on, his expression cold, almost lifeless. Her resolution weakening and her burning lungs constricting, Ebony's head began to spin and she could no longer feel her fingers or toes. Unable to cling on any longer, one hand slipped from the granite and she swung around. As her back hit the wall, her other hand lost its grip and she began to plummet, face first and barely conscious, towards the fiery home of the Deus-Umbra.

Without warning, she felt claws grab her from behind, gripping tightly around her waist, and hoist her into the air. She could hear yelling but was too dazed to make sense of it. All she could think was *The Deus-Umbra has me*.

Fighting to stay conscious as she swung through the air, the speed and motion making her disoriented and unable to focus, Ebony felt the heat drop away and a blast of cold air strike her face. The tang of salt assaulted her nostrils; she was back outside, over the sea. Helpless, she sailed through the sky, dangling by her middle, her back curved, head and feet trailing, her vision slowly improving. Behind her, the shadowy outline of Gallows Island grew smaller and smaller. The sky was now eggshell blue; a pale yellow sun shimmering above the horizon. But caught in the grip of the Deus-Umbra, she knew that there was no saving her this time.

'Noooooo!' screamed Ebony in her mind, unable to muster the energy to call out.

In the distance, she heard a crazed roar and an explosion. Her vision clearing, Ebony looked back towards the island. She could just make out the figure of the Deus-Umbra bursting out of the cave, its wings spread and its red eyes flaring as it hurtled skyward. But that meant something else was carrying her!

Gathering enough energy to look up, she saw a strong, muscular chest, striped white and black. The peregrine figurehead that had broken free of the ship had come to her rescue – and it had Chiyoko dangling from its other set of claws, pale and limp but alive. It must have snatched her up too, out of Zach's grip.

Ebony closed her eyes, concentrating on calming her nerves. As she felt the bird dipping down towards the ocean, she opened them again: she was heading straight towards a small fishing boat. And not just any fishing boat – in it were Uncle Cornelius and Aunt Ruby, as well as four of the Order's men, the cowgirl and Icarus Bean.

The peregrine dropped Ebony and Chiyoko into the boat, circled once to check they had landed safely and then flew off. One of the men knelt down and gave them both the once over. 'They're weak but not seriously hurt,' he said.

Seeing her family and friends, Ebony felt her heart warm and the strength in her limbs start to return.

'Thank goodness Winston managed to attract the peregrine in time. Get them water,' ordered Aunt Ruby, 'and give them some air.'

As Uncle Cornelius and the cowgirl leapt into action, Ebony asked, 'Where's Winston? And Seamus?', but her voice was so slight and faint no one heard her. She was too weak to ask about Mr O'Hara's whereabouts. And right now, he was the least of her worries.

Ebony heard Chiyoko coughing and spluttering as her uncle poured water onto the girl's lips. Feeling the cool water from the cowgirl's canteen revive her, Ebony pushed herself into a seated position. Looking up, she saw the giant wings of the peregrine swoop down. The bird dropped Winston at her feet before powering high into the sky again, its head swivelling this way and that. As Ebony scooped Winston up in a tight hug, several geese flew by in a V formation, honking.

'The battle is upon us,' said Aunt Ruby, her face dark and brooding.

'Do you feel strong enough to fight?' asked Icarus.

But a giant shadow silenced him and prevented Ebony from replying.

The red-gold dragon was above them, with Zach in its claws. He screamed cruel threats as he whizzed overhead, pointing at Ebony. The dragon swooped but, holding its master, it could only blast a length of icy breath across the boat, making everyone duck. It then took off at top speed. Ebony could still hear the threats from Zach raining down as he was lifted into the air. Following their path, Ebony watched as the dragon dropped her enemy on board his own ship before powering back up to the sky. As he landed, Ambrose appeared, a desperate look on his face. There was no sign of the Deus-Umbra or the peregrine – were they locked in battle somewhere? Their absence chilled Ebony to her bones. Aunt Ruby tipped her head back and, mouth cupped with both hands, sounded the vulture signal.

At the front of the boat, the cowgirl stared out to sea, straight-backed and one hand hovering over her coiled lasso. As the fishing boat pushed through the water, Winston leapt from Ebony's grip and took cover near the cabin. Ebony checked on Chiyoko; the girl was starting to come round.

'We should get to land,' cried one of the Order's men. 'It's safer.'

Hearing a loud groan like a whale's distress cry, Ebony followed the noise. *The Black Peregrine* pirate ship was tilted, its masts at a dangerous angle, close to tipping the whole boat. The groan was issuing from its hull. The ship wouldn't stay afloat for much longer; water was rushing through a hole in its side and would soon pull it down into the dark depths of the Atlantic.

'Is anyone still alive on board that ship?' asked Ebony, her voice louder as her strength grew.

'We think so,' replied her aunt.

'Then we have to help them first. They're only here because of me. We can't abandon them.'

Moving to the front of the boat, rising and falling with the waves as the vessel powered its way through, Ebony shielded her eyes and looked out across the sea. Icarus joined her, handing her a bow and then her rucksack.

'I saw Ambrose hurl it over the side,' he said, as Ebony quickly checked the contents then secured it across both shoulders. 'I dived in to get it, then swam to meet the fishing boat.'

'What happened to make the ship sink?' asked Ebony, nodding across the ocean, picking up her bow, hoping it wasn't her mistake at Battleships that had caused the situation.

As though in reply, the dragon hurtled from the sky, its nose pointed like a missile. Seconds later, it was ripping right through it and then it was gone.

'I don't understand,' said Ebony. 'Why is it attacking that ship?'

'Those people on board are your allies,' replied Icarus, 'and Ambrose knows you care what happens to them.'

High in the sky, Ebony caught a glimpse of the peregrine, its wings outstretched, turning its head this way and that.

'Where did the dragon go?' cried Ebony.

A whooshing sound from behind made Ebony and Icarus look back: the King Vulture had answered Ruby's call and was powering its way towards the troubled ship. Nearby, the ocean bubbled and broiled, and looking down into the deep water, Ebony saw two white eyes hurtling their way up from the seabed.

'Look out!' she cried.

Uncle Cornelius clung on to the wheel as everyone else in the fishing boat flung themselves down, hands over their heads. As the dragon ripped its way out of the ocean, huge waves crashed all around, slamming over the top of the small fishing boat and swamping it inches deep in water.

As the boat steadied, everyone climbed to their feet. Having heard the commotion, the vulture stretched out its wings and circled back; catching sight of the dragon it gave an immense screech. Up above, the peregrine pulled up and hovered, then hurtled downwards, its wings pinned back and its beak thrust forward.

The cowgirl aimed her gun and fired at the dragon, but the bullet pinged off the creature's back as though it were made of bulletproof glass. Ebony reached for her bow and fired also; the first arrow missed but the second stuck fast in its side, golden blood oozing from the wound. Before she could draw again, the peregrine attacked, striking the dragon with its beak. The dragon roared and somersaulted in the air, spinning out of control into the vulture's path. Sticking out its long neck, the vulture jabbed its beak into one of the dragon's eyes. Half blind, the dragon lashed out with its claws and its jaws. The vulture tried to glide out of the way, but the dragon lunged, grabbing the vulture's neck in its teeth. Crunching down and twisting to one side, there was a loud snap as the vulture's neck broke in two. The dragon opened its jaws and let the bird fall; its heavy body made a loud splash as it hit the waves and sank to the ocean's depths.

As the last glimpse of the vulture's bright orange wattle slipped away from sight in the crashing waves, the peregrine raced by, slicing the dragon's back with its claws and snapping off the arrow shaft, leaving the tip still lodged in the creature's side. Screaming, the dragon shot into the sky at bullet speed and the peregrine quickly followed, but not before glancing back at Chiyoko.

It does recognise her, thought Ebony as she watched its progress.

Everyone on board the fishing boat stared skyward, breath held, trying to guess what would happen next as the falcon and dragon arced through the air high above. A fireball suddenly exploded in their path, and the two creatures broke to either side of it. The dragon flew on but the peregrine swept its wings back and began to plummet towards the ocean. A creature with sharp, pointed wings burst through the smoke of the fireball and followed in close pursuit. Ebony recognised the murderous glint in its eye: too wary to tackle the peregrine alone, the Deus-Umbra had joined forces with the dragon and was after the bird's blood.

42

As Ebony pulled on the bowstring, making an arrow appear, Chiyoko pointed to the water and shouted, 'Winston!'

Splashing around in the water, his legs waving frantically, Winston gasped for breath. The huge waves had carried him overboard unnoticed by the others, and he was tiring quickly. Uncle Cornelius steered the boat closer and Chiyoko moved quickly. Grabbing a nearby bucket on a rope, she threw it out to sea and Winston climbed in. Hauling the bucket up over the side, Chiyoko extracted Winston and cupped him in her hands. As he coughed and spluttered, she hummed to him gently. Recognising the tune – it was the one Seamus had sung – Ebony suddenly remembered the box.

'Where's the silver box I gave you?' she shouted to Chiyoko, her arrow poised.

The girl stopped humming and reached into her sleeve. Turning it inside out, revealing a secret pocket, she pulled out the box and showed it to Ebony.

'Open it!' cried Ebony. 'You have to open it!'

Chiyoko tried, but the lid wouldn't open. 'There's something wrong,' she cried. 'It's never been stuck before.'

'Keep trying,' cried Ebony, her voice cracking with desperation. 'I think it will help us.'

With the legend she had read about the Silent Peregrine, and seeing the way the bird looked at Chiyoko, she was certain they were somehow linked to the box – and that this was the key to beating the Deus-Umbra of which Mrs O'Hara had spoken. Ambrose and Zach had been determined to find it, so whatever the box did it must be powerful.

A cry rang out as the dragon smashed into the hull of *The Black Peregrine* from the side. The ship groaned and creaked, lolling even more towards the sea. Ebony could now see that on board a battle still raged, although it looked like the Shadow Walkers had turned on each other. Lines of smaller Shadow Walkers were attacking the larger ones, picking them off so they were separated from their comrades and holding them captive, keeping them away from the shadows so they couldn't return to the Shadowlands. Injured pirates and the Order's men who had stayed to fight were strewn around the edges of the deck. Ebony spied her pirate self being tended by a girl in a white nightdress – another one of her past selves.

'We haven't got long before she goes down,' said one of the Order's men to Icarus. 'We'd better get our men and the pirates off quickly.'

Uncle Cornelius, Icarus and Aunt Ruby sprang into action. Cornelius gunned the engine of their little boat, while Icarus and Ruby started shouting and waving to the injured to attract their attention. They were soon close enough to *The Black*

Peregrine for the survivors to be able to jump into the boat. A gust of wind rushed over the fishing boat as the peregrine raced past, the Deus-Umbra just behind its tail feathers, screeching. As it raced by, the Deus-Umbra caught Ebony's eye and hissed.

'How's that box coming along?' Ebony shouted.

A determined growl from Chiyoko provided the reply she needed.

The peregrine flew high into the sky, flapping its wings and opening its beak as though trying to cry out.

'Is it OK?' asked Chiyoko, her eyes wide.

'Just concentrate on getting that box open!' shouted Ebony. Turning to the others, she called out. 'Hurry – if the ship sinks when we're nearby, the sea will suck us down with it.'

One of the men from the Order managed to stand and shuffle his way across the deck. Aunt Ruby and Icarus used a fishing net to hoist him down. Behind him, a Shadow Walker tried to grab him but lost its balance and fell from the ship with a cry. Moments later, its shadowy hand gripped on to their fishing boat. The cowgirl fired, splattering it into a hundred pieces.

'That should hold it off for a while,' she said, although the pieces had already begun to re-form on the surface of the sea, like a living oil slick.

Ebony watched as the peregrine circled the ship, now with the dragon on its tail. Where had the Deus-Umbra gone? Every now and again the dragon let out a burst of icy breath, but the peregrine was too fast and too swift and managed to evade the freezing blasts. A sudden screech gave away the Deus-Umbra's position: it was perched on top of the main mast on Ambrose's ship, sucking in deep breaths of sea air. The ship had turned its prow towards them and was racing their way. Lifting off, the Deus-Umbra hurtled towards the fishing boat dangerously fast. Everyone cowered – even the cowgirl.

Peeping out from under her arms, Ebony watched as the Deus-Umbra changed course and flew straight into the peregrine, making the bird tumble through the air like a bowling ball. Regaining control of its wings and using them as brakes, the peregrine righted itself and chased after the Deus-Umbra. Catching up, it rammed its pointed beak into the creature's behind, taking the demon completely by surprise and making it roar with pain.

But the Deus-Umbra wasn't going to be easily beaten. Turning in mid air, it lashed out at the peregrine. The bird dodged out of the way just in time, but a second attempt caught one of its tail feathers. Flinging the feather away, the Deus-Umbra roared in frustration and returned to its pursuit. Ebony willed the peregrine on; even if it turned out to be no match for the Deus-Umbra, it was at least a distraction while they tried to open the box.

Behind her, Chiyoko gave a frustrated growl and began to sob.

Turning, Ebony called out, 'Let me have a try!'

Before handing it over, Chiyoko raised the box to her lips and kissed it. 'For luck,' she said.

As her words died away, the lid sprang open and something was released. A bright blue semi-quaver floated into the air and with it a sweet but melancholic tune – one that Ebony had heard before. It was the song that Chiyoko had been singing to Winston moments earlier.

While the others concentrated on hauling another survivor into the fishing boat, Ebony and Chiyoko watched the blue musical note float higher and higher into the air. It was almost at the same height as the ship's tilted edge. Instinctively, Chiyoko started to sing along and at that moment another voice rang out across the skies, singing the same melody. The second voice seemed to fill the air around them, echoing slightly, but clear. As she listened, Ebony recognised the voice.

'It's Seamus,' she cried. 'He must be using the conch – but why? What does the song mean?'

Feeling something tug on her trousers, Ebony looked down to see Winston pointing into the distance. Squinting into the gentle daylight to see what he was looking at, she saw the peregrine hurtling their way, its wings pulled back and its neck stretched forward as it pushed itself to the limits of its speed. On its tail was the Deus-Umbra, talons outstretched and eyes gleaming. Just as the Deus-Umbra was about to grab the peregrine, the bird dodged left. The demon, pulled on by its own momentum, missed its mark and the peregrine dived straight for the blue semi-quaver. Turning, the Deus-Umbra followed its prey, screeching angrily as it tried to get there first, its body moving so fast it was just a blur. In a blaze of red-gold, the dragon swooped back onto the scene and chased after them.

The Peregrine reached the blue note and gulped it down; the second it had the note swallowed, the tune ceased. Chiyoko and Seamus also stopped singing and Ebony realised that their song had simply been to attract the peregrine to the note: Seamus had been helping Chiyoko to alert it to the open box and its contents.

Turning, the peregrine falcon faced its attackers.

As the Deus-Umbra and dragon drew close, their momentum carrying them on towards the bird, the falcon opened its mouth and let out the loudest, shrillest shriek Ebony had ever heard. Dropping to the deck, she covered her ears, everyone around her doing the same. The sound was so penetrating, it made her eyes sting and her toes tingle. But she had to see what effect the noise had; peering up, she saw the Deus-Umbra had frozen in its tracks, roaring like it was in immense pain, writhing and thrashing in the air. A loud beating sound filled the air and a King Vulture appeared. Just as Ebony was wondering how it had resurrected itself, another arrived on the scene. And behind it, a flock of honking geese and several gannets, their heads swivelling and their beady eyes searching. The beating sound grew even louder as a murmuration of starlings arrived, so big that the sky darkened. Looking around her, Ebony could see birds flocking from all directions.

'The peregrine has called for help!' cried Ebony. 'That's what the box contained: its call.'

The peregrine continued screeching, moving closer and closer as hundreds of birds surrounded the Deus-Umbra and began to attack. Hundreds soon became thousands, and although the demon lashed out with its claws and snapped its teeth, the power had shifted and there were too many birds for it to fend off. With a loud screech, it bolted up into the sky, leaving the dragon alone to face the angry birds. The peregrine followed.

'Sink that boat!' came a cry, just barely audible over the noise of the birds. 'But bring me the guardian!'

Locating the noise, Ebony saw Zach balancing on the prow of his approaching ship, his face ablaze with fury. But the dragon couldn't free itself from the cloud of birds that pecked and clawed at its scales. As a raven caught the dragon's remaining eye and pulled it from its socket, the other birds attacked en masse and the dragon fell from the sky. Hitting the ocean with a splash, its bloodied corpse floated briefly on the waves before sinking into the depths of the ocean. The falcon gave its loudest screech yet and all the birds flocked in its direction, towards the fast-retreating Deus-Umbra.

'This isn't over yet, Ebony!' cried Ambrose, appearing next to Zach, gun in hand. 'Your soul still belongs to us.'

Before she could reply, he rained bullets towards the others on the fishing boat. Ebony ducked behind the cabin. As the men from the Order fired back, she realised how close the enemy ship was, ploughing its way through the water towards them. Looking up, Ebony saw the Deus-Umbra racing across the sky, the peregrine chasing after it, its continuous screech belting out. Seconds later, the demon changed tack and suddenly hurtled out of the sky, ploughing back towards the ships at top speed. It smashed through *The Black Peregrine* and, this time, the boat split in two. As the wood groaned and screeched, debris smattering the cold Atlantic, the falcon and its battalion of birds raced back down, filling the sky. They swooped and dived, hovered and swirled, their eyes peeled and alert, lying in wait for the Deus-Umbra to resurface.

'Over there!' cried Ebony, spying the creature's head pop out of the water.

But, realising it was outnumbered and couldn't win, the Deus-Umbra was too cunning and fast; like a bullet, it flew up out of the water and raced at top speed towards the heavens. Up, up, up it went, higher than the birds could follow, until it was out of sight.

'All Shadow Walkers, return to the ship!' cried Ambrose, still firing at the fishing boat. In response to Ambrose's order, the larger Shadow Walkers that could break free began to leap across back to their ship, which was now alongside the dangerously damaged *Black Peregrine*. As they departed, Ebony noticed something strange about the smaller Shadow Walkers that remained on board *The Black Peregrine*; they were all joined, with heads that wobbled. They weren't real Shadow Walkers after all: they were puppets, like those Mrs O'Hara had used in her show.

With his army back on board, Ambrose leaned over the

side and spat into the sea. 'This still isn't over,' he yelled.

'You killed my mother,' screamed Zach, the ship coming closer. 'For that, you'll pay.'

Ebony lifted her bow and held it rigid, ready to fire once they were in range. But as soon as the ship touched the shadow of the fishing boat, it appeared to dive into the darkness and vanished. It had returned to the Shadowlands. It seemed that with the dragon dead and the Deus-Umbra gone, Ambrose wasn't willing to continue the fight.

Overhead, the peregrine closed its beak, no longer making its cry, and the birds began to disperse. Looking around, Ebony saw that most of *The Black Peregrine* had sunk, taking with it all of its crew, including one of their own men. Only the top of the tallest mast was still visible. Seconds later, a body bobbed up to the surface; Icarus pointed, and the Order's men stared silently at their comrade. One crossed his torso in a blessing, while another sobbed quietly. Aunt Ruby and Uncle Cornelius threw out a fishing net and hauled him in.

As his lifeless body flopped over the side onto the deck, a tear slipped from Ebony's eye and crystallised, just like in the Reflectory, hitting the water with a splash. The peregrine swooped down and snatched the tear from the frothing waves. Feeling her rucksack vibrate, Ebony peered inside. Her bronze rose was sizzling and shaking, a blue glow emanating from one petal, just like the first time it had come into contact with the silver box that belonged to Chiyoko. As Ebony lifted the rose out, it began to glow phosphorous blue, sizzling and crackling as its colour brightened. Holding the rose higher, Ebony watched as the blue glow shot out like a beam, hitting what remained of *The Black Peregrine*'s sinking main mast. At the same time, the peregrine swooped, dropping her tear onto the mast also.

For a moment nothing happened and then, as Ebony and the others in the fishing boat watched, the water began to churn and the two halves of the ship began to rise back out of the water. The pieces moved together. The split began to mend, with holes patching themselves. Before long *The Black Peregrine* floated before them again in all her original glory.

Ebony gasped as the phosphorous glow from her rose spread to the ends of the masts, along the edges of the hull and to the tip of the prow. When the ship was once again complete, a huge hook swung out towards them on a fat, twisted rope.

'Time to go,' said the cowgirl, and before Ebony could say thank you, the girl was swinging her way back to the ship where her other past selves were waiting.

Along the sides of the ship, the pirates lined up and lifted their bloodied and battered weapons in salute.

Returning to its ship, the peregrine took hold of a rope swinging from the prow in its beak. With the ship glowing blue, the peregrine pulled it down into the depths of the ocean. Only when the glow had disappeared did Ebony look towards home.

As they reached the cottage, the front door sprang open and Mulligan burst out, his teeth bared and saliva dripping from his tongue, the silver-grey streaks in his fur shining in the early morning sun. Satisfied it was all clear, he led the way inside; as she followed, Ebony kept a close eye on the rhythmic swish of the wildcat's tail.

Inside, a fire was roaring, yet the air was damp. An old, hunched body sat next to the fireplace, nursing one arm. Ebony did a double take before she realised who it was.

'Joe!' she cried, rushing to his side. 'Are you OK?' Noticing his arm was wrapped in a bandage dotted with pus and bloodstains, she opened her eyes wide. 'Who did this to you?'

'Those mangy Shadow Walkers a few days ago – but I'm fine. It's already healing.'

'During the ambush I spoke of,' added Icarus.

Mulligan padded over and sat next to the old man, gently purring.

Aunt Ruby moved closer and unravelled the bandage a little to inspect the wound. 'I have just the thing!' she said, dashing off to the first-aid box.

Mulligan gave a small growl and nudged Joe's leg as Aunt Ruby raced back into the room. Pulling out a small vial, she popped off the cork and took a deep sniff. A faint whiff of *Ebonius Tobinius* roses filled Ebony's nostrils, mixed with strong alcohol and pungent herbs.

'There we are,' said Aunt Ruby, sprinkling the liquid onto Joe's arm. He took a sharp intake of breath as the liquid made contact with the wound, but didn't flinch. 'It stings, but it'll stop infection.'

Next, she whipped out a needle and thread. Mulligan took one look and swiped it away, showing his pointy canines. Icarus laughed.

'Would any of that work on this?' asked Ebony, holding out her palm.

On it, the black skull – the sign of the Shadow Walkers – was now as big as a two euro coin. Uncle Cornelius cowered, but Aunt Ruby rushed in to take a look.

'Where did you get this?' asked Aunt Ruby.

'In the tunnel below Mercury Lane that leads to the Hideout.'

'A tunnel?'

'They've marked her,' growled Icarus. 'So they can find her whenever they want.' Looking up, he fixed Ebony with a serious stare. 'But you did it again, Ebony. You stopped them from swapping your soul!'

'I smashed the soul-swapping machine, but they'll just build another. And Zach's mum, your wife …' She couldn't finish. But Icarus had heard what Zach said on the ship and he understood. As he turned away, Ebony saw his shoulders shaking with sobs.

'You saved my daughter,' said Mrs O'Hara, appearing from one of the other rooms. 'And by keeping your soul intact, you saved the Order.'

Seeing her mother, Chiyoko burst into tears and ran across the room for a hug.

'I still don't know what happened exactly,' said Ebony.

'It seems,' replied Aunt Ruby, 'that Chiyoko was the one who originally discovered how to chase the Deus-Umbra away. That figurehead you raised was a replica of an extinct bird that was once revered in these parts; it was thought they kept the village of the original Nine Lives families safe. When the Deus-Umbra terrorised the village, a past incarnation of Chiyoko released the village's last peregrine so it could call for allies from far and wide.'

Ebony nodded. 'I read about the legend – I take it she was the handler? I saw the bird look at her like she was a friend. But how did they manage to capture the Deus-Umbra?'

'We still don't know. That creature has such strong magic! But we need to find out because ...'

'It's still out there, somewhere,' finished Ebony. 'And it'll be back.'

An uncomfortable silence fell upon the group.

'How did the peregrine's song end up in a box?' asked Chiyoko, shyly.

'The head of one of the original Nine Lives families wanted

to be able to control the Deus-Umbra,' explained Mrs O'Hara, 'and protect our people if it should return. So once the Deus-Umbra was imprisoned, he captured the peregrine and stole its voice, sealing it up in the box as a safety precaution. That man was a past incarnation of my husband.'

'Mr O'Hara? But he doesn't even believe any of this stuff!'

'Yes. But this was so many lifetimes ago, he has no recollection. None of us had; but I have been patrolling the shadows for years, watching and listening. I heard Ambrose and Zach talking about a powerful box, and after a while, I realised it was in our possession.'

'I had no idea,' said Chiyoko, holding the box out on her palm. 'But why didn't you just let me keep it and explain?'

'I heard Ambrose say that he knew where it was. I didn't want you in harm's way – and seeing as Ebony is guardian, I thought it best to give her the box to protect.'

'But that doesn't explain why you couldn't tell me,' said Ebony, her teeth chattering. 'All those riddles!'

'With Zach able to read minds, I thought it best not to tell you everything. It was a risk, but under the circumstances, we had everything to gain and nothing to lose.'

'And how did the silent peregrine survive?' asked Ebony.

'Even though the legend was almost forgotten, some of the original bird statues were saved. Their significance was lost, but thankfully someone preserved one of them by attaching it as a figurehead on the front of a ship. Whether they knew what they were doing or not, we cannot be certain, but thank goodness they did. *The Book of Learning* brought the bird to life, and the music note added the spirit of the last peregrine. Without the figurehead, I don't know what we'd have done.'

'But a ship from the 1600s coming to our rescue? All my past selves, in fact – how is that possible?'

'It's not just distance you can travel in the Shadowlands, Ebony,' came Icarus's reply. 'You can also travel through time. How else do you think your past selves have been coming to your aid?'

Ebony nodded, too exhausted to ask more. 'But once again, I figured the clues out too late. If you hadn't sent the shadow puppet to the cave–'

'Not me,' said Mrs O'Hara, pointing towards Ebony's old bedroom. 'That was Seamus. I had those Shadow Walker puppets to manage; it turns out that when something really matters, my son's skill is greater than he thought.'

Rushing towards her bedroom door, Ebony stopped, her hand stifling a gasp.

There, in her old lumpy bed, lay Seamus. His eyes were shut and his breathing was shallow. She could tell from the sheen on his skin that he had a fever. The conch was carefully placed on the bedside table and next to him knelt his father. His face was grey and wan; he looked like he hadn't slept for days. He was gripping his son's hand tightly.

'Is this because he helped me?' asked Ebony, dropping to her knees and letting her chin fall.

'If I had only listened,' replied Mr O'Hara, distractedly. 'If

I hadn't stopped Seamus from doing what he loved, if I had encouraged him … he would have been stronger.' He paused and held his palm to his son's forehead. 'I was on my way to help you but when my wife and Seamus arrived, and I found out what they were planning, I had to stay with them. To make sure they were safe.' He turned to face Ebony. 'I'm sorry I ever doubted you. There's no way they would have put themselves at risk like this if you weren't the true guardian. I've been foolish. I should have known you'd be just like your parents.'

'Will he be OK?' asked Ebony, feeling a tear run down her cheek.

'His mother assures me he will be; he's just exhausted.'

Returning to the living room, closing the door quietly to let Seamus sleep, Ebony and Mr O'Hara joined the others. As bright sunshine crept through the window and along the floor, Ebony stared into the fire, letting the warm flames reach into her bones.

'Will it ever be over?' asked Ebony. 'I've released the souls, but it will be years before they'll be reborn and able to help us. In the meantime do we have enough power to defeat the judge and the Deus-Umbra when they return?'

Aunt Ruby came to her side and held her hand. 'We will vote Ambrose out the instant we return to Dublin and we'll put someone trustworthy in his place. But whether that will reduce his power enough for us to beat him entirely? We cannot be certain. And as for the demon, it will be even harder, maybe even impossible.'

'So, we're doomed, no matter what?' asked Ebony, pulling back her hand and stroking the mark on her palm.

'Not quite,' said Mr O'Hara. 'I have made an important discovery.' Clearing his throat, he fought to say the words. 'Your parents are alive and I know where they are.'